Also by Patricia Highsmith

RIPLEY'S
GAME

PATRICIA HIGHSMITH

| RIPLEY'S |
| GAME |

 ALFRED A. KNOPF   NEW YORK   1974

THIS IS A BORZOI BOOK
PUBLISHED BY ALFRED A. KNOPF, INC.

Library of Congress Cataloging in Publication Data

Highsmith, Patricia (Date)   Ripley's game.

    I. Title.
PZ3.H53985Rk   [PS3558.I366]
813'.5'4   73–20739
ISBN 0–394–49005–3

MANUFACTURED IN THE UNITED STATES OF AMERICA
FIRST AMERICAN EDITION

RIPLEY'S GAME

"There's no such thing as a perfect murder," **| 1 |**
Tom said to Reeves. "That's just a parlor
game, trying to dream one up. Of course you could say there
are a lot of unsolved murders. That's different." Tom was
bored. He walked up and down in front of his big fireplace,
where a small but cozy fire crackled. Tom felt he had spoken
in a stuffy, pontificating way. But the point was he couldn't
help Reeves, and he'd already told him that.

"Yes, sure," said Reeves. He was sitting in one of the yellow
silk armchairs, his lean figure hunched forward, hands clasped
between his knees. He had a bony face, short light brown hair,
cold gray eyes—not a pleasant face but a face that might have
been rather handsome if it hadn't borne a scar that traveled
five inches from his right temple across his cheek almost to his
mouth. Slightly pinker than the rest of his face, the scar
looked like a bad job of stitching, or as if perhaps it had never
been stitched. Tom had never asked about the scar, but
Reeves had volunteered once, "A girl did it with her compact.
Can you imagine?" (No. Tom couldn't.) Reeves had given
Tom a quick, sad smile, one of the few smiles Tom could recall from Reeves. And, on another occasion, "I was thrown
from a horse—dragged by the stirrup for a few yards." Reeves
had said that to someone else, but Tom had been present.
Tom suspected a dull knife in a very nasty fight somewhere.

Now Reeves wanted Tom to provide someone—suggest
someone—to do one or perhaps two "simple murders" and
perhaps one theft, also safe and simple. Reeves had come from
Hamburg to Villeperce to talk to Tom, and he was going to
stay the night and go to Paris tomorrow to talk to someone
else, then return to his home in Hamburg, presumably to do
some more thinking if he failed. Reeves was primarily a fence,
but lately he had been dabbling in the illegal gambling world
of Hamburg, which he was now undertaking to protect. Protect from what? Italian sharks who wanted to come in. One

Italian in Hamburg was a Mafia button man, sent out as a
feeler, Reeves thought, and the other might be one—from a
different family. By eliminating one or both of these in-
truders, Reeves hoped to discourage further Mafia attempts,
and also to draw the attention of the Hamburg police to a
Mafia threat. Then let the police handle the rest; which was
to say, throw the Mafia out. "These Hamburg boys are a
decent batch," Reeves had declared fervently. "Maybe what
they're doing is illegal, running a couple of private casinos,
but as clubs they're not illegal, and they're not taking out-
rageous profits. It's not like Las Vegas, *all* Mafia-controlled,
and right under the noses of the American cops!"

Tom took the poker, pushed the fire together, and put
another neatly cut third of a log on. It was nearly six. Soon be
time for a drink. And why not now? "Would you—"

Mme. Annette, the Ripleys' housekeeper, came in from
the kitchen hall. "Excuse me, Messieurs. Would you like your
drinks now, M. Tome, since the gentleman has not wanted
any tea?"

"Yes, thank you, Mme. Annette. Just what I was thinking.
And ask Mme. Héloïse to join us, would you?" Tom wanted
Héloïse to lighten the atmosphere a little. He had said to
Héloïse, before he went to Orly at three to fetch Reeves, that
Reeves wanted to talk to him about something, so Héloïse
had pottered about in the garden or stayed upstairs all after-
noon.

"You wouldn't consider taking it on yourself?" Reeves said
with a last-minute urgency and hope. "You're not connected,
you see, and that's what we want. Safety. And after all, the
money—ninety-six thousand bucks—isn't bad."

Tom shook his head. "I'm connected with *you*—in a way."
Dammit, he'd done little jobs for Reeves Minot, such as
mailing small stolen items, or recovering tiny objects like
microfilm rolls from toothpaste tubes where Reeves had
planted them. "How much of this cloak-and-dagger stuff do
you think I can get away with? I've got my reputation to protect, you know." Tom felt like smiling at that, but at the

same time his heart had quickened with genuine feeling, and he stood taller, conscious of the fine house in which he lived, of his secure existence now, six whole months after the Derwatt episode, a near catastrophe from which he had escaped with no worse than a bit of suspicion upon him. Thin ice, yes, but the ice hadn't broken through. Tom had accompanied the English Inspector Webster and a couple of forensic men to the Salzburg woods where he had cremated the body of the man presumed to be the painter Derwatt. Why had he crushed the skull, the police had asked. Tom still winced when he thought of it, because he had done it to try to scatter and hide the upper teeth. The lower jaw had come away easily, and Tom had buried it at a distance. But the upper teeth—some of them had been gathered by one of the forensic men. Fortunately there had been no record of Derwatt's teeth with any dentist in London, Derwatt having been living (it was believed) in Mexico for the preceding six years. "It seemed part of the cremation, part of the idea of reducing him to ashes," Tom had replied. The cremated body had been Bernard's. Yes, Tom could still shudder, as much at the danger of that moment as at the horror of his act, dropping a big stone on the charred skull. But he hadn't killed Bernard. Bernard Tufts had been a suicide.

Tom said, "Surely among all the people you know, you can find somebody who can do it."

"Yes, and that would be a connection—more than you. Oh, the people I know are sort of known," Reeves said with sad defeat in his voice. "You know a lot of respectable people, Tom, people really in the clear, people above reproach."

Tom laughed. "How're you going to *get* such people? Sometimes I think you're out of your mind, Reeves."

"No! You know what I mean. Someone who'd do it for the money, just the money. They don't have to be experts. We'd prepare the way. It'd be like—public assassinations. Someone who, if he was questioned, would look—absolutely incapable of doing such a thing."

Mme. Annette came in with the bar cart. The silver ice

bucket shone. The cart squeaked slightly. Tom had been meaning to oil it for weeks. Tom might have gone on bantering with Reeves because Mme. Annette, bless her soul, didn't understand English, but Tom was tired of the subject, and delighted by Mme. Annette's interruption. Mme. Annette was in her sixties, from a Normandy family, fine of feature and sturdy of body, a gem of a servant. Tom could not imagine Belle Ombre functioning without her.

Then Héloïse came in from the garden, and Reeves got to his feet. Héloïse was wearing bell-bottom pink-and-red striped dungarees with LEVI printed vertically on all the stripes. Her blond hair swung long and loose. Tom saw the firelight glow in it and thought, What purity compared to what we've been talking about! The light in her hair was gold, however, which made Tom think of money. Well, he didn't really need any more money, even if the Derwatt picture sales, of which he got a percentage, would soon come to an end because there would be no more pictures. He still got a percentage from the Derwatt Art Supplies Company, and that would continue. Then there was the modest but slowly increasing income from the Greenleaf securities which he had inherited in a will forged by Tom himself. Not to mention Héloïse's generous allowance from her father. No use being greedy. Tom detested murder unless it was absolutely necessary.

"Did you have a good talk?" Héloïse asked in English, and fell back gracefully onto the yellow sofa.

"Yes, thank you," said Reeves.

The rest of the conversation was in French, because Héloïse was not comfortable in English. Reeves did not know much French but he got along, and they were not talking about anything important: the garden, the mild winter, which seemed really to have passed because here it was early March and the daffodils were opening. Tom poured champagne for Héloïse from one of the little bottles on the cart.

"How ees eet in Hambourg?" Héloïse ventured again in English, and Tom saw amusement in her eyes as Reeves struggled to get out a conventional response in French.

It was not too cold in Hamburg, either, and Reeves added that he had a garden also, as his *petite maison* found itself on the Alster, which was water; that was to say, a sort of bay where many people had homes with gardens and water, meaning they could have small boats if they wished.

Tom knew that Héloïse disliked Reeves Minot, distrusted him, that Reeves was the kind of person Héloïse wanted Tom to avoid. Tom reflected with satisfaction that he could honestly say to Héloïse tonight that he had declined to cooperate in the scheme that Reeves had proposed. Héloïse was always worried about what her father would say. Her father, Jacques Plissot, was a millionaire pharmaceutical manufacturer, a Gaullist, the essence of French respectability. And he had never cared for Tom. "My father will not stand for much more!" Héloïse often warned Tom, but Tom knew she was more interested in his own safety than in hanging on to the allowance her father gave her—an allowance he frequently threatened to cut off, according to Héloïse. She had lunch with her parents at their home in Chantilly once a week, usually Friday. If her father ever severed her allowance, they could not quite make it at Belle Ombre, Tom knew.

The dinner menu was médaillons de boeuf, preceded by cold artichokes with Mme. Annette's own sauce. Héloïse had changed into a simple dress of pale blue. She sensed already, Tom thought, that Reeves had not got what he had come for. Before they all retired, Tom made sure that Reeves had everything he needed, and at what hour he would like tea or coffee brought to his room. Coffee at eight, Reeves said. Reeves had the guest room in the left center of the house, which gave him the bathroom that was usually Héloïse's, but from which Mme. Annette had already removed Héloïse's toothbrush to Tom's bathroom, off his room.

"I am glad he is going tomorrow. Why is he so tense?" Héloïse asked while brushing her teeth.

"He's always tense." Tom turned off the shower, stepped out, and quickly enveloped himself in a big yellow towel. "That's why he's thin—maybe." They were speaking in English, because Héloïse was not shy about speaking English with him.

"How did you meet him?"

Tom couldn't remember. When? Maybe five or six years ago. In Rome? Who was Reeves a friend of? Tom was too tired to think hard, and it didn't matter. He had five or six such acquaintances, and would have been hard pressed to say where he had met each one.

"What did he want from you?"

Tom put his arm around Héloïse's waist, pressing the loose nightdress close to her body. He kissed her cool cheek. "Something impossible. I said no. You can see that. He is disappointed."

That night there was an owl, a lonely owl calling somewhere in the pines of the communal forest behind Belle Ombre. Tom lay with his left arm under Héloïse's neck, thinking. She fell asleep, and her breathing became slow and soft. Tom sighed, and went on thinking. But he was not thinking in a logical, constructive way. His second coffee was keeping him awake. He was remembering a party he had been to a month ago in Fontainebleau, an informal birthday party for a Mme.—who? It was her husband's name that Tom was interested in, an English name that might come to him in a few seconds. The man, the host, had been in his early thirties, and they had a small son. The house was a straight-up-and-down three-story, on a residential street in Fontainebleau, a patch of garden behind it. The man was a picture framer; that was why Tom had been dragged along by Pierre Gauthier, who had an art-supply shop in the Rue Grande, where Tom bought his paints and brushes. Gauthier had said, "Oh, come along with me, M. Reeply. Bring your wife! He wants a lot of people. He's a little depressed. . . . And anyway, since he makes frames, you might give him some business."

Tom blinked in the darkness, and moved his head back a little so his eyelashes would not touch Héloïse's shoulder. He recalled a tall blond Englishman with a certain resentment and dislike, because in the kitchen—that gloomy kitchen with worn-out linoleum and a smoke-stained tin ceiling with a nineteenth-century bas-relief pattern—this man had made an unpleasant remark to Tom. The man—Trewbridge, Tewksbury?—had said, in an almost sneering way, "Oh, yes, I've heard of you." Tom had said, "I'm Tom Ripley. I live in Villeperce," and Tom had been about to ask him how long he'd been in Fontainebleau, thinking that perhaps an Englishman with a French wife might like to make acquaintance with an American with a French wife living not far away, but Tom's venture had been met with rudeness. Trevanny? Wasn't that his name? Blond straight hair, rather Dutch-looking—but then the English often looked Dutch and vice versa.

What Tom was thinking of now, however, was what Gauthier had said later the same evening: "He's depressed. He doesn't mean to be unfriendly. He's got some kind of blood disease—leukemia, I think. Pretty serious. Also, as you can see from the house, he's not doing too well." Gauthier had a glass eye of a curious yellow-green color, obviously an attempt to match the real one, but a failure. In fact, Gauthier's false eye suggested the eye of a dead cat. You avoided looking at it, yet you were hypnotically drawn to it. Gauthier's gloomy words, combined with the glass eye, had made a strong impression of death upon Tom, and Tom had not forgotten.

Oh, yes, I've heard of you. Did that mean that Trevanny, or whatever his name was, thought he was responsible for Bernard Tufts's death, and before that Dickie Greenleaf's? Or was the Englishman merely embittered against everyone because of his ailment? Dyspeptic, like a man with a constant stomach ache? Now Tom recalled Trevanny's wife, not pretty, but rather an interesting-looking woman with chestnut hair, friendly and outgoing, making an effort at that party in the small living room and the kitchen where no one sat down on the few chairs available.

Tom was thinking, Would this man take on such a job as Reeves was proposing? An interesting approach to Trevanny had occurred to Tom. It was an approach that might work with any man, if one prepared the ground, but in this case the ground was already prepared. Trevanny was seriously worried about his health. Tom's idea was nothing more than a practical joke, he thought, a nasty one, but the man had been nasty to him. The joke might not last more than a day or so, until Trevanny could consult his doctor.

Tom was amused by his thoughts, and eased himself gently from Héloïse, so that if he shook with repressed laughter for an instant he wouldn't awaken her. Suppose Trevanny was vulnerable, and carried out Reeves's plan like a soldier, like a dream? Was it worth a try? Yes, because Tom had nothing to lose. Neither had Trevanny. Trevanny might gain. Reeves might gain—according to Reeves, but let Reeves figure that out, because what Reeves wanted seemed as vague to Tom as Reeves's microfilm activities, which presumably had to do with international spying. Were governments aware of the insane antics of some of their spies? Of those whimsical, half-demented men flitting from Bucharest to Moscow and Washington with guns and microfilm—men who might with the same enthusiasm have put their energies into stamp-collecting, or acquiring secrets of miniature electric trains?

| 2 | So it was that some ten days later, Jonathan Trevanny, who lived in the Rue Saint-Merry, Fontainebleau, received a curious letter from his good friend Alan McNear. Alan, a Paris representative of an English electronics firm, had written the letter just before leaving for New York on a business assignment, and oddly the day after he had visited the Trevannys in Fontainebleau. Jonathan had expected—or, rather, not expected—a sort of thank-you letter from Alan for the send-off party Jonathan and Simone had given him, and Alan did write a few words

of appreciation, but the paragraph that puzzled Jonathan went:

> Jon, I was shocked at the news in regard to the old blood ailment, and am even now hoping it isn't so. I was told that you knew but weren't telling any of your friends. Very noble of you, but what are friends for? You needn't think we'll avoid you or that we'll think you'll become so melancholy that we won't want to see you. Your friends (and I'm one) are here—always. But I can't write anything I want to say, really. I'll do better when I see you next, in a couple of months when I wangle myself a vacation, so forgive these inadequate words.

What was Alan talking about? Had his doctor, Périer, said something to his friends, something he wouldn't tell him? Something about not living much longer? Dr. Périer hadn't been to the party for Alan, but could Dr. Périer have said something to someone else?

Had Dr. Périer spoken to Simone? And was Simone keeping it from him, too?

As Jonathan thought of these possibilities, he was standing in his garden, at eight-thirty in the morning, chilly under his sweater, his fingers smudged with earth. He'd best speak with Dr. Périer today. No use with Simone. She might put on an act. *But, darling, what're you talking about?* Jonathan wasn't sure he'd be able to tell if she was putting on an act or not.

And Dr. Périer—could he trust him? Dr. Périer was always bouncing with optimism, which was fine if you had something minor—you felt fifty percent better, even cured. But Jonathan knew he didn't have anything minor. He had myelocytic leukemia, characterized by an excess of yellow matter in the bone marrow. In the past five years, he'd had at least four blood transfusions per year. Every time he felt weak, he was supposed to get to his doctor, or to the Fontainebleau hospital, for a transfusion. Dr. Périer had said (and so had a specialist in Paris) that there would come a time when the decline might be swift, when transfusions wouldn't do the trick any longer. Jonathan had read enough about his ailment to know that himself. No doctor had yet come up with a cure for myelocytic leukemia. On the average, you died after six to twelve years, or even six to eight. Jonathan was entering his sixth year.

Jonathan set his fork back in the little brick structure, formerly an outside toilet, that served as a tool shed, then walked to his back steps. He paused with one foot on the first step and drew the fresh morning air into his lungs, thinking, How many weeks will I have to enjoy such mornings? He remembered thinking the same thing last spring, however. Buck up, he told himself, he'd known for six years that he might not live to see thirty-five. Jonathan mounted the iron steps with a firm tread, thinking that it was already eight-fifty-two, and that he was due in his shop at nine or a few minutes after.

Simone had gone off with Georges to the École Maternelle, and the house was empty. Jonathan washed his hands at the sink and made use of the vegetable brush, which Simone would not have approved of, but he left the brush clean. The only other sink was in the bathroom on the top floor. There was no telephone in the house. He'd ring Dr. Périer from his shop the first thing.

Jonathan walked to the Rue de la Paroisse and turned left, then went on to the Rue des Sablons, which crossed it. In his shop, Jonathan dialed Dr. Périer's number, which he knew by heart.

The nurse said the doctor was booked up today, which Jonathan had expected.

"But this is urgent. It's something that won't take long. Just a question, really—but I must see him."

"You are feeling weak, M. Trevanny?"

"Yes, I am," Jonathan said at once.

He got an appointment for twelve noon. The hour had a certain doom about it.

Jonathan was a picture framer. He cut mats and glass, made frames, chose frames from his stock for clients who were undecided, and once in a blue moon, when buying old frames at auctions and from junk dealers, he got a picture that was of some interest with the frame, a picture which he could clean and put in his window and sell. But it wasn't a lucrative business. He scraped along. Seven years ago he'd had a partner, another Englishman, from Manchester, and they had started an antique shop in Fontainebleau, dealing mainly in junk which they refurbished and sold. This hadn't paid enough for two, and Roy had pushed off and got a job as a garage mechanic somewhere near Paris. Shortly after that, a Paris doctor had said the same thing that a London doctor had told Jonathan: "You're inclined to anemia. You'd better have frequent checkups, and it's best if you don't do any heavy work." So from handling armoires and sofas, Jonathan had turned to the lighter work of handling picture frames and glass. Before Jonathan had married Simone, he had told her that he might not live more than another six years, because just at the time he met Simone, he'd had it confirmed by two doctors that his periodic weakness was caused by myelocytic leukemia.

Now, Jonathan thought as he calmly, very calmly, began his day, Simone might remarry if he died. Simone worked five afternoons a week from two-thirty until six-thirty at a shoe-shop in the Avenue Franklin Roosevelt, which was within walking distance of their house. She had begun working only in the past year, when Georges had been old enough to be put into the French equivalent of kindergarten. They needed the two hundred francs a week that Simone earned, but Jonathan was irked by the thought that Brezard, her boss, was a bit of a lecher, liked to pinch his employees' behinds, and doubtless to try his luck in the back room where the stock was. Simone was a married woman, as Brezard well knew, so there was a limit as to how far he could go, Jonathan supposed, but that never stopped his type from trying. Simone was not at all a flirt; she had a curious shyness, in fact, that suggested she thought herself not attractive to men. It was a quality that endeared her to Jonathan. In Jonathan's opinion, Simone was supercharged with sex appeal, though of the kind that might not be apparent to the average man, and it especially annoyed Jonathan that that swine Brezard must have become aware of Simone's very different kind of attractiveness and wanted some of it for himself. Not that Simone talked much about Brezard. Once she had mentioned that he tried it on with his women employees—two besides Simone. For an instant that morning, as Jonathan presented a framed watercolor to a client, he imagined Simone, after a discreet interval, succumbing to the odious Brezard, who, after all, was a bachelor and financially better off than Jonathan. Absurd, Jonathan thought. Simone hated his type.

"Oh, it's lovely! Excellent!" said the young woman holding the watercolor at arm's length.

Jonathan's long, serious face slowly smiled, as if a small and private sun had come out of clouds and begun to shine within him. She was so genuinely pleased! Jonathan didn't know her; in fact, she was picking up the picture that an older woman, perhaps her mother, had brought in. The price should have been twenty francs more than he had first es-timated, because the framing was not the same kind the older woman had chosen (Jonathan had not had enough in stock), but he didn't mention this and accepted the eighty francs agreed upon.

Then Jonathan pushed a broom over his wooden floor, and feather-dusted the three or four pictures in his small front window. His shop was positively shabby, Jonathan thought that morning. No color anywhere, frames of all sizes leaning against unpainted walls, samples of frame wood hang-ing from the ceiling, a counter with an order book, ruler, pencils. At the back of the shop stood a long wooden table where Jonathan worked with his miter boxes, saws, and glass cutters. Also on the big table were his carefully protected sheets of matboard, a great roll of brown paper, string, wire, pots of glue, and boxes of variously sized nails, and above the table on the walls were racks of knives and hammers. In principle, Jonathan liked the nineteenth-century atmosphere, the lack of commercial frou-frou. He wanted his shop to look as if a good craftsman ran it, and in that he had succeeded, he thought. He never overcharged; he did his work on time, or if he was going to be late, he notified his clients by postcard or a telephone call. People appreciated that, Jonathan had found.

At eleven-thirty-five, having framed two small pictures and fixed their owners' names to them, Jonathan washed his hands and face at the cold-water tap in his sink, combed his hair, stood up straight, and tried to brace himself for the worst. Dr. Périer's office was not far away in the Rue Grande. Jonathan turned his door card to OUVERT at 14:30, locked his front door, and set out.

Jonathan had to wait in Dr. Périer's front room with its sickly, dusty rose laurel plant. The plant never flowered; it didn't die, and never grew, never changed. Jonathan identified himself with the plant. Again and again his eyes were drawn to it, though he tried to think of other things. There were copies of *Paris-Match* on the oval table, out of date and much thumbed; Jonathan found them more depressing than the laurel plant. Dr. Périer also worked at the big Hôpital de Fontainebleau, Jonathan reminded himself; otherwise it would have seemed an absurdity to entrust one's life to, to believe a life-or-death diagnosis of, a doctor who worked in such a wretched little place as this looked.

The nurse came out and beckoned.

"Well, well, how's the interesting patient, my most interesting patient?" said Dr. Périer, rubbing his hands, then extending one to Jonathan.

Jonathan shook his hand. "I feel quite all right, thank you. But what this is about—I mean the tests of two months ago. I understand they are not favorable?"

Dr. Périer looked blank, and Jonathan watched him intently. Then Dr. Périer smiled, showing yellowish teeth under his carelessly trimmed mustache.

"What do you mean unfavorable? You saw the results."

"But—you know I'm not an expert in understanding them —perhaps."

"But I explained them to you. Now, what is the matter? You're feeling tired again?"

"In fact, no." Since Jonathan knew the doctor wanted to get away for lunch, he said hastily, "To tell the truth, a friend of mine has learned somewhere that—I'm due for a crisis. Maybe I haven't long to live. Naturally, I thought this information must have come from you."

Dr. Périer shook his head, then laughed, hopped about like a bird, and came to rest with his skinny arms lightly outspread on the top of a glass-enclosed bookcase. "My dear sir—first of all, if it were true, I would not have said it to anybody. That is not ethical. Second, it is not true, as far as I know from the last test. . . . Do you want another test today? Late this afternoon at the hospital, maybe I—"

"Not necessarily. What I really wanted to know is—is it true? You wouldn't just not tell me?" Jonathan said, with a laugh. "Just to make me feel better?"

"What nonsense! Do you think I'm that kind of a doctor?"

Yes, Jonathan thought, looking Dr. Périer straight in the eye. And God bless him, maybe, in some cases, but Jonathan thought he deserved the facts, because he was the kind of man who could face the facts. Jonathan bit his underlip. He could go to the lab in Paris, he thought, insist on seeing the specialist Moussu again. Also he might get something out of Simone today at lunchtime.

Dr. Périer was patting his arm. "Your friend—and I won't ask who he is!—is either mistaken or not a very nice friend, I think. Now, then, you should tell me when and if you become tired. *That* is what counts."

Twenty minutes later, Jonathan was climbing the front steps of his house, carrying an apple tart and a long loaf of bread. He let himself in with his key and walked down the hall to the kitchen. He smelled frying potatoes, a mouthwatering smell signifying lunch, not dinner, and Simone's potatoes would be in long slender pieces, not short chunks like the chips in England. Why had he thought of English chips?

Simone was at the stove, wearing an apron over her dress, wielding a long fork. "Hello, Jon. You're late."

Jonathan put an arm around her and kissed her cheek, then held up the paper box and swung it toward Georges, who was sitting at the table, blond head bent, cutting out parts for a mobile from an empty box of corn flakes.

"Ah, a cake! What kind?" Georges asked.

"Apple." Jonathan set the box on the table.

They had a small steak each, the delicious fried potatoes, a green salad.

"Brezard is starting inventory," Simone said. "The summer stock comes in next week, so he wants to have a sale Friday and Saturday. I might be a little late tonight."

She had warmed the apple tart on the asbestos plate. Jonathan waited impatiently for Georges to go in the living room, where a lot of his toys were, or out to the garden.

When Georges left finally, Jonathan said, "I had a funny letter today from Alan."

"Alan? Funny how?"

"He wrote it just before he went to New York. It seems he's heard—" Should he show her Alan's letter? She could read English well enough. Jonathan decided to go on. "He's heard somewhere that I'm worse, due for a bad crisis—or something. Do you know anything about it?" Jonathan watched her eyes.

Simone looked genuinely surprised. "Why, no, Jon. How would I hear—except from you?"

"I spoke with Dr. Périer just now. That's why I was late. Périer says he doesn't know of any change in the situation, but you know Périer!" Jonathan smiled, still watching Simone anxiously. "Well, here's the letter," he said, pulling it from his back pocket. He translated the paragraph.

"*Mon Dieu!* Well, where did *he* hear it from?"

"Yes, that's the question. I'll write him and ask, don't you think?" Jonathan smiled again, a more genuine smile. He was sure Simone didn't know anything about it.

Jonathan carried a second cup of coffee into the small square living room where Georges was now sprawled on the floor with his cut-outs. Jonathan sat down at the writing desk, which always made him feel like a giant. It was a rather dainty French *écritoire*, a present from Simone's family. Jonathan was careful not to put too much weight on the writing shelf. He addressed an airmail letter to Alan McNear at the Hotel New Yorker, began the letter breezily enough, and wrote a second paragraph:

> I don't know quite what you mean in your letter about the news (about me) which shocked you. I feel all right, but this morning spoke with my doctor here to see if he was giving me the whole story. He disclaims any knowledge of a worse condition. So, dear Alan, what does interest me is where did you hear it? Could you possibly drop me a line soon? It sounds like a misunderstanding, and I'd be delighted to forget it, but I hope you can understand my curiosity as to where you heard it.

He dropped the letter in a mailbox en route to his shop. It would probably be a week before he heard from Alan.

That afternoon, Jonathan's hand was as steady as ever as he pulled his razor knife down the edge of his steel ruler. He thought of his letter, making its progress to Orly airport maybe by this evening, maybe by tomorrow morning. He thought of his age, thirty-four, and of how pitifully little he would have done if he were to die in another couple of months. He'd produced a son, and that was something, but hardly an achievement worthy of special praise. He would not leave Simone very secure. If anything, he had lowered her standard of living slightly. Her father was only a coal merchant, but somehow over the years her family had gathered a few conveniences around them—a car, for instance, and decent furniture. They vacationed in June or July down South in a villa which they rented, and last year they had paid a month's rent so that Jonathan and Simone could go there with Georges. Jonathan had not done as well as his brother Philip, two years older than himself, though Philip had looked physically weaker and had been a dull, plodding type all his life. Philip was a professor of anthropology at Bristol University—not brilliant, Jonathan was sure, but a good solid man with a solid career, a wife, and two children. Jonathan's mother, a widow now, had a happy existence with her brother and sister-in-law in Oxfordshire, taking care of the big garden there and doing all the shopping and cooking. Jonathan felt himself the failure of his family, both physically and as to his work. He had first wanted to be an actor. At eighteen he'd gone to a drama school for two years. He didn't have a bad face for an actor, he thought—not too handsome, with his big nose and wide mouth, but good-looking enough to play romantic roles and heavy enough to play heavier roles in time. What pipedreams! He'd hardly got two walk-on parts in the three years he'd hung around London and Manchester theatres—supporting himself by odd jobs, including one as a veterinary's assistant. "You take up a lot of space and you're not even sure of yourself," a director once said to him. And then, working for an antique dealer in another of his odd jobs, Jonathan had thought he might like the antique business. He had learned all he could from his boss, Andrew Mott. Then the grand move to France with his friend Roy Johnson, who had had enthusiasm, if not much knowledge, about starting an antique shop via the junk trade. Jonathan remembered his dreams of glory and adventure in a new country, France; dreams of freedom, of success. And instead of success, instead of a series of educational mistresses, instead of making friends with bohemians, or with some stratum of French society which Jonathan had imagined existed but perhaps didn't—instead of all this, Jonathan had continued to limp along, no better off really than when he'd been trying to get jobs as an actor and had supported himself any old way.

The only successful thing in his whole life was his marriage to Simone, Jonathan thought. The news of his disease had come in the same month he had met Simone Foussadier. He'd begun to feel strangely weak, and had romantically thought that it might be due to falling in love. But a little extra rest hadn't shaken the weakness; he had fainted once in a street in Nemours, so he had gone to a doctor—Dr. Périer in Fontainebleau, who had suspected a blood condition and sent him to a specialist in Paris. The specialist, Dr. Moussu, after two days of tests, had confirmed myelocytic leukemia, and said that he might have from six to eight—or, with luck, twelve—years to live. There would be an enlargement of the spleen, which in fact Jonathan already had without having noticed it. Thus Jonathan's proposal to Simone had been a declaration of love and death in the same awkward speech. It would have been enough to put most young women off, or to have made them say they needed some time to think about it. Simone had said yes, she loved him, too. "It is the love that is important, not the time," Simone had said. None of the calculation that Jonathan had associated with the French, and with Latins in general. Simone said she had already spoken to her family. And this after they had known each other only two weeks. Jonathan felt himself suddenly in a world more secure than any he had ever known. Love—in a real and not a merely romantic sense, love that he had no control over—had miraculously rescued him. In a way, he felt that it had rescued him from death, but he realized that he meant that love had taken the terror out of death. And here was death six years later, as Dr. Moussu in Paris had predicted. Perhaps. Jonathan didn't know what to believe.

He must make another visit to Moussu in Paris, he thought. Three years ago, Jonathan had had a complete change of blood under Dr. Moussu's supervision in a Paris hospital. The treatment was called Vincainestine, the idea or the hope being that the excess of white with accompanying yellow components would not return to the blood. But the yellow excess had reappeared in about eight months.

Before he made an appointment with Dr. Moussu, however,

Jonathan preferred to wait for a letter from Alan McNear. Alan would write at once, Jonathan felt sure. One could count on Alan.

Jonathan, before he left his shop, cast one desperate glance around its Dickensian interior. It wasn't really dusty; it was just that the walls needed repainting. He wondered if he should make an effort to spruce the place up, start soaking his customers as so many picture framers did, sell lacquered brass items with big markups? Jonathan winced. He wasn't the type.

That day was Wednesday. On Friday, while bending over a stubborn screw eye that had been in an oak frame for perhaps a hundred and fifty years and had no intention of yielding to his pliers, Jonathan suddenly had to drop the pliers and look for a seat. The seat was a wooden box against the wall. He got up almost at once and went to the sink to wet his face, bending as low as he could. In five minutes or so, the faintness passed, and by lunchtime he had forgotten about it. Such moments came every two or three months, and Jonathan was glad if they didn't catch him on the street.

On Tuesday, six days after he had posted his letter to Alan, he received a letter from the Hotel New Yorker.

Saturday, March 25th

Dear Jon,

Believe me, I'm glad you spoke with your doctor and that the news is good! The person who told me you were in a serious way was a little balding fellow with a mustache and a glass eye—early forties, maybe. He seemed really concerned, and perhaps you shouldn't hold it too much against him, as he may have heard it from someone else.

I'm enjoying this town and wish you and Simone were here, esp. as I'm on an expense account. . . .

The man Alan meant was obviously Pierre Gauthier, who

had the art-supply shop in the Rue Grande. He was not a friend of Jonathan's, just an acquaintance. Gauthier often sent people to Jonathan to have their pictures framed. He had been at the house the night of Alan's send-off party, Jonathan remembered distinctly, and must have spoken to Alan then. It was out of the question that Gauthier had spoken maliciously. Jonathan was only a little surprised that Gauthier even knew he had a blood ailment, though word did get around, Jonathan realized. Jonathan thought the thing to do was speak to Gauthier and ask him where he'd heard the story.

It was ten to nine. Jonathan had waited for the mail, as he had yesterday morning. His impulse was to go straight to Gauthier, but he felt this would show unseemly anxiety, and that he'd better get his bearings by going to his shop and opening as usual.

Because of three or four customers, Jonathan didn't have a break till ten-thirty. He left his clock card in the glass of his door indicating that he would be open again at eleven.

When Jonathan entered the art-supply shop, Gauthier was busy with two women customers. Jonathan pretended to browse among racks of paintbrushes until Gauthier was free. Then he said, "M. Gauthier! How goes it?" and extended a hand.

Gauthier clasped Jonathan's hand in both his own and smiled. "And you, my friend?"

"Well enough, thank you. . . . *Écoutez*. I don't want to take your time—but there is something I would like to ask you."

"Yes? What's that?"

Jonathan beckoned Gauthier farther away from the door, which might open at any minute. There was not much standing room in the little shop. "I heard from a friend—my friend Alan, you remember? The Englishman. At the party at my house a few weeks ago."

"Yes! Your friend the Englishman. Alain." Gauthier remembered and looked attentive.

Jonathan tried to avoid even glancing at Gauthier's false

eye by concentrating on the other eye. "Well, it seems you told Alan that you'd heard I was very ill, maybe not going to live much longer."

Gauthier's soft face grew solemn. He nodded. "Yes, M'sieur, I did hear that. I hope it's not true. I remember Alain, because you introduced him to me as your best friend. So I assumed he knew. Perhaps I should have said nothing. I am sorry. It was perhaps tactless. I thought you were—in the English style—putting on a brave face."

"It's nothing serious, M. Gauthier, because as far as I know, it's not true! I've just spoken with my doctor. But—"

"Ah, *bon!* Ah, well, that's different! I'm delighted to hear that, M. Trevanny! Ha! Ha!" Pierre Gauthier gave a peal of laughter as if a ghost had been laid and he found not only Jonathan but himself back among the living.

"But I'd like to know where you heard this. Who told you I was so ill?"

"Ah—yes!" Gauthier pressed a finger to his lips, thinking. "Who? A man. Yes—of *course!*" He had it, but he paused.

Jonathan waited.

"But I remember he said he wasn't sure. He'd heard it, he said. An incurable blood disease, he said."

Jonathan felt warm with anxiety again, as he had felt several times in the past week. He wet his lips. "But who? How did he hear it? Didn't he say?"

Gauthier again hesitated. "Since it isn't true—shouldn't we best forget it?"

"Someone you know very well?"

"No! Not at all well, I assure you."

"A customer?"

"Yes. Yes, he is. A nice man, a gentleman. But since he *said* he wasn't sure— Really, M'sieur, you shouldn't bear a resentment, although I can understand how you could resent such a remark."

"Which leads to the interesting question of how the gentleman came to hear I was very ill," Jonathan went on, laughing now.

"Yes. Exactly. Well, the point is, it isn't true. Isn't that the main thing?"

Jonathan saw in Gauthier a French politeness, an unwillingness to alienate a customer, and—which was to be expected—an aversion to the subject of death. "You're right. That's the main thing." Jonathan shook hands with Gauthier, both of them smiling now, and bade him adieu.

That very day at lunch, Simone asked Jonathan if he had heard from Alan. Jonathan said yes.

"It was Gauthier who said something to Alan."

"Gauthier? The art-shop man?"

"Yes." Jonathan was lighting a cigarette over his coffee. Georges had gone out into the garden. "I went to see Gauthier this morning and I asked him where he'd heard it. He said from a customer. A man. . . . Funny, isn't it? Gauthier wouldn't tell me who, and I can't really blame him. It's some mistake, of course. Gauthier realizes that."

"But it's a shocking thing," said Simone.

Jonathan smiled, knowing Simone wasn't really shocked, since she knew Dr. Périer had given him rather good news. "As we say in English, one mustn't make a mountain out of a molehill."

In the following week, Jonathan bumped into Dr. Périer in the Rue Grande, the doctor in a hurry to enter the Société Générale before it shut at twelve sharp. But he paused to ask him how he was.

"Quite well, thank you," said Jonathan, whose mind was on buying a plunger for the toilet from a shop, a hundred yards away, which also shut at noon.

"M. Trevanny." Dr. Périer paused with one hand on the big knob of the bank's door. He moved away from the door, closer to Jonathan. "In regard to what we were talking about the other day, no doctor can be *sure*, you know. In a situation like yours. I don't want you to think I've given you a guarantee of perfect health, immunity for years. You know yourself—"

"Oh, I didn't assume that!" Jonathan interrupted.

"Then you understand," said Dr. Périer, smiling, and dashed at once into his bank.

Jonathan trotted on in quest of the plunger. It was the kitchen sink that was stopped up, not the toilet, he remembered, and Simone had lent a neighbor their plunger months ago and . . . Jonathan was thinking of what Dr. Périer had said. *Did* he know something, suspect something from the last test, something not sufficiently definite to warrant telling him about?

At the door of the *droguerie,* Jonathan encountered a smiling, dark-haired girl who was just locking up, removing the outside door handle.

"I'm sorry. It's five minutes past twelve," she said.

Tom, during the last week in March, was | 3 | engaged in painting a full-length portrait of Héloïse horizontal on the yellow satin sofa. And Héloïse seldom agreed to pose. But the sofa stayed still, and Tom had it satisfactorily on his canvas. He had also made seven or eight sketches of Héloïse with her head propped upon her left hand, her right hand resting on a big art book. He kept the two best sketches and threw the others away.

Reeves Minot had written him a letter asking if he had come up with a helpful idea—as to a person, Reeves meant. The letter had arrived a couple of days after Tom had spoken with Gauthier, from whom Tom usually bought his paints. Tom had replied to Reeves: "Am trying to think, but meanwhile you should go ahead with your own ideas, if you have any." The "am trying to think" was merely polite, even false, like a lot of phrases that served to oil the machinery of social intercourse, as Emily Post might say. Reeves hardly kept Belle Ombre oiled financially; in fact, Reeves's payments to Tom for occasional services as go-between and fence would hardly cover the dry-cleaning bills, but it never hurt to maintain friendly relations. Reeves had procured a false passport for Tom and had got it to Paris fast when Tom had needed it to help defend the Derwatt industry. Tom might one day need Reeves again.

The business with Jonathan Trevanny was merely a game for Tom. He was not doing it for Reeves's gambling interests. Tom happened to dislike gambling and had no respect for people who chose to earn their living, or even part of their living, from it. It was pimping, of a sort. Tom had started the Trevanny game out of curiosity, and because Trevanny had once sneered at him—and because Tom wanted to see if his own wild shot would find its mark, and make Jonathan Trevanny, who Tom sensed was priggish and self-righteous, uneasy for a time. Then Reeves could offer his bait, hammering in the point that Trevanny was soon to die anyway. Tom doubted that Trevanny would bite, but it would be a period of discomfort for the man, certainly. Unfortunately Tom couldn't guess how soon the rumor would get to Jonathan Trevanny's ears. Gauthier was gossipy enough, but it just might happen, even if Gauthier told two or three people, that no one would have the courage to broach the subject to Trevanny himself.

So Tom, although he was busy as usual with his painting, his spring planting, his German and French studies (Schiller and Molière now), plus supervising a crew of three masons who were constructing a greenhouse along the right side of Belle Ombre's back lawn, still counted the passing days and imagined what might have happened after that afternoon in the middle of March when he had said to Gauthier that he'd heard Trevanny wasn't long for this world. Not too likely that Gauthier would speak to Trevanny directly, unless they were closer than Tom thought. Gauthier would more likely tell someone else about it. Tom counted on the fact (he was sure it was a fact) that the possibility of anyone's imminent death was a fascinating subject to everyone.

Tom went to Fontainebleau, some twelve miles from Ville-perce, every two weeks or so. Fontainebleau was better than

Moret for shopping, for having suède coats cleaned, for buying radio batteries and the rarer things that Mme. Annette wanted for her cuisine. Jonathan Trevanny had a telephone in his shop, Tom had noted in the directory, but apparently not in his house in the Rue Saint-Merry. Tom had been trying to look up the house number, although he thought he would recognize the house when he saw it. Around the end of March, Tom became curious to see Trevanny again—from a distance, of course. So on a trip to Fontainebleau one morning, a market day, for the purpose of buying two round terracotta flower tubs, Tom, after putting these items in the back of the green Renault station wagon, walked through the Rue des Sablons where Trevanny's shop was. It was nearly noon.

Trevanny's shop looked in need of paint and a bit depressing, as if it belonged to an old man, Tom thought. Tom had never patronized Trevanny, because there was a good framer in Moret, closer to Tom. The little shop with "Encadrement" in fading red letters on the wood over the door stood in a row of shops—a launderette, a cobbler's, a modest travel agency—with its door on the left side and to the right a square window with assorted frames and two or three paintings with handwritten price tags on them. Tom crossed the street casually, glanced into the shop, and saw Trevanny's tall, Nordic-looking figure behind the counter some twenty feet away. Trevanny was showing a man a length of frame, slapping it into his palm, talking. Then Trevanny glanced at the window, saw Tom for an instant, but continued talking to the customer with no change in his expression.

Tom strolled on. Trevanny hadn't recognized him. Tom turned right, in to the Rue de France, the second important street after the Rue Grande, and continued till he came to the Rue Saint-Merry, where he turned right. Or had Trevanny's house been to the left? No, right.

Yes, there it was, surely, the narrow, cramped-looking gray house with slender black handrails going up the front steps. The tiny areas on either side of the steps were cemented, and no flowerpots relieved the barrenness. But there was a garden behind, Tom recalled. The windows, though sparkling clean, showed rather limp curtains. Yes, this was where he'd come on the invitation of Gauthier that evening in February. There was a narrow passage on the left side of the house that must lead to the garden beyond. A green plastic garbage bin stood in front of the padlocked iron gate to the garden, and Tom imagined that the Trevannys usually got to the garden via the back door off the kitchen, which Tom remembered.

Tom was on the other side of the street, walking slowly, but careful not to appear to be loitering, because he couldn't be sure that the wife, or someone else, was not even now looking out one of the windows.

Was there anything else he needed to buy? Zinc white. He was nearly out of it. And that purchase would take him to Gauthier, the art-supply man. Tom quickened his step, congratulating himself because his need of zinc white was a real need, so he'd be entering Gauthier's on a real errand, while at the same time he might be able to satisfy his curiosity.

Gauthier was alone in the shop.

"*Bonjour,* M. Gauthier!" said Tom.

"*Bonjour,* M. Reepley!" Gauthier replied, smiling. "And how are you?"

"Very well, thank you, and you? . . . I find I need some zinc white."

"Zinc white." Gauthier pulled a flat drawer from his cabinet against a wall. "Here they are. And you like the Rembrandt, as I recall."

Tom did. Derwatt zinc white and other Derwatt-made colors were available, too, their tubes emblazoned with the bold, downward-slanting signature of Derwatt in black on the label, but somehow Tom didn't want to paint at home with the name Derwatt catching his eye every time he reached for a tube of anything.

Tom paid, and as Gauthier was handing him his change and the little bag with the zinc white in it, Gauthier said, "Ah, M. Reepley, you recall M. Trevanny, the framer in the Rue Saint-Merry?"

"Yes, of course," said Tom, who had been wondering how to bring Trevanny up.

"Well, the rumor that you heard, that he is going to die soon, is not true at all." Gauthier smiled.

"No? Well, very good! I'm glad to hear that."

"Yes. M. Trevanny went to see his doctor, even. I think he was a bit upset. Who wouldn't be, eh? Ha-ha! But you said somebody told *you*, M. Reepley?"

"Yes. A man who was at the party—in February. Mme. Trevanny's birthday party. So I assumed it was a fact and everybody knew it, you see."

Gauthier looked thoughtful.

"You spoke to M. Trevanny?" Tom asked.

"No-no. But I did speak to his best friend one evening, another evening at the Trevannys' house, this month. Evidently he spoke to M. Trevanny. How these things get around!"

"His best friend?" Tom asked with an air of innocence.

"An Englishman. Alain something. He was going to America next day. But—do you recall who told *you*, M. Reepley?"

Tom shook his head slowly. "Can't recall his name, not even how he looked. There were so many people that night."

"Because"—Gauthier bent closer and whispered, as if there were someone else present—"M. Trevanny asked *me*, you see, who had told me. Of course I didn't say it was *you*. These things can be misinterpreted. I didn't want to get *you* into trouble. Ha!" Gauthier's shiny glass eye did not laugh but looked out from his head with a bold stare, as if there were a different brain controlling that eye, a computer kind of brain that would know everything at once, if someone just programmed it properly.

"I thank you for that, because it is not nice to make remarks which are not true about people's health, eh?" Tom was grinning now, ready to take his leave, but he added, "M. Trevanny does have a blood condition, however, didn't you say?"

"That is true. I think it's leukemia. But that's something he lives with. He once told me he'd had it for years."

Tom nodded. "At any rate, I'm glad he's not in danger. *À bientôt,* M. Gauthier. Many thanks."

Tom walked in the direction of his car. Trevanny's shock, though it may have lasted only a few hours until he consulted his doctor, must at least have put a little crack in his self-confidence. A few people had believed—and maybe Trevanny himself had believed—that he was not going to live more than a few weeks. That was because such a possibility wasn't out of the question for a man with Trevanny's ailment. A pity Trevanny was now reassured, but that little crack might be all that Reeves needed. The game could now enter its second stage. Trevanny would probably say no to Reeves. End of game, in that case. On the other hand, Reeves would approach him as if he was a doomed man. It would be amusing if Trevanny weakened. That day after lunch with Héloïse and her Paris friend Noëlle, who was going to stay overnight, Tom left the ladies and wrote a letter to Reeves on his typewriter.

March 28th

Dear Reeves,

I have an idea for you, in case you have not yet found what you are looking for. His name is Jonathan Trevanny, early thirties, English, a picture framer, married to Frenchwoman with small son. [Here Tom gave Trevanny's home and shop addresses and shop telephone number.] He looks as if he could use some money, and although he may not be the *type* you want, he looks the picture of decency and innocence, and, what is more important for you, I have found out that he has only a few months or weeks to live. He's got leukemia, and has just heard the bad news. He might be willing to take on a dangerous job to earn some money now.

I don't know Trevanny personally. Need I emphasize that I don't wish to make his acquaintance, nor do I wish you to mention my name? My suggestion

is if you want to sound him out, come to F'bleau,
put yourself up at a charming hostelry called L'Aigle
Noir for a couple of days, ring Trevanny at his shop,
make an appointment, and talk it over. And do I
have to tell you to give another name besides your
own?

Tom felt a sudden optimism about the project. The vision
of Reeves with his disarming air of uncertainty and anxiety
—almost suggestive of probity—laying such an idea before
Trevanny, who looked as upright as a saint, made Tom laugh.
Did he dare occupy a table in L'Aigle Noir's dining room or
bar when Reeves made his date with Trevanny? No, that
would be too much. This reminded him of another point, and
he added to his letter:

If you come to F'bleau, please don't telephone or
write a note to me under any circumstances. De-
stroy my letter now, please.

Yours ever,

Tom

The telephone rang in Jonathan's shop on | **4** |
Friday afternoon, March 31st. He was just
gluing brown paper to the back of a large picture, and he
had to find suitable weights—an old sandstone saying LONDON,
the glue pot itself, a wooden mallet—before he could lift the
telephone.

"Hello?"

"*Bonjour*, M'sieur. M. Trevanny? . . . You speak English,
I think. My name is Stephen Wister, W-i-s-t-e-r. I'm in Fontainebleau for a couple of days, and I wonder if you could
find a few minutes to talk with me about something—something that I think would interest you."

The man had an American accent. "I don't buy pictures," Jonathan said. "I'm a framer."

"I didn't want to see you about anything connected with your work. It's something I can't explain over the phone. . . . I'm staying at the Aigle Noir."

"Oh?"

"I was wondering if you have a few minutes this evening after you close your shop. Around seven? Six-thirty? We could have a drink or a coffee."

"But—I'd like to know why you want to see me." A woman had come into the shop—Mme. Tissot, Tissaud?—to pick up a picture. Jonathan smiled apologetically to her.

"I'll have to explain when I see you," said the soft, earnest voice. "It'll take only ten minutes. Have you any time? At seven today, for instance?"

Jonathan shifted. "Six-thirty would be all right."

"I'll meet you in the lobby. I'm wearing a gray plaid suit. But I'll speak to the porter. It won't be difficult."

Jonathan usually closed around six-thirty. At six-fifteen, he stood at his cold-water sink, scrubbing his hands. It was a mild day, and Jonathan had worn a polo-neck sweater with an old beige corduroy jacket, not elegant enough for L'Aigle Noir, and the addition of his second-best mack would have made things worse. Why should he care? The man wanted to sell him something. It couldn't be anything else.

The hotel was only a five-minute walk from the shop. It had a small front court enclosed by high iron gates, and a few steps led up to its front door.

Jonathan saw a slender, tense-looking man with crew-cut hair move toward him with a faint uncertainty, and Jonathan said, "Mr. Wister?"

"Yes." Reeves gave a twitch of a smile and extended his hand. "Shall we have a drink in the bar here, or do you prefer somewhere else?"

The bar was pleasant and quiet. Jonathan shrugged. "As you like." He noticed an awful scar the length of Wister's cheek.

They went to the wide door of the hotel's bar, which was empty except for a man and a woman at a small table.

Wister turned away as if put off by the quietude, and said, "Let's try somewhere else."

They walked out of the hotel and turned right. Jonathan knew the next bar, the Café du Sport or some such, roistering at this hour with boys at the pinball machines and workmen at the counter. On the threshold of the bar-café, Wister stopped as if he had come unexpectedly upon a battlefield in action.

"Would you mind," Wister said, turning away, "coming up to my room? It's quiet and we can have something sent up."

They went back to the hotel, climbed a flight of stairs, and entered an attractive room in Spanish décor—black ironwork, a raspberry-colored bedspread, a pale green carpet. A suitcase on the rack was the only sign of the room's occupancy. Wister had entered without a key.

"What'll you have?" Wister went to the telephone. "Scotch?"

"Fine."

The man ordered in clumsy French. He asked for the bottle to be brought up, and for plenty of ice, please.

Then there was a silence. Why was the man uneasy, Jonathan wondered. Jonathan stood by the window where he had been looking out. Evidently Wister didn't want to talk until the drinks arrived. Jonathan heard a discreet tap at the door.

A white-jacketed waiter came in with a tray and a friendly smile. Stephen Wister poured generous drinks.

"Are you interested in making some money?"

Jonathan smiled, settled in a comfortable armchair now, with the huge iced Scotch in his hand. "Who isn't?"

"I have a dangerous job in mind—well, an important job—for which I'm prepared to pay quite well."

Jonathan thought of drugs: the man probably wanted something delivered or held. "What business are you in?" Jonathan inquired politely.

"Several. Just now one you might call—gambling. . . .
Do you gamble?"

"No." Jonathan smiled.

"I don't, either. That's not the point." The man got up
from the side of the bed and walked slowly about the room.
"I live in Hamburg."

"Oh?"

"Gambling isn't legal in the city limits, but it goes on in
private clubs. However, whether it's legal or not is not the
point. I need a person eliminated, possibly two—and maybe
a theft done. Now, that's putting my cards on the table." He
looked at Jonathan with a serious, hopeful expression.

Killed, the man meant. Jonathan was startled; then he
smiled and shook his head. "I wonder where you got my
name!"

Stephen Wister didn't smile. "Never mind that." He continued walking up and down with his drink in his hand, and
his gray eyes glanced at Jonathan and away again. "I wonder
if you're interested in ninety-six thousand dollars? That's
about forty thousand pounds, and about four hundred and
eighty thousand francs—new francs. Just for shooting a man
—maybe two; we'll have to see how it goes. It'll be an arrangement that's safe and foolproof for you."

Jonathan shook his head again. "I don't know where you
heard that I'm a—a gunman. You've got me confused with
someone else."

"No. Not at all."

Jonathan's smile faded under the man's intense stare. "It's
a mistake. —Do you mind telling me how you came to
ring me?"

"Well, you're—" Wister looked more pained than ever.
"You're not going to live more than a few months. You know
that. You've got a wife and a small son—haven't you?
Wouldn't you like to leave them a little something when
you're gone?"

Jonathan felt the blood drain from his face. How did
Wister know so much? Then he realized it was all connected,

that whoever told Gauthier he was going to die soon knew this man, was connected with him somehow. Jonathan was not going to mention Gauthier. Gauthier was an honest man, and Wister was a crook. Suddenly Jonathan's Scotch didn't taste so good. "There was a crazy rumor—recently—"

Now Wister shook his head. "It is not a crazy rumor. It may be that your doctor hasn't told you the truth."

"And you know more than my doctor? My doctor doesn't lie to me. It's true I have a blood disease, but I'm in no worse state now—" Jonathan broke off. "The essential thing is, I'm afraid I can't help you, Mr. Wister."

As Wister bit his underlip, the long scar moved in a distasteful way, like a live worm.

Jonathan looked away from him. Was Dr. Périer lying, after all? Jonathan thought he should ring up the Paris laboratory tomorrow morning and ask some questions, or simply go to Paris and demand another examination.

"Mr. Trevanny, I'm sorry to say it's evidently you who aren't informed. At least you've heard what you call the rumor, so I'm not the bearer of bad tidings. It's your own choice, but under the circumstances, a considerable sum like this, I would think, should sound rather pleasant. You could stop working and enjoy your— Well, for instance, you could take a cruise around the world with your family and still leave your wife—"

Jonathan felt slightly faint. He stood up and took a deep breath. The sensation passed, but he preferred to be on his feet. Wister was talking, but Jonathan barely listened.

". . . my idea. There're a few men in Hamburg who would contribute toward the ninety-six thousand dollars. The man, or men, we want out of the way are Mafia men."

Jonathan had only half recovered. "Thanks, I am not a killer. You may as well get off the subject."

Wister went on. "But exactly what we want is someone not connected with any of us, or with Hamburg. Although the first man, only a button man, must be shot in Hamburg. The reason is that we want the police to think that two Mafia gangs are fighting each other in Hamburg. In fact, we want the police to step in on our side." He continued to walk up and down, looking at the floor mostly. "The first man ought to be shot in a crowd, a U-bahn crowd. That's our subway— 'underground' you'd call it. The gun would be dropped at once, the—the assassin blends into the crowd and vanishes. An Italian gun, with no fingerprints on it. No clues." He brought his hands down like a conductor finishing.

Jonathan moved back to the chair, in need of it for a few seconds. "Sorry. No." He would walk to the door as soon as he got his strength back.

"I'm here all tomorrow, and probably till late Sunday afternoon. I wish you'd think about it. . . . Another Scotch? Might do you good."

"No, thanks." Jonathan hauled himself up. "I'll be pushing off."

Wister nodded, looking disappointed.

"And thanks for the drink."

"Don't mention it." Wister opened the door for Jonathan.

Jonathan went out. He had expected Wister to press a card with his name and address into his hand. Jonathan was glad he hadn't.

The streetlights had come on in the Rue de France. Seven twenty-two. Had Simone asked him to buy anything? Bread, perhaps. Jonathan went into a *boulangerie* and bought a long stick. The familiar chore was comforting.

The supper consisted of vegetable soup, a couple of slices of leftover fromage de tête, a salad of tomatoes and onions. Simone talked about a wallpaper sale at a shop near where she worked. For a hundred francs, they could paper the bedroom, and she had seen a beautiful mauve and green pattern, very light and art nouveau.

"With only one window, that bedroom's very dark, you know, Jon."

"Sounds fine," Jonathan said. "Especially if it's a sale."

"It *is* a sale. Not one of these silly sales where they reduce something five percent—like my stingy boss." She wiped bread crust in her salad oil and popped it into her mouth. "You're worried about something? Something happened today?"

Jonathan smiled suddenly. He wasn't worried about anything. He was glad Simone hadn't noticed he was a little late, and that he'd had a big drink. "No, darling. Nothing happened. The end of the week, maybe. Almost the end."

"You feel tired?"

It was like a question from a doctor, routine now. "No. —I've got to telephone a customer tonight between eight and nine." It was eight-thirty-seven. "I may as well do it now, dear. Maybe I'll have some coffee later."

"Can I go with you?" Georges asked, dropping his fork, sitting back ready to leap out of his chair.

"Not tonight, *mon petit copain.* I'm in a hurry. And you just want to play the pinball machines—I know you."

"Hollywood Chewing Gum!" Georges shouted, pronouncing it in the French manner, "Ollyvoo Schvang Gom!"

Jonathan winced as he lifted his jacket from the hall hook. Hollywood Chewing Gum, whose green and white wrappers littered the gutters and occasionally Jonathan's garden, had mysterious attractions for infants of the French nation. "*Oui,* M'sieur," Jonathan said, and went out the door.

Dr. Périer had a home number in the directory, and Jonathan hoped he was in tonight. A certain *bar-tabac,* which had a telephone, was closer than Jonathan's shop. Panic was taking hold of him, and he began to trot toward the slanting lighted red cylinder that marked the tabac two streets away. He would insist on the truth. Jonathan nodded a greeting to the young man behind the bar, whom he knew slightly, and pointed to the telephone and also to the shelf where the directories lay. "*Fontainebleau!*" Jonathan shouted. The place was noisy, and the jukebox was going. Jonathan searched out the number and dialed.

Dr. Périer answered and recognized Jonathan's voice.

"I would like to have another test. Even tonight. Now—if you could take a sample."

"Tonight?"

"I could come to see you at once. In five minutes."

"Are you— You are weak?"

"Well—I thought if the test went to Paris tomorrow—" Jonathan knew that Dr. Périer was in the habit of sending various samples to Paris on Saturday mornings. "If you could take a sample either tonight or early tomorrow morning—"

"I am not in my office tomorrow morning. I have visits to make. If you are so upset, M. Trevanny, come to my house now."

Jonathan paid for his call, and remembered just before he went out the door to buy two packages of Hollywood Chewing Gum. Périer lived way over on the Boulevard Maginot, which would take nearly ten minutes. Jonathan trotted and walked. He had never been to the doctor's house.

It was a big, gloomy building, and the concierge was an old, slow, skinny woman who was watching television in a little glass-enclosed room full of plastic plants.

While Jonathan waited for the lift to descend into the rickety cage, the concierge crept into the hall and asked curiously, "Your wife is having a baby, M'sieur?"

"No. No," Jonathan said, smiling, and recalled that Dr. Périer was a general practitioner.

He rode up.

"Now what is the matter?" Dr. Périer asked, beckoning him through the dining room. "Come into this room."

The apartment was dimly lighted. The television set was on somewhere. The room they went into was like a little office, with medical books on the shelves, and a desk on which the doctor's black bag now sat.

"*Mon Dieu,* one would think you are on the brink of collapse. You've just been running, obviously, and your cheeks are pink. Don't tell me you've heard another rumor that you're on the edge of the grave!"

Jonathan made an effort to sound calm. "It's just that I

want to be sure. I don't feel so splendid, to tell the truth. I know it's been only two months since the last test but—since the next is due the end of April, what's the harm—" He broke off, shrugging. "Since it's easy to take some marrow, and since it can go off tomorrow early—" Jonathan was aware that his French was clumsy at that moment, aware of the word *moelle,* marrow, which had become revolting, especially when Jonathan thought of his as being abnormally yellow. He sensed Dr. Périer's attitude of humoring his patient.

"Yes, I can take the sample. The result will probably be the same as last time. You can never have complete assurance from medical men, M. Trevanny. . . ." The doctor continued to talk while Jonathan removed his sweater, obeyed Dr. Périer's gesture, and lay down on an old leather sofa. The doctor jabbed the anesthetizing needle in. "But I can appreciate your anxiety," Dr. Périer said seconds later, pressing and tapping on the tube that was going into Jonathan's sternum.

Jonathan disliked the crunching sound of it, but found the slight pain quite bearable. This time, perhaps, he'd learn something. Jonathan could not refrain from saying before he left, "I must know the truth, Dr. Périer. You don't think that the laboratory might not be giving us a proper summing up? I'm ready to believe their *figures* are correct—"

"This summing up or prediction is what you can't get, my dear young man!"

Jonathan then walked home. He thought of telling Simone that he'd gone to see Périer, that he again felt anxious, but he couldn't: he'd put Simone through enough. What could she say if he told her? She would only become a little more anxious herself.

Georges was already in bed upstairs, and Simone was reading to him. Asterix again. Georges, propped against his pillows, and Simone, on a low stool under the lamplight, were like a tableau vivant of domesticity. The year might have been 1880, Jonathan thought, except for Simone's slacks. Georges's hair was as yellow as corn silk under the light.

"Le schvang gom?" Georges asked, grinning.

Jonathan smiled and produced one packet. The other could wait for another occasion.

"You were gone a long time," said Simone.

"I had a beer at the café," Jonathan said.

The next afternoon between four-thirty and five, as Dr. Périer had told him to do, Jonathan telephoned the Ebberle-Valent Laboratoires in Neuilly. He gave his name and spelled it and said he was a patient of Dr. Périer's in Fontainebleau. Then he waited to be connected with the right department, while the telephone gave a *blup* every minute for the pay units. Jonathan had pen and paper ready. Could he spell his name again, please? Then a woman's voice began to read the report, and Jonathan jotted figures down quickly. Hyperleukocytose 190,000. Wasn't that bigger than before?

"We shall, of course, send a written report to your doctor, which he should receive by Tuesday."

"This report is less favorable than the last, is it not?"

"I have not the previous report here, M'sieur."

"Is there a doctor there? Could I speak with a doctor, perhaps?"

"*I* am a doctor, M'sieur."

"Oh. Then this report—whether you have the old one or not—is not a good one, is it?"

Like a textbook, she said, "This is a potentially dangerous condition involving lowered resistance. . . ."

Jonathan had telephoned from his shop. He had turned his sign to FERMÉ and drawn his door curtain, though he had been visible through the window. Now, as he went to remove the sign, he realized he hadn't locked his door. Since no one else was due to call for a picture that afternoon, Jonathan thought he could afford to close. It was five to five.

He walked to Dr. Périer's office, prepared to wait more than an hour if he had to. Saturday was a busy day, because most people didn't work and were free to see the doctor. There were three people ahead of Jonathan, but the nurse asked if he would be long, Jonathan said no, and the nurse squeezed him in with an apology to the next patient. Had Dr. Périer spoken to his nurse about him Jonathan wondered.

Dr. Périer raised his black eyebrows at Jonathan's scribbled notes, and said, "But this is incomplete."

"I know, but it tells something, doesn't it? It's slightly worse —isn't it?"

"One would think you want to get worse!" Dr. Périer said with his customary cheer, which now Jonathan mistrusted. "Frankly, yes, it is worse, but only a little worse. It is not crucial."

"In percentage—ten percent worse, would you say?"

"M. Trevanny, you are not an automobile! Now, it is not reasonable for me to make a remark until I get the full report Tuesday."

Jonathan walked homeward rather slowly, walked through the Rue des Sablons just in case he saw someone who wanted to go into his shop. There wasn't anyone. Only the launderette was doing a brisk business. People with bundles of laundry were bumping into each other at the door. It was nearly six. Simone would be quitting the shoeshop sometime after seven, later than usual, because Brezard wanted to take in every franc possible before closing for Sunday and Monday. And Wister was still at L'Aigle Noir. Was he only waiting for him, waiting for him to change his mind and say yes? Wouldn't it be funny if Dr. Périer was in conspiracy with Stephen Wister, if between them they might have fixed the Ebberle-Valent Laboratoires to give him a bad report? And if Gauthier were in on it, too, the little messenger of bad tidings? Like a nightmare in which the strangest elements join forces against—against the dreamer. But Jonathan knew he wasn't dreaming. He knew that Dr. Périer wasn't in the pay of Stephen Wister. Nor was Ebberle-Valent. And it was not a dream that his condition was worse, that death was a little closer, or sooner, than he had thought. It was, however, true of everyone who lived one more day, Jonathan reminded himself. Jonathan thought of death, and the process of aging, as a decline, literally a downward path. Most people had a chance to take it slowly, starting at fifty-five or whenever they slowed up, descending until seventy or whatever year was their number. Jonathan realized that his death was going to be like falling over a cliff. When he tried to "prepare" himself, his mind wavered and dodged. His attitude, or his spirit, was still thirty-four years old and wanted to live.

The Trevannys' narrow house, blue-gray in the dusk, showed no lights. It was a rather somber house, and that fact had amused Jonathan and Simone when they had bought it five years ago. "The Sherlock Holmes house," Jonathan used to call it when they were debating against another in Fontaine-bleau. "I still prefer the Sherlock Holmes house," Jonathan remembered saying once. The house had an 1890 air, sugges-tive of gaslights and polished banisters, though none of the wood anywhere had been polished when they moved in. The house had looked as if it could be made into something with turn-of-the-century charm, however. The rooms were small but interestingly arranged, the garden a rectangular patch full of wildly overgrown rosebushes, but at least the rosebushes were there, and all the garden had needed was a clearing out. And the scalloped glass portico over the back steps, its little glass-enclosed porch, had made Jonathan think of Vuillard, Bonnard. Now it struck Jonathan that five years of occupancy hadn't really defeated the gloom. New wallpaper would brighten the bedroom, yes, but that was only one room. The house wasn't yet paid for: they had three more years to go on the mortgage. An apartment such as they'd had in the first year of their marriage would have been cheaper, but Simone was used to a house with a bit of garden—she'd had a garden all her life in Nemours—and as an Englishman, Jona-than liked a bit of garden, too. He had never regretted that the house took such a hunk of their income.

What Jonathan was thinking of as he climbed the front steps was not so much the remaining mortgage but the fact that he was probably going to die in this house. More than likely, he would never know another, more cheerful house with Simone. He was thinking that the Sherlock Holmes house had been standing for decades before he had been born, and that it would stand for decades after his death. It had been his fate to choose this house, he felt. One day they would carry him out feet first, maybe still alive but dying, and he would never enter the house again.

To Jonathan's surprise, Simone was in the kitchen playing some kind of card game with Georges. She looked up, smiling; then Jonathan saw her remember: the Paris laboratory this afternoon. He had told her he was going to call, to try to speak to Moussu again. But she couldn't mention that in front of Georges.

"The old creep closed early today," Simone said. "No business."

"Good!" Jonathan said brightly. "What goes on in this gambling den?"

"I'm winning!" Georges said in French.

Simone got up and followed Jonathan into the hall as he hung his raincoat. She looked at him inquiringly.

"Nothing to worry about," Jonathan said, but she beckoned him farther down the hall to the living room. "It seems to be a trifle worse, but I don't feel worse, so what the hell? I'm sick of it. Let's have a Cinzano."

"You were worried because of that story, weren't you, Jon?"

"Yes. That's true."

"I wish I knew who started it." Her eyes narrowed bitterly. "It's a nasty story. Gauthier never told you who said it?"

"No. As Gauthier said, there was some mistake somewhere, some kind of exaggeration." Jonathan was repeating what he had said to Simone before. But he knew it was no mistake, that it was a quite calculated story.

Jonathan stood at the first-floor bedroom window, watching Simone hang the wash on the | 5 |

garden line. There were pillowcases, Georges's sleep suits, a dozen pairs of Georges's and Jonathan's socks, two white nightdresses, bras, Jonathan's beige work trousers—everything except sheets, which Simone sent to the laundry, because well-ironed sheets were important to her. Simone wore tweed slacks and a thin red sweater that clung to her body. Her back looked strong and supple as she bent over the big oval basket, pegging out dishcloths now. It was a fine, sunny morning with a hint of summer in the breeze.

Jonathan had wriggled out of going to Nemours to have lunch with Simone's parents, the Foussadiers. He and Simone went every other Sunday as a rule. Unless Simone's brother Gérard fetched them, they took the bus to Nemours. Then, at the Foussadiers' house, they had a big lunch with Gérard and his wife and two children, who also lived in Nemours. Simone's parents always made a fuss over Georges, always had a present for him. Around three, Simone's father, Jean-Noël, would turn on the TV. Jonathan was frequently bored, but he went with Simone because it was the correct thing to do, and because he respected the closeness of French families.

"Do you feel all right?" Simone had asked when Jonathan had begged off.

"Yes, darling. It's just that I'm not in the mood today, and I'd also like to get that patch ready for the tomatoes. So why don't you go with Georges?"

So Simone and Georges went on the bus at noon. Simone had put the remains of a boeuf bourguignon into a small red casserole on the stove, and all Jonathan had to do was heat it when he felt hungry.

Jonathan had wanted to be alone. He was thinking about the mysterious Stephen Wister and his proposal. Jonathan was very much aware that Wister was still there, at L'Aigle Noir, not three hundred yards away. He certainly had no intention of getting in touch with Wister, though the idea was curiously exciting and disturbing, a bolt from the blue, a shaft of color in his uneventful existence, and he wanted to observe it—to enjoy it, in a sense. Jonathan also had the feeling (it had been proved quite often) that Simone could read his thoughts, or at least knew when something was pre-occupying him. If he appeared absent-minded that Sunday, he didn't want Simone to notice it and ask him what was the matter. So Jonathan gardened with a will, and daydreamed. He thought of forty thousand pounds, a sum which meant the mortgage could be paid off at once, a couple of installment items taken care of, the interior of their house painted where it needed it, a television set acquired, a nest egg put aside for Georges's university, a few new clothes for Simone and himself—ah, mental ease! Simply freedom from anxiety! He thought of one—maybe two Mafia figures—burly, dark-haired thugs exploding in death, arms flailing, their bodies falling. What Jonathan was incapable of imagining, as his spade sank into the earth of his garden, was himself pulling a trigger, having aimed a gun at a man's back, perhaps. More interesting, more mysterious, more dangerous was how Wister had got hold of his name. There was a plot against him in Fontainebleau, and it had somehow got to Hamburg. Impossible that Wister had him mixed up with someone else, because even Wister had spoken of his illness, of his wife and small son. Someone, Jonathan thought, whom he considered a friend, or at least a friendly acquaintance, was not friendly at all toward him.

Wister would probably leave Fontainebleau around five this afternoon, Jonathan thought. By three, Jonathan had eaten his lunch, and had tidied up papers and old receipts in the catchall drawer of the round table in the center of the living room. Then—he was happily aware that he was not tired at all—he tackled with broom and dustpan the exterior of the pipes and the floor around their oil furnace.

A little after five, as Jonathan was scrubbing soot from his hands at the kitchen sink, Simone arrived with Georges, her brother Gérard, and his wife Yvonne, and they all had a drink in the kitchen. Georges had been presented by his grand-parents with a round box of Easter goodies, including an egg wrapped in gold foil, a chocolate rabbit, and colored gum-

drops—all under yellow cellophane and as yet unopened because Simone had forbade him to open it, in view of the other
sweets he had eaten in Nemours. Georges went with the
Foussadier children into the garden.

"Don't step on the soft part, Georges!" Jonathan shouted.
He had raked the turned ground smooth, but left the pebbles
for Georges to pick up. Georges would probably get his two
friends to help him fill the red wagon. Jonathan gave him
fifty centimes for a wagonful of pebbles—not ever full, but
full enough to cover the bottom.

It was starting to rain. Jonathan had brought the laundry
in a few minutes ago.

"The garden looks marvelous!" Simone said. "Look,
Gérard!" She beckoned her brother onto the little back
porch.

By now, Jonathan thought, Wister was probably on a train
from Fontainebleau to Paris, or maybe he'd taken a taxi from
Fontainebleau to Orly, considering the money he seemed to
have. Maybe he was already in the air, en route to Hamburg.
Simone's presence, the voices of Gérard and Yvonne seemed
to erase Wister from the Hôtel de L'Aigle Noir, seemed to turn
Wister almost into a quirk of Jonathan's imagination. Jonathan felt a mild triumph in the fact that he had not telephoned Wister, as if by not telephoning him he had successfully resisted some kind of temptation.

Gérard Foussadier, an electrician, was a neat, serious man
a little older than Simone, with fairer hair than hers, and a
carefully clipped brown mustache. His hobby was naval his-
tory, and he made model nineteenth-century and eighteenth-
century frigates in which he installed miniature electric lights
that he could put completely or partially on by a switch in his
living room. Gérard himself laughed at the anachronism of
electric lights in his frigates, but the effect was beautiful when
all the other lights in the house were turned out and eight
or ten ships seemed to be sailing on a dark sea around the living room.

"Simone said you were a little worried—as to your health, Jon," Gérard said earnestly. "I am sorry."

"Not particularly. Just another checkup," Jonathan said. "The report's about the same." Jonathan was used to these clichés, which were like saying, "Very well, thank you," when someone asked you how you felt. What Jonathan said seemed to satisfy Gérard, so evidently Simone had not said much.

Yvonne and Simone were talking about linoleum. The kitchen linoleum was wearing out in front of the stove and the sink. It hadn't been new when they bought the house.

"You're really feeling all right, darling?" Simone asked Jonathan when the Foussadiers had left.

"Better than all right. I even attacked the boiler room. The soot." Jonathan smiled.

"You are mad. . . . Tonight you'll have a decent dinner, at least. Mama insisted that I bring home three paupiettes from lunch and they're delicious!"

Then close to eleven, as they were about to go to bed, Jonathan felt a sudden depression, as if his legs, his whole body had sunk into something viscous, as if he were walking hip-deep in mud. Was he simply tired? But it seemed more mental than physical. He was glad when the light was turned out, when he could relax with his arms around Simone, her arms around him, as they always lay when they fell asleep. He thought of Stephen Wister (was that his real name?) maybe flying eastward now, his thin figure stretched out in an airplane seat. Jonathan imagined Wister's face with the pinkish scar, puzzled, tense; but Wister would no longer be thinking of Jonathan Trevanny. He'd be thinking of someone else. He must have two or three more prospects, Jonathan thought.

The morning was chill and foggy. Just after eight, Simone went off with Georges to the École Maternelle, and Jonathan stood in the kitchen, warming his fingers on a second bowl of café au lait. The heating system wasn't adequate. They'd got rather uncomfortably through another winter, and even now in spring the house was chilly in the morning. The furnace had been in the house when they bought it, adequate for the five radiators downstairs, but not for the other five upstairs which they had hopefully installed. They'd been warned, Jonathan remembered, but a bigger furnace would have cost three thousand new francs, and they hadn't had the money.

Three letters had fallen through the slot in the front door. One was an electricity bill. Jonathan turned a square white envelope over and saw "Hôtel de L'Aigle Noir" on its back. He opened the envelope. A business card fell out and dropped. Jonathan picked it up and read "Stephen Wister *chez*," which had been written above:

REEVES MINOT
159 AGNESSTRASSE
WINTERHUDE (ALSTER)
HAMBURG 56
629–6757

There was also a letter.

April 1st

Dear Mr. Trevanny,

I was sorry not to hear from you this morning, or so far this afternoon. In case you change your mind, I enclose a card with my address in Hamburg. If you have second thoughts about my proposition, please telephone me collect at any hour. Or come to talk to me in Hamburg. Your round-trip transportation can be wired to you at once if I hear from you.

In fact, wouldn't it be a good idea to see a Hamburg specialist about your blood condition and get another opinion? This might make you feel more comfortable.

I am returning to Hamburg Sunday night.

Yours sincerely,
Stephen Wister

Jonathan was surprised, amused, annoyed all at once. *More comfortable.* That was a bit funny, since Wister was sure he

was going to die soon. If a Hamburg specialist said, "*Ach, ja,
you have just one or two more months,*" would that make him
feel more comfortable? Jonathan pushed the letter and the
card into a back pocket of his trousers. A return trip to Hamburg gratis. Wister was thinking of every enticement. Interesting that he'd sent the letter Saturday afternoon, so that
he would receive it early Monday, though Jonathan might
have rung him at any time Sunday. There was no mailbox
collection on Sunday.

It was 8:52 a.m. Jonathan thought of what he had to do.
He needed more mat paper from a firm in Melun. There were
at least two clients he should write a postcard to, because their
pictures had been ready for more than a week. Jonathan
usually went to his shop on Mondays and spent his time doing
odds and ends, though the shop was not open since it was
against French law to be open six days a week.

Jonathan got to his shop at nine-fifteen, drew the green
shade of the door, and locked the door again, leaving the
FERMÉ sign on it. He pottered about, still thinking about
Hamburg. The opinion of a German specialist might be a
good thing. Suppose he accepted Wister's offer of a round
trip? (Jonathan was copying an address onto a postcard.) But
then he'd be beholden to Wister. Jonathan realized he was
toying with the idea of killing someone for Wister—not for
Wister, but for the money. A Mafia member. They were all
criminals themselves, weren't they? Of course, Jonathan reminded himself, he could always pay Wister back if he accepted his round-trip fare. The point was, Jonathan couldn't
pay for the trip himself just now; there wasn't enough money
in the bank. If he really wanted to make sure of his condition,
Germany (or Switzerland, for that matter) could tell him.
They still had the best doctors in the world, hadn't they?
Jonathan put the card of the paper supplier of Melun beside
his telephone to remind him to call tomorrow, because the
paper place wasn't open today either. And who knew,
mightn't Stephen Wister's proposal be feasible? For an instant, Jonathan saw himself blown to bits by the crossfire of

German police officers: they'd caught him just after he fired on the Italian. But even if he was dead, Simone and Georges would get the forty thousand quid. Jonathan came back to reality. He wasn't going to kill anybody, no. But Hamburg—going to Hamburg seemed a lark, a break, even if he learned some bad news. He'd learn *facts*, anyway. And if Wister paid now, Jonathan could pay him back in a matter of three months, if he scrimped, didn't buy any clothes—not even a beer in a café. Jonathan rather dreaded telling Simone, though she'd agree, of course, since it had to do with seeing another doctor, presumably an excellent doctor. The scrimping would come out of Jonathan's own pocket.

Around eleven, Jonathan put in a call to Wister's number in Hamburg, direct, not collect. Three or four minutes later, his telephone rang, and Jonathan had a clear connection, much better than the one to Paris usually sounded.

". . . Yes, this is Wister," Wister said, in his light, tense voice.

"I had your letter this morning," Jonathan began. "The idea of going to Hamburg—"

"Yes, why not?" said Wister casually.

"But I mean the idea of seeing a specialist—"

"I'll cable you the money right away. You can pick it up at the Fontainebleau post office. It should be there in a couple of hours."

"That's—that's kind of you. Once I'm there, I can—"

"Can you come today? This evening? There's room here for you to stay."

"I don't know about today." And yet why not?

"Call me again when you've got your ticket. Tell me what time you're coming in. I'll be in all day."

Jonathan's heart was beating a little fast when he hung up.

At home during lunchtime, Jonathan went upstairs to the bedroom to see if his suitcase was handy. It was, on top of the wardrobe where it had been since their last holiday, nearly a year ago, in Arles.

He said to Simone, "Darling, something important. I've decided to go to Hamburg and see a specialist."

"Oh, yes? . . . Périer suggested it?"

"Well—in fact, no. My idea. I wouldn't mind having a German doctor's opinion. I know it's an expense."

"Oh, Jon! Expense! . . . Did you have any news this morning? The laboratory report comes tomorrow, doesn't it?"

"Yes. What they say is always the same, darling. I want a fresh opinion."

"When do you want to go?"

"Soon. This week."

Just before five, Jonathan called at the Fontainebleau post office. The money had arrived. Jonathan presented his *carte d'identité* and received six hundred francs. He went from the post office to the Syndicate d'Initiative in the Avenue Franklin Roosevelt, just a couple of streets away, and bought a round-trip ticket to Hamburg on a plane that left Orly airport at 9:25 p.m. that evening. He would have to hurry, he realized, and he liked that, because it precluded thinking, hesitating. He went to his shop and telephoned Hamburg, this time collect.

Wister again answered. "Oh, that's fine. At eleven fifty-five, right. Take the airport bus to the city terminus, would you? I'll meet you there."

Then Jonathan made a telephone call to a client who had an important picture to pick up, and said that he would be closed Tuesday and Wednesday for "family reasons," a common excuse. He'd have to leave a sign to that effect in his door for a couple of days. Not a very unusual matter, Jonathan thought, since shopkeepers in town frequently closed for a few days for one reason or another. Jonathan had once seen a sign saying, "Closed because of hangover."

Jonathan shut up shop and went home to pack. It would be a two-day stay at most, he thought, unless the Hamburg hospital or whatever insisted that he stay longer for tests. He had checked the trains to Paris, and there was one around 7 p.m. that would do nicely. He had to get to Paris, then to Les Invalides for a bus to Orly. When Simone came home with Georges, Jonathan had his suitcase downstairs.

"Tonight?" Simone said.

"The sooner the better, darling. I had an impulse. I'll be back Wednesday, maybe even tomorrow night."

"But—where can I reach you? You arranged for a hotel?"

"No. I'll have to telegraph you, darling. Don't worry."

"You've got everything arranged with the doctor? Who is the doctor?"

"I don't know yet. I only know the hospital." Jonathan dropped his passport as he tried to stick it into the inside pocket of his jacket.

"I never saw you like this," said Simone.

Jonathan smiled at her. "At least—I'm not collapsing!"

Simone wanted to go with him to the Fontainebleau-Avon station, and take the bus back, but Jonathan begged her not to.

"I'll telegraph right away," Jonathan said.

"Where is Hamburg?" Georges demanded for the second time.

"*Allemagne!* Germany!" Jonathan said.

Jonathan found a taxi in the Rue de France luckily. The train was pulling into the Fontainebleau-Avon station as he arrived, and he barely had time to buy his ticket and hop on. He took a taxi from the Gare de Lyon to Les Invalides. Jonathan had some money left from the six hundred francs. For a while, he was not going to worry about money.

On the plane, he half slept, with a magazine in his lap. He was imagining being another person. The rush of the plane seemed to be rushing this new person away from the man left behind in the dark gray house in the Rue Saint-Merry. He imagined another Jonathan helping Simone with the dishes at this moment, chatting about boring things such as the price of linoleum for the kitchen floor.

The plane touched down. The air was sharp and much colder. There was a long lighted speedway, then the city's streets, massive buildings looming up into the night sky, street-lights of different color and shape from those of France.

And there was Wister smiling, walking toward him with his right hand extended. "Welcome, Mr. Trevanny! Have a good trip? . . . My car is just outside. Hope you didn't mind coming to the terminus. My driver—not my driver but one I use sometimes—was tied up till just a few minutes ago."

They were walking out to the curb. Wister droned on in his American accent. Except for his scar, nothing about Wister suggested violence. He was, Jonathan decided, overly calm, which from a psychiatric point of view might be ominous. Or was he merely nursing an ulcer? Wister stopped beside a well-polished black Mercedes-Benz. An older man, wearing no cap, took care of Jonathan's medium-sized suit-case and held the door for him and Wister.

"This is Karl," Wister said.

"Evening," Jonathan said.

Karl smiled, and murmured something in German.

It was quite a long drive. Wister pointed out the Rathaus, "the oldest in all Europe, and the bombs didn't get it," and a great church or cathedral whose name Jonathan didn't catch. He and Wister were sitting together in the back. They entered a part of town with a more country-like atmosphere, went over a bridge, and onto a darker road.

"Here we are," Wister said. "My place."

The car had turned onto a climbing driveway and stopped beside a large house with a few lighted windows and a lighted, well-kept entrance.

"It's an old house with four flats, and I have one," Wister explained. "Lots of such houses in Hamburg. Reconverted. Here I have a nice view of the Alster. It's the Aussenalster, the big one. You'll see more tomorrow."

They rode up in a modern lift, Karl taking Jonathan's suitcase. Karl pressed a bell, and a middle-aged woman in a black dress and white apron opened the door, smiling.

"This is Gaby," said Wister to Jonathan. "My part-time housekeeper. She works for another family in the house and sleeps with them, but I told her we might want some food tonight. Gaby, Herr Trevanny *aus Frankreich.*"

The woman greeted Jonathan pleasantly and took his coat. She had a round, pudding-like face, and looked the soul of good will.

"Wash up in here, if you like," said Wister, gesturing to a bathroom whose light was already on. "I'll get you a Scotch. Are you hungry?"

When Jonathan came out of the bathroom, the lights—four lamps—were on in the big square living room. Wister was sitting on a green sofa, smoking a cigar. Two Scotches stood on the coffee table in front of him. Gaby came in at once with a tray of sandwiches and a round pale yellow cheese.

"Ah, thank you, Gaby." Wister said to Jonathan, "It's late for Gaby, but when I told her I had a guest coming, she insisted on staying up to serve the sandwiches." Wister, though making a cheerful remark, didn't smile. In fact his straight eyebrows drew together anxiously as Gaby arranged the plates and the silverware. When she departed, he said, "You're feeling all right? Now, the main thing is—the visit to the specialist. I have a good man in mind, Dr. Heinrich Wentzel, a hematologist at the Eppendorfer Krankenhaus, which is the principal hospital here. World famous. I've made an appointment for you for tomorrow at two, if that's agreeable."

"Certainly. Thank you," Jonathan said.

"That gives you a chance to catch up on your sleep. Your wife didn't mind your taking off on such short notice, I hope? . . . After all, it's only intelligent to consult more than one doctor about a serious ailment."

Jonathan felt a bit dazed, and he was also distracted by the décor, by the fact that it was all supposed to be *German,* and that it was the first time he'd been in Germany. The furnishings were quite conventional and more modern than antique, though there was a handsome Biedermeier desk against the wall opposite Jonathan. There were low bookshelves along all the walls, long green curtains at the windows, and the lamps in the corners spread the light pleasantly. A purple wooden box lay open on the glass coffee table, presenting a variety of cigars and cigarettes in compartments. The white fireplace had brass accessories, but there was no fire now. A rather interesting painting that looked like a Derwatt hung over the fireplace. And where was Reeves Minot? Wister was Minot, Jonathan supposed. Was Wister going to announce this, or assume that Jonathan realized it? It occurred to Jonathan that he and Simone ought to paint or paper their whole house white. He should discourage the idea of the art-nouveau wall-paper in the bedroom. If they wanted to achieve more light, white was the logical—

". . . You might've given some thought to the other proposition," Wister was saying, in his soft voice. "The idea I was talking about in Fontainebleau."

"I'm afraid I haven't changed my mind about that," Jonathan said. "And so this leads to—obviously I owe you six hundred francs." Jonathan forced a smile. Already he felt the Scotch, and as soon as he realized this, he nervously drank a little more from his glass. "I can repay you within three months. The specialist is the essential thing for me now. . . . First things first."

"Of course," said Wister. "And you mustn't think about repayment. That's absurd."

Jonathan didn't want to argue, but he felt vaguely ashamed. More than anything, Jonathan felt odd, as if he were dreaming, or somehow not himself. It's only the foreignness of everything, he thought.

"This Italian we want eliminated," Wister said, folding his hands behind his head and looking up at the ceiling, "has a routine job. Ha! That's funny! He only makes out that it's a regular job with regular hours. He hangs around the clubs off the Reeperbahn, pretending he has a taste for gambling, just as he's pretending he's an oenologist. I'm sure he has a friend at the—whatever they call the wine factory here. He goes to the wine factory every afternoon, but he spends his evenings in one or another of the private clubs, playing the tables a little and seeing who he can meet. Mornings he sleeps because he's up all night. Now, the point is," Wister said, sitting up, "he takes the U-bahn every afternoon to get home, home being a rented flat. He's got a six-month lease and a real six-month job with the wine place to make it look legitimate. . . . Have a sandwich!" Wister extended the plate as if he had just realized the sandwiches were there.

Jonathan took a tongue sandwich. There was also coleslaw and dill pickle.

"The important point is, he gets off the U-bahn at the Steinstrasse station every day around six-fifteen by himself, looking like any other businessman coming back from the office. That's the time we want to get him." Wister spread his bony hands palm downward. "The assassin fires once if you can get the middle of his back—twice for sure, maybe—drops the gun, and bob's your uncle, as the English say, isn't that right?"

The phrase was indeed familiar, out of the long-ago past. "If it's so easy, why do you need me?" Jonathan managed a polite smile. "I'm an amateur, to say the least. I'd botch it."

Wister might not have heard. "The crowd in the U-bahn *may* be rounded up. Some of them. Who can tell? Thirty, forty people, perhaps, if the cops get there fast enough. It's a huge station, the station for the main railway terminus. They might look people over. But suppose they look you over?" Wister shrugged. "You'll have dropped the gun. You'll have used a thin stocking over your hand, and you'll drop the stocking a few seconds after you fire. No powder marks on you, no fingerprints on the gun. You have no connection with the man who's dead. Oh, it really won't come to all that. But one look at your French identity card, the fact of your appointment with Dr. Wentzel—you're in the clear. My point is—*our* point—we don't want anyone connected with us or the clubs. . . ."

Jonathan listened and made no comment. On the day of the shooting, he was thinking, he would have to be in a hotel, he could hardly be a houseguest of Wister, in case a policeman asked him where he was staying. And what about Karl and the housekeeper? Did they know anything about this? Were they trustworthy? It's all a lot of nonsense, Jonathan thought, and wanted to smile, but he wasn't smiling.

"You're tired," Wister informed him. "Want to see your room? Gaby already took your suitcase in."

Fifteen minutes later, Jonathan was in pajamas after a hot shower. His room had a window on the front of the house like the living room, which had two windows on the front, and Jonathan looked out on a body of water with white lights along the near shore, and some red and green from the tied-up boats. It looked dark, peaceful, and spacious. A searchlight's beam swept protectively across the sky. His bed was a three-quarter width, neatly turned down. There was a glass of what looked like water on his bed table and a package of Gitanes maize, his brand, and an ashtray and matches. Jonathan took a sip from the glass and found that it was indeed water.

Jonathan sat on the edge of his bed, sipping coffee which Gaby had just brought. It was coffee the way he liked it, strong with a dash of thick cream. Jonathan had awakened at 7 a.m., then gone back to sleep until Wister had knocked on the door at ten-thirty.

| 6 |

"Don't apologize. I'm glad you slept," Wister had said. "Gaby is ready to bring you some coffee. Or do you prefer tea?"

Wister had also added that he'd made a reservation for Jonathan at a hotel—Hotel Viktoria in midtown—where they would go before lunch. Jonathan thanked him. No further conversation about the hotel. But that was the beginning, Jonathan thought, as he had thought last night. If he was to carry out Wister's plan, he mustn't be a houseguest here. Jonathan, however, felt glad he was going to be out from under Wister's roof in a couple of hours.

A friend or acquaintance of Wister's named Rudolf some-thing arrived at noon. Rudolf was young and slender with straight black hair; he was nervous and polite. Wister said he was a medical student. Evidently he didn't speak English. He reminded Jonathan of photographs of Franz Kafka. They all got into the car, driven by Karl, and set off for Jonathan's hotel. Now Jonathan could see the bridges, large and small, which spanned the narrow divide between the two Alsters. Everything looked so new compared to France, Jonathan thought, and then recalled that Hamburg had been flattened by bombs. The car stopped in a commercial-looking street, in front of the Hotel Viktoria.

"They all speak English," Wister said. "We'll wait for you."

Jonathan went in. A bellhop had taken his suitcase at the door. He registered, looking at his English passport to get the number right. He asked for his suitcase to be sent up to his room, as Wister had told him to do. The hotel was ap-propriately of middle category, Jonathan saw.

Then they drove to a restaurant for lunch, where Karl did not join them. They had a bottle of wine at their table before the meal, and Rudolf became more merry. Rudolf spoke in German and Wister translated a few of his pleasantries. Jona-than was thinking of two o'clock, when he was due at the hospital.

At one point, Rudolf addressed Wister as Reeves.

Jonathan thought Rudolf had said it once before, and this time there was no mistake. Wister—Reeves Minot—took it calmly. And so did Jonathan.

"Anemic," said Rudolf to Jonathan.

"Worse." Jonathan smiled.

"Schlimmer," said Reeves Minot, and continued speaking to Rudolf in German, which to Jonathan sounded as clumsy as his French, but was probably equally adequate.

The food was excellent, the portions enormous. Reeves had brought his cigars, but before they could finish them they had to leave for the hospital. Karl again drove them.

The hospital was a vast assembly of buildings set among

trees and pathways lined with flowers. The wing of the hospital where Jonathan had to go looked like a laboratory of the future: rooms on either side of a corridor as in a hotel, except that these rooms held chromium chairs or beds and were illuminated by fluorescent and variously colored lamps. The smell was not of disinfectant but like that of some unearthly gas, resembling the smell Jonathan had known under the X-ray machine which five years ago had done no good with the leukemia. It was the kind of place where laymen surrendered utterly to the omniscient specialists, Jonathan thought, and at once he felt weak enough to faint. He was walking at that moment down a seemingly endless corridor of soundproofed floor surface with Rudolf, who was to interpret if Jonathan needed it. Reeves had remained in the car with Karl. Jonathan was not sure if they were going to wait, or how long the examination would take.

Dr. Wentzel, a heavy man with gray hair and walrus mustaches, knew a little English, but he didn't try to construct long sentences. "How long?" Six years. Jonathan was weighed and asked if he had had any weight loss recently; then he stripped to the waist and his spleen was palpated. All the while, the doctor murmured in German to a nurse who was taking notes. His blood pressure was taken, his eyelids looked at, urine and blood samples taken; finally the sternum marrow sample was taken with a punchlike instrument that operated faster and with less discomfort than Dr. Périer's. Jonathan was told he could have the results tomorrow morning. The examination had taken only about forty-five minutes.

Jonathan and Rudolf walked out. The car was several yards away among some other cars in a parking area.

"How was it? . . . When will you know?" Reeves asked. "Would you like to come back to my place or go to your hotel?"

"I think to my hotel, thanks." Jonathan sank with relief into a corner of the car.

Rudolf seemed to be singing Wentzel's praises to Reeves. They arrived at the hotel.

"We'll pick you up for dinner," said Reeves cheerfully. "At seven."

Jonathan got his key and went to his room. He took off his jacket and fell onto the bed face down. After two or three minutes, he pushed himself up and went to the writing desk. There was notepaper in a drawer. He sat down and wrote:

April 4th

My dear Simone,

I have just had an examination and will know the results tomorrow morning. Very efficient hospital, doctor looking like Emp. Franz Josef, said to be the best hematologist in the world! Whatever the result tomorrow, I shall feel more at ease knowing it. With luck I may be home tomorrow before you get this, unless Dr. Wentzel wants to do some other tests.

Will telegraph now, just to say I am all right. I miss you, I think of you and Cailloux.

À bientôt, with all my love,

Jon

Jonathan hung up his best suit, which was dark blue, left the rest of his things in his suitcase, and went downstairs to post his letter. He had changed a ten-pound traveler's check, from an old folder holding three or four, last evening at the airport. He wrote a short telegram to Simone saying he was all right and that a letter was arriving. Then he went out, took note of the street's name and the look of the neighborhood—a huge beer advertisement struck him most forcibly—and set out for a walk.

The pavements bustled with shoppers and pedestrians, with dachshunds on leads, with hawkers of fruit and newspapers. Jonathan gazed into a window full of beautiful sweaters. There was also a handsome blue silk dressing gown set off against a background of creamy-white sheep pelts. He started to figure out its price in francs and gave it up, not being really interested. He crossed a busy avenue where there were both streetcars and buses, came to a canal with a foot-bridge, and decided not to cross it. A coffee, perhaps. Jona-than approached a pleasant-looking coffee bar which had pastry in the window and a counter as well as small tables inside, but then could not bring himself to go in. He realized that he was terrified of what the report tomorrow morning would say. He suddenly had a hollow feeling that was fa-miliar, a feeling of thinness as if he had become tissue paper, a coolness on his forehead as if life itself were evaporating.

What Jonathan knew also, or at least suspected, was that tomorrow morning he would receive a phony report. Jona-than distrusted Rudolf's presence. A medical student. Ru-dolf had been no help, because he hadn't been needed. The doctor's nurse had spoken English. Mightn't Rudolf write up a phony report tonight? Substitute it somehow? Jona-than even imagined Rudolf pinching hospital stationery that afternoon. Or maybe he was losing his mind, Jonathan warned himself.

He turned back in the direction of his hotel, taking the shortest way possible. He reached the Viktoria, claimed his key, and let himself into his room. Then he took his shoes off, went into the bathroom and wet a towel, and lay down with the towel across his forehead and eyes. He didn't feel sleepy, just odd. Reeves Minot was odd. To advance a total stranger six hundred francs, to make the insane proposal that he had—promising more than forty thousand pounds. It couldn't be true. Reeves Minot would never deliver. Reeves Minot seemed to live in a world of fantasy. Maybe he wasn't even a crook, merely a bit cracked, a type that lived on delusions of importance and power.

The telephone awakened Jonathan. A man's voice said in English, "A chentleman waits on you below, sir."

Jonathan looked at his watch and saw that it was a minute or two past seven. "Would you tell him I'll be down in two minutes?"

Jonathan washed his face, put on a polo-neck sweater, then a jacket. He also took his topcoat.

Karl was alone in the car. "You had a nice afternoon, sir?" he asked in English.

In the course of the small talk, Jonathan found that Karl had quite a vocabulary in English. How many other strangers had Karl ferried around for Reeves Minot, Jonathan wondered. What business did Karl think Reeves was in? Maybe it simply didn't matter to Karl. What business was Reeves supposed to be in?

Karl stopped the car in the sloping driveway again, and this time Jonathan took the lift alone to the second floor.

Reeves Minot, in gray flannels and a sweater, greeted Jonathan at the door. "Come in! Did you take it easy this afternoon?"

They had Scotch. The table was set for two, and Jonathan assumed that they were going to be alone this evening.

"I would like you to see a picture of the man I have in mind," Reeves said, hauling his thin form from the sofa and going to his Biedermeier desk. He took something from a drawer. He had two photographs of the Italian, one a front view, the other a profile, in a group of several people bending over a table.

The table was a roulette table. Jonathan looked at the front-view picture, which was as clear as a passport photograph. The man looked about forty-five, with the square, fleshy face of lots of Italians, creases already curving from the flanges of his nose down to the level of his thick lips. His dark eyes looked wary, almost startled, yet in the faint smile there was an air of "So what've *I* done, eh?" Salvatore Bianca, Reeves said his name was.

"This picture," Reeves said, pointing to the group picture, "was taken in Hamburg about a week ago. He doesn't gamble, just watches. This is a rare moment when he's actually looking at the wheel. . . . Bianca's probably killed half a dozen men himself, or he wouldn't be a button man. But he's not an important Mafioso. He's expendable. Just to start the ball rolling, you see . . ." Reeves went on, while Jonathan finished his drink, and Reeves made him another. "Bianca wears a hat all the time—outdoors, that is—a homburg. A tweed overcoat, usually . . ."

Reeves had a stereo, and Jonathan would have enjoyed some music but felt it would have been rude to ask, though he could imagine Reeves flying to the stereo to play precisely what he wanted. Jonathan interrupted finally, "An ordinary-looking man, homburg pulled down and coat collar turned up—and one's supposed to spot him in a crowd after seeing these two pictures?"

"A friend of mine is going to ride the same underground from the Rathaus stop, where Bianca gets on, to the Messberg, which is the next stop, and the only stop before the Steinstrasse. Look!"

This had set Reeves off again, and he showed Jonathan a street map of Hamburg which folded like an accordion and had the U-bahn routes marked in blue dots.

"You'll get on the U-bahn with Fritz at the Rathaus. Fritz is coming over after dinner."

I'm sorry to disappoint you, Jonathan wanted to say. He felt a twinge of guilt for having led Reeves on to this extent. Or had he led Reeves on? No. Reeves was taking a crazy gamble. Reeves was probably used to such things; he might not be the first person Reeves had approached. Jonathan was tempted to ask if he were the first person, but Reeves's voice droned on.

"There is definitely the possibility of a second shooting. I don't want to mislead you. . . ."

Jonathan was glad to hear the bad side of it. Reeves had been presenting it all in a rosy light, the bob's-your-uncle shooting followed by pocketsful of money and a better life in France or wherever, a cruise around the world, the best of everything for Georges (Reeves had asked his son's name), a more secure life for Simone. How would I ever explain all the lolly to her, Jonathan wondered.

"This is *Aalsuppe*," Reeves said as he picked up his spoon. "Specialty of Hamburg and Gaby loves to make it."

The eel soup was very good. There was an excellent cool Moselle.

"Hamburg has a famous zoo, you know. Hagenbeck's Tierpark, in Settlingen. A nice drive from here. We might go tomorrow morning. That is"—Reeves looked suddenly troubled—"if something doesn't turn up for me. I'm halfway expecting something. I should know by tonight or early tomorrow."

One would have thought the zoo was an important matter. Jonathan said, "Tomorrow morning I get the results from the hospital. I'm supposed to be there at eleven." Jonathan felt despair, as if eleven might be the hour of his death.

"Yes, of course. Well, the zoo in the afternoon, maybe. The animals are in a natural—natural habitat. . . ."

Sauerbraten. Red cabbage.

The doorbell rang. Reeves did not get up, and in a moment Gaby came in and announced that Herr Fritz had arrived.

Fritz had a cap in his hand and wore a rather shabby overcoat. He was about fifty.

"This is Paul," said Reeves to Fritz, indicating Jonathan. "An Englishman. Fritz."

"Good evening," Jonathan said.

Fritz gave a friendly wave to Jonathan. Fritz was a tough one, Jonathan thought, but he had an amiable smile.

"Sit down, Fritz," said Reeves. "Glass of wine? Scotch?" Reeves spoke in German. "Paul is our man," he added in English to Fritz. He handed Fritz a tall-stemmed glass of white wine.

Fritz nodded.

Jonathan was amused. The oversized wineglasses looked like something out of Wagnerian opera. Reeves was sitting sidewise in his chair now.

"Fritz is a taxi driver," Reeves said. "Taken Herr Bianca home many an evening, eh, Fritz?"

Fritz murmured something, smiling.

"Not many an evening, twice," Reeves said. "Sure, we don't—" Reeves hesitated, as if not knowing in what language to speak, then continued to Jonathan, "Bianca probably doesn't know Fritz by sight. It doesn't matter too much if he does, because Fritz gets off at Messberg. The point is, you and Fritz will meet outside the Rathaus U-bahn station tomorrow, and then Fritz will indicate our—our Bianca."

Fritz nodded, apparently understanding everything.

Tomorrow now. Jonathan listened in silence.

"You both get on at the Rathaus stop; that'll be around six-fifteen. Best to be there before six, because Bianca for some reason might be early, though he's pretty regular at six-fifteen. Karl will drive you—Paul—so there's nothing to worry about. You don't go anywhere near each other, you and Fritz, but it may be that Fritz will have to get on the train, the same train as Bianca and you, in order to point him out definitely. In any case, Fritz gets off at Messberg, the next stop." Then Reeves said something in German to Fritz and extended a hand.

Fritz produced from an inside pocket a small black gun and gave it to Reeves. Reeves looked at the door, as if anxious lest Gaby come in, but he didn't seem very anxious, and the gun was hardly bigger than his palm. After fumbling a little, Reeves got the gun open and peered at its cylinders.

"It's loaded. Has a safety. Here. You know a little about guns, Paul?"

Jonathan had a smattering. Reeves showed him, with assistance from Fritz. The safety—that was the important thing. Be sure how to get it off. This was an Italian gun.

Fritz had to leave. He said goodbye, nodding to Jonathan. *"Bis Morgen! Um sechs!"*

Reeves walked with him to the door. Then Reeves came back from the hall with a brownish-red tweed topcoat, not new. "This is very loose," he said. "Try it on."

Jonathan didn't want to, but he got up and put the coat on. The sleeves were longish. Jonathan put his hands into the pockets and found, as Reeves was now informing him, that the right-hand pocket was cut through. He was to carry the gun in his jacket pocket, reach for it through the pocket of the coat, fire the gun once, preferably, and drop it.

"You'll see the crowd," Reeves said, "a couple of hundred people. You step back afterward, like everybody else, recoiling from an explosion." Reeves illustrated, his body leaning backward, walking backward.

They drank Steinhäger with their coffee. Reeves asked him about his home life, Simone, Georges. Did Georges speak English or only French?

"He's learning some English," Jonathan said. "I'm at a disadvantage, since I'm not with him a lot."

| 7 | Reeves telephoned Jonathan at his hotel the next morning just after nine. Karl would pick him up at twenty to eleven to drive him to the hospital. Rudolf would come along, too. Jonathan had been sure of that.

"Good luck," said Reeves. "I'll see you later."

Jonathan was downstairs in the lobby, reading a London *Times*, when Rudolf walked in a few minutes early. Rudolf was smiling a shy, mouselike smile, looking more like Kafka than ever.

"Morning, Herr Trevanny!" he said.

Rudolf and Jonathan got into the back of the big car.

"Luck with report!" said Rudolf pleasantly.

"I intend to speak with the doctor, too," said Jonathan just as pleasantly.

He was sure Rudolf understood this, but Rudolf looked a little confused and said, *"Wir werden versuchen—"*

Jonathan went with Rudolf into the hospital, though Rudolf had said he could fetch the report and also find out if the doctor was free. Karl had translated, so that Jonathan understood perfectly. Karl, in fact, seemed neutral, Jonathan

thought, and probably was. The atmosphere was strange to
Jonathan, however, as if everyone were acting, acting badly,
even himself. Rudolf spoke with a nurse at the desk in the
front hall and asked for the report of Herr Trevanny.

The nurse looked in a box of sealed envelopes of various
sizes and produced one of business-letter size with Jonathan's
name on it.

"And Dr. Wentzel? Is it possible to see him?" Jonathan
asked the nurse.

"Dr. Wentzel?" She consulted a ledger with isinglass slots,
pushed a button, and lifted a telephone. Then she spoke in
German for a minute, put the telephone down, and said to
Jonathan in English, "Dr. Wentzel is busy all day today, his
nurse says. Would you care to make an appointment for tomorrow morning at ten-thirty?"

"Yes, I would," Jonathan said.

"Very good, I will make it. But his nurse says you will
find a—a lot of information in the report."

Then Jonathan and Rudolf walked back to the car. Rudolf was disappointed, Jonathan thought, or was he imagining it? Anyway, Jonathan had the thick envelope in his
hand, the genuine report.

In the car, Jonathan said "Excuse me" to Rudolf, and
opened the envelope. It was three typewritten pages, and
Jonathan saw at a glance that many of the words were the
same as the French and English terms he was familiar with.
The last page, however, was two long paragraphs in German.
There was the same long word for the yellow components.
Jonathan's pulse faltered when he read 210,000 leukocytes,
which was higher than the last French report, and higher than
it had ever been. Jonathan did not struggle with the last page.
As he refolded the sheets, Rudolf said something in a polite
tone, extending his hand, and Jonathan handed him the report, hating it, and yet what else could he do, and what did
it matter?

Rudolf told Karl to drive on.

Jonathan looked out the window. He had no intention of

asking Rudolf to explain anything. Jonathan preferred to work it out with a dictionary, or to ask Reeves. Jonathan's ears began to ring, and he leaned back and made an effort to breathe deeply. Rudolf glanced at him and at once lowered a window.

Karl said over his shoulder, *"Meine Herrn*, Herr Minot expects you both to come to lunch. Then perhaps to the zoo." Rudolf gave a laugh and replied in German.

Jonathan thought of asking to be driven back to his hotel. But to do what? Stew over the report, not understanding all of it? Rudolf wanted to be let out somewhere. Karl dropped him near a bridge, and Rudolf gave back the report and shook Jonathan's hand firmly. Then Karl drove on to Reeves Minot's house. Sunlight twinkled on the Alster's water. Little boats bobbed gaily at anchor, and two or three boats were sailing about, simple and clean as brand-new toy boats.

Gaby opened the door for Jonathan. Reeves was on the telephone, but he soon finished.

"Hello, Jonathan! What's the news?"

"Not too good," said Jonathan, blinking. The sunlight in the white room was dazzling.

"And the report? Can I see it? Can you understand all of it?"

"No—not all of it." Jonathan handed the envelope to Reeves.

"You saw the doctor, too?"

"He was busy."

"Sit down, Jonathan. Maybe you could use a drink." Reeves went to the bottles on one of his bookshelves.

Jonathan sat on the sofa and put his head back. He felt blank and discouraged, but at least not faint.

"A worse report than you've been getting from the French?" Reeves returned with a Scotch-and-water.

"That's about it," Jonathan said.

Reeves looked at the back page, the prose. "You've got to watch out for minor wounds. That's interesting."

And nothing new, Jonathan thought. He bled easily.

Jonathan waited for Reeves's comment, in fact for Reeves's translation.

"Rudolf translated this for you?"

"No. I didn't ask him to."

". . . 'cannot tell if this represents a worsened condition, not having seen a former—diagnosis . . . sufficiently dangerous in view of the length of time—et cetera.' I'll go through it word for word, if you like," said Reeves. "One or two words I'll need the dictionary for, these compound words, but I've got the essentials."

"Then just tell me the essentials."

"They really might've written this out for you in English," Reeves said, then scanned the page again. ". . . 'a considerable granulation of cells as well as—of the yellow—matter. As you have had X-ray treatment, this is not to be advised again at the moment, as the leukemia cells become resistant to it. . . .' "

Reeves went on for a few moments. There was no prediction of remaining time, Jonathan noticed, no hint of a deadline.

"Since you couldn't see Wentzel today, would you like me to try to make an appointment for you tomorrow?" Reeves sounded genuinely concerned.

"Thanks, but I made an appointment for tomorrow morning. Ten-thirty."

"Good. And you said his nurse speaks English, so you don't need Rudolf. . . . Why don't you stretch out for a few minutes?" Reeves pulled a pillow to the corner of the sofa.

Jonathan lay back with one foot on the floor, the other dangling over the sofa's edge. He felt weak and drowsy, as if he could sleep for several hours. Reeves strolled toward the sunny window, talking about the zoo. He spoke of a rare animal—the name went out of Jonathan's mind as soon as he heard it—that had recently been sent from South America. A pair of them. Reeves said they should see these animals. Jonathan was thinking of Georges tugging his wagon of peb bles. Cailloux. Jonathan knew he would not live to see Georges much older—never, by any means, see him grow tall, hear his voice break. Jonathan sat up abruptly, clenched his teeth, and tried to will his strength back.

Gaby came in with a large tray.

"I asked Gaby to make a cold lunch, so we can eat whenever you feel up to it," Reeves said.

They had cold salmon with mayonnaise. Jonathan couldn't eat much, but the brown bread and butter and the wine tasted good. Reeves was talking about Salvatore Bianca, of the Mafia's connection with prostitution, of their custom of employing prostitutes in their gambling establishments, and of taking ninety percent of the girls' earnings from them. "Extortion," Reeves said. "Money's their objective—terror's their method. See Las Vegas! Actually, Hamburg boys don't *want* prostitutes," Reeves said with an air of righteousness. "Girls are there—a few, helping at the bar, for instance. Maybe they're available, but not on the premises—no, indeed." Jonathan was hardly listening, certainly not thinking about what Reeves was saying. He poked at his food, felt the blood rise to his cheeks, and held a quiet debate with himself. He would try the shooting. And it was not because he thought he was going to die in a few days or weeks; it was simply because the money was useful, because he wanted to give it to Simone and Georges. Forty thousand pounds, or ninety-six thousand dollars—or, Jonathan supposed, only half of that if there wasn't another shooting to do, or if he got caught on the first shooting.

"But you will, I think, won't you?" Reeves asked, wiping his lips on a crisp white napkin. He meant fire the gun this evening.

"If something happens to me," Jonathan said, "can you see that my wife gets the money?"

"But"—Reeves's scar twitched—"what can happen? Yes, I'll see that your wife gets the money."

"But if something does happen—if there's only one shooting—"

Reeves pressed his lips together as if he didn't like replying. "Then it's half the money. But there'll likely be two, to be honest. Full payment after the second. . . . But that's splendid!" He smiled, and it was the first time Jonathan had seen a real smile from him. "You'll see how easy it is tonight. And later we'll celebrate—if you're in the mood." He clapped his hands over his head, Jonathan thought as a gesture of jubilation, but it was a signal to Gaby.

Gaby arrived and took away the plates.

Twenty thousand pounds, Jonathan was thinking. Not so impressive, but better than a dead man with funeral expenses.

Coffee. Then the zoo. The animals Reeves had wanted him to see were two small bear-like creatures the color of butterscotch. There was a small crowd in front of them, and Jonathan never got a good view. He also was not interested. Jonathan had a good view of some lions walking in apparent freedom. Reeves was concerned that Jonathan didn't become tired. It was nearly 4 p.m.

Back at Reeves's house, he insisted on giving Jonathan a tiny white pill, which he called a "mild sedative."

"But I don't need a sedative," Jonathan said. He felt quite calm—in fact, well.

"It's best. Please take my word for it."

Jonathan swallowed the pill. Reeves told him to lie down in the guest room for a few minutes. Jonathan didn't fall asleep, and Reeves came in at five to say it would soon be time for Karl to drive him to his hotel. The topcoat was at the hotel. Reeves gave him a cup of tea with sugar, which tasted all right, and Jonathan assumed there was nothing in it but tea. Reeves gave him the gun, and showed him the safety catch again. Jonathan put the gun in his trousers pocket.

"See you tonight!" Reeves said cheerily.

Karl drove him to his hotel and said he would wait. Jonathan supposed he had five or ten minutes. He brushed his teeth—with soap, because he'd left the toothpaste at home for Simone and Georges and hadn't bought any more—then lit a Gitane and stood looking out the window until he realized he wasn't seeing anything, wasn't even thinking of anything. He went to the closet and got the topcoat. It had been worn, but not much. Whose had it been? Appropriate, Jonathan thought, because he could pretend to be acting in someone else's clothes, pretend the gun was a blank gun in a play. But Jonathan knew that he knew exactly what he was doing. Toward the Mafioso he was going to kill (he hoped), he felt no mercy. And Jonathan realized he felt no pity for himself, either. Death was death. For different reasons, Bianca's life and his own life had lost value. The only interesting detail was that Jonathan stood to be paid for his act of killing Bianca. Jonathan put the gun in his jacket pocket and the nylon stocking in the same pocket. He found he could draw the stocking onto his hand with the fingers of the same hand. Nervously, he wiped the gun of fingerprints real and imaginary with his stocking-covered fingers. He would have to hold the coat aside slightly when he fired; otherwise there'd be a bullet hole in the coat. He had no hat. Curious that Reeves hadn't thought of a hat. It was too late now to worry about it.

Jonathan left his room and pulled the door firmly shut.

Karl was standing on the pavement by his car. He held the door for Jonathan. Jonathan wondered how much Karl knew—if he knew everything.

Jonathan was leaning forward in the back seat to ask Karl to go to the Rathaus U-bahn station when Karl said over his shoulder, "You are to meet Fritz at the Rathaus station. That is correct, sir?"

"Yes," said Jonathan, relieved. He sat back in a corner and lightly fingered the little gun. He pushed the safety on and off, remembering that forward was off.

"Herr Minot suggested here, sir. The entrance is across the street." Karl opened the door but didn't get out, because the street was crowded with cars and people. "Herr

Minot said I am to find you at your hotel at seven-thirty, sir," said Karl.

"Thank you." Jonathan felt lost for an instant, hearing the thud of the car door closing. He looked around for Fritz. Jonathan was at a huge intersection marked "Gr. Johannes-strasse" and "Rathausstrasse." As in London—Piccadilly, for instance—there seemed to be at least four entrances to the U-bahn here because so many streets intersected. Jonathan looked around for the short figure of Fritz, who would be wearing a cap. A group of men, like a football team in top-coats, dashed down the U-bahn steps, revealing Fritz stand-ing calmly by the metal post of the stairs, and Jonathan's heart gave a leap as if he had met a lover at a secret rendez-vous. Fritz gestured toward the steps, and went down himself.

Jonathan kept an eye on Fritz's cap, though there were now fifteen or more people between them. Fritz moved to one side of the throng. Evidently Bianca had not come yet, and they had to wait. There was a hubbub of German around Jonathan, a burst of laughter, a shouted *"Wiedersehen, Max!"*

Fritz stood against a wall some twelve feet from the train. Jonathan drifted in his direction but kept a safe distance away. As Jonathan approached the wall, Fritz nodded and moved diagonally toward a ticket gate. Jonathan bought a ticket. Fritz shuffled on in the crowd. Tickets were punched. Jonathan knew Fritz had sighted Bianca, but Jonathan hadn't.

A train was standing. When Fritz made a dash for a car, Jonathan did, too. In the car, which was not particularly crowded, Fritz remained standing, holding onto a vertical chromium bar. He pulled a newspaper from his pocket. Fritz nodded forward, not looking at Jonathan.

Then Jonathan saw the Italian, closer to Jonathan than to Fritz—a dark, square-faced man, in a gray homburg and a smart gray topcoat with brown leather buttons, staring rather angrily straight ahead, lost in thought. Jonathan looked again at Fritz, who was only pretending to read his newspaper, and when Jonathan's eyes met his, Fritz nodded and smiled slightly in confirmation.

At the next stop, Messberg, Fritz got off. Jonathan looked at the Italian again, briefly, although his glance seemed in no danger of distracting the Italian from his rigid stare into space. Suppose Bianca didn't get off at the next stop but rode on and on to a remote station where there'd be almost no people getting off?

But Bianca moved to the door as the train slowed. Steinstrasse. Jonathan had to make an effort, without bumping anyone, to stay just behind Bianca. There was a flight of steps up. The crowd, perhaps eighty to a hundred people, flowed together more tightly in front of the stairway and began to creep upward. Bianca's gray topcoat was just in front of Jonathan, and they were still a couple of yards from the stairs. Jonathan could see gray hairs among the black at the back of the man's neck, and a jagged dent in his flesh like a carbuncle scar.

Jonathan had the gun in his right hand, out of his jacket pocket. He removed the safety. He pushed his coat aside and aimed at the center of the man's topcoat.

The gun made a raucous *"Ka-boom!"*

Jonathan dropped the gun. He had stopped, and now he recoiled, genuinely, backward and to the left, as a collective *"Oh-h-h—ah-h-h!"* rose from the crowd. Jonathan was perhaps one of the few people who did not utter an exclamation.

Bianca had sagged and fallen.

An uneven circle of people surrounded Bianca.

". . . *Pistole* . . ."

". . . *erschossen!* . . ."

The gun lay on the cement. Someone started to pick it up, and was stopped by at least three people from touching it. Many people—not enough interested, or in a hurry—were going up the stairs. Jonathan was moving a little to the left to circle the group around Bianca. He reached the stairs. A man was shouting, *"Polizei!"* Jonathan walked briskly, but no faster than several other people who were making their way to pavement level.

Jonathan arrived on the street and simply walked on, straight ahead, not caring where he went. He walked at a moderate pace and as if he knew where he was going, though he didn't. He saw a huge railway station on his right. Reeves had mentioned that. There were no footsteps behind him, no sounds of pursuit. With the fingers of his right hand, he wriggled the piece of stocking off. But he didn't want to drop it so close to the U-bahn station.

"Taxi!" Jonathan had seen a free one making for the railway station. It stopped, and he got in. He gave the name of the street where his hotel was.

Jonathan sank back, but he found himself glancing to right and left out the windows of the cab, as if expecting to see a policeman gesticulating, pointing to the cab, demanding that the driver stop. Absurd! He was absolutely in the clear.

Yet the same sensation came to him as he entered the Viktoria—as if the law must have got his address somehow and would be in the lobby to meet him. But, no. Jonathan walked quietly into his own room and closed the door. He felt in his pocket, the jacket pocket, for the bit of stocking. It was gone, had fallen somewhere.

Twenty past seven. Jonathan took off the topcoat, dropped it in an upholstered chair, and went for his cigarettes, which he had forgotten to take with him. He inhaled the comforting smoke of caporal. Then, putting the cigarette on the edge of the basin in the bathroom, he washed his hands and face, stripped to the waist, and washed with a face towel and hot water.

As he was pulling on a sweater, the telephone rang.

"Herr Karl waits on you below, sir."

Jonathan went down. He carried the topcoat over his arm. He wanted to give it back to Reeves, wanted to see the last of it.

"*Good* evening, sir!" said Karl, beaming as if he had heard the news and deemed it good.

In the car, Jonathan lit another cigarette. It was Wednesday evening. He'd said to Simone that he might be home tonight, but she probably wouldn't have his letter till tomorrow. He thought of the two books due back Saturday at the Bibliothèque Pour Tous near the church in Fontainebleau.

Jonathan was again in Reeves's comfortable apartment. He handed the topcoat to Reeves, rather than to Gaby. Jonathan felt awkward.

"*How* are you, Jonathan?" Reeves asked, tense and concerned. "How did it go?"

Gaby went away. Jonathan and Reeves walked into the living room.

"All right," Jonathan said. "I think."

Reeves smiled a little—even the little making his face look radiant. "*Very* good. Fine! I hadn't heard, you know? May I offer you champagne, Jonathan? Or Scotch? Sit down!"

"Scotch."

Reeves bent over the bottles. He asked, in a soft voice, "How many—how many shots, Jonathan?"

"One." And what if he wasn't dead, Jonathan thought suddenly. Wasn't that quite possible? Jonathan took the drink from Reeves.

Reeves had a stemmed glass of champagne, and he raised the glass to Jonathan and drank. "No difficulties? Fritz did well?"

Jonathan nodded, and glanced at the door where Gaby would appear if she came back. "Let's hope he's dead. It just occurs to me—he might not be."

"Oh, this'll do all right even if he's *not* dead. You saw him fall?"

"Oh, yes." Jonathan gave a sigh, and realized he had been hardly breathing for several minutes.

"The news may have reached Milan already," Reeves said cheerfully. "An Italian bullet. Not that the Mafia always use Italian guns, but it was a nice touch. He was of the Di Stefano family. There are a couple of the Genotti family in Hamburg, too, and we hope these two families will now start shooting at each other."

Reeves had said that before. Jonathan sat down on the sofa. Reeves walked about in a glow of satisfaction.

"If it suits you, we'll have a quiet evening here," Reeves said. "If anyone telephones, Gaby's going to say I'm out."

"Does Karl or Gaby—how much do they know?"

"Gaby—nothing. Karl, it doesn't matter if he does. Karl simply isn't interested. He works for other people besides me, and he's well paid. It's in his interest *not* to know anything, if you follow me."

Jonathan understood. But Reeves's information did not make Jonathan feel any more comfortable. "By the way— I'd like to go back to France tomorrow." This meant two things, that Reeves could pay him or make the arrangement to pay him tonight, and that any other assignment ought to be discussed tonight. Jonathan intended to say no to any other assignment, whatever the financial arrangement, but he thought he was entitled to half the forty thousand pounds for what he had done.

"Why not, if you like," said Reeves. "Don't forget you have the appointment tomorrow morning."

But Jonathan didn't want to see Dr. Wentzel again. He wet his lips. His report was bad, and his condition was worse. And there was another element: Dr. Wentzel with his walrus mustaches represented "authority" somehow, and Jonathan felt that he would be putting himself in a dangerous position by confronting him again. He knew he wasn't thinking logically, but that was the way he felt. "I don't really see any reason to see him again—since I'm not staying any longer in Hamburg. I'll cancel the appointment early tomorrow. He's got my Fontainebleau address for the bill."

"You can't send francs out of France," Reeves said, with a smile. "Send me the bill when you get it. Don't worry about that."

Jonathan let it go. He certainly didn't want Reeves's name on a check to Wentzel, however. He told himself to come to the point, which was his own payment from Reeves. Instead, Jonathan sat back on the sofa and asked rather pleasantly, "What do you do here—for work, I mean?"

"Work—" Reeves hesitated, but looked not at all disturbed by the question. "Various things. I scout for New York art dealers, for example. All those books over there—" He indicated the bottom row of books in a bookshelf. "They're art books, mainly German art, with names and addresses of individuals who own things. There's a demand in New York for German painters. Then, of course, I scout among the young painters here, and recommend them to galleries and buyers in the States. Texas buys a lot. You'd be surprised."

Jonathan was surprised. Reeves Minot—if what he said was true—must judge paintings with the coldness of a Geiger counter. Was Reeves possibly a *good* judge? Jonathan had realized that the painting over the fireplace, a pinkish scene of a bed with an old person lying in it—male or female?—apparently dying, really *was* a Derwatt. It must be extremely valuable, Jonathan thought, and evidently Reeves owned it.

"Recent acquisition," Reeves said, seeing Jonathan looking at his painting. "A gift—from a grateful friend, you might say." He had an air of wanting to say more, but of thinking he shouldn't.

During dinner, Jonathan wanted to bring up the money again, and couldn't. Reeves started talking about something else. Ice-skating on the Alster in the winter, and iceboats that went like the wind and occasionally collided.

Then nearly an hour later, when they were sitting on the sofa over coffee, Reeves said, "This evening I can't give you more than five thousand francs, which is absurd. No more than pocket money." Reeves went to his desk and opened a drawer. "But at least it's in francs." He came back with the francs in his hand. "I could give you an equal amount in marks tonight, too."

Jonathan didn't want marks, didn't want to have to change them in France. The francs, he saw, were in hundred-franc notes, pinned together in batches of ten, the way French banks issued them. Reeves laid the five stacks on the coffee table, but Jonathan did not touch them.

"I can't get any more until the rest contribute. Four or five people," Reeves said. "But there's no doubt at all that I can get the marks."

Jonathan was thinking, somewhat vaguely because he was anything but a bargainer himself, that Reeves was in a weak position asking other people for money after the deed was done. Shouldn't his friends have put up the money first—in trust, maybe, or at least more down payment? "I don't want it in marks, thanks," said Jonathan.

"No, of course. I understand. Another thing, your money ought to be in Switzerland in a secret account, don't you think? You don't want it showing on your account in France, and you don't want to keep it in a sock like the French, do you?"

"Hardly. —When can you get the half?" Jonathan asked, as if he was sure it was coming.

"Within a week. Don't forget there might be a second job—in order to make the first job count for something. We'll have to see."

Jonathan was irked and tried to conceal it. "When will you know that?"

"Also within a week. Maybe even in four days. I'll be in touch."

"But—to be frank—I think more money than this is only fair, don't you? Now, I mean." Jonathan felt his face grow warm.

"I do. That's why I apologized for this paltry sum. I tell you what. I'll do the best I can, and the next you hear from me—via me—will be the pleasant news of a Swiss bank account and a statement of the sum you have in it."

That sounded better. "When?" Jonathan asked.

"Within a week. My word of honor."

"That is—a half?" Jonathan said.

"I'm not sure I can get a half before— You know I explained to you, Jonathan, that this is a double-barreled deal. The boys who are paying this kind of money want a certain kind of result." Reeves looked at him.

Jonathan could see that Reeves was asking silently whether he was going to do the second shooting or not. And if he wasn't, say so now. "I understand," Jonathan said. A little more, even a third of the money, wouldn't be bad, Jonathan was thinking. Something like fourteen thousand pounds. For what he had done, that was a comfortable little sum. Jonathan decided to sit tight tonight and stop arguing.

He flew back to Paris the next day on a midday plane. Reeves had said he would cancel Dr. Wentzel, and Jonathan had left it for him to do. Reeves had also said he would telephone him Saturday, the day after tomorrow, in his shop. Reeves had accompanied Jonathan to the airport, and had shown him the morning paper with a picture of Bianca on the U-bahn platform. Reeves had an air of quiet triumph: there was not a clue except the Italian gun, and a Mafia killer was suspected. Bianca was labeled a Mafia soldier or button man. Jonathan had seen the front pages of the newspapers on the stands that morning when he went out to buy cigarettes, but he'd had no desire to buy a newspaper. Now in the plane, he was handed one by the smiling stewardess. Jonathan left it folded on his lap and closed his eyes.

It was nearly 7 p.m. when Jonathan got home, via train and taxi, and he let himself into the house with his key.

"Jon!" Simone came down the hall to greet him.

He put his arms around her. "Hello, darling!"

"I was expecting you!" she said, laughing. "Somehow. Just now. . . . What's the news? Take off your coat. I had your letter this morning that you might be home last night. Are you out of your mind?"

Jonathan flung his overcoat on the hook and picked up Georges, who had just crashed against his legs. "And how's my little pest? How's Cailloux?" He kissed Georges's cheek. Jonathan had brought Georges a dump truck, which was in a plastic bag with the whiskey he had brought, but Jonathan thought the truck could wait, and he pulled out the drink.

"Ah, *quel luxe!*" Simone said. "Shall we open it now?"

"I insist!" said Jonathan.

They went into the kitchen. Simone liked ice with Scotch and Jonathan was indifferent.

"Tell me what the doctors said." Simone took the ice tray to the sink.

"Well—they say about the same as the doctors here. But they want to try out some drugs on me. They're going to let me know." On the plane, Jonathan had decided to say this to Simone. It would leave the way open for another trip to Germany. And what was the real *use* of telling her things were a trifle worse, or looked worse? What could she do about it but worry a little more? Jonathan's optimism had risen on the plane: if he'd come through the first episode, he might make it through the second.

"You mean you'll have to go back?" she asked.

"That's possible." Jonathan watched her pour the two Scotches, generous ones. "But they're willing to pay me for it. They're going to let me know."

"Really?" said Simone, surprised.

"Is that Scotch? What do *I* get?" Georges said in English, with such clarity that Jonathan burst out laughing.

"Want some? Take a sip," Jonathan said, holding out his glass.

Simone restrained his hand. "There's orange juice, Georgie!" She poured orange juice for him. "They're trying out a cure, you mean?"

Jonathan frowned, but he still felt master of the situation. "Darling, there's no cure. They're—they're going to try a lot of new pills. That's about all I know. Cheers!" Jonathan felt a bit euphoric. He had the five thousand francs in his inside jacket pocket. He was safe, for the moment, safe in the bosom of his family. If all went well, the five thousand was merely pocket money, as Reeves Minot had said.

Simone leaned on the back of one of the straight chairs. "They'll *pay* for your going back? That means there's some danger attached?"

"No. I think—there's some inconvenience attached. Going back to Germany. I only mean they'll pay my transportation." Jonathan hadn't worked it out: he could say that Dr. Périer would give the injections, administer the pills. But for the moment he thought he was saying the right thing.

"You mean—they consider you a special case?"

"Yes. In a way. Of course I'm not," he said, smiling. He wasn't, and Simone knew he wasn't. "They just *might* want to try some tests. I don't know yet, darling."

"Anyway, you look awfully happy about it. I'm glad, darling."

"Let's go out to dinner tonight. The restaurant on the corner here. We can take Georges," he protested over her dissent. "Come on, we can afford it!"

| 8 | Jonathan put four thousand of the francs into an envelope in a drawer among eight such drawers in a wooden cabinet at the back of his shop. This drawer was next to the bottom, and held nothing but ends of wire and string and some tags with reinforced holes—junk that only a frugal person or an eccentric would save, Jonathan thought. It was a drawer, like the one below it, that Jonathan didn't open ordinarily. Neither would Simone, he thought, on the rare occasions when she helped out in the shop. Jonathan's real cash drawer was the top one on the right under the wooden counter. The remaining thousand francs Jonathan put into their joint account at the Société Générale

on Friday morning. It could be two or three weeks before Simone noticed the extra thousand, and she probably wouldn't comment even if she saw it in their checkbook. If she did, Jonathan could say that a few customers had suddenly paid up. He usually signed the checks to pay their bills, and the bankbook stayed in the drawer of the *écritoire* in the living room, unless one or the other of them had to take it out of the house to pay for something, which happened only about once a month.

By Friday afternoon, Jonathan had found a way to use a little of the thousand. He bought a mustard-colored tweed suit for Simone from a shop in the Rue de France for three hundred and ninety-five francs. He'd seen the suit days ago, before Hamburg, and thought of Simone; the rounded collar, the dark yellow tweed flecked with brown, the four brown buttons set in a square on the jacket had seemed created just for her. The price had been shocking, more than a bit out of line, he'd thought. Now it seemed almost a bargain, and Jonathan gazed with pleasure at the new material being folded with care between snowy sheets of tissue paper. And Simone's appreciation gave Jonathan pleasure all over again. Jonathan thought it was the first new thing she'd had, the first pretty outfit, in a couple of years, because the dresses from the market or the Prisunic didn't count.

"But it must've been terribly expensive, Jon!"

"No—not really. The Hamburg doctors gave me an advance—in case I have to go back. Quite generous. Don't think about that."

Simone smiled. She didn't want to think about money, Jonathan saw. Not just now. "I'll count this as one of my birthday presents."

Jonathan smiled, too. Her birthday had been almost two months ago.

Saturday morning Jonathan's telephone rang. It had rung a few times already, but this was the irregular ring of a long-distance call.

"This is Reeves. . . . How is everything?"

"All right, thanks." Jonathan was suddenly tense and alert. There was a customer in his shop, a man staring at lengths of sample frame wood on Jonathan's wall. But Jonathan was speaking in English.

Reeves said, "I'm coming to Paris tomorrow and I'd like to see you. I have something for you—you know." Reeves sounded calm, as usual.

Simone wanted Jonathan to go to her parents' home in Nemours tomorrow. "Can we make it in the evening—around six, say? I've got a long lunch."

"Oh, sure, I understand. French Sunday lunches! Sure, around six. I'll be at the Hotel Cayré. That's on Raspail."

Jonathan had heard of the hotel. He said he would try to be there by six or seven. "There're fewer trains on Sunday."

Reeves said not to worry. "See you tomorrow."

Reeves was bringing some money, evidently. Jonathan gave his attention to the man who wanted a frame.

Simone looked marvelous on Sunday in the new suit. Jonathan asked her, before they left for the Foussadiers', not to say that he was being paid anything by the German doctors.

"I am not a fool!" Simone declared with such quick duplicity that Jonathan was amused and felt Simone really was more with him than with her parents. Often he felt the opposite.

"Even today," Simone said at the Foussadiers', "Jon has to go to Paris to talk to a colleague of the Germans."

It was a particularly cheerful Sunday lunch. Jonathan and Simone had brought a bottle of Johnny Walker.

Jonathan got the 4:49 p.m. train from Fontainebleau, because there had been no convenient train from Saint-Pierre-Nemours, and arrived in Paris around five-thirty. He took the Métro; there was a stop right beside the hotel.

Reeves had left a message for Jonathan to be sent up to his room. He was in shirt sleeves, and had apparently been lying on the bed reading newspapers. "Hello, Jonathan! How's life? Sit down—somewhere. I have something to show you." He went to his suitcase. "This—as a starter." Reeves held up a square white envelope, took a typewritten page from it, and handed it to Jonathan.

The letter was in English, addressed to the Swiss Bank Corporation, and it was signed by Ernst Hildesheim. The letter requested a bank account to be opened in the name of Jonathan Trevanny, gave Jonathan's shop address in Fontainebleau, and said that a check for eighty thousand marks was enclosed. The letter was a carbon, but it was signed.

"Who's Hildesheim?" Jonathan asked, meanwhile thinking that the German mark was worth about one and six-tenths French francs, so that eighty thousand marks would convert to something over a hundred and twenty thousand French francs.

"A Hamburg businessman—for whom I've done a few favors. Hildesheim's not under any kind of surveillance and this won't appear on his company books, so there's nothing for him to worry about. He sent a personal check. The point is, Jonathan, this money has been deposited in your name, posted yesterday from Hamburg, so you'll be getting your private number next week. That's a hundred and twenty-eight thousand French francs." Reeves didn't smile, but he had an air of satisfaction. He reached for a box on the writing table. "Dutch cigar? They're very good."

Because the cigars were something different, Jonathan took one, smiling. "Thanks." He puffed it alight from the match that Reeves held. "Thanks also for the money." It wasn't half. It wasn't quite a third, Jonathan realized. But he couldn't say so.

"Nice start, yes. The casino boys in Hamburg are quite pleased. The other Mafia who're cruising around, a couple of the Genotti family, claim they don't know anything about Salvatore Bianca's death, but of course they would say that. What we want to do now is knock off a Genotti as if in retaliation for Bianca. And we want to get a big shot, a *capo*—a chief just under the boss, you know? There's one named Vito Marcangelo, who travels nearly every weekend from Munich to Paris. He has a girl friend in Paris. He's the chief of the dope business in Munich—at least for the family there. Munich, by the way, is even more active than Marseilles now, as far as dope goes. . . ."

Jonathan listened uneasily, waiting for an opening in which he could say that he didn't care to take on another job. Jonathan's thoughts had changed in the last forty-eight hours. And it was curious how Reeves's very presence stripped Jonathan of a sense of daring—maybe made the deed more real. Then there was the fact that he apparently had a hundred and twenty-eight thousand francs in Switzerland already. As they talked, Jonathan had sat down on the edge of an armchair.

". . . a moving train, a day train, the Mozart Express . . ."

Jonathan shook his head. "Sorry, Reeves. I really don't think I'm up to it." Reeves could block the check to Switzerland, Jonathan thought suddenly. Reeves could simply cable Hildesheim. Well, so be it.

Reeves looked crestfallen. "Oh. Well—I am sorry. Really. We'll just have to find another man—if you won't do it. And—I'm afraid he'll get the better part of the money, too." Reeves shook his head, puffed his cigar, and stared out the window for a moment. Then he leaned over and gripped Jonathan's shoulder firmly. "Jon, the first part went so well!"

Jonathan sat back, and Reeves released him. Jonathan squirmed like someone forced to make an apology. "Yes, but—to shoot somebody on a train?" Jonathan could see himself unable to escape anywhere.

"Not a shooting, no. We couldn't have the noise. I was thinking of a garrote."

Jonathan could hardly believe his ears.

Reeves said calmly, "It's a Mafia method. A slender cord, silent—a noose! You pull it tight. That's all."

Jonathan thought of his fingers touching a warm neck. It was revolting. "Absolutely out of the question. I couldn't."

Reeves took a breath, going into another gear, shifting.

"This man is well guarded—two bodyguards, as a rule. But on a train—people get bored sitting and walk in the aisle a bit, or they go to the men's room once or twice, or the dining car, maybe alone. It might not work, Jonathan. You might not—find the occasion, but you could try. . . . Then there's pushing, just pushing him out the door. Those doors can open when the train's moving, you know. But he'd yell— and it might not kill him, either."

Ludicrous, Jonathan thought. But he didn't feel like laughing. Reeves dreamed on silently, looking up at the ceiling. Jonathan was thinking that if he was caught as a murderer or in an attempt at murder, Simone wouldn't touch any of the money from it. She'd be appalled, ashamed. "I simply cannot help you," Jonathan said. He stood up.

"But—you could at least *ride* the train. If the right moment doesn't present itself, we'll just have to think of something else—another *capo,* maybe, another method. But we'd love to get this guy! He's going to move from Munich dope to the Hamburg casinos—organizing. That's the rumor, anyway." Reeves said, on another note, "Would you try a gun, Jon?"

Jonathan shook his head. "I haven't the nerve, for God's sake. On a train? No."

"Look at this garrote!" Reeves pulled his left hand quickly from his trousers pocket.

He held what looked like a thin whitish string. The end, slipped through a loop, was prevented from going all the way through by a small lump at the end of the cord. Reeves tossed it around the bedpost and pulled, jerking the cord to one side.

"You see? Nylon. Strong as wire, almost. He couldn't even grunt more than once—" Reeves broke off.

Jonathan was disgusted. You would have to touch the victim with your other hand—somehow. And wouldn't it take about three minutes?

Reeves seemed to give it up. He strolled to a window and turned. "Think about it. You can ring me or I'll ring you in a couple of days. Marcangelo usually leaves Munich around noon on Fridays. It would be ideal if it could be done next weekend."

Jonathan drifted toward the door. He put his cigar out in an ashtray on the bed table.

Reeves was looking at him shrewdly, yet he might have been gazing behind him, thinking already of someone else for the job. His long scar seemed, as it did in certain lights, thicker than it was. The scar had probably given him an inferiority complex with women, Jonathan thought. Yet how long had he had it? Maybe just a couple of years, one couldn't tell.

"Like a drink downstairs?"

"No, thanks," Jonathan said.

"Oh, I have a book to show you!" Reeves went to his suitcase again and pulled a book with a bright red jacket from a back corner. "Take a look. Keep it. It's a wonderful piece of journalism. Documentary. You'll see the kind of people we're dealing with. But they're flesh and blood like everyone else. Vulnerable, I mean."

The book was called *The Grim Reapers: The Anatomy of Organized Crime in America*.

"I'll telephone you Wednesday," Reeves said. "You'd come to Munich Thursday and spend the night. I'd be there at some hotel also. Then you'd return Friday night to Paris by train."

Jonathan's hand was on the doorknob, and now he turned it. "Sorry, Reeves, but I'm afraid it's no go. Bye-bye."

Jonathan walked out of the hotel and directly across the street to the Métro. On the platform, awaiting a train, he read the blurb on the book jacket. On the back of the jacket were police photographs, front and profile, of several unpleasant-looking men with downturned mouths, faces loose and grim at once, all with dark, staring eyes. It was curious, the similarity of their expressions, whether the faces were plump or lean. There was a section of seven or eight pages of photographs in the book. The chapters were titled by American cities—Detroit, New York, New Orleans, Chicago—and at the back of the book, besides an index, was a section of Mafia families like family trees, except that these people were all contemporaries: bosses, sub-bosses, lieutenants, button men, the latter numbering fifty or sixty for the Genovese family which Jonathan had heard of. The names were real, and for many of them addresses were given. Jonathan browsed in the book on the train to Fontainebleau. There was "Icepick Willie" Alderman, whom Reeves had spoken of in Hamburg, who killed his victims by bending over their shoulders, as if to speak to them, and sticking an ice pick through their eardrums. "Icepick Willie" was photographed, grinning, among a Las Vegas gambling fraternity of half a dozen men with Italian names, as well as a cardinal, a bishop, and a monsignor (their names were also given), after the clergy had "received a pledge of $7,500 to be spread over five years." Jonathan closed the book in brief depression, then opened it again after a few minutes of staring out the window. The book held facts, after all, and the facts were fascinating.

Jonathan rode the bus from the Fontainebleau-Avon station to the plaza near the château, and walked up the Rue de France to his shop. He had his shop key with him, and he went in to leave the Mafia book in the seldom-used drawer with the hidden francs before he walked to his house in the Rue Saint-Merry.

Tom Ripley had noticed the sign FERMETURE PROVISOIRE POUR RAISONS DE FAMILLE in the window of Jonathan Trevanny's shop on a certain Tuesday in April, and had thought that Trevanny might have gone to Hamburg. Tom was very curious to know if he had, but not curious enough to telephone Reeves to ask.

Then, on a Thursday morning around ten, Reeves had

telephoned from Hamburg and said in a voice tense with repressed jubilation, "Well, Tom, it's done! It's all—everything's fine. Tom, I thank you!"

Ripley had been wordless for a moment. Trevanny had really come through? Héloïse had been in the living room with him, so there had been little he could say except "Good. Glad to hear it."

"No need of the phony doctor's report. Everything went fine! Last night."

"So—and—he's coming back home now?"

"Yes. Due tonight."

Tom had cut the conversation short. He had been the one who had thought of Reeves's substituting a report of Trevanny's condition that would be worse than the truth, and had suggested it in jest, although Reeves was the type to have tried it—a dirty, humorless trick, Tom thought. And it hadn't even been necessary. Tom smiled with amazement. He could tell from Reeves's joy that his intended victim was actually *dead*. Killed by Trevanny. Tom was indeed surprised. Poor Reeves had so wanted a word of praise from Tom for his organization of the coup, but Tom hadn't been able to say anything: Héloïse knew quite a bit of English, and Tom didn't want to take any chances. He thought suddenly of looking at Mme. Annette's *Le Parisien Libéré*, which she bought every morning, but Mme. Annette was not yet back from her shopping.

"Who was that?" Héloïse asked. She was looking over magazines on the coffee table, weeding out old ones to be thrown away.

"Reeves," Tom said. "Nothing of importance."

Reeves bored Héloïse. He had no talent for small talk, and he looked as if he didn't enjoy life.

Tom heard Mme. Annette's steps crunching briskly on the gravel in front of the house, and he went into the kitchen to meet her. She came in through the side door, and smiled at him.

"You would like some more coffee, M. Tome?" she asked,

setting her basket on the wooden table. An artichoke toppled from the peak.

"No, thank you, Mme. Annette, I came to have a look at your *Parisien Libéré*, if I may. The horses—"

Tom found the item on the second page. There was no photograph. An Italian named Salvatore Bianca, 48, had been shot dead in an underground station in Hamburg. The assassin was unknown. A gun found on the scene was of Italian manufacture. The victim was known to be of the De Stefano family of Mafiosi of Milan. The account was hardly three inches long. But it might be an interesting beginning, Tom thought. It might lead to much greater things. Jonathan Trevanny—the innocent-looking, positively square Trevanny—had succumbed to the temptation of money (what else?) and committed a successful murder! Tom had succumbed himself, in the case of Dickie Greenleaf. Could it be that Trevanny was one of *us?* But "us" to Tom was only Tom Ripley. He smiled.

Last Sunday, Reeves had rung Tom from Orly in a dejected state, saying that Trevanny was declining the job, and could Tom come up with anybody else? Tom had said no. Reeves said he had written Trevanny a letter that would arrive Monday morning, inviting him to Hamburg for a medical examination. That was when Tom had said, "If he comes, you could perhaps see that the report is slightly worse."

Tom might have gone to Fontainebleau on Friday or Saturday to satisfy his curiosity and catch a glimpse of Trevanny in his shop, perhaps bringing a drawing to be framed (unless Trevanny was taking the rest of the week off to recuperate). In fact, Tom had intended to go to Fontainebleau Friday for stretchers from Gauthier's shop, but Héloïse's parents had been due for the weekend—they had stayed Friday and Saturday nights—and on Friday the household had been in a slight tizzy preparing for them. Mme. Annette was worried, unnecessarily, about her menu—the quality of the fresh moules for Friday night—and after Mme. Annette had prepared the guest room to perfection, Héloïse had made her change the bed linens and the bathroom towels, because they all bore Tom's monogram, TPR, and not the Plissot family's. The Plissots had given the Ripleys two dozen magnificent heavy linen sheets from the family stock as a wedding present, and Héloïse thought it only courteous and also diplomatic to use them when the Plissots visited. Mme. Annette had suffered a slight slip of memory about this, for which she certainly wasn't reprimanded by either Héloïse or Tom. Tom knew the change of bed linen was also due to the fact that Héloïse didn't want her parents to be reminded by his monogram that she was married to him when they got into bed. The Plissots were critical and stuffy—a fact made some-how worse by the fact that Arlene Plissot, a slender, still at-tractive woman of fifty, made a real effort to be informal, tolerant of the young, and all that. It just wasn't in her. The weekend had been a real ordeal, in Tom's opinion, and by Christ, if Belle Ombre wasn't a well-run household, then what was? The silver tea service (another wedding gift of the Plissots) was kept polished to perfection by Mme. Annette. Even the birdhouse in the garden was swept of droppings daily, as if it were a miniature guesthouse on the property. Everything of wood in the house gleamed and smelled pleas-antly of lavender-scented wax that Tom brought over from England. Yet Arlene had said, while stretched out on the bearskin before the fireplace in a mauve trouser suit, warm-ing her naked feet, "Wax is not enough for such floors, Héloïse. From time to time, they need a treatment with lin-seed oil and white spirits—*warm,* you know, so it soaks into the wood better."

When the Plissots left on Sunday afternoon after tea, Héloïse had snatched off her middy top and flung it at a French window, which had given an awful crack because of a heavy pin on the middy, although the glass had not broken.

"Champagne!" Héloïse cried, and Tom dashed down to the cellar to fetch it.

They'd had champagne, though the tea things were not

cleared away (Mme. Annette was, for once, putting her feet up), and then the telephone had rung.

It was Reeves Minot's voice, sounding downcast. "I'm at Orly. Just leaving for Hamburg. I saw our mutual friend in Paris today and he says no to the next—the next, you know. There's got to be one more, I know that. I explained that to him."

"You've paid him something?" Tom watched Héloïse waltzing with her champagne glass in hand. She was humming the grand waltz from *Der Rosenkavalier*.

"Yes, about a third, and I think that's not bad. I've put it in Switzerland for him."

Tom thought he recalled a promised sum of nearly five hundred thousand francs. A third was not munificent, but it was reasonable, Tom supposed. "You mean another shooting," Tom said.

Héloïse was singing and twirling. "La-da-da, la-dee-dee . . ."

"No." Reeves's voice cracked. He said softly, "It's got to be a garrote. On a train. I think that's the hitch."

Tom was shocked. Of course Trevanny wouldn't do it. "Must it be on a train?"

"I've got a plan. . . ."

Reeves always had a plan. Tom listened politely. Reeves's idea sounded dangerous and uncertain. Tom interrupted. "Maybe our friend has had enough at this stage."

"No, I think he's interested. But he won't agree—to come to Munich, and we need the job done by next weekend."

"You've been reading *The Godfather* again, Reeves. Make some arrangement with a gun."

"A gun makes noise," Reeves said without a flicker of humor. "I'm wondering—either I come up with someone else, Tom, or—Jonathan's got to be persuaded."

Impossible to persuade him, Tom thought, and said rather impatiently, "There's no better persuasion than money. If that doesn't work, I can't help you." Tom was unpleasantly reminded of the visit of the Plissots. Would he and Héloïse have bent over backward, strained themselves for nearly three days, if they didn't need the twenty-five thousand francs a year that Jacques Plissot gave Héloïse as an allowance?

"I'm afraid if he's paid any more," Reeves said, "he really will quit. I've told you, maybe I can't get it—the rest of the dough—until he does the second job."

Tom was thinking that Reeves didn't understand Trevanny's type at all. If Trevanny was paid in full, he'd either do the job or return half the money.

"If you think of something in regard to *him*," Reeves said with apparent difficulty, "or if you know of anyone else who could do it, telephone me, will you? In the next day or so?"

Tom was glad when they'd hung up. He shook his head quickly, and blinked his eyes. Reeves Minot's ideas often gave Tom the feeling of being befogged by some heavy dream that hadn't even the reality of most dreams.

Héloïse hurdled the back of the yellow sofa, one hand gently touching the sofa back, the other holding her champagne glass, and she landed silently, seated. Elegantly, she lifted her glass to him. *"Tu a bien réussi ce weekend, mon trésor!"*

"Thank you, my darling!"

Yes, life was sweet again; they were alone again—they could dine tonight barefoot if they chose. Freedom!

Tom thought of Trevanny. He didn't really care about Reeves, who always scraped through, or pulled out of a situation that became too dangerous in the nick of time. But Trevanny—there was a bit of a mystery. Tom cast about for a way of making better acquaintance with Trevanny. The situation was difficult, because he knew that Trevanny didn't like him. But there was nothing simpler than taking a picture to Trevanny to frame.

On Tuesday, Tom drove to Fontainebleau and went first to Gauthier's art-supply shop to buy stretchers. Gauthier might volunteer some news about Trevanny, something about his Hamburg trip, Tom thought, since ostensibly Trevanny had gone to consult a doctor. Tom made his purchase, but Gauthier didn't mention Trevanny.

Just as he was leaving, Tom said, "And how is our friend— M. Trevanny?"

"Ah, *oui*. He went to Hamburg last week to see a specialist." Gauthier's glass eye glared at Tom, while the live eye glistened and looked a bit sad. "I understand the news was not good. A little worse, perhaps, than what his doctor here tells him. But he is courageous. You know these English—they never show their real feelings."

"I'm sorry to hear he's worse," Tom said.

"Yes, well—that's what he told me. But he carries on."

Tom put his stretchers in his car and took a portfolio from the back seat. He had brought a watercolor for Trevanny to frame. His conversation with Trevanny might not go well today, Tom thought, but the fact that he would have to pick up his picture at some future date would insure that he had a second chance to see him. Tom walked to the Rue des Sablons and went into the little shop. Trevanny was discussing a frame with a woman, holding a strip of wood against the top of an etching. He glanced at Tom, and Tom was sure Trevanny recognized him.

"It may look heavy now, but with a white mat—" Trevanny was saying. Trevanny's accent was quite good.

Tom looked for some change in Trevanny—a sign of anxiety, perhaps—but saw none. At last it was Tom's turn. "*Bonjour*. Good morning. Tom Ripley," Tom said, smiling. "I was at your house in—in February, wasn't it? Your wife's birthday."

"Oh, yes."

Tom could see in Trevanny's face that his attitude hadn't changed since that night in February when he had said, "Oh, yes, I've heard of you." Tom opened his portfolio. "I have a watercolor. Done by my wife. I thought perhaps a narrow dark brown frame, a mat—say, two and a half inches at the widest, at the bottom."

Trevanny gave his attention to the watercolor which lay on the notched, worn counter between them.

The picture was mainly green and purple, Héloïse's free interpretation of a corner of Belle Ombre, with a background of pine woods in winter. It was not bad, Tom thought, because Héloïse had known when to stop. She had no idea Tom had saved it, and to see it framed was going to be a pleasant surprise for her, Tom hoped.

"Something like this, perhaps," Trevanny said, pulling down a length of wood from a shelf with a confusion of pieces. He laid it above the picture at the distance that the mat would take up.

"I think that's nice, yes."

"Mat off-white or white? Such as this one?"

Tom made his decision. Trevanny printed Tom's name and address carefully on a pad. He gave his telephone number, too.

What to say now? Trevanny's coolness was almost palpable. Tom knew Trevanny would decline, but he felt he had nothing to lose, so he said, "Perhaps you and your wife would come to my house for a drink sometime. Villeperce isn't far. Bring your little boy, too."

"Thanks. I have no car," Trevanny said, with a polite smile. "We don't go out very much, I'm afraid."

"A car's no problem. I could fetch you. And of course count on having dinner with us, too." The words tumbled out of Tom. Trevanny shoved his hands into the pockets of his coat sweater and shifted on his feet as if his will were shifting. Tom sensed that Trevanny was curious about him.

"My wife's shy," said Trevanny, smiling for the first time. "She doesn't speak much English."

"Neither does my wife, really. She's French, too, you know. However—if my house is too far away, what's the matter with a pastis now? Aren't you about to close?"

Trevanny was. It was a little after noon.

They walked to a bar-restaurant at the corner of the Rue de France and the Rue Saint-Merry. Trevanny had stopped at a bakery to buy bread. He ordered a draft beer, and Tom had the same. Tom put a ten-franc note on the counter.

"How did you happen to come to France?" Tom asked.

Trevanny told Tom about starting an antique shop in France with an English friend. "And you?" asked Trevanny.

"Oh, my wife likes it here. And so do I. I can't think of a more pleasant life, really. I can travel if I wish. I have lots of free time—leisure, you'd call it. Gardening and painting. I paint like a Sunday painter, but I enjoy it. Whenever I feel like it, I go to London for a couple of weeks." That was cards on the table, in a way, naïve, harmless. Except that Trevanny might wonder where the money came from. Tom thought it probable that Trevanny had heard the Dickie Greenleaf story, forgotten most of it, as people did, except that certain things stayed in the memory, like Dickie Greenleaf's "mysterious disappearance," though later Dickie's suicide had been accepted as fact. Possibly Trevanny knew that Tom got some income from what Dickie Greenleaf had left in his will (the will that Tom had forged), because this had been in the papers. Then there'd been the Derwatt affair last year, not so much about Derwatt in the French papers as the strange disappearance of Thomas Murchison, the American who'd been a guest at Tom's home.

"Sounds a pleasant life," Trevanny remarked dryly, and wiped foam from his upper lip.

Trevanny wanted to ask him something, Tom felt. What? Tom was wondering whether, for all his English cool, Trevanny would suffer a fit of conscience and either tell his wife or go to the police and confess. Tom thought he was right to think Trevanny hadn't told—and wouldn't tell—Simone what he had done. Just six days ago, Trevanny had pulled a trigger and killed a man. Of course Reeves would have given Trevanny pep talks, morale-building lectures on the viciousness of the Mafia and the positive good Trevanny or anybody would do by eliminating one of them. Then Tom thought of the garrote. No, he couldn't see Trevanny using a garrote. How did Trevanny feel about the killing he had done? Or had he had time to feel anything yet? Maybe not. Jonathan lit a Gitane. He had large hands. He was the type who could wear old clothes, unpressed trousers, and still have the air of a gentleman. He had rugged good looks that he himself seemed quite unaware of.

"Do you happen to know," said Trevanny, looking at Tom with his calm blue eyes, "an American called Reeves Minot?"

"No," Tom said. "Lives here in Fontainebleau?"

"No. But he travels a lot, I think."

"No." Tom drank his beer.

"I'd better push off. My wife's expecting me."

They went out. They had to go in different directions.

"Thanks for the beer," Trevanny said.

"A pleasure!"

Tom walked to his car, which was in the parking area in front of L'Aigle Noir, and drove off for Villeperce. He was thinking about Trevanny, thinking that he was a rather disappointed man, disappointed about his present situation. Surely Trevanny had had aspirations in his youth. Tom remembered Trevanny's wife, an attractive woman who looked steady and devoted, the kind of woman who would never push her husband to better his situation, never nag at him to earn more money. In her way, Trevanny's wife was probably as upright and decent as Trevanny himself. Yet Trevanny had succumbed to Reeves's proposal. That meant that Trevanny was a man who could be pushed or pulled in any direction if one did it intelligently.

Mme. Annette greeted Tom with the message that Héloïse would be a little late, because she had found an English *commode de bateau* in an antique shop in Chilly-en-Bière, had signed a check for it, but had to accompany the antique man to the bank. "She will be home with the commode at any minute!" said Mme. Annette, her blue eyes sparkling. "She asks you to wait lunch for her, M. Tome."

"But of course!" said Tom just as cheerily. The bank account was going to be slightly overdrawn, he thought, which was why Héloïse had to go to the bank and talk to someone—and how would she manage that during lunch when the bank was closed? Mme. Annette was joyous because still another piece of furniture was entering the house which she could get to work on with her indefatigable waxing. Héloïse had been looking for a nautical, brassbound chest of drawers for Tom for months. It was a whim of hers to see a *commode de bateau* in his room.

Tom decided to seize the opportunity to try Reeves, and he ran up to his room. It was one-twenty-two. Belle Ombre had had two new dial telephones for about three months, and it was no longer necessary to get a long-distance number through the operator.

Reeves's housekeeper answered. Tom used his German and asked if Herr Minot was in. He was.

"Reeves, hello! Tom. I can't talk long. I just wanted to say I've seen our friend. Had a drink with him. . . . In a bar in Fontainebleau. I think—" Tom was standing up, tense, staring through the window at the trees across the road, at the empty blue sky. He was not sure what to say, except that he wanted to tell Reeves to keep trying. "I don't know but I think it might work with him. It's only a hunch. But try again."

"Yes?" said Reeves, hanging on his words as if he were an oracle that never failed.

"When do you expect to see him?"

"Well, I'm hoping he'll come Thursday to Munich. Day after tomorrow. I'm trying to persuade him to consult another doctor there. Then—on Friday the train from Munich to Paris leaves around two-ten."

Tom had once taken the Mozart Express, boarding it at Salzburg. "I would say, give him a choice of a gun and— the other thing, but advise him not to use the gun."

"I *did* try that!" Reeves said. "But you think he might still come around, eh?"

Tom heard a car, two cars, roll onto the gravel in front of the house. No doubt it was Héloïse with the antique dealer. "I've got to sign off, Reeves. Right now."

Tom put the telephone down gently. He felt uneasy. Trevanny might either freeze on the train job or bollix it. Was Trevanny going to need some help?

Later that day, alone in his room, Tom examined the handsome commode which had been installed between his two front windows. The chest was of oak, low and solid, with shining brass corners and countersunk brass drawer pulls. The polished wood looked alive, as if animated by the hands of the maker, or maybe by the hands of the captain, or captains, who had used it. A couple of shiny, dark dents in the wood were like the odd scars that every living thing acquired in the course of life. An oval plaque of silver was set into the top, and on it was engraved in scrolly letters, "Captain Archibald L. Partridge, Plymouth, 1734," and in much smaller letters the name of the carpenter, which Tom thought a nice touch of pride.

| 10 | On Wednesday, as Reeves had promised, he telephoned Jonathan at his shop. Jonathan was unusually busy and had to ask Reeves to ring back just after noon.

Reeves did ring back and, after his usual courtesies, asked if Jonathan would be able to come to Munich the following day.

"There are doctors in Munich, too, you know—very good ones. I have one in mind, Dr. Max Schröder. I've found out he could see you early Friday, around eight in the morning. All I have to do is confirm it. If you—"

"All right," said Jonathan, who had anticipated that the conversation would go exactly like this. "Very good, Reeves. I'll see about my ticket."

"One way, Jonathan. . . . Well, that's up to you."

Jonathan knew. "When I find out the plane time, I'll ring you back."

"I know the times. There's a plane leaving Orly at 1:15 p.m. direct to Munich, if you can make it."

"All right. I'll aim for that."

"If I don't hear from you, I'll assume you're on it. I'll meet you at the city terminus, as before."

Absent-mindedly, Jonathan went to his sink, smoothed his hair with both hands, then reached for his mack. It was raining a little and rather chilly. Jonathan had made his decision yesterday. He would go through the same movements again, visit a doctor in Munich this time, and he would board the train. The dubious part to Jonathan was his own nerve. Just how far would he be able to go? He left the shop, locking the door with his key.

Jonathan bumped into a trash can on the pavement, and realized that he was trudging along instead of walking. He raised his head a little. He'd demand to have a gun as well as the noose, and if he balked at using the noose because of a failure of nerve (which Jonathan fully expected), and he used the gun, then that was that. Jonathan would make an arrangement with Reeves: if he used the gun and it was obvious that he was going to be caught, then he would use the next bullet or two for himself. That way he could never possibly betray Reeves and the other people Reeves was connected with. For this, Reeves would pay the rest of the money to Simone. Jonathan realized that his corpse couldn't be taken for that of an Italian, but he supposed it was possible that the Di Stefano family would have hired a non-Italian killer.

Jonathan said to Simone, "I had a telephone call from the Hamburg doctor this morning. He wants me to go to Munich tomorrow."

"Oh? So soon?"

Jonathan remembered he had told Simone it might be a fortnight before the doctors wanted to see him again. He had said Dr. Wentzel had given him some pills and would want to check the result. There had, in fact, been a conversation about pills with Dr. Wentzel—there was nothing one could do with leukemia except try to slow it up with pills—but Dr. Wentzel had not given him any. Jonathan was sure the doctor would have given him pills if he had seen him a second time. "There's another doctor in Munich—someone called Schröder—Dr. Wentzel wants me to see."

"Where is Munich?" asked Georges.

"In Germany," Jonathan said.

"How long will you be gone?" Simone asked.

"Probably—till Saturday morning," Jonathan said, thinking the train might come in so late Friday night that there wouldn't be a train out of Paris to Fontainebleau.

"And what about the shop? Would you like me to be there tomorrow morning? And Friday morning? What time must you leave tomorrow?"

"There's a plane at one-fifteen. Yes, darling, it would be a help if you could look in tomorrow morning and Friday morning—even for an hour. There'll be a couple of people calling for pictures." Jonathan stabbed his knife gently into a piece of Camembert which he had taken and didn't want.

"You're worried, Jon?"

"Not really. No, on the contrary, any news I get ought to be slightly better news." Polite cheerfulness, Jonathan thought, and it was really rubbish. The doctors couldn't do anything against time. He glanced at his son, who looked a bit puzzled, but not puzzled enough to ask another question, and Jonathan realized that Georges had been overhearing such conversations ever since he could understand speech. Georges had been told: "Your father has a germ. Like a cold. It makes him tired sometimes. But you cannot catch it. Nobody can catch it, so it is not going to hurt you."

"Will you sleep at the hospital?" Simone asked.

Jonathan didn't understand what she meant at first. "No.

Dr. Wentzel—his secretary said they'd booked a hotel for me."

Jonathan left the house the next morning just after nine in order to catch the nine-forty-two to Paris, because the next train would have made him too late for Orly. He had bought his ticket, one way, the preceding afternoon, and he had put another thousand francs into the account at the Société Générale, and five hundred in his wallet, which left two thousand five hundred in the drawer in his shop. He had also removed *The Grim Reapers* from the drawer and put it into his suitcase to give back to Reeves.

Just before 5 p.m., Jonathan got off the bus that had brought him to the Munich city terminus. It was a sunny day, the temperature pleasant. There were a few sturdy, middle-aged men in leather shorts and green jackets, and a hurdy-gurdy played on the pavement. He saw Reeves trotting toward him.

"I'm a little late—sorry!" Reeves said. "How are you, Jonathan?"

"Quite well, thank you," Jonathan said, smiling.

"I've got you a hotel room. We'll get a taxi now. I'm in a different hotel, but I'll come up with you and we'll talk."

They got into a taxi. Reeves talked about Munich. He talked as if he really knew the city and liked it, not as if he were talking out of nervousness. Reeves had a map and pointed out "the English Garden," which their taxi was not going to pass, and the section bordering the Isar River, where Reeves told him his appointment was tomorrow morning at eight. Both their hotels were in the central area, Reeves said. The taxi stopped at a hotel, and a boy in a dark red uniform opened the taxi door.

Jonathan registered. The lobby had lots of modern stained-glass panels depicting German knights and troubadours. He was pleasantly aware that he felt unusually well, and there-

fore cheerful. Was it a prelude to some awful news tomorrow, some awful catastrophe? It struck Jonathan as insane to
feel cheerful, and he cautioned himself as he might if he
were on the verge of taking a drink too many.

Reeves came with him to his room. The bellhop was just
leaving, having deposited Jonathan's suitcase. Jonathan hung
his topcoat on a hook in the hall.

"Tomorrow morning—even this afternoon, we might get
you a new topcoat," Reeves said, looking with a somewhat
pained expression at Jonathan's.

"Oh?" Jonathan had to admit his coat was pretty shabby.
He smiled a little, unresentful. At least he'd brought his
good suit, his rather new black shoes. He hung up the blue
suit.

"After all, you'll be in the first class on the train," Reeves
said. He walked to the door and slid the latch, which made
it impossible for anyone outside to enter. "I've got the gun.
Another Italian gun, a little different. I couldn't get a silencer, but I thought—to tell you the truth—a silencer
wouldn't make that much difference."

Jonathan understood. He looked at the small gun that
Reeves had pulled from a pocket, and felt for an instant
empty, stupid. To fire this gun at all meant that he'd have
to shoot himself immediately afterward. That was the only
meaning the gun had for him.

"And this, of course," said Reeves, pulling the garrote
from his pocket.

In the bright light of Munich, the cord had a pallid,
fleshlike color.

"Try it on the—back of that chair," Reeves said.

Jonathan took the cord and dropped its loop over a pro-
jection on the back of the chair. Indifferently, he pulled it
until it was tight. He was not disgusted now; he merely
felt blank. Would the average person, he wondered—finding
the cord in his pocket, or anywhere—know at once what it
was? Probably not, Jonathan thought.

"You must jerk it, of course," said Reeves solemnly, "and keep it tight."

Jonathan felt suddenly annoyed, started to say something ill-tempered, and checked himself.

He took the cord off the chair and was about to drop it on the bed when Reeves said, "Keep that in your pocket. Or the pocket of whatever suit you're going to wear tomorrow."

Jonathan started to put it in the trousers he was wearing, then went and stuck it in a pocket of the trousers of his blue suit.

"I'd like to show you these two pictures." Reeves took an unsealed white envelope from his jacket pocket. The envelope held two photographs, one glossy and the size of a postcard, the other a neatly clipped newspaper picture folded twice. "Vito Marcangelo."

Jonathan looked at the glossy photograph, which was cracked in a couple of places. It showed a man with a round head and face, heavy curvaceous lips, and wavy black hair. A streak of gray at either temple gave an impression of steam spewing from his head.

"He's about five feet six," Reeves said. "His hair is still gray there, he doesn't touch it up. And here he is partying."

The newspaper photograph was of three men and a couple of women standing behind a dinner table. An inked-in arrow pointed to a short, laughing man with a gray blaze at his temple. The caption was in German.

Reeves took the pictures back. "Let's go out for the topcoat. Something'll be open. By the way, the safety on that gun works the same as the other one. It's loaded with six bullets. I'll put it in here, all right?" Reeves took the gun from the foot of the bed and put it in a corner of Jonathan's suitcase.

"Briennerstrasse's very good for shopping," Reeves said as they rode down in the elevator. They walked. Jonathan had left his topcoat in the hotel room.

Jonathan chose a dark green tweed. Who was paying for it didn't seem to matter much. Also, Jonathan thought that he might have only about twenty-four hours to wear it. Reeves insisted on paying for the coat, though Jonathan said he could pay him back when he changed some francs into marks.

"No, no, my pleasure," said Reeves, jerking his head a little, which was sometimes his equivalent of a smile.

Jonathan wore the coat out of the shop. Reeves pointed things out to him as they walked—Odeonsplatz, the beginning of Ludwigstrasse, which Reeves said went on to Schwabing, the district where Thomas Mann had had his house. They walked to the Englischer Garten, then took a taxi to a beer hall. Jonathan would have preferred tea. He realized that Reeves was trying to make him relax. Jonathan felt relaxed enough, and was not even worried about what Dr. Max Schröder would say tomorrow morning. Rather, whatever Dr. Schröder said simply wouldn't matter.

They dined in a noisy restaurant in Schwabing, and Reeves informed him that practically everyone in the place was "an artist or a writer." Jonathan was amused by Reeves. He felt a bit swimmy in the head from all the beer, and now they were beginning to drink Gumpoldskirchen.

Before midnight, Jonathan stood in his hotel room in his pajamas. He had just had a shower. The telephone would ring at seven-fifteen tomorrow morning, followed at once by a continental breakfast. Jonathan sat down at the writing table, took some notepaper from the drawer, and addressed an envelope to Simone. Then he remembered he'd be home the day after tomorrow, perhaps even late tomorrow night. He crumpled the envelope and tossed it into the wastebasket. Tonight during dinner, he had said to Reeves, "Do you know a man called Tom Ripley?" Reeves had looked blank and said, "No. Why?" Jonathan got into bed and pressed a button that, conveniently, extinguished all the lights, including the one in the bathroom. Had he taken his pills tonight? Yes. Just before his shower. He'd put the pill bottle in his jacket pocket, so he could show them to Dr. Schröder tomorrow, in case the doctor was interested.

Reeves had asked, "Has the Swiss bank written you yet?" They hadn't, but a letter might well have come to his shop this morning, Jonathan thought. Would Simone open it? The chances were fifty-fifty, depending on how busy she was. The Swiss letter would confirm a deposit of eighty thousand marks, and there'd probably be cards for him to sign for samples of his signature. The envelope, Jonathan supposed, would have no return address, or nothing identifiable as a bank. Since he was due back Saturday, Simone might leave any letters unopened. Fifty-fifty, he thought again, and slid gently into sleep.

In the hospital the next morning, the atmosphere seemed strictly routine and curiously informal. Reeves was present the whole time, and Jonathan could tell, though the conversation was all in German, that Reeves didn't tell Dr. Schröder about the previous examination in Hamburg. The Hamburg report had been sent to Dr. Périer in Fontainebleau, who must by now have sent it to the Ebberle-Valent Laboratoires, as he had promised.

Again a nurse spoke perfect English. Dr. Max Schröder was about fifty, with black hair modishly down to his shirt collar.

"He says," Reeves told Jonathan, "that it is more or less a classic case with—not so cheerful predictions for the future."

No, there was nothing new for Jonathan. Not even the message that the results of the examination would be ready for him tomorrow morning.

It was nearly eleven when Jonathan and Reeves left the hospital. They walked along an embankment of the Isar, where there were children in carriages, stone apartment buildings, a pharmacy, a grocery shop—all the appurtenances of living which Jonathan felt not the least part of that morning. He even had to remember to breathe. Today was going to be a day of failure, he thought. He wanted to plunge into the river and drown, or become a fish. Reeves's presence and his sporadic talking irked him; finally he managed not to hear him. Jonathan felt that he was not going to kill anyone today, not by the string in his pocket, not by the gun either.

"Shouldn't I think about getting my suitcase," Jonathan interrupted, "if the train's at two-something?"

They found a taxi.

Almost beside the hotel there was a shopwindow full of twinkling objects, glowing with gold and silver lights like a German Christmas tree. Jonathan drifted toward the window. It was mostly tourist trinkets, he saw with disappointment, but then he noticed a gyroscope poised at a slant against its square box.

"I want to buy something for my son," Jonathan said, and went into the shop. He pointed and said, *"Bitte,"* and acquired the gyroscope without noticing the price. He had changed two hundred francs at the hotel that morning.

Jonathan had already packed, so all he had to do was close his suitcase. He took it down himself. Reeves stuck a hundred-mark note into Jonathan's hand and asked him to pay the hotel bill, because it might look odd if Reeves paid it. Money had ceased to matter to Jonathan.

They were early at the station. In the buffet, Jonathan didn't want anything to eat, only coffee.

So Reeves ordered coffee, too. "You'll have to make the opportunity yourself, Jon. It may not work out, I know, but this man we *want*. . . . Stay near the restaurant car. Smoke a cigarette; stand at the end of the carriage next to the restaurant car, for instance. . . ."

Jonathan had a second coffee. Reeves bought a *Daily Telegraph* and a paperback for Jonathan to take with him.

Then the train pulled in, daintily clicking on the rails, sleek gray and blue—the Mozart Express. Reeves was looking for Marcangelo, who was supposed to board with at least two bodyguards. There were perhaps sixty people getting on all along the platform, and as many getting off. Reeves grabbed Jonathan's arm and pointed. Jonathan was standing with suitcase in hand by the carriage he was supposed to enter, according to his ticket. Jonathan saw—or did he?— the group of men that Reeves was talking about: three rather short men in hats, climbing the steps two carriages away from his, toward the front of the train.

"It's him. I even saw the gray in his hair," Reeves said. "Now where's the restaurant car?" He stepped back to see better, trotted along the platform and came back. "It's the one in front of Marcangelo's."

The train's departure was being announced in French.

"You've got the gun in your pocket?" Reeves asked.

Jonathan nodded. Reeves had reminded him, when he went up to his hotel room for his suitcase, to put it in his pocket. "See that my wife gets the money, whatever happens to me."

"That's a promise." Reeves patted his arm.

The whistle blew for a second time, and doors banged. Jonathan got on the train and didn't look back at Reeves, who he knew would be following him with his eyes. Jonathan found his seat. There were only two other people in the compartment, which was for eight passengers. The upholstery was dark red plush. Jonathan put his suitcase on an overhead rack, then his new coat, folded inside out. A young man entered the compartment and hung out the window, talking to someone in German. Jonathan's other companions were a middle-aged man sunk in what looked like office papers, and a neat little woman wearing a small hat and reading a novel. Jonathan was next to the businessman, who had the window seat facing the way the train was moving. Jonathan opened his *Telegraph*.

It was 2:11 p.m.

Jonathan watched the outskirts of Munich glide past, office buildings, onion towers. Opposite Jonathan were three framed photographs—a château somewhere, a lake with a couple of swans, some snow-topped Alps. The train purred over the smooth rails and rocked gently. Jonathan closed his eyes. By locking his fingers and putting his elbows on the armrests, he could almost doze. There was time, time to make up his mind, change his mind, change back again. Marcangelo was going to Paris, like him, and the train didn't arrive until 11:07 tonight. There was a stop at Strasbourg around 6:30 p.m., he remembered Reeves saying. A few minutes later, Jonathan woke up and realized there was a thin but regular stream of people in the aisle. A man came partway into the glass-doored compartment with a trolley of sandwiches, bottles of beer and wine. The young man bought a beer. A stocky man stood smoking a pipe in the aisle, and from time to time pushed himself against the window to let others pass him.

No harm in strolling past Marcangelo's compartment, as if en route to the restaurant car, just to size up the situation, Jonathan thought. But it took him several minutes to muster his initiative, during which time he smoked a Gitane. He put his ashes into the metal receptacle fixed under the window, careful not to drop any on the knees of the man reading office papers.

At last Jonathan got up and walked forward. The door at the end of the carriage was sticky to open. There were two more doors before he reached Marcangelo's carriage. Jonathan walked slowly, bracing himself against the gentle but irregular swaying of the train, glancing into each compartment. Marcangelo was instantly recognizable, because he was facing Jonathan in a center seat, asleep with hands folded across his abdomen, jowls sunk into his collar, the gray streak at the temples flowing back and up. Jonathan had a quick impression of two other Italian types leaning toward each other, talking and gesticulating. There was no one else in the compartment. He went on to the end of the carriage and onto the platform, where he lit another cigarette and stood looking out the window. This end of the carriage had a rest room, or *toilette,* which now showed a red tag in its circular lock, indicating that it was occupied. Another man, bald and slender, stood by the opposite window, perhaps waiting for the toilet. The idea of trying to kill anyone here was absurd, because there were bound to be witnesses. Or if only killer and victim were on the platform, wouldn't someone very likely appear in a matter of seconds? The train was not at all noisy, and if a man cried out, even with the garrote already around his neck, wouldn't the people in the first compartment hear him?

A man and a woman came out of the restaurant car and went along the carriage aisle, not closing the doors, though a white-jacketed waiter did so at once.

Jonathan walked back in the direction of his own carriage and glanced once more into Marcangelo's compartment, but very briefly. Marcangelo was awake and smoking a cigarette: fat, leaning forward, talking.

If it was done, it ought to be done before Strasbourg, Jonathan thought. He imagined quite a lot of people getting on there to go to Paris. But maybe that was wrong. In about half an hour, he thought, he ought to put on his topcoat and go and stand on the platform at the end of Marcangelo's carriage and wait. Suppose Marcangelo used the toilet at the *other* end of his carriage? There were toilets at both ends. And suppose he didn't go to the toilets at all? That was possible, even though it wasn't likely. And suppose the Italians simply didn't choose to patronize the restaurant car? No, they would logically go there to eat, but they'd all go together. If he couldn't do anything today, Reeves would simply have to make another plan, a better one, Jonathan thought. But Marcangelo, or someone comparable, would have to be killed, by him, if he was to collect any more money.

Just before four, Jonathan forced himself to get up, to haul down his topcoat carefully. In the aisle, he put it on the coat with its heavy right-hand pocket, and went with his paperback to stand on the platform at the end of Marcangelo's carriage.

11 When Jonathan passed the Italians' compartment, he had seen out of the corner of his eye a confusion of figures, men pulling down a suitcase, or perhaps struggling playfully. And he had heard laughter.

A minute later, Jonathan stood leaning against a metal-framed map of Central Europe, facing the half-glass door of the corridor. Through the glass, Jonathan saw a man approaching, bumping the door open. This man looked like one of Marcangelo's bodyguards, dark-haired, in his thirties, with the sour expression and the sturdy build that insured he would one day look like a disgruntled toad. Jonathan recalled the photographs on the jacket of *The Grim Reapers*. The man went straight to the rest-room door and entered. Jonathan continued to look at his open paperback. After a very short time, the man reappeared and went back into the corridor.

Jonathan took a deep breath. Suppose it'd been Marcangelo, wouldn't it have been a perfect opportunity, with no one passing from the carriage or the restaurant car? Jonathan realized that he would've stood just where he was, pretending to read, if it *had* been Marcangelo. Jonathan's right hand, in his pocket, pushed the safety of the little gun on and off. After all, what was the risk? What was the loss? Merely his own life.

Marcangelo might come lumbering forward at any minute, push the door open, and then—it could be like before, in the German underground. Couldn't it? Then a bullet for himself. But Jonathan imagined firing at Marcangelo and immediately tossing the gun out the door beside the toilet—or out the door's window, which looked as if it opened—then walking casually into the restaurant car, sitting down, and ordering something.

It was quite impossible.

I'll order something now, Jonathan thought, and went

into the restaurant car, where there were plenty of free tables. On one side, the tables were for four people, on the other side for two. Jonathan took one of the smaller tables. A waiter came. Jonathan ordered a beer, then quickly changed it to wine.

"*Weisswein, bitte,*" Jonathan said.

A quarter bottle of cold Riesling appeared. The *cluckety-cluck* of the train sounded more muffled and luxurious here. The window was bigger, yet somehow more private, making the forest—the Black Forest?—look spectacularly rich and verdant. There were endless tall pines, as if Germany had so many it didn't need to cut them down for any purpose. Not a scrap of debris or paper was to be seen, or any human figure caring for the forest, which was equally surprising to Jonathan. When did the Germans do their tidying? Jonathan tried to summon courage from the wine. Somewhere along the line he had lost his momentum; it was just a matter of getting it back. He drank off the last of the wine as if it were an obligatory toast, paid his bill, and pulled on his coat, which he had laid on the opposite chair. He would stand on the platform until Marcangelo appeared, and whether Marcangelo was alone or with two bodyguards, he would shoot.

Jonathan tugged at the carriage door, sliding it open. He was back in the prison of the platform, leaning against the map again, looking at the stupid paperback. . . . *David had wondered, did Elaine suspect? Desperate now, David went over the events of* . . . Jonathan's eyes moved over the print like an illiterate's. He remembered something he'd thought of before, days ago. Simone would refuse the money if she knew how he had got it, and of course she'd know how he had got it if he shot himself on the train. He wondered if Simone could be persuaded by Reeves—by somebody—convinced that what he had done wasn't exactly like murder. Jonathan almost laughed. It was quite hopeless. What was he doing standing here? He could walk straight ahead now, back to his seat.

A figure was approaching. Jonathan looked up and then blinked. The man coming toward him was Tom Ripley.

Ripley pushed open the half-glass door, smiling a little. "Jonathan," he said softly. "Give me the thing, would you? The garrote." He stood sidewise to Jonathan, looking out the window.

Jonathan felt suddenly blank with shock. Whose side was Tom Ripley on? Marcangelo's? He started at the sight of three men approaching in the corridor.

Tom moved a bit closer to Jonathan to get out of their way.

The men were talking in German, and they went on into the restaurant car.

Tom said over his shoulder to Jonathan, "The string. We'll give it a try, all right?"

Jonathan understood, or partly understood. Ripley was a friend of Reeves. He knew Reeves's plan. Jonathan was wadding the garrote up in his left-hand trousers pocket. He pulled his hand out and gave the garrote to Tom, then looked away and was aware of a sense of relief.

Tom pushed the garrote into a pocket. "Stay there. I might need you." He went over to the toilet, saw that it was empty, and went in.

He locked the door. The garrote wasn't even through its loop. Tom adjusted it for action, and put it carefully into the pocket of his jacket. He smiled a little. Jonathan had gone pale as a sheet. Tom had rung up Reeves two days ago, and had learned that Jonathan was coming but would probably hold out for a gun. Jonathan must have a gun now, Tom thought, but a gun in such conditions was impossible.

Stepping on the water pedal, Tom wet his hands, shook them, and passed his palms over his face. He was feeling a bit nervous himself. His first Mafia effort!

Tom had felt that Jonathan might botch the job, and, having got Jonathan into the situation, he thought it behooved him to try to help him out. So Tom had flown to Salzburg yesterday in order to board the train today. He had asked Reeves what Marcangelo looked like, but rather casually, and Tom didn't think Reeves suspected that he was going to be on the train. On the contrary, he had told Reeves that he thought his scheme was harebrained, that he should let Jonathan off with half the money and find someone else for the second job if he wanted to make a success of it. But Reeves wouldn't. Reeves was like a small boy playing a game he had invented himself, a rather obsessive game with severe rules—for other people. Tom wanted to help Trevanny, and what a great cause it was! Killing a big-shot Mafioso! Maybe even two Mafiosi!

Tom hated the Mafia, hated their loan-sharking, their blackmail, their bloody Church, their cowardliness in forever delegating their dirty work to underlings, so that the law couldn't get its hands on the bigger bastards among them, could never get them behind bars except on charges of income-tax evasion or some other triviality. The Mafiosi made Tom feel almost virtuous by comparison. At this thought, Tom laughed aloud, a laugh that rang in the tiny metal-and-tile room in which he stood. (He was aware that he just might be keeping Marcangelo himself waiting outside the door.) Yes, there were people more dishonest, more corrupt, decidedly more ruthless than himself, and these were the Mafiosi—that charming, squabbling batch of families which the Italian-American League claimed did not exist, claimed were a figment of fiction writers' imagination. Why, the Church itself, with its bishops making blood liquefy at the festival of San Gennaro, and little girls seeing visions of the Virgin Mary—all *this* was more real than the Mafia! Yes, indeed! Tom rinsed his mouth and spat and ran water into the basin and let it drain. Then he went out.

On the platform there was no one but Jonathan Trevanny, smoking a cigarette which he dropped at once like a soldier who wanted to appear efficient under the eyes of a superior officer. Tom gave him a reassuring smile and faced the side window by Jonathan.

"Did they go by, by any chance?" Tom had not wanted to peer through the doors into the restaurant car.

"No."

"We may have to wait till after Strasbourg, but I hope not."

A woman was emerging from the restaurant car, having trouble with the doors, and Tom sprang to help her.

"*Danke schön,*" she said.

"*Bitte,*" Tom replied.

Tom drifted to the other side of the platform and pulled a *Herald Tribune* from his jacket. It was now eleven minutes past five. They were to arrive at Strasbourg at six-thirty-three. Tom supposed the Italians had had a big lunch and were not going to go into the restaurant car.

A man went into the toilet.

Jonathan was looking down at his book, but Tom's glance made Jonathan look at him, and Tom smiled reassuringly. When the man came out, Tom moved over toward Jonathan. There were two men standing in the aisle of the carriage, several yards away, one smoking a cigar. Both were looking out the window and paying no attention to him and Jonathan.

"I'll try to get him *in* the john," Tom said. "Then we'll have to heave him out the door." Tom jerked his head to indicate the door on the toilet side. "If I'm in there with him, knock twice on the door when the coast is clear. Then we'll give him the old heave-ho as fast as pos." Very casually Tom lit a Gauloise, and slowly and deliberately yawned.

Jonathan's panic, which had reached a peak when Tom had been in the toilet, was subsiding a little. Tom wanted to go through with it. Why he did was beyond Jonathan's power to imagine just now. Jonathan also had a feeling that Tom might intend to bungle the thing and leave Jonathan holding the bag. And yet why? More likely, Tom Ripley wanted a cut of the money—maybe all the rest of it. At that moment, Jonathan simply didn't care. It didn't matter. Now Tom himself looked a bit worried, Jonathan thought. He was leaning against the wall opposite the john door, newspaper in hand, but he wasn't reading.

Then Jonathan saw two men approaching. The second man was Marcangelo. The first man was not one of the Italians. Jonathan glanced at Tom, who looked at him immediately, and Jonathan nodded once.

The first man looked around on the platform, saw the toilet, and made for it. Marcangelo passed in front of Jonathan, then, finding the john occupied, he turned and went back to the carriage aisle. Jonathan saw Tom grin and make a sweeping gesture with his right arm, as if to say, "Dammit, the fish got away!"

Marcangelo was in plain view of Jonathan, waiting just a few feet away in the aisle, looking out the window. It occurred to Jonathan that Marcangelo's guards, who were in the middle of the carriage, wouldn't know that Marcangelo had had to wait, and that this extra time would arouse their anxiety soon if Marcangelo didn't come back. Jonathan nodded slightly at Tom, which he hoped Tom would understand to mean that Marcangelo was waiting nearby.

The man in the rest room came out and returned to the carriage.

Now Marcangelo approached, and Jonathan glanced at Tom, but he was sunk in his newspaper.

Tom was aware that the dumpy figure entering the platform was Marcangelo again, but he didn't look up from his newspaper. Just in front of Tom, Marcangelo opened the door of the toilet, and Tom sprang forward, like a person who was determined to get into the toilet first, and flipped the garrote over Marcangelo's head. Tom hoped he stifled his cry as he dragged him, with a jerk of the garrote like a boxer's right cross, into the little room and closed the door. He yanked the garrote viciously—one of Marcangelo's own weapons in his prime, Tom supposed—and saw the nylon disappear in the flesh of his neck. He gave it another whirl behind the man's head and pulled still tighter. With his left hand, Tom flicked the lever that locked the door. Marcangelo's gurgles stopped, his tongue began to protrude from the awful wet mouth, and his eyes closed in misery, then opened in horror and began to have the blank, what's-happening-to-me stare of the dying. His lower false teeth clattered to the tiles. Tom was almost cutting his thumb and the side of his forefinger with the force he was exerting on the string, but he felt it a pain worth enduring. Marcangelo had slumped to the floor, but the garrote—or, rather, Tom —was holding him in a more or less seated position. Marcangelo was now unconscious, Tom thought, and it was impossible for him to be breathing at all. He picked up the teeth, dropped them into the toilet, and managed to step on the pedal which dumped the pan. He wiped his fingers with disgust on Marcangelo's padded shoulder.

Jonathan had seen the flick of the latch that changed the color from green to red. The silence was alarming. How long would it last? What was happening? How much time had passed? Jonathan kept glancing through the glass half of the door into the carriage.

A man came from the restaurant car, started for the toilet, and, seeing that it was occupied, went on into the carriage.

Jonathan was thinking that Marcangelo's friends would appear if he was in the least long in getting back to his compartment. Now the coast was clear, was it time to knock? There *must* have been time for Marcangelo to die. Jonathan went and rapped twice on the door.

Tom calmly stepped out, closed the door, and surveyed the situation. A woman in a reddish tweed suit approached just then—a smallish, middle-aged woman who was plainly headed for the toilet. The indicator was now showing green.

"Sorry," Tom said to her. "Someone—a friend of mine— is being sick in there, I'm afraid."

"*Bitte?*"

"*Mein Freund ist da drinnen ziemlich krank,*" Tom said, with an apologetic smile. "*Entschuldigen Sie, gnädige Frau. Er kommt sofort heraus.*"

She nodded and smiled, and went back into the carriage.

"Okay, give me a hand!" Tom whispered to Jonathan, and started for the john.

"Another one's coming," Jonathan said. "One of the Italians."

"Oh, Christ." The Italian might simply wait on the platform, Tom thought, if he went into the toilet and locked the door.

The Italian, a sallow chap of about thirty, gave Jonathan and Tom a look, saw that the toilet said *libre*, then went into the restaurant car, no doubt to see if Marcangelo was there.

Tom said to Jonathan, "Can you bash him with the gun after I hit him?"

Jonathan nodded. The gun was small, but Jonathan's adrenaline was stirring at last.

"As if your life depended on it," Tom added. "Maybe it does."

The bodyguard came back from the restaurant car, moving more quickly. Tom was on the Italian's left, and pulled him by the shirtfront suddenly, out of view of the restaurant car's door. He hit him in the jaw, then followed it with a left fist in the man's abdomen, and Jonathan cracked the Italian on the back of the head with the gun butt.

"The door!" Tom said, jerking his head and trying to catch the Italian, who was falling forward.

The man was not unconscious, his arms flailed weakly, but Jonathan already had the side door open, and Tom's instinct was to get him out without spending a second on another blow. The noise of the train wheels came with a sudden roar. They pushed, kicked, and poured the bodyguard out. Tom lost his balance and would have toppled out if Jonathan hadn't caught him by his jacket tails. *Bang*, the door shut again.

Jonathan pushed his fingers through his tousled hair.

Tom motioned for him to go to the other side of the platform, where he could see down the aisle. Jonathan went, and Tom could see him making an effort to collect himself and look like an ordinary passenger again.

Tom raised his eyebrows in a question, Jonathan nodded, and Tom nipped into the toilet and swung the latch, trusting that Jonathan would have the wit to knock again when it was safe. Marcangelo lay crumpled on the floor, head next to the basin pedestal, his face pale now with a touch of blue in it. Tom looked away from him, heard the rustle of doors outside—the restaurant car door—and then a welcome two knocks. This time Tom opened the door just a crack.

"Looks all right," Jonathan said.

Tom kicked the toilet door open past Marcangelo's shoes, which the door bumped, and signaled for Jonathan to open the side door of the train. They worked together, Jonathan having to help Tom with some of Marcangelo's weight before the door was in a fully open position. The door tended to close because of the direction of the train. They tumbled Marcangelo through it headfirst, heels over head, and Tom, trying to give him a final kick, didn't touch him at all, because his body had already fallen clear onto a cinder bank so close that Tom could see individual ashes and blades of grass. Now he held Jonathan's right arm while Jonathan reached for the door's lever and caught it.

Tom pulled the toilet door shut, breathless, trying to assume a calm air. "Go back to your seat and get off at Strasbourg," he said. "They'll be looking at everyone on this train." He gave Jonathan a nervous pat on the arm. "Good luck, my friend." He watched Jonathan open the door that went into the carriage aisle.

Then Tom started to enter the restaurant car, but a party of four was coming out, and he had to step aside while they waddled, talked, and laughed through the two doors. At last he entered and took the first vacant table. He sat down in a chair facing the door he had just come through. He was expecting the second bodyguard at any moment. Casually he drew the menu toward him and studied it. Coleslaw. Tongue salad. Gulaschsuppe. The menu was in French, English, and German.

Jonathan, walking down the aisle of Marcangelo's carriage, come face to face with the second Italian bodyguard, who rudely bumped into him in getting past. Jonathan was glad that he felt a bit dazed, otherwise he might have reacted with alarm at the physical contact. The train gave a whistle followed by two shorter ones. Did that mean something? He got back to his seat and sat down without removing his overcoat, careful not to glance at any of the other people in the compartment. His watch said five-thirty-one. It seemed more than an hour since he had looked at it and it had said eleven minutes past five. Jonathan squirmed, closed his eyes, cleared his throat, imagining the bodyguard and Marcangelo, having rolled under the train wheels, being chewed to bits. Or maybe they hadn't rolled under. Was the bodyguard even dead? Maybe he'd be rescued and would describe him and Tom Ripley with accuracy. Why had Ripley helped him? Or should he call it help? What did Ripley want out of it? He was now under Ripley's thumb, he realized. Ripley probably wanted only money, however. Or was he due for worse? Some kind of blackmail? Blackmail had a lot of forms.

Should he try to get a plane from Strasbourg to Paris tonight, or stay at a hotel in Strasbourg? Which was safer? And safer from what, the Mafia or the police? Wouldn't some passenger, looking out the window, have seen one body, maybe two, falling beside the train? Or had the two bodies fallen too close to the train to be seen? If anybody had seen anything, the train wouldn't have stopped, but word could be radioed, Jonathan supposed. He was on the alert for a train guard in the aisle, for any sign of agitation, but he saw none.

At that moment, having ordered Gulaschsuppe and a bottle of Carlsbad, Tom was looking at his newspaper, which he had propped against a mustard pot, and nibbling a crisp roll. And he was amused by the anxious Italian who had waited patiently outside the occupied john until, to the Italian's surprise, a woman had emerged. Now the bodyguard was for the second time peering down the dining car through the two glass doors. Here he came, still trying to keep his cool, looking for his *capo* or his thug chum or both, walking the whole length of the car as if he might find Marcangelo sprawled under one of the tables or chatting with the chef at the other end of the car.

Tom had not lifted his eyes as the Italian came through, but he had felt his glance. Now he risked a look over his shoulder, like a man who was expecting the waiter with his food, and saw the bodyguard—a blondish, crinkly-haired type in a chalk-stripe suit, broad purple tie—talking with a waiter at the back of the car. The busy waiter was shaking his head and pushing past him with a tray. The body-guard bustled down the aisle between the tables again and went out.

Tom's paprika-red soup arrived with the beer. He was hungry, as he had had only a small breakfast in his Salzburg hotel—not the Goldener Hirsch this time, because the staff knew him there. Tom had flown to Salzburg instead of Munich, not wanting to encounter Reeves and Jonathan Trevanny at the railway station. He'd had time in Salzburg to buy a green leather jacket with green felt trim for Héloïse, which he intended to hide away until her birthday in October. He had told her he was going to Paris for one night, maybe two, to see some art exhibits, and since he did this now and then, staying at the Inter-Continental or the Ritz or the Pont-Royal, Héloïse had not been surprised. Tom, in fact, varied his hotels, so that if he told Héloïse he was in Paris when he wasn't, she wouldn't be alarmed at not finding him at, say, the Inter-Continental, if she telephoned. He had also bought his ticket at Orly, instead of at the travel agencies at Fontainebleau or Moret, where he was known, and he had used the false passport provided by Reeves last year:

Robert Fiedler Mackay, American, engineer, born in Salt Lake City, no wife. It had occurred to Tom that with a bit of effort the Mafia could get the passenger list of the train. Was he on the Mafia's list of interesting people? Tom hesitated to attribute such an honor to himself, but some of Marcangelo's family might have noticed his name in the newspapers. Not recruitable material, not promising as an extortion victim, either, but still a man on the borderline of the law.

But this Mafia bodyguard, or button man, hadn't given Tom as long a look as he'd given a husky young man in a leather jacket across the aisle from Tom. Perhaps all was well.

Jonathan Trevanny would need some reassuring. Trevanny no doubt thought he wanted money, that he was intending to blackmail him somehow. Tom had to laugh a little (he was still looking at his newspaper and might have been reading Art Buchwald) at the memory of Trevanny's face when Tom had walked onto the platform, and at that particular moment when Trevanny had realized that he meant to help him. Jonathan should at least collect the money that had been promised, Tom felt. Tom was vaguely ashamed of himself, in fact, for having got Jonathan into this, and so coming to Jonathan's aid relieved a bit of his guilt.

Yes, if all went well, Trevanny would be a lucky and much happier man, Tom was thinking, and Tom believed in positive thinking. Don't hope, *think* the best, and things would work out for the best, he felt. He would have to see Trevanny again to explain a few things—above all, that Trevanny should take full credit for the Marcangelo murder in order to collect the rest of the money from Reeves. He and Trevanny mustn't seem to be friendly; that was a vital point. They mustn't *be* friendly at all. (Tom wondered now what was happening to Trevanny, if the second bodyguard was cruising the whole train.) The dear old

Mafia would try to track the killer—or killers—down. The Mafia often took years, but they never gave up. Even if the man they wanted fled to South America, the Mafia would try to get him, Tom knew. But it seemed to him that at the moment Reeves Minot was in more danger than either himself or Trevanny.

He'd try to ring Trevanny tomorrow morning in his shop. Or tomorrow afternoon, in case Trevanny didn't make it to Paris tonight. Tom lit a Gauloise and glanced at the woman in the reddish tweed suit, whom he and Trevanny had seen on the platform. She was now dreamily eating a dainty salad of lettuce and cucumber. Tom felt euphoric.

When Jonathan got off at Strasbourg, he imagined that there were more police in evidence than might be usual—six, perhaps, instead of the usual two or three. One police officer seemed to be examining a man's papers. Or had the man simply asked a direction and the cop was consulting a guidebook? Jonathan walked straight out of the station with his suitcase. He had decided to stay in Strasbourg, which, for no real reason, seemed a safer place than Paris tonight. The remaining bodyguard was probably going on to Paris to join his friends—unless by some chance he was at this moment tailing him, ready to plug him in the back. Jonathan felt a light sweat breaking out, and he was suddenly aware of being tired. He set his suitcase down on a curb at a street intersection and gazed around at the unfamiliar buildings. The scene was busy with pedestrians and cars. It was twenty to seven, no doubt the Strasbourg rush hour. Jonathan thought of registering under another name. If he wrote a false name plus a false identity-card number, no one would ask to see his real card. Then he realized that a false name would make him even more uneasy. He was becoming aware of what he had done. He suffered a brief nausea. Then he picked up his suitcase and trudged on. The gun weighed heavily in his overcoat pocket. He was afraid to drop it down a street drain, or into a trash can. Jonathan saw himself getting all the way to Paris and into his own house with the little gun still in his pocket.

Tom, having left the Renault station wagon near the Porte d'Italie in Paris, got home to Belle Ombre a little before 1 a.m. Saturday. There was no light visible at the front of the house, but when Tom climbed the stairs with his suitcase, he was delighted to see that there was one on in Héloïse's room. He went in to see her.

| **12** |

"Back finally! How was Paris? What did you do?" Héloïse was in green silk pajamas with a pink satin eiderdown pulled up to her waist.

"Ah, I chose a bad film tonight." Tom saw that the book she was reading was one he had bought, on the French Socialist movement. That would not improve relations with her father, Tom thought. Often Héloïse came out with very leftist remarks, principles which she had no idea of practicing. Tom felt he was slowly pushing her to the left. Push with one hand, take with the other, Tom thought.

"Did you see Noëlle?" Héloïse asked.

"No. Why?"

"She was having a dinner party—tonight, I think. She needed one more man. Of course she invited us both, but I told her you were probably at the Ritz and to telephone you."

"I was at the Crillon this time," Tom said, pleasantly aware of the scent of Héloïse's cologne mingled with Nivea. And he was unpleasantly aware of his own grubbiness after the train ride. "Is everything all right here?"

"Very all right," said Héloïse in a manner that sounded seductive, though Tom knew she didn't mean it that way. She meant she had had a happy and ordinary day and she was happy herself.

"I feel like a shower. See you in ten minutes." Tom went to his room, where he had a real shower in the tub, not the telephone-type shower of Héloïse's bathroom.

A few minutes later—Héloïse's Austrian jacket having been tucked away in a bottom drawer under sweaters—Tom was dozing in bed beside Héloïse, too tired to look at *L'Express* any longer. He wondered if *L'Express* might have a picture of one of the two Mafiosi, or both, beside the railway track in the next week's edition. Was that bodyguard dead? Tom devoutly hoped he had fallen under the rails somehow, because he was afraid he hadn't been dead when they tossed him out. Tom recalled Jonathan pulling him back when he'd been about to fall out, and with his eyes closed he winced at the memory. Trevanny had saved his life, or at least saved him from an awful fall, and possibly from having a foot cut off by the train wheels.

Tom slept well, and got up around eight-thirty, before Héloïse was awake. He had coffee downstairs in the living room and, in spite of his curiosity, didn't switch on the radio for the nine-o'clock news. He took a stroll around the garden, gazed with some pride at the strawberry patch, which he had recently snipped and weeded, and stared at three burlap sacks of dahlia roots that had been kept over the winter and were due for planting. Tom was thinking of trying Trevanny by telephone this afternoon. The sooner he saw him, the better for Trevanny's peace of mind. Tom wondered if he had noticed the blondish bodyguard who had been in such a tizzy. Tom had passed the man in the aisle when he was making his way from the restaurant car back to his seat, the bodyguard looking ready to explode with frustration, and Tom had had a great desire to say, in his best gutter Italian, "You'll get the sack if this kind of work keeps up, eh?"

Mme. Annette returned before eleven from her morning shopping, and, hearing her close the door into the kitchen, Tom went in to have a look at *Le Parisien Libéré*.

"The horses," Tom said with a smile, picking up the newspaper.

"Ah, *oui!* You have a bet, M. Tome?"

Mme. Annette knew he didn't bet. "No, I want to see how a friend made out."

Tom found what he was looking for at the bottom of page 1, a short item. Italian garroted. Another gravely wounded. The garroted man was identified as Vito Marcangelo, 52, of Milan. Tom was more interested in the gravely wounded Turoli, 31, who had also been pushed from the train and suffered multiple concussions, broken ribs, and a damaged arm that might require amputation in a Strasbourg hospital. Turoli was said to be in a coma, in critical condition. The report went on to say that a passenger had seen one body on the train embankment and alerted a train official, but not before kilometers had been covered by the luxurious Mozart Express, which had been going *à toute vitesse* toward Strasbourg. Then two bodies had been discovered by the rescue team. It was estimated that four minutes had elapsed between the fall of each body, and police were actively pursuing their inquiries.

Obviously there would be more on the subject, probably with photographs, in later editions, Tom supposed. That was a nice Gallic touch of detection, the four minutes—like a problem in arithmetic for children, Tom thought. If a train is going at one hundred kilometers per hour, and one Mafioso is tossed out, and a second Mafioso is found tossed out six and two-thirds of a kilometer distant from the first Mafioso, how much time has elapsed between the tossing out of each Mafioso? Answer: four minutes. There was no mention of the second bodyguard, who was evidently keeping his mouth shut and lodging no complaints about the service on the Mozart Express.

But Turoli wasn't dead. Tom realized that Turoli had perhaps had a look at him before Tom hit him in the jaw, had some idea of him. He might be able to describe him or identify him if he ever saw him again. But Turoli had probably not seen Jonathan at all, since Jonathan had hit him from behind.

Around 3:30 p.m., when Héloïse had gone off to visit Agnès Grais, on the other side of Villeperce, Tom looked up Trevanny's shop number in Fontainebleau, and found that he had it correct in his memory.

Trevanny answered.

"Hello. This is Tom Ripley. Um-m—about my picture— Are you alone just now?"

"Yes."

"I'd like to see you. I think it's important. Can you meet me, say—after you close today? Around seven? I can—"

"Yes." Trevanny sounded as tense as a cat.

"Suppose I hold my car around the Salamandre Bar? You know the bar I mean on the Rue Grande?"

"Yes, I know it."

"Then we'll drive somewhere and have a talk. Quarter to seven?"

"Right," said Trevanny as if through his teeth.

Trevanny was going to be pleasantly surprised, Tom thought as he hung up.

A little later that afternoon, when Tom was in his atelier, Héloïse telephoned.

"Hello, Tome! I am not coming home, because Agnès and I are going to cook something wonderful and we want you to come. Antoine is here, you know. It's Saturday! So come around seven-thirty, all right?"

"How is eight, darling? I'm working a little."

"*Tu travailles?*"

Tom smiled. "I'm sketching. I'll be there at eight."

Antoine Grais was an architect, with a wife and two small children. Tom looked forward to a pleasant, relaxing evening with his neighbors. He drove off to Fontainebleau early so that he could buy a plant—he chose a camellia—as a present for the Graises, and could give this as an excuse for being a little late, in case he was.

In Fontainebleau, Tom also bought a *France-Soir* for the latest news about Turoli. There was nothing about any change in his condition, but the paper did say that the two

Italians were believed to be members of the Genotti family of Mafia, and might have been victims of a rival gang. That would please Reeves, Tom thought, as that was Reeves's objective. Tom found a vacant spot at the curb a few yards from the Salamandre. He looked through his back window and saw Trevanny walking toward him in his rather slow stride. Then Trevanny caught sight of Tom's car. He was wearing a raincoat of impressive decrepitude.

"Hello!" Tom said, opening the door. "Get in and we'll go to Avon—or somewhere."

Trevanny got in, barely mumbling hello.

Avon was a twin town of Fontainebleau, though smaller. Tom drove down the slope toward the Fontainebleau-Avon railway station and bore to the right on the curve that led into Avon.

"Everything all right?" Tom asked pleasantly.

"Yes," Trevanny said.

"You've seen the papers, I suppose."

"Yes."

"That bodyguard isn't dead."

"I know." Jonathan had imagined, since eight o'clock that morning when he had seen the papers in Strasbourg, that Turoli was going to come out of his coma at any moment and give a description of him and Tom Ripley, the two men on the platform.

"You got back to Paris last night?"

"No, I—I stayed in Strasbourg and got a plane this morning."

"No trouble in Strasbourg? No sign of that second bodyguard?"

"No," Jonathan said.

Tom was driving slowly, looking for a quiet spot. He slid up to a curb in a little street of two-story houses, stopped, and switched off his lights. "I think," Tom said, pulling out his cigarettes, "considering the papers haven't reported clues —not the right ones, anyway—we did a rather good job. That comatose bodyguard is the only rub." Tom offered Jonathan a cigarette, but Jonathan took out his own. "Have you heard from Reeves?" Tom asked.

"Yes. This afternoon. Before you rang." Reeves had rung this morning, and Simone had answered. "Someone in Hamburg—an American," Simone had said. That was also making Jonathan nervous, simply the fact that Simone had spoken with Reeves, although he hadn't given his name.

"I hope he's not being sticky about the money," Tom said. "I prodded him, you know. He ought to come up with all of it right away."

And how much would you like, Jonathan wanted to ask, but decided to let Ripley get to it himself.

Tom smiled and slumped behind the wheel. "You're probably thinking that I want some of the—forty thousand quid, isn't it? But I don't."

"Oh. —Frankly I was thinking you wanted some. Yes."

"That's why I wanted to see you today. One of the reasons. The other reason is to ask if you're worried." Jonathan's tension was making Tom feel awkward, almost tongue-tied. He gave a laugh. "Of course you're worried! But there're worries and worries. I might be able to help—that is, if you talk to me."

What *did* he want, Jonathan wondered. He surely wanted something. "I don't quite understand, I suppose, why you were on the train."

"Because it was a pleasure! A pleasure for me to eliminate, or help to eliminate, such people as those two yesterday. Simple as that! Also a pleasure for me to help you put a little money in your pocket. —However, I meant worried about what we did—in any way. It's hard for me to put into words. Maybe because I'm not at all worried. Not yet, anyway."

Jonathan felt off balance. Tom Ripley was being evasive—somehow—or joking. Jonathan still felt hostility toward Ripley, a wariness. Now it was too late. Yesterday on the train, seeing Ripley about to take over the job, Jonathan might have said, "All right, it's all yours," and walked off, back to his seat. That wouldn't have erased the Hamburg affair, which Ripley knew about, but—yesterday the money hadn't been the motivation. Jonathan had simply been in a panic, even before Ripley had arrived. Now Jonathan felt he couldn't find the right weapon for his defense. "I gather it was you," Jonathan said, "who put out the story that I was on my last legs. You gave my name to Reeves."

"Yes," Tom said a little contritely but firmly. "But it was a choice, wasn't it? You could've said no to Reeves's idea." Tom waited, but Jonathan didn't answer. "However, the situation is considerably better now, isn't it? I hope you're not anywhere near dying, and you've got quite a bit of dough —lolly, you'd call it."

Jonathan saw Tom's face light up with his innocent-looking American smile. No one, seeing Tom Ripley's face now, could imagine that he would kill anyone, garrote someone, and yet he'd done just that about twenty-four hours ago. "You have a habit of playing practical jokes?" Jonathan asked with a smile.

"No. No, certainly not. This might be the first time."

"And you want—nothing at all."

"I can't think of anything I want from you. Not even friendship, because that'd be dangerous."

Jonathan squirmed. He made himself stop drumming his fingers on a matchbox.

Tom could imagine what he was thinking, that he was under Tom Ripley's thumb, in a way, whether Ripley wanted anything or not. Tom said, "You're no more in my grip than I am in yours. I did the garroting, didn't I? You could as well say something against me as I against you. Think of it that way."

"True," Jonathan said.

"If there's one thing I'd like to do, it's protect you."

Now Jonathan laughed and Ripley didn't.

"Of course, it may not be necessary. Let's hope not. The

trouble is always other people. Ha!" Tom stared through the windshield for an instant. "For instance, your wife. What've you told her about the money coming in?"

That was a problem—real, tangible, and unsolved. "I said I was being paid something by the German doctors. That they're making tests—using me."

"Not bad," Tom said musingly, "but maybe we can think of something better. Because obviously you can't account for the whole sum like that, and you both may as well enjoy it. —How about somebody dying in your family? In England? A recluse cousin, for instance."

Jonathan smiled and glanced at Tom. "I've thought of that, but frankly there isn't anybody."

Tom could see that Jonathan wasn't in the habit of inventing. Tom could have invented something for Héloïse if he'd suddenly come into a great deal of money. He would create an eccentric tucked away in Santa Fe or Sausalito all these years, a third cousin of his mother's or something like that, and embroider the personage with details remembered from a brief meeting in Boston when Tom had been a small boy—orphaned, as Tom really had been. Little had he known that this cousin had a heart of gold. "Still it ought to be easy with your family so far away in England. We'll think about it," Tom added when he saw that Jonathan was about to say something negative. Tom looked at his watch. "I'm afraid I'm due for dinner, and I suppose you are, too. Ah, one more thing, the gun. A small matter, but did you get rid of it?"

The gun was in the pocket of the raincoat Jonathan was wearing. "I've got it now. I'd very much like to get rid of it."

Tom extended his hand. "Let's have it. One thing out of the way." Jonathan handed it to him, and Tom stuck it into the glove compartment. "Never used, so it's not too dangerous, but I'll get rid of it because it's Italian." Tom paused for thought. There must be something else. Now was the time to think of it, because he didn't intend to see

Jonathan again. Then it came to him. "By the way, I assume that you will tell Reeves you did this job alone. Reeves doesn't know I was on the train. It's much better that way."

Jonathan had rather assumed the opposite, and took a moment to digest this. "I thought you were a rather good friend of Reeves's."

"Oh, we're friendly. Not too. We keep a distance." In a way Tom was thinking out loud, and also trying to say the right thing in order not to scare Trevanny, in order to make him feel more sure of himself. It was difficult. "No one knows I was on that train but you. I bought my ticket under another name. In fact, I was using a false passport. I realized you were having trouble with the garrote idea. I spoke with Reeves on the telephone." Tom started his motor and put on the lights. "Reeves is a bit cracked."

"How so?"

A motorcycle with a strong headlight came roaring around the corner and passed them, drowning out the car's hum for a moment.

"He plays games," Tom said. "He's mainly a fence, as you may know—receives goods, passes them on. It's as silly as spy games, but at least Reeves hasn't been caught yet— caught and released and all that. I understand he's doing quite well in Hamburg, but I haven't seen his place there. —He shouldn't be dabbling in *this* sort of thing. Not his dish."

Jonathan had imagined Tom Ripley a frequent visitor at Reeves Minot's place in Hamburg. He remembered Fritz had a small package with him at Reeves's that night. Jewelry? Dope? Jonathan watched the familiar viaduct, then the dark green trees near the railway station come into view, their tops bright under the streetlights. Only Tom Ripley next to him was unfamiliar. Jonathan's fear rose afresh. "If I may ask—how did you come to pick on me?"

Tom was just then making the difficult turn at the top of the hill in to the Avenue Franklin Roosevelt, and had to pause for oncoming traffic. "For a petty reason, I'm sorry to say. That night in February at your party—you said something I didn't like." Now Tom was clear of traffic. "You said, 'Yes, I've heard of you,' in a rather nasty way."

Jonathan remembered. He also remembered he'd been feeling particularly tired and consequently bloody-minded that evening. So for a slight rudeness, Ripley had got him into the mess he was in now. Rather, he'd got himself into it, Jonathan realized.

"You won't have to see me again," Tom said. "The job has been a success, I think, if we don't hear anything from that bodyguard." Should he say "I'm sorry" to Jonathan? To hell with it, Tom thought. "And, from a moral point of view, I trust you don't reproach yourself. Those men were murderers, too. They often murder innocent people. So we took the law into our own hands. The Mafia would be the first to agree that people should take the law into their own hands. That's their cornerstone." Tom turned in to the Rue de France. "I won't take you all the way to your door."

"Anyplace here. Thanks very much."

"I'll try to send a friend to pick up my picture." Tom stopped his car.

Jonathan got out. "As you like."

"Do ring me if you're in straits," Tom said with a smile.

At least Jonathan smiled back as if he were amused.

Jonathan walked toward the Rue Saint-Merry, and in the next seconds began to feel better—relieved. Much of his relief was due to the fact that Ripley didn't seem to be worried—not by the bodyguard's still being alive, not by the fact that they'd both stood for what seemed an unlikely length of time on that platform in the train. And the money situation—that was as incredible as the rest of it.

Jonathan slowed his steps as he approached the Sherlock Holmes house, though he knew he was later than usual. The signature cards from the Swiss bank had come to his shop yesterday, Simone had not opened the letter, and Jonathan had signed the cards and put them into the post at once this afternoon. He had a four-figure number for his account, which he had thought he would remember but which he had already forgotten. Simone had accepted his second visit to Germany to see a specialist, but there wouldn't be any more visits, and Jonathan would have to account for the money—not all of it, but a good deal of extra money—by stories of injections and pills, and perhaps he'd have to make another trip or two to Germany just to substantiate his story that the doctors were continuing their tests. It was difficult—not at all Jonathan's style. He was hoping that some better explanation might occur to him, but he knew it wouldn't unless he racked his brains to think of one.

"You're late," Simone said as he came in. She was in the living room with Georges, picture books spread all over the sofa.

"Customers," Jonathan said, and hung his raincoat on a hook. The absence of the gun's weight was a relief. He smiled at his son. "And how are you, Pebble Boy? What're you up to?" Jonathan spoke in English.

Georges grinned like a little blond pumpkin. One front tooth had vanished while Jonathan had been on the Munich trip. "I am weeding," Georges said.

"Reading. You weed in the garden. Unless, of course, you have a speech defect."

"Wot's a peach defect?"

Worms, for example. But that could go on forever. What's worms? A town in Germany. "Speech defect—like when you st-stutter. _B-b-bégayer_—that's a—"

"Oh, Jon, look at this," Simone said, reaching for a newspaper. "I didn't notice it at lunch. Look. Two men—no, one man was killed on the train from Germany to Paris yesterday. Murdered and pushed off the train! Do you think that was the train you were on?"

Jonathan looked at the photograph of the dead man on the slope of ground, looked at the account of it as if he had not seen it before: ". . . garroted . . . an arm of the second victim may require amputation. . . ." He said, "Yes—the Mozart Express. I didn't notice anything on the train. But then there were about thirty carriages." Jonathan had told Simone he had come in too late last night to make the last train to Fontainebleau, and that he had stayed at a small hotel in Paris.

"The Mafia," Simone said, shaking her head. "They must've had a compartment with the shades drawn to do that garroting. Ugh!" She got up and went to the kitchen.

Jonathan glanced at Georges, who was bent over an Asterix picture book at that instant. Jonathan would not have wanted to explain what garroting meant.

Tom, though he felt a bit tense, was in the best of spirits that evening. Antoine and Agnès Grais lived in a round stone house with a turret, surrounded by climbing roses. Antoine was in his late thirties, neat and rather severe, master in his own house, and tremendously ambitious. He worked in a modest studio in Paris all week, came to the country on weekends to join his family, and knocked himself out further with gardening. Tom knew that Antoine considered him lazy, because if Tom's garden was equally neat, what miracle was it, since Tom had nothing else to do all day? The spectacular dish that Agnès and Héloïse had created was lobster casserole with a great variety of seafood in the rice, and a choice of two sauces to go with it.

"I've thought of a wonderful way to start a forest fire," Tom said musingly when they were having coffee. "Especially good down in the South of France, where there're so many dry trees in summer. You fix a hand lens in a pine tree— you could do it even in winter—and then when the summer comes, the sun shines through it and the magnifying glass starts a little blaze in the pine needles. You place it near the house of somebody you dislike and—snap, crackle, pop!— the whole thing goes up in blazes! The police or the insurance people very likely wouldn't find the hand lens in all the charred wood, and even if they did—perfect, isn't it?"

Antoine chuckled grudgingly, while the women gave appreciative shrieks of horror.

"If that happens to my property down South, I will know who did it!" said Antoine in his deep baritone.

The Graises owned a small place near Cannes, which they rented in July and August, when rents were highest, and used themselves in the other summer months.

Mainly, however, Tom was thinking of Jonathan Trevanny. A stiff, repressed kind of fellow, but basically decent. He was going to need some more assistance. Merely moral assistance, Tom hoped.

Because of Filippo Turoli's uncertain state, Tom drove to Fontainebleau Sun-

| 13 |

day to buy the London papers, the *Observer* and the *Sunday Times,* which he usually bought from the Villeperce *journaux-tabac* on Monday morning. The news kiosk in Fontainebleau was in front of L'Aigle Noir. Tom glanced around for Trevanny, who probably bought the London papers habitually, too, but he didn't see him. It was 11 a.m., and perhaps Trevanny already had them. Tom got into his car and looked at the *Observer* first. It had nothing about the train incident. Tom wasn't sure the English papers would bother to report the story, but he looked into the *Sunday Times* and found an item on page 3, one short column, that he fell upon eagerly. The writer had given it a light touch: ". . . It must have been an exceptionally fast Mafia job. . . . Filippo Turoli, of the Genotti family, one arm missing, one eye damaged, regained consciousness early Saturday, and his condition is improving so rapidly he may soon be flown to a Milan hospital. But if he knows anything, he is not talking." That was no news to Tom, that he wasn't talking, but plainly he was going to live. Which was unfortunate. Tom was thinking that Turoli had probably already given a description of him to his pals. Turoli would have been visited in Strasbourg by family members. Important Mafiosi in the hospital were protected day and night by guards, and Tom thought that Turoli would get this treatment, too, when the idea of eliminating Turoli crossed his mind. He recalled the Mafia-guarded hospitalization of Joe Colombo, head of the Profaci family in New York. Despite overwhelming evidence to the contrary, Colombo denied that he was a member of the Mafia or that the Mafia existed. Nurses had had to step over the legs of bodyguards sleeping in the halls when Colombo had been in the hospital. Best not to think about getting rid of Turoli. He had probably already said that a man in his thirties with brown hair, a little over average height, had socked him in the jaw and the stomach, and that there must have been another man behind him, because he had got a crack on the back of the head. The question was would Turoli be absolutely sure if he spotted him again; Tom thought there was a good chance he would. Oddly, Turoli might recall Jonathan a little more clearly, simply because Jonathan didn't look like other men, was taller and blonder than most people. Turoli, of course, would compare notes with the second bodyguard, who was alive and well.

"Darling," Héloïse said when Tom walked into the living room, "how would you like to go cruising on the Nile?"

Tom's thoughts were so far away that he had to think for a moment what the Nile was and where. Héloïse was barefoot on the sofa, browsing in travel brochures. Periodically she received a slew of them from an agency in Moret, sent on the agency's initiative, because Héloïse was such a good customer. "I don't know. Egypt—"

"Doesn't this look *séduisant?*" She showed Tom a picture of a little boat called the *Isis,* which rather resembled a Mississippi steamboat, sailing past a reedy shore.

"Yes. It does."

"Or somewhere else. If you don't want to go anywhere, I will see how Noëlle feels," she said, returning to the brochures.

Spring was stirring in Héloïse's blood. Tickling her feet.

They had not been anywhere since just after Christmas, when they'd had a rather pleasant time on a yacht sailing from Marseilles to Portofino and back. The owners of the yacht, friends of Noëlle and rather elderly, had a house in Portofino. Tom didn't want to go anywhere just now, but he didn't say so to Héloïse.

It was a quiet and pleasant Sunday, and Tom made two good preparatory sketches of Mme. Annette at her ironing board. She ironed in the kitchen on Sunday afternoons, watching her TV, which she wheeled into position against the cupboards. There was nothing more domestic, more French, Tom thought, than Mme. Annette's sturdy little figure bent over her iron on a Sunday afternoon. He wanted to capture the spirit of this on canvas—the very pale orange of the kitchen wall in sunlight and the delicate blue-lavender of one of Mme. Annette's dresses, which set off her fine blue eyes.

The telephone rang just after 10 p.m., when Tom and Héloïse were lying in front of the fireplace looking at the Sunday papers. Tom answered.

It was Reeves, sounding extremely upset. The connection was bad.

"Can you hold on? I'll try it from upstairs," Tom said.

Reeves said he would, and Tom went running up the stairs, saying to Héloïse, "Reeves! A lousy connection!" Not that the telephone was better upstairs, but Tom wanted to be alone for the call.

Reeves said, "I said my apartment. In Hamburg. It was *bombed* today."

"What? My God!"

"I'm ringing you from Amsterdam."

"Were you hurt?" Tom asked.

"*No!*" Reeves shouted, his voice cracking. "That's the miracle. I just happened to be out around 5 p.m. So was Gaby, because she doesn't work Sundays. These guys, they— they must've tossed a bomb through the *window*. Quite a feat.

The people below heard a car rush up and pull away after a minute, then two minutes later an *awful* explosion—which knocked all the pictures off their walls, too."

"Look—how much are they onto?"

"I thought I better get elsewhere for my health. I was out of town in less than an hour."

"How did they *find out?*" Tom yelled into the telephone.

"I dunno. I really dunno. They might've got something out of Fritz, because Fritz failed to keep a *date* with me today. I sure hope old Fritz is okay. But he doesn't know—you know, our friend's name. I always called him Paul when he was here. An Englishman, I said, so Fritz thinks he lives in England. I honestly think they're doing this on suspicion, Tom. I think our plan has essentially *worked*."

Good old optimistic Reeves; with his apartment bombed, his possessions lost, his plan was a success. "Listen, Reeves, what about—what are you doing with your stuff in Hamburg? Your papers, for instance?"

"Strongbox at the bank," Reeves said promptly. "I can have those sent. Anyway, what papers? If you're worried—I just have *one* little address book, and that's always on me. I'm sure as hell sorry to lose a lot of records and paintings I've got there, but the police said they'd protect everything they could. Naturally they questioned me—nicely, of course—for a few minutes, but I explained I was in a state of shock, damn near true, and I had to go somewhere for a while. They know where I am."

"Do the police suspect the Mafia?"

"Didn't say so if they did. Tom, old boy, I'll ring you again tomorrow maybe. Take my number, will you?"

Half reluctantly, though he realized he might need it for some reason, Tom took down Reeves's hotel's name, the Zuyder Zee, and its number.

"Our mutual friend sure did one hell of a grand job, even if that second bastard is still alive. For a fellow who's ane-mic—" Reeves broke off with a laugh that was almost hysteri-cal.

"You've paid him in full now?"

"Did that yesterday," said Reeves.

"So you don't need him any more, I suppose."

"No. We've got the police interested here. I mean in Hamburg. That's what we wanted. I heard more Mafia have *arrived*. So that's—"

They were cut off abruptly. Tom felt a swift annoyance, a sense of stupidity, as he stood there with the buzzing, dead telephone in his hand. He hung up and stood in his room for a few seconds, wondering if Reeves would ring back, thinking he probably wouldn't, trying to digest the news. From what Tom knew of the Mafia, he thought they might leave it at bombing Reeves's flat. They might not be out for Reeves. But obviously the Mafia knew that Reeves had had something to do with the killings, so the idea of creating the impression of rival Mafia gang-war had failed. On the other hand, the Hamburg police would make an extra effort to clear the Mafia out of the town—out of private gambling clubs, too. Like everything Reeves did, or dabbled in, this situation was vague, Tom thought. The verdict ought to be: not quite successful.

The only happy fact was that Trevanny had his money. He should be informed of that by Tuesday or Wednesday. Good news from Switzerland!

The next days were quiet. No more telephone calls and no letter from Reeves Minot. Nothing in the newspapers about Filippo Turoli in the hospital at Strasbourg or Milan, not even in the Paris *Herald Tribune* and the London *Daily Telegraph,* which Tom bought in Fontainebleau. Tom planted his dahlias one afternoon, a three-hour job because he had them in smaller lots within the burlap bags, labeled for color, and he tried to plan his color patches as carefully as if he were imagining a canvas. Héloïse spent three nights at Chantilly; her mother was undergoing a minor operation for a tumor, which luckily turned out to be benign. Mme. Annette, thinking Tom was lonely, comforted him with American food, which she had learned to prepare to please him: spareribs with barbecue sauce, clam chowder, and fried chicken. Tom wondered from time to time about his own safety. In the peaceful atmosphere of Villeperce, this sleepy, rather proper little village, and through the tall iron gates of Belle Ombre that appeared to guard the castle-like house but actually didn't—anyone might scale them—a murderer might arrive, one of the Mafia boys, who would knock on the door or ring the bell, push past Mme. Annette, dash up the stairs, and plug Tom. It would probably take the police from Moret a good fifteen minutes to get here, assuming Mme. Annette could telephone them at once. A neighbor hearing a shot or two might assume a hunter was trying his luck with owls, and probably wouldn't attempt to investigate.

During the time that Héloïse was in Chantilly, Tom decided to acquire a harpsichord for Belle Ombre—for himself, too, of course, and possibly for Héloïse. Once, somewhere, he had heard her playing some simple ditty on a piano. Where? When? He suspected she was a victim of childhood lessons, and, knowing her parents, Tom assumed they had knocked any joy out of her endeavors. And although a harpsichord might cost a goodly sum (it would be cheaper to buy it in London, of course, but not with the hundred-percent tax the French would demand for bringing it in), it certainly came in the category of cultural acquisitions, so Tom did not reproach himself for the desire. A harpsichord was not a swimming pool. He telephoned an antique dealer in Paris whom he knew fairly well, and though the man dealt only in furniture, he was able to give Tom the name of a reliable place in Paris where he might buy a harpsichord.

Tom went up to Paris and spent a whole day listening to harpsichord lore from the dealer, looking at instruments, trying them out with timid chords, and making his decision. The one he chose, a gem of beige wood embellished with gold leaf here and there, cost more than ten thousand francs, and would be delivered on Wednesday, April 26th, accompanied by the tuner, who would have to get to work at once because the instrument would have been disturbed by the move.

This purchase gave Tom a heady lift, made him feel invincible as he walked back to his Renault, impervious to the eye and maybe even the bullets of the Mafia.

And Belle Ombre had not been bombed in his absence. Villeperce's tree-bordered, sidewalkless streets looked as quiet as ever. No strange characters loitered. Héloïse returned in a good mood on Friday, and there was the surprise of the harpsichord for Tom to look forward to. The large and delicately handled crate containing the instrument was due on Wednesday. It was going to be more fun than Christmas.

Tom hadn't told Mme. Annette about the harpsichord, either. But on Monday he said, "Mme. Annette, I have a request. On Wednesday we have a special guest coming for lunch—maybe for dinner, too. Let's have something nice."

Mme. Annette's blue eyes lit up. She liked nothing better than extra effort, extra trouble, if it was in the cooking department. *"Un vrai gourmet?"* she asked hopefully.

"I would think so," Tom replied. "Now, you reflect. I am not going to tell you what to prepare. Let it be a surprise for Mme. Héloïse also."

Mme. Annette smiled mischievously. One would have thought she had been given a present.

The gyroscope Jonathan bought for Georges in Munich turned out to be **14** the most appreciated toy Jonathan had ever given his son. Its magic remained every time Georges pulled it from the square box where Jonathan insisted that he keep it.

"Careful not to drop it!" Jonathan said, lying on his stomach on the living-room floor. "It's a delicate instrument."

The gyroscope was forcing Georges to learn some new English words, because in his absorption with the toy Jonathan didn't bother speaking French. The wonderful wheel spun on the tip of Georges's finger, or leaned sidewise from the top of a plastic castle turret—the latter an object resurrected from Georges's toybox, pressed into service instead of the Eiffel Tower shown on the pink page of instructions for the gyroscope.

"A larger gyroscope," Jonathan said, "keeps ships from rolling on the sea." Jonathan did a fairly good job of explaining, and thought if he fixed the gyroscope inside a toy boat in a bathtub of tossing water, he might be able to illustrate what he meant. "Big ships have lots of gyroscopes going at once."

"Jon, the sofa." Simone was standing in the living-room doorway. "You didn't tell me what you think. Dark green?"

Jonathan rolled over on the floor, propped on his elbows. In his eyes the beautiful gyroscope still spun and kept its miraculous balance. Simone meant for the re-covering of the sofa. "What I think is that we should buy a new sofa," Jonathan said, getting up. "I saw an advertisement today for a black Chesterfield for five thousand francs. I'll bet I can get the same thing for three thousand five hundred, if I look around."

"Three thousand five hundred *new* francs?"

Jonathan had known she would be shocked. "Consider it an investment. We can afford it." Jonathan did know of an antique dealer some five kilometers out of town who dealt in nothing but large, well-restored pieces of furniture. Up to now, he hadn't been able to think of buying anything from this shop.

"A Chesterfield would be magnificent—but don't go overboard, Jon. You're on a spree!"

Jonathan had talked today about buying a television set, too. "I won't go on a spree," he said calmly. "I wouldn't be such a fool."

Simone beckoned him into the hall, as if she wanted to be out of Georges's hearing. Jonathan embraced her. Her hair got mussed against the hanging coats.

She whispered in his ear, "All *right*. But when is your next trip to Germany?"

She didn't like the idea of his trips. He had told her they were trying new pills, that Périer was giving them to him, that though he might stay in the same condition, there was a chance the condition would improve, and certainly it wouldn't get worse. Because of the money Jonathan said he was being paid, Simone couldn't believe that he wasn't taking a risk of some kind. Even so, Jonathan hadn't told her how much money was now in the Swiss Bank Corporation in Zurich. Simone knew only that there was six thousand francs or so in the Société Générale in Fontainebleau, instead of their usual four to six hundred—which often went down to two hundred when they paid a mortgage installment.

"I'd love a new sofa. But are you sure it's the best thing to buy now? At such a price? Don't forget the mortgage."

"Darling, how could I? Bloody mortgage!" He laughed. He wanted to pay off the mortgage at a whack. "All right, I'll be careful. I promise."

Jonathan knew he had to think of a better story, or elaborate on the story he'd already told. But for the moment he preferred to relax, to enjoy merely the thought of his new fortune—because spending it wasn't easy. And he could still die within a month. The three-dozen pills that Dr. Schröder of Munich had given him, pills that Jonathan was now taking at the rate of two a day, were not going to save his life or bring about any great change. A sense of security might be a fantasy of sorts, but wasn't it as real as anything else while it lasted? What else was there? What else was happiness but a mental attitude?

And there was the other unknown, the fact that the bodyguard called Turoli was still alive.

On April 29th, a Saturday evening, Jonathan and Simone

went to a Schubert and Mozart concert played by a string quartet at the Fontainebleau Theatre. Jonathan had bought the most expensive tickets and had wanted to take Georges, who could behave well if he were sufficiently cautioned beforehand, but Simone had been against it. She was more embarrassed than Jonathan if Georges was not a model child. "In another year, yes," said Simone.

During the intermission, they went into the big foyer where there was smoking. It was full of familiar faces, among them Pierre Gauthier, the art-supply dealer, who to Jonathan's surprise was sporting a wing collar and black tie.

"You are an embellishment of the music this evening, Madame!" he said to Simone, with an admiring look at her Chinese-red dress.

Simone acknowledged the compliment gracefully. She did look especially well and happy, Jonathan thought. Gauthier was alone. Jonathan suddenly remembered that his wife had died a few years ago, before Jonathan had become acquainted with him.

"All of Fontainebleau is here tonight!" said Gauthier, making an effort to speak above the hubbub. His good eye roved over the scores of people in the domed hall, and his bald head shone under the gray and black hair he had carefully combed over it. "Shall we have a coffee afterward? In the café across the street?" Gauthier asked. "I shall be pleased to invite you."

Simone and Jonathan were about to say yes when Gauthier stiffened a little. Jonathan followed Gauthier's glance and saw Tom Ripley in a group of four or five, only a few yards away. Ripley's eyes met Jonathan's and he nodded; he looked as if he might come over to say hello, and at the same time Gauthier sidled to the left, leaving. Simone turned her head to see who Jonathan and Gauthier had been looking at.

"*Tout à l'heure, peut-être!*" said Gauthier.

Simone looked at Jonathan and her eyebrows went up a little.

Ripley stood out, not so much because he was tall as because he looked un-French with his brown hair touched with gold under the lights of the chandeliers. He wore a plum-colored satin jacket. The striking blond girl who seemed to be wearing no makeup at all must be his wife.

"So?" Simone said. "Who is that one?"

Jonathan knew she meant Ripley. Jonathan's heart was beating faster. "I don't know. I've seen him before but I don't know his name."

"He was at our house—that man," Simone said. "I remember him. Gauthier doesn't like him?"

A bell rang, the signal for people to return to their seats. "I don't know. Why?"

"Because he seemed to want to get away!" Simone said, as if the fact were obvious.

The pleasure of the music had vanished for Jonathan. Where was Tom Ripley sitting? In one of the boxes? Jonathan didn't look up at the boxes. Ripley might have been across the aisle from him, for all Jonathan knew. He realized that it wasn't Ripley's presence that had spoiled the evening, but Simone's reaction. And Simone's reaction had been caused, Jonathan knew, by his own uneasiness at seeing Ripley. Jonathan deliberately tried to relax in his seat, propped his chin on his fingers, knowing all the while that his efforts were not deceiving Simone. Like a lot of other people, she had heard stories about Tom Ripley (even though at this moment she might not recall his name), and she was perhaps going to connect Tom Ripley with—with what? At the moment, Jonathan really didn't know. But he dreaded what would come. He reproached himself for having shown his nervousness so plainly, so naïvely. Jonathan realized he was in a mess, a very dangerous situation, and that he had to play it coolly if he possibly could. He had to be an actor. A little different from his effort to succeed on the stage when he'd been younger. This situation was quite real. Or, if one liked, quite phony. Jonathan had never before tried to be phony with Simone.

"Let's try to find Gauthier," Jonathan said when they were moving up the aisle. The applause was still pattering around them, gathering itself into the coordinated palm-pounding of a French audience that wanted still another encore.

But somehow they didn't find Gauthier. Jonathan missed Simone's reply. She didn't seem interested in finding him. They had a baby-sitter—a girl who lived in their street—at home with Georges. It was almost eleven. Jonathan didn't look for Tom Ripley and didn't see him.

On Sunday, Jonathan and Simone had lunch in Nemours with Simone's parents and her brother Gérard and his wife. As usual, there was television after lunch, which Jonathan and Gérard did not watch.

"That's excellent that the boches are subsidizing you for being one of their guinea pigs!" Gérard said with one of his rare laughs. "That is, if they don't do you any harm." He said this in rapid slang, and it was the first thing he had said that really caught Jonathan's attention.

They were both smoking cigars. Jonathan had bought a box at a *tabac* in Nemours. "Yes. Lots of pills. Their idea is to attack with eight or ten drugs all at once. Confuse the enemy, you know. It also makes it more difficult for the enemy cells to become immune." Jonathan rambled on quite well in this vein, half convinced he was inventing it as he went along, half recollecting it as a proposed method for combating leukemia that he had read about months ago. "Of course, there's no guarantee. There could be side effects, which is why they're willing to pay me a bit of money for going through with it."

"What kind of side effects?"

"Maybe—a decrease in blood-congealing level." Jonathan was getting better and better at the meaningless phrases, and his attentive listener inspired him. "Nausea—not that I've noticed any so far. Then, of course, they don't know all the side effects as yet. They're running a risk. So am I."

"And if it succeeds? If they call it a success?"

"A couple of more years of life," Jonathan said pleasantly.

On Monday morning, Jonathan and Simone drove with a neighbor, Irène Pliesse—the woman who kept Georges afternoons after school until Simone could fetch him— to the antique dealer on the outskirts of Fontainebleau where Jonathan thought they might find a sofa. Irène Pliesse was easygoing, large-boned, and always struck Jonathan as rather masculine, though perhaps she wasn't. She was the mother of two small children, and her house in Fontaine-bleau was more than commonly full of frilly doilies and organdy curtains. At any rate, she was generous with her time and her car, and had often volunteered to drive the Trevannys to Nemours on the Sundays when they went, but Simone, with characteristic scrupulousness, had never once accepted, because Nemours was a regular family affair. There-fore the pleasure of using Irène Pliesse's services for the sofa-hunting was an unguilty one, and Irène took as much interest in the purchase as if the sofa was to be her own.

There was a choice of two Chesterfields, both with old frames and both recently covered in new black leather. Jona-than and Simone preferred the larger one, and Jonathan managed to knock the price down five hundred to three thousand francs. He knew it was a bargain, because he had seen the same sized sofa advertised, with a picture, for five thousand. Now this vast sum, three thousand, nearly his and Simone's combined monthly earnings, seemed positively tri-fling. It was amazing, Jonathan thought, how quickly one could adjust to having a little money.

Even Irène, whose house looked opulent compared to the Trevannys', was impressed by the sofa. And Jonathan no-ticed that Simone didn't at first know what to say to pass it off smoothly.

"Jon had a little windfall from a relative in England.

Not much but—we wanted to get something really nice with it."

Irène nodded.

All was well, Jonathan thought.

The next evening, before dinner, Simone said, "I dropped in to say hello to Gauthier today."

Jonathan felt on guard at once because of Simone's tone of voice. He was drinking a Scotch-and-water and looking at the evening paper. "Oh, yes?"

"Jon—wasn't it this M. Ripley who told Gauthier that— that you hadn't long to live?" Simone spoke softly, though Georges was upstairs, probably in his room.

Had Gauthier admitted it when Simone asked him a direct question? Jonathan didn't know how Gauthier would behave being asked a direct question—and Simone could be gently persistent until she got her answer. "Gauthier told me," Jonathan began, "that— Well, as I told you, he wouldn't say who told him. So I don't know."

Simone looked at him. She was sitting on the handsome black Chesterfield sofa, which had since yesterday transformed their living room. It was due to Ripley, Jonathan was thinking, that Simone was sitting where she was. It didn't help Jonathan's state of mind.

"Gauthier told you it was Ripley?" Jonathan asked with an air of surprise.

"Oh, he wouldn't say. But I simply asked him—was it M. Ripley. I described Ripley, the man we saw at the concert. Gauthier knew whom I meant. You seem to know, too —his name." Simone sipped her Cinzano.

Jonathan fancied her hand shook slightly. "It could be, of course," Jonathan said, with a shrug. "Don't forget, Gauthier told me whoever told him—" Jonathan gave a laugh. "All this talebearing! Anyway Gauthier said, whoever it was— the man said he could have been mistaken, that things get exaggerated. —Darling, it really is best forgotten. It's silly to blame strangers. Silly to make too much out of it."

"Yes, but—" Simone tilted her head. Her lips twisted somewhat bitterly, in a way Jonathan had seen only once or twice before. "The curious thing is, it *was* Ripley. I know that. Not that Gauthier said it—no. He didn't. But I could tell. —Jon?"

"Yes, dear."

"It's because—Ripley is very close to being a crook. Maybe he is a crook. Lots of crooks are not caught, you know. That is the reason I ask. I ask *you*. Are you—all this money, Jon —are you getting it by any chance, somehow, from this M. Ripley?"

Jonathan made himself look straight at Simone. He felt that he had to protect what he already had, and it wasn't *so* connected with Ripley that it would be a lie if he said it wasn't. "How could I? For what, darling?"

"Just because he is a crook! Who knows for what? What has he got to do with these German doctors? Are they really doctors you are talking about?" She was beginning to sound hysterical. The color had risen to her cheeks.

Jonathan frowned. "Darling, Périer has my two reports!"

"There is something very dangerous about the tests, Jon, or they wouldn't pay you so much—isn't that true? —I have the feeling you're not telling me the whole truth."

Jonathan laughed a little. "What could Tom Ripley, that do-nothing— He's an American, anyway. What could he have to do with German doctors?"

"You saw the German doctors because you were afraid you were going to die soon. And it was Ripley—I'm pretty sure—who started the story you were going to die soon."

Georges was bumping his way down the stairs, talking to some toy that he was dragging along. Georges in his dream-world, but he was a presence, just a few yards away, and it rattled Jonathan. He found it incredible that Simone had discovered so much, and his impulse was to deny all of it, at any cost.

Simone was waiting for him to say something.

Jonathan said, "I don't know who it was told Gauthier."

Georges was standing at the door. Now his arrival was a

relief for Jonathan. It effectively stopped the conversation. Georges was asking a question about a tree outside his window. Jonathan didn't listen, and let Simone answer.

During dinner, Jonathan had the feeling Simone didn't quite believe him; that she wanted to believe him but couldn't. Yet Simone (maybe because of Georges) was almost her usual self. She wasn't sulking or cool. But the atmosphere for Jonathan was uncomfortable. And it was going to continue, he realized, unless he could come up with some more specific reason for extra money from the German hospitals. Jonathan hated the idea of lying, exaggerating the danger for himself in order to account for the money.

It even crossed Jonathan's mind that Simone would speak to Tom Ripley himself. Mightn't she telephone him? Make an appointment to see him? Jonathan dismissed that idea. Simone didn't like Tom Ripley. She wouldn't want to come anywhere near him.

That same week, Tom Ripley came to Jonathan's shop. His picture had been ready for several days. Jonathan had a customer in his shop when Ripley arrived, and Ripley proceeded to look over some ready-made frames that leaned against a wall, obviously content to wait till Jonathan was free. At last the customer left.

"Morning," Tom said pleasantly. "It wasn't so easy, after all, to get someone to pick up my picture, so I thought I'd come myself."

"Yes, fine. It's ready," Jonathan said, and went to the back of his shop to get it. It was wrapped in brown paper, but the paper wasn't tied, and it was marked "Ripley," the label fastened with Scotch tape to the paper. Jonathan carried it to the counter. "Like to see it?"

Tom was pleased with it. He held it at arm's length. "That's great. Very nice. What do I owe you?"

"Ninety francs."

Tom pulled his billfold out. "Is everything all right?"

Jonathan was aware that he took a couple of breaths before he answered. "Since you ask—" He accepted the hundred-franc note with a polite nod, pulled out his cash drawer, and got the change. "My wife—" Jonathan looked at the door and was glad to see that no one was approaching at the moment. "My wife spoke to Gauthier. He didn't tell her that you started that story about my—demise. But my wife seems to have guessed it. I really don't know how. Intuition."

Tom had foreseen this happening. He was aware of his reputation, that many people mistrusted him, avoided him. Tom had often thought that his ego would have been shattered long ago—the ego of the average person would have been shattered—except for the fact that people, once they got to know him, once they came to Belle Ombre and spent an evening, liked him and Héloïse well enough, and the Ripleys were invited back. "And what did you say to your wife?"

Jonathan tried to speak quickly because there might not be much time. "What I've said from the start—that Gauthier always refused to tell me who started the story. That's true."

Tom knew. Gauthier had gallantly refused to tell his name. "Well, keep cool. If we don't see each other— Sorry about the other night at the concert," Tom added, with a smile.

"Yes. But—it's unfortunate. The worst is, she associates you—she's trying to—with the money we've got now. Not that I've told her how much it is."

Tom had thought of that, too. It *was* irritating. "I won't bring you any more pictures to frame."

A man with a large canvas on a stretcher was struggling through the door.

"*Bon,* M'sieur!" Tom said, waving his free hand. "*Merci. Bonsoir.*"

Tom went out. If Trevanny was seriously worried, Tom thought, Trevanny could telephone him. Tom had already said that at least once. It was unfortunate, troublesome for Trevanny, that his wife suspected that Tom had started the nasty rumor. On the other hand, the rumor wasn't easily connected with money from hospitals in Hamburg and Munich, still less with the murder of two Mafiosi.

| 15 | On Sunday morning, when Simone was hanging laundry on the garden line, and Jonathan and Georges were making a stone border, the doorbell rang.

It was one of their neighbors, a woman of about sixty, whose name Jonathan wasn't sure of—Delattre? Delambre? She looked distressed.

"Excuse me, M. Trevanny."

"Come in," said Jonathan.

"It is M. Gauthier. Have you heard the news?"

"No."

"He was hit last night by a car. He is dead."

"Dead? Here in Fontainebleau?"

"He was coming home around midnight from an evening with a friend, someone in the Rue de la Paroisse. You know M. Gauthier lives in the Rue de la République, just off the Avenue Franklin Roosevelt. It was that crossroads with the little triangle of green where there is a traffic light. Someone saw the people who did it—two boys in a car. They didn't stop. They went through a red light and hit M. Gauthier and *didn't stop!*"

"Good lord! Won't you sit down, Mme.—"

Simone had come into the hall. "Ah, *bonjour,* Mme. Delattre!" she said.

"Simone, Gauthier is dead," Jonathan said. "Run over by a hit-and-run driver."

"Two boys," said Mme. Delattre. "They didn't stop!"

Simone gasped. "When?"

"Last night. He was dead when they got him to the hospital here. Around midnight."

"Won't you come in and sit down, Mme. Delattre?" Simone asked.

"No, no, thank you. I must be off to see a friend. Mme. Mockers. I am not sure if she knows yet. We all knew him so well, you know?" She was near tears, and set her shopping basket down for a moment to wipe her eyes.

Simone pressed her hand. "Thank you for coming to tell us, Mme. Delattre. That was kind of you."

"The funeral is on Monday," Mme. Delattre said. "At Saint-Louis." Then she departed.

The news somehow didn't register with Jonathan. "What's her name?"

"Mme. *Delattre*. Her husband's a plumber," Simone said, as if of course Jonathan should know.

Delattre wasn't the plumber they used. Gauthier was dead. What would happen to his shop, Jonathan wondered. He found himself staring at Simone. They were standing in the narrow front hall.

"Dead," Simone said. She put her hand out and gripped Jonathan's wrist, not looking at him. "We should go to the funeral on Monday, you know."

"Of course." A Catholic funeral. It was all in French now, not Latin. He imagined the neighbors, faces familiar and unfamiliar, in the cool church full of candles.

"Hit-and-run," Simone said. She walked stiffly down the hall, and looked back over her shoulder at Jonathan. "It's really shocking."

Jonathan followed her through the kitchen, out into the garden. It was good to get back into the sunlight.

Simone had finished hanging her washing. She straightened some things on the line, then picked up the empty basket. "Hit-and-run. —Do you really think so, Jon?"

"That's what she said." They were both talking softly. Jonathan still felt a bit dazed, but he knew what Simone was thinking.

She came a step closer, carrying the basket. Then she beckoned him toward the steps that led to the little porch, as if neighbors on the other side of the garden wall might hear them. "Do you think he could've been killed purposely? By someone hired to kill him?"

"Why?"

"Because perhaps he knew something. That's why. Isn't

it possible? . . . Why should an innocent person be struck down like that—accidentally?"

"Because—these things happen sometimes," Jonathan said.

Simone shook her head. "You don't think that M. Ripley possibly had something to do with it?"

Jonathan saw an irrational anger in her. "Absolutely not. I certainly don't think so." Jonathan could have bet his life that Tom Ripley hadn't had anything to do with it. He started to say that, but it would've sounded a bit strong—and, if he wanted to look at it in another way, a rather comical bet.

Simone started to pass him and enter the house, but she stopped close to him. "It's true Gauthier didn't tell me anything definite, Jon, but he might have known something. I think he did. —I have the feeling he was killed on purpose."

Simone was simply shocked, Jonathan thought, like himself. She was putting into words ideas that she hadn't thought out. He followed her into the kitchen. "Known something about what?"

Simone was putting the basket away in the corner cupboard. "That's just it. I don't know."

The funeral service for Pierre Gauthier took place at 10 a.m. Monday in the Church of Saint-Louis, the main church of Fontainebleau. The church was filled, and people even stood on the pavement outside where two black automobiles waited dismally—one a shiny hearse, the other a box-like bus to carry family relations and friends who had no car of their own. Gauthier was a widower without children. He perhaps had a brother or sister, and maybe some nieces or nephews. Jonathan hoped so. The funeral seemed a lonely thing, despite all the people.

"Do you know he lost his glass eye on the street?" a man next to Jonathan whispered to him in church. "It fell out when he was hit."

"Oh?" Jonathan shook his head in sympathy. The man who had spoken to him was a shopkeeper. Jonathan knew his face, but couldn't connect him with a shop. Jonathan could clearly see Gauthier's glass eye on the black tar road, maybe crushed by a car wheel by now, maybe found in the gutter by some curious children. What did the back of a glass eye look like?

Candles twinkled yellow-white, barely illuminating the church's dreary gray walls. It was an overcast day. The priest intoned the formal phrases in French. Gauthier's coffin stood, short and thick, in front of the altar. At least, if Gauthier had little family, he had many friends. Several women, a few men, were wiping away tears. And other people were murmuring to each other, as if their own exchanges could give them more comfort than the rote the priest was reciting.

There were some soft bells, like chimes.

Jonathan looked to his right, at the people in the rows of chairs across the aisle, and his eyes were caught by the profile of Tom Ripley. Ripley was looking straight ahead toward the priest, who was speaking again, and he seemed to be following the ceremony with concentration. His face stood out among the faces of the French. Or did it? Was it merely because he knew Tom Ripley? Why had Ripley troubled to come? In the next instant, Jonathan wondered if Tom Ripley might be putting on an act by coming. If, as Simone suspected, he really had had something to do with Gauthier's death, even arranged it and paid for it.

When the people all stood up to file out of the church, Jonathan tried to avoid Tom Ripley. He thought the best way to succeed in this was not to try to avoid him, above all not to glance in his direction. But on the steps in front of the church, Tom Ripley suddenly dashed up to one side of Jonathan and Simone and greeted them.

"Good morning!" Ripley said in French. He wore a black muffler around his neck, a dark blue raincoat. *"Bonjour,*

Madame. I'm glad to see you both. You were friends of M. Gauthier, I think."

They were all walking slowly down the steps because of the dense crowd, so slowly it was hard for them to keep their balance.

"Oui," Jonathan replied. "He was one of our neighborhood shopkeepers, you know. A very nice man."

Tom nodded. "I haven't seen the papers this morning. A friend in Moret rang me and told me. Have the police any idea who did it?"

"I haven't heard," Jonathan said. "Just 'two boys.' Did you hear anything else, Simone?"

Simone shook her head, which was covered in a dark scarf. "No. Not a thing."

Tom nodded. "I was hoping you might've heard something—living closer than I do."

Tom Ripley seemed genuinely concerned, Jonathan thought, not just putting on a show for them.

"I must buy a paper. —Are you going to the cemetery?" Tom asked.

"No, we're not," said Jonathan.

Tom nodded. They had all now reached the pavement level. "Nor am I. I'll miss old Gauthier. It's too bad. —Very nice to have seen you." With a quick smile, Ripley went away.

Jonathan and Simone walked on, around the corner of the church into the Rue de la Paroisse, the direction of their house. Neighbors nodded to them, gave them brief smiles, and some said, "Good morning, Madame, M'sieur," in a way they wouldn't have done on ordinary mornings. Car motors started up, ready to follow the hearse to the cemetery, which, Jonathan recalled, was just behind the Fontainebleau Hospital where he had so often gone for transfusions.

"Bonjour, M. Trevanny! *Et Madame!"* It was Dr. Périer, sprightly as ever, and almost as beaming. He pumped Jonathan's hand, at the same time making a small bow to Simone. "What a dreadful thing, eh? —No, no, no, they haven't

found the boys at all. But someone said there was a Paris license on the car. A black D.S. That's all they know. . . . And how are you feeling, M. Trevanny?" Dr. Périer's smile was confident.

"About the same," Jonathan said. "No complaints." He was glad that Dr. Périer took off at once, because Jonathan was aware that Simone knew he was supposed to be seeing Dr. Périer rather frequently now for pills and injections; he hadn't been to Périer for at least a fortnight, when he had delivered Dr. Schröder's report that had come to him at his shop.

"We must buy a paper," said Simone.

"Up at the corner," Jonathan said.

They bought a paper, and Jonathan stood on the pavement, which was still a bit crowded with people dispersing from Gauthier's service, and read about "the disgraceful and wanton act of young hoodlums" that had taken place late Saturday evening in a street in Fontainebleau. Simone looked over his shoulder. The weekend paper had not had time to print the story, so this was the first account they had seen. Someone had seen a large, dark car with at least two young men in it, but no mention was made of a Paris license number. The car had gone on in the direction of Paris but had vanished by the time police tried to give pursuit.

"It *is* shocking," said Simone. "It isn't often, you know, that there are hit-and-run accidents in France."

Jonathan detected a note of chauvinism.

"That's what makes me suspect—" She shrugged. "Of course, I could be completely wrong. But it is quite in character for this type Ripley to make an appearance at M. Gauthier's funeral service!"

"He—" Jonathan stopped. He had been going to say that Tom Ripley had certainly seemed concerned that morning, and also that he bought his art supplies at Gauthier's shop, but Jonathan realized that he was not supposed to know this. "What do you mean by 'in character'?"

Simone shrugged again, and Jonathan knew that, in the

mood she was in, she might refuse to say another word on the subject. "I think it is just possible this Ripley found out from M. Gauthier that I spoke with him, asking him who started this story about you. I told you I thought it was Ripley, even though M. Gauthier wouldn't say so. And now—this—the *very* mysterious death of M. Gauthier."

Jonathan was silent. They were nearing the Rue Saint-Merry. "But that story, darling—it couldn't possibly be worth killing a man for. Be reasonable."

Simone suddenly remembered they needed something for lunch. She went into a *charcuterie,* and Jonathan waited on the pavement. For a few seconds, Jonathan realized—in a different way, as if he saw it through Simone's eyes—what he had done in killing one man and in helping to kill another. Jonathan had rationalized it by telling himself that the two men had been gunmen themselves, murderers. Simone, of course, wouldn't see it that way. They were human beings, after all. Simone was sufficiently upset because Tom Ripley might have hired someone to kill Gauthier—just might have. If she knew that her own husband had pulled a trigger— Or was he influenced at the moment by the funeral service he had just been to? After all, the service had been about the sanctity of human life, despite saying that the next world was even better. Jonathan smiled ironically. It was the word "sanctity"—

Simone came out of the *charcuterie,* awkwardly holding little packages because she didn't have her shopping net with her. Jonathan took a couple of them. They walked on.

Sanctity. Jonathan had given the Mafia book back to Reeves. If ever he had serious qualms about what he had done, all he needed to do was remember some of the murderers he had read about.

Nevertheless, Jonathan felt apprehensive as he climbed the steps of the house behind Simone. It was because Simone was now so hostile toward Ripley. She hadn't cared for Pierre Gauthier that much, to be so affected by his death. Her attitude was composed of a sixth sense, conventional morality, and wifely protectiveness. She believed that Ripley had started the story about his dying soon, and Jonathan foresaw that nothing would shake her, because no other person could easily be substituted as a source of the story, especially now that Gauthier was dead and couldn't back Jonathan up if he tried to invent another person.

Tom shed his black muffler in his car and drove southward toward Moret and home. It was a pity about Simone's hostility. She might even suspect that he had arranged Gauthier's death. Tom lit a cigarette with the lighter from his dashboard. He was in the red Alfa Romeo and felt tempted to go fast, but he held his speed back prudently.

Gauthier's death had been an accident, Tom was sure. A nasty, unfortunate thing, but still an accident, unless Gauthier was mixed up in stranger things than Tom knew about.

A big magpie swooped across the road, beautiful against a background of a pale green weeping willow. The sun had begun to come out. Tom thought of stopping in Moret to buy something—there always seemed something that Mme. Annette needed or might like—but today he couldn't recall anything that she'd asked for, and he didn't really feel like stopping. It was his usual framer in Moret who had rung him yesterday to tell him about Gauthier. Tom must have mentioned to him at some point that he bought his paints at Gauthier's in Fontainebleau. Tom let his foot down on the accelerator and passed a truck, then two speeding Citroëns, and soon he was at the turnoff to Villeperce.

"Ah, Tome, you had a long-distance telephone call," Héloïse said when he came into the living room.

"From where?" But Tom knew. It was probably Reeves.

"Germany, I think." Héloïse went back to the harpsichord, which now had a place of honor near the French windows.

Tom recognized a Bach chaconne whose treble she was reading. "They'll ring back?" he asked.

Héloïse turned her head and her long blond hair swung out. "I don't know, *chéri*. It was only the operator I spoke to, because they wanted person-to-person. There it is!" she said as the telephone rang on her last words.

Tom dashed upstairs to his room.

The operator ascertained that he was M. Ripley; then Reeves's voice said, "Hello, Tom. Can you talk?" Reeves sounded calmer than the last time.

"Yes. You're in Amsterdam?"

"Yeah, and I have a little news you won't find in the newspaper that I thought you might like to hear. That body-guard died. You know, the one they took to Milan."

"Who said he died?"

"Well, I heard it from one of my friends in Hamburg. A usually reliable friend."

It was the kind of story the Mafia might put out, Tom thought. He would believe it when he saw the corpse. "Anything else?"

"I thought it might be good news for our mutual friend, that this guy is dead. You know."

"Sure. I do understand, Reeves. And how are you?"

"Oh, still alive." Reeves forced the sound of a laugh. "Also I'm arranging for my things to be sent to Amsterdam. I like it here. I feel much safer than in Hamburg, I can tell you that. Oh, there is one thing. My friend Fritz. He telephoned me, got my number from Gaby. He's now with his cousin in some little town near Hamburg. But he got beaten up—lost a couple of teeth, poor guy. Those swine beat him up for what they could get out of him."

That was close to home, Tom thought, and felt a pang of sympathy for this unknown Fritz—Reeves's driver, or package-runner.

"Fritz never knew our friend as anything else but 'Paul,'" Reeves went on. "Also Fritz gave them an opposite description—black hair, short, and plump—but I'm afraid they might not believe him. Fritz did pretty well, considering he was getting the treatment. He said he stuck to his story—the way our friend looks, and that's all he knows about him. *I'm* the one in a mess, I think."

That was certainly true, Tom thought, because the Italians knew what Reeves looked like, all right. "Very interesting news. I don't think we should talk all day, my friend. What're you really worried about?"

Reeves's sigh was audible. "Getting my things here. But I sent Gaby some money, and she's going to get them shipped. I've written my bank, and all that. I'm even growing a beard. And of course I'm using a—another name."

Tom had supposed Reeves would be using another name, with one of his false passports. "And what's your name?"

"Andrew Lucas—of Virginia," Reeves said, with a "Hah" by way of a laugh. "By the way, have you seen our mutual friend?"

"No. Why should I? —Well, Andy, let me know how things go." Tom was sure Reeves would ring if he were in trouble, if it was the kind of trouble where he was still able to ring, because Reeves thought Tom Ripley could pull him out of anything. But mainly for Trevanny's sake, Tom wanted to know if Reeves was in trouble.

"I'll do that, Tom. Oh, one more thing! A Di Stefano man was plugged in Hamburg! Saturday night. You might see it in the papers and you might not. But the Genotti family must've got him. That's what we wanted. . . ."

Reeves signed off at last.

If the Mafia got to Reeves in Amsterdam, Tom was thinking, they'd torture some facts out of him. Tom doubted if Reeves could stand up as well as Fritz apparently had done. He wondered which family, the Di Stefanos or the Genottis, had got hold of Fritz? Fritz probably knew only about the first operation, the shooting in Hamburg. That victim had been merely a button man. The Genottis would be far more livid: they had lost a *capo* and, if what Reeves said was true, a button man or bodyguard. Didn't both families know by now that the murders had started with Reeves and the Hamburg casino boys and not through family warfare? Were they finished with Reeves? Tom felt quite incapable of protecting him if he should need protection. If it was only one man they

were up against, how easy it would be! But the Mafia were beyond count.

Reeves had said that he had been calling from a post office.
At least that was safer than calling from his hotel. Tom was
thinking about Reeves's first call. Hadn't that been from a
hotel called the Zuyder Zee? Tom thought so.

Harpsichord notes came purely from belowstairs, a message
from another century. Tom went down. Héloïse would want
him to tell her about the funeral service, say something about
it, though when he had asked her if she wanted to go with
him, she had said that funeral services depressed her.

| 16 | Jonathan stood in his living room, gazing out the
front window. It was just after twelve noon. He
had turned on the portable radio for the midday news, and it
was playing pop music. Simone was in the garden with
Georges, who had stayed in the house alone while he and
Simone went to the funeral service. On the radio a man's voice
sang, "Runnin' on along . . . runnin' on along . . ." Jonathan watched a young dog that looked like an Alsatian loping
after two small boys on the opposite pavement. He had a sense
of the temporariness of everything, of life of all kinds—not
only of the dog and the two boys but of the houses behind them,
a sense that everything would perish, finally crumble, shapes
destroyed and even forgotten. Jonathan thought of Gauthier
in his casket being lowered into the ground perhaps at this
moment, and then he didn't think about Gauthier again but
about himself. He hadn't the energy of the dog that had
trotted past. If he'd had any prime, he felt past it. It was too
late, and Jonathan felt that he wasn't able to enjoy what was
left of his life, now that he had a little wherewithal to do so.
He ought to close up his shop; sell it or give it away—what
did it matter? Yet on second thought he couldn't simply
squander the money, because what would Simone and Georges

have when he died? Forty thousand quid wasn't a fortune. His ears were ringing. Calmly Jonathan took deep, slow breaths. He made an effort to raise the window in front of him and found he hadn't the strength. He turned to face the center of the room, his legs heavy and nearly uncontrollable. The ringing in his ears had completely drowned the music.

He came to, sweating and cool, on the living-room floor. Simone was on her knees beside him, lightly passing a damp towel across his forehead, down his face.

"Darling, I just *found* you! How are you? . . . Georges, it is all right. Papa is *all right!*" But Simone sounded frightened.

Jonathan put his head down again on the carpet.

"Some water?"

Jonathan managed to sip from the glass she held. He lay back again. "I think I might have to lie here all afternoon!" His voice warred with the ringing in his ears.

"Let me straighten this." Simone pulled at his jacket, which was bunched under him.

Something slipped out of a pocket. He saw Simone pick it up; then she looked back at him with concern, and Jonathan kept his eyes open, focusing on the ceiling, because things were worse if he closed his eyes. Minutes passed, minutes of silence. Jonathan was not worried, because he knew he would hang on; this wasn't death, merely a faint. Maybe first cousin to death, but death wouldn't come like this. Death would probably have a sweeter, more seductive pull, like a wave sweeping out from a shore, sucking hard at the legs of a swimmer who'd already ventured too far, and who mysteriously had lost his will to struggle. Simone went away, urging Georges out with her, then returned with a cup of hot tea.

"This has a lot of sugar. It will do you good. Do you want me to telephone Dr. Périer?"

"Oh, no, darling. Thanks." After some sips of the tea, Jonathan got himself to the sofa and sat down.

"Jon, what's this?" Simone asked, holding up the little blue book that was the Swiss bank's passbook.

"Oh—that—" Jonathan shook his head, trying to make himself more alert.

"It's a bankbook. Isn't it?"

"Well—yes." The sum was in six figures, more than four hundred thousand francs, which were indicated by an "f" after them. He knew that Simone had looked into the little book in all innocence, assuming it was a record of some household purchase, some kind of record they had in common.

"It says francs. French francs? . . . Where did you get it? What *is* it, Jon?"

The sum was in French francs. "Darling, that's sort of an advance—from the German doctors."

"But—" Simone looked at a loss. "It's French *francs,* isn't it? This sum!" She laughed a little, nervously.

Jonathan's face was suddenly warm. "I told you where I got it, Simone. Naturally—I know it's a biggish sum. I didn't want to tell you at once. I—"

Simone laid the little blue book carefully on top of his billfold on the low table in front of the sofa. Then she pulled the chair from in front of the writing table and sat down on it, sidewise, holding to its back with one hand. "Jon—"

Georges suddenly appeared in the hall doorway, and Simone got up with determination and turned him by the shoulders. *"Chouchou,* Papa and I are talking. Now leave us alone for a minute." She came back and said quietly, "Jon, I don't believe you."

Jonathan heard a trembling in her voice. It wasn't only the amount of money, startling though it was, but also his secrecy lately—the trips to Germany. "Well—you've got to believe me," Jonathan said. Some strength had returned. He stood up. "It's an advance. They don't think I'm going to be able to use it. I won't have time. But you can."

Simone did not respond to his laugh. "It's in your name. Jon, whatever you are doing, you are not telling me the truth." And she waited, just those few seconds when he might have told her, but he didn't speak.

Simone left the room.

Lunch was a sort of duty. They barely talked. Jonathan could see that Georges was puzzled. He could foresee the days ahead: Simone perhaps not questioning him again, just coolly waiting for him to tell the truth, or to explain—somehow. Long silences in the house, no more lovemaking, no more affection or laughter. He had to come up with something else, something better. Even if he said he ran the risk of dying under the German doctors' treatment, was it logical that they'd paid him this much? Not really. Jonathan realized that his life wasn't worth as much as the lives of two Mafiosi.

Friday morning was lovely, with a light rain alternating with sunlight every half hour or so, | **17** | just the thing for the garden, Tom thought. Héloïse had driven up to Paris, because there was a dress sale at a certain boutique in the Faubourg Saint-Honoré, and Tom felt sure she would come back with a scarf or something more important from Hermès as well. Tom sat at the harpsichord playing the bass of a Goldberg variation, trying to get the fingering in his head and in his hand. He had bought a few music books in Paris the same day he had acquired the harpsichord. He knew how the variation should sound, because he had Landowska's recordings. As he was going over it for the third or fourth time and feeling that he had made progress, the telephone jangled.

"Hello?" said Tom.

" 'Ello—ah—to whom am I speaking, please?" a man's voice asked in French.

Tom felt uneasy. "You wished to speak to whom?" he asked with equal politeness.

"M. Anquetin?"

"No, this is not his house," said Tom, and put the telephone back in its cradle.

The man's accent had been perfect—hadn't it? But then

the Italians would get a Frenchman to make the call, or an Italian whose French accent was perfect. Or was he overly anxious? Frowning, Tom turned to face the harpsichord and the windows, and shoved his hands into his back pockets. Had the Genotti family found Reeves in his hotel, and were they checking all the telephone numbers he had called? If so, this caller wouldn't be satisfied with his answer. An ordinary person would have said, "You are mistaken. This isn't the number you want." Sunlight came through the windows slowly, like something liquid pouring between the red curtains onto the rug. It was like an arpeggio that Tom could almost hear—Chopin, perhaps. He realized that he was afraid to ring Reeves in Amsterdam and ask what was happening. The call hadn't sounded like a long-distance call, but it wasn't always possible to tell. It could have come from Paris. Or Amsterdam. Or Milan. Tom had an unlisted number. The operator wouldn't give his name or address, but from the exchange—424—it would be easy for someone who had the number to find the district if he cared to. It was part of the Fontainebleau area. Tom knew it wouldn't be impossible for the Mafia to find out that Tom Ripley lived in this area, even in Villeperce, because the Derwatt affair had been in the newspapers, with his photograph, just six months ago. Much depended, of course, on the second bodyguard, alive and uninjured, who had walked the train in search of his *capo* and his colleague. This one might remember Tom's face from the restaurant car.

Tom was on the Goldberg variation bass again when the telephone rang a second time. Ten minutes had passed since the first call. This time he was going to say it was the house of Robert Wilson. There was no concealing his American accent.

"*Oui,*" Tom said in a bored tone.

"Hello—"

"Yes. Hello," Tom said, recognizing Jonathan Trevanny's voice.

"I'd like to see you," Jonathan said, "if you've got some time."

"Yes, of course. Today?"

"If you could, yes. I can't—I don't want to make it around the lunch hour, if you don't mind. Later today?"

"Seven?"

"Even six-thirty. Can you come to Fontainebleau?"

Tom agreed to meet Jonathan at the Salamandre Bar. He could guess what it was about: Jonathan couldn't explain the money properly to his wife. Jonathan sounded worried, but not desperate.

At six o'clock, Tom took the Renault, because Héloïse was not back with the Alfa. She had telephoned to say she was going to have cocktails with Noëlle and might also have dinner with her. And she had bought a beautiful suitcase at Hermès, because it had been on sale. Héloïse thought the more she bought at sales, the more she was being economical and positively virtuous.

Tom found Jonathan already in the Salamandre, standing at the counter drinking dark beer—probably good old Whitbread's ale, Tom thought. The place was unusually busy and noisy this evening, and Tom supposed it would be all right to talk at the counter. He nodded and smiled in greeting, and ordered the same dark beer for himself.

Jonathan told him what had happened. Simone had seen the Swiss bankbook. Jonathan had told her it was an advance from the German doctors and that he was running a risk in taking their drugs, and that this was a kind of payment for his life.

"But she doesn't really believe me." Jonathan smiled. "She's even suggested I impersonated somebody in Germany to get an inheritance for a gang of crooks—something like that—and that this is my cut. Or that I've borne false witness for something." Jonathan gave a laugh. He actually had to shout to be heard, but he was sure no one in the vicinity was listening, or could understand if they did. Three barmen were working frantically behind the counter, pouring Pernods and red wine and drawing glasses of lager from the tap.

"I can understand," Tom said, glancing at the noisy fray around him. He was still concerned about the telephone call he had got that morning, though it hadn't been repeated in the afternoon. He had even looked around Belle Ombre and Villeperce as he drove out at six for any strange figures on the streets. It was odd how you knew everybody in the village by their figures, even at a distance, so that a newcomer at once caught your eye. Also Tom had been a little afraid, when he started the motor of the Renault: fixing dynamite to the ignition was a favorite Mafia prank. "We'll have to think!" Tom shouted earnestly.

Jonathan nodded and quaffed his beer. "Funny she's suggested nearly everything I might've done short of murder!"

Tom put his foot on the rail and tried to think in all the din. He looked at a pocket of Jonathan's old corduroy jacket where a rip had been neatly mended, no doubt by Simone. Tom said in sudden desperation, "I wonder what's the matter with telling her the truth? After all, these Mafiosi, these *morpions*—"

Jonathan shook his head. "I've thought of that. Simone—she's Catholic. *That*—" Being regularly on the pill was a concession for Simone to have made. Jonathan saw the Catholic retreat as a slow one: they didn't want to be seen to be routed, even if they gave in here and there. Georges was being raised as a Catholic—inevitable in this country—but Jonathan tried to make him see that it wasn't the only religion in the world, tried to make him understand that he would be free to make his own choice when he grew a little older, and his efforts had so far not been opposed by Simone. "It's so different for her," Jonathan shouted, getting used to the noise, almost liking its protective wall. "It'd be really a shock—something she couldn't forgive, you know. Human life and all that."

"Human! Ha-ha!"

"The thing is," Jonathan said, serious again, "it's almost like my whole marriage. I mean, as if my marriage itself was at stake." He looked at Tom, who was trying to follow him. "What a hell of a place to talk about something serious!" Jonathan began again with determination, "Things are not the same between us, to put it mildly. And I don't see how they're going to get any better. I was simply hoping you might have an idea—as to what I should do or say. On the other hand, I don't know why you *should*. It's my problem."

Tom was thinking they might find a quieter place, or sit in his car. But would he be able to think any better in a quieter place? "I'll try to think of something!" Tom yelled. Why did everyone—even Jonathan—suppose that he could come up with an idea for them? Tom often thought he had a hard enough time trying to steer a course for himself. His own welfare often required ideas: those inspirations that came sometimes while he was under the shower, or gardening, those gifts of the gods that were presented only after anxious pondering. A single person hadn't the mental equipment to take on the problems of another and maintain the same degree of excellence, Tom thought. Then he reflected that his own welfare was tied up with Jonathan's, and if Jonathan cracked up . . . But Tom couldn't imagine Jonathan saying to anyone that Tom had been on the train with him, helping him. There shouldn't be any need to say it, and as a matter of principle Jonathan wouldn't. How does one suddenly acquire *ninety-two thousand dollars?* That was the problem. It was the question Simone was asking Jonathan.

"If we could only make a double-barreled thing out of it," Tom said finally.

"What do you mean?"

"Something added to the sum the doctors might have paid you. —How about a *bet?* One doctor has bet another in Germany, and they've both deposited the money with you, a sort of trust fund—I mean it's in *trust* with you. That could account for—let's say fifty thousand dollars of it, more than half. Or are you thinking in francs? Um-m—more than two hundred and fifty thousand francs, perhaps."

Jonathan smiled. The idea was amusing, but rather wild. "Another beer?"

"Sure," said Tom, and lit a Gauloise. "Look. You might say to Simone that—that because the bet seemed so frivolous, or ruthless or whatever, you hadn't wanted to tell her, but there's a bet on your life. One doctor has bet that you'll live

—a full life span, for instance. That would leave you and Simone with a little more than two hundred thousand francs of your own—which, by the way, I hope you've already begun to enjoy!"

Tock! Tock! A hectic barman set down Tom's fresh glass and bottle. Jonathan was already on his second.

"We've bought a sofa—much needed," Jonathan said. "We could treat ourselves to a TV, too. Your idea *is* better than nothing. Thank you."

A stocky man of about sixty greeted Jonathan with a brief handshake and walked on toward the back of the bar with no glance at Tom. Tom stared at two blond girls who were being chatted up by a trio of boys in bell-bottom trousers standing by their table. A roly-poly old dog with skinny legs looked miserably up at Tom as he waited on the leash for his master to finish his *petit rouge.*

"Heard from Reeves lately?" Tom asked.

"Lately—not in about a month, I think."

Then Jonathan didn't know about Reeves's apartment being bombed, and Tom saw no reason to tell him. It would only shake his morale.

"Have you? Is he all right?"

Tom said casually, "I really don't know," as if Reeves was not in the habit of writing or telephoning. Tom was suddenly ill at ease, feeling that someone was watching him. "Let's take off, shall we?" He beckoned to the barman to take his two ten-franc notes, though Jonathan had also pulled out his money. "My car's outside to the right."

On the pavement, Jonathan began awkwardly, "You feel you're all right yourself? Nothing to worry about?"

Now they were beside the car. "I'm the worrying type," Tom said. "You'd never think so, would you? I try to think of the worst before it happens. Not quite the same as being pessimistic." Tom smiled. "You going home? I'll drop you off."

Jonathan got into the car.

When Tom got in and closed the door, he at once had a sense of privacy, as if they were in a room in his house. And how long would his house be safe? He had an unpleasant vision of the ubiquitous Mafia, like black cockroaches darting everywhere, coming from everywhere. If he fled his house, getting Héloïse and Mme. Annette out before him or with him, the Mafia might simply set fire to Belle Ombre. He thought of the harpsichord burning, or going up in pieces from a bomb. Tom admitted that he had a love of house and home usually found only in women.

"I'm in more danger than you if that bodyguard, the second one, can identify my face. I've had a few pictures in the newspapers, that's the trouble," Tom said.

Jonathan knew. "I apologize for asking to see you today. I'm afraid I'm awfully worried about my wife. It's because —how *we* get along is the most important thing in my life. It's the first time I've ever tried to deceive her about anything, you see. And I've rather failed—so it's shattering to me. But—you were a help. Thanks."

"Yes. It's all right this time," Tom said pleasantly. He meant their seeing each other this evening. "But it occurs to me—" Tom opened the glove compartment and took out the Italian gun. "I think you ought to have this handy. In your shop, for instance."

"Really? To tell you the truth, I'm afraid I'd be hopeless in a shoot-out."

"It's better than nothing. If someone comes into your shop who looks odd— Haven't you got a drawer just behind your counter?"

A tingle went up Jonathan's spine, because he'd had a dream a few nights ago of exactly that: a Mafia gunman coming into his shop and shooting him point-blank in the face. "But why do you think I'll need it? There's some reason, isn't there?"

Suddenly Tom thought, Why not tell Jonathan? It might inspire him to more caution. At the same time, Tom knew that caution wasn't of much help. It also occurred to him that Jonathan would be safer if he took his wife and child away on a trip for a while. "Yes, I had a telephone call today that bothered me. A man who sounded French, but that doesn't mean anything. He asked for some French name. It may not mean anything and yet I can't be sure. Because as soon as I open my mouth, I sound like an American, and he may have been verifying. . . ." Tom trailed off. "To fill you in further, Reeves's place in Hamburg was bombed—I suppose it was around the middle of April."

"His apartment. Good God! Was he injured?"

"No one was in the place at the time. But Reeves went to Amsterdam in a hurry. He's still there, as far as I know, under another name."

Jonathan thought of Reeves's apartment being looked over for names and addresses, of his and maybe Tom Ripley's also being found. "Then how much does the enemy know?"

"Oh, Reeves says he has all his important papers under control. They got hold of Fritz—I suppose you know Fritz—and beat him up a bit, but according to Reeves, Fritz was heroic. He gave them an opposite description of you—you being the man Reeves hired, or somebody hired." Tom sighed. "I'm assuming they suspect Reeves and a few casino club men. Only." He glanced at Jonathan's wide eyes. Jonathan didn't look so much frightened as jolted.

"Good Christ!" Jonathan whispered. "Do you suppose they got hold of my address—or yours?"

"No," Tom said, smiling, "or they'd have been here already, I can tell you that." Tom wanted to get home. He turned on the ignition and maneuvered himself into the traffic of the Rue Grande.

"Then—assuming the man who phoned you was one of them, how did he get your number?"

"Now we enter the realm of guesswork," Tom said, getting his car into the clear at last. He was still smiling. Yes, it was dangerous, and this time he wasn't getting a penny out of it, not even protecting his own money, which was what he had done in the Derwatt near fiasco. "Maybe because Reeves was stupid enough to ring me from Amsterdam. I'm toying with the possibility that the Mafia boys might've traced him to Amsterdam, because for one thing he's having his housekeeper send his possessions there. Pretty stupid move, so soon," Tom said, as if in parentheses. "I'm wondering, you see, if—even if Reeves got out of his Amsterdam hotel, the Mafia didn't check on the phone calls he made. In which case my number might be there. By the way, he didn't ring you, I trust, when he was in Amsterdam? You're sure?"

"I know the last call I had was from Hamburg." Jonathan remembered Reeves's cheerful voice, telling him his money, all of it, would be deposited at once in the Swiss bank. Jonathan was worried about the bulge of the gun in his pocket. "Sorry, but I'd better go to my shop first to get rid of this gun. Drop me anywhere here."

Tom pulled up to a curb. "Take it easy. If you're seriously —alarmed about anything, go ahead and ring me. I mean that."

Jonathan gave an awkward smile, because he felt scared. "If I can be of help—do the same."

Tom drove on.

Jonathan walked toward his shop, one hand in his pocket supporting the weight of the gun. He put the gun into his cash drawer, which slid under the heavy counter. Tom was right, the gun was better than nothing, and Jonathan knew he had another advantage: he didn't care much about his own life. It wouldn't be like Tom Ripley getting shot or whatever, losing his life while in the best of health—and for literally nothing, it seemed to Jonathan.

If a man walked into his shop with intent to shoot him, and if he was lucky enough to be able to shoot the man first, it would be the end of the game anyway. Jonathan didn't need Tom Ripley to tell him that. The shot would bring people, the police, the dead man would be identified, and the question would be asked: "Why should a Mafia man want to shoot at Jonathan Trevanny?" The train journey would be exposed next, because the police would ask about his movements in the last weeks, would want to see his passport. He'd be finished.

Jonathan locked his shop door and walked on toward the Rue Saint-Merry. He was thinking of Reeves's apartment bombed, all those books, the records, the paintings. He was thinking of Fritz, who had guided him to the button man called Salvatore Bianca, of Fritz beaten up and not betraying him.

It was nearly seven-thirty, and Simone was in the kitchen. *"Bonsoir!"* Jonathan said, smiling.

"Bonsoir," Simone said. She turned the oven down, then straightened and removed her apron. "And what were you doing with M. Ripley this evening?"

Jonathan's face tingled a little. Where had she seen them? When he'd got out of Tom's car? "He came to talk about some framing," Jonathan said. "So we had a beer. It was near closing time."

"Oh?" She looked at Jonathan, not moving. "I see."

Jonathan hung his jacket in the hall. Georges was coming down the stairs to greet him, saying something about his hovercraft. He was assembling a model Jonathan had bought for him, and it was a little too complicated. Jonathan swung him up over his shoulder. "We'll have a look at it after dinner, all right?"

The atmosphere didn't improve. They had a delicious purée of vegetable soup, made in a six-hundred-franc mixer that Jonathan had just bought: it made fruit juices and pulverized almost everything, including small chicken bones. Jonathan tried without success to talk about other things. Simone soon brought any subject to a halt. It wasn't impossible, Jonathan was thinking, that Tom Ripley should want him to frame some pictures. After all, Tom had said he painted.

Jonathan said, "Ripley is interested in framing several things. I might have to go to his house to look at them."

"Oh?" in the same tone. Then she said something pleasant to Georges.

Jonathan disliked Simone when she was like this, and hated himself for disliking her. He had been planning to plunge into the explanation—the bet explanation—of the money in the Swiss bank. He simply couldn't that evening.

After dropping Jonathan, Tom had an impulse to stop at a bar-café and ring his house. He | **18** | wanted to know if all was well, and if Héloïse was home. To his great relief, Héloïse answered.

"*Oui, chéri,* I just got home. Where are you? . . . No, I only had a drink with Noëlle."

"Héloïse, my pet, let's do something nice tonight. Maybe the Graises or the Berthelins are free. . . . I know it's late to ask anyone for dinner, but for after dinner. Maybe the Cleggs. . . . Yes, I feel like seeing some people." Tom said he would be home in fifteen minutes.

Tom drove fast, but carefully. He felt curiously shaky about tonight. He wondered whether Mme. Annette had got any telephone calls since he left the house.

Héloïse, or Mme. Annette, had put the front light on at Belle Ombre, though dusk had not yet fallen. A big Citroën cruised slowly past just before Tom turned in at the gates, and he looked at it carefully: dark blue, lumbering on the slightly uneven road, with a license plate ending in 75, meaning a Paris car. There had been at least two people in it. Was it casing Belle Ombre? He was probably over-anxious.

"Hello, Tome! *Les Clegg* can come for a quick drink, and *les Grais* can come for dinner, because Antoine didn't go to Paris today. Does that please you?" Héloïse kissed his cheek. "Where were you? Look at the suitcase! I admit it's not very big—"

Tom looked at the dark purple suitcase with a red canvas band around it. The clasps and the lock appeared to be brass. The purple leather looked like kid, and perhaps was. "Yes. It *is* pretty." It really was, like their harpsichord, or like his *commode de bateau* upstairs.

"And look—inside." Héloïse opened it. "Really str-rong," she said in English.

Tom leaned over and kissed her hair. "Darling, it's lovely. We can celebrate the suitcase—and the harpsichord. The Cleggs and the Graises haven't seen the harpsichord, have they? No. How is Noëlle?"

"Tome, something is making you nervous," Héloïse said in a soft voice, in case Mme. Annette might hear.

"No," said Tom. "I just feel like seeing some people. I had a very quiet day. Ah, Mme. Annette, *bonsoir!* People tonight. Two for dinner. Can you manage?"

Mme. Annette had just arrived with the bar cart. "*Mais oui,* M. Tome. It will have to be *à la fortune du pot,* but I shall try a ragout—my Normandy style, if you remember. . . ."

Tom didn't listen to her ingredients—there was beef, veal, and kidney, because she'd had time to pop out to the butcher's this evening, and it was not going to be potluck at all, Tom was sure. But he had to wait until she finished. Then he said, "By the way, Mme. Annette, have there been any telephone calls since I left at six?"

"No, M. Tome." With expertise Mme. Annette extracted the cork from a small bottle of champagne.

"None at all? Not even a wrong number?"

"*Non,* M. Tome." Mme. Annette poured champagne carefully into a wide glass for Héloïse.

Héloïse was watching him. But Tom decided to persist, rather than go into the kitchen to speak with Mme. Annette. Or should he go into the kitchen? Yes. That was quite easy. When Mme. Annette had gone back, Tom said to Héloïse, "I think I'll get a beer." Mme. Annette had left him to make his own drink, as Tom often preferred to do.

In the kitchen, Mme. Annette had her dinner in full swing, vegetables washed and ready, and something already boiling on the stove. "Madame," Tom said, "it's very important—today. Are you quite sure nobody telephoned at all? Even somebody—even by error?"

This seemed to jog her memory, to Tom's alarm. "Ah, *oui,* the telephone rang around six-thirty. A man asked for—some other name I can't recall, M. Tome. Then he hung up. An error, M. Tome."

"What did you say to him?"

"I said it was not the residence of the person he wanted."

"You told him it was the Ripley residence?"

"Oh, no, M. Tome. I simply said it was not the right number. I thought that was the correct thing to do."

Tom beamed at her. It had been the correct thing to do. Tom had reproached himself for going off today without asking her not to give his name under any circumstances, but she'd handled everything properly on her own initiative. "Excellent. That's always the correct thing to do," Tom said with admiration. "That's why I have an unlisted number, in order to have a little privacy, *n'est-ce pas?*"

"*Bien sûr,*" said Mme. Annette, as if it were the most natural thing in the world.

Tom went back to the living room, forgetting all about the beer. He poured a Scotch for himself. He was not reassured. If it had been a Mafioso looking for him, he might be doubly suspicious because two people at the house had refrained from giving the name of the proprietor. Tom wondered if some checking was going on in Milan or Amsterdam or perhaps Hamburg. Didn't Tom Ripley live in Villeperce? Couldn't this 424 number be a Villeperce number? Yes, indeed. Fontainebleau numbers began with 422, but 424 was an area southward, including Villeperce.

"What is worrying you, Tome?" Héloïse asked.

"Nothing, darling. What's happening with your cruise plans? Have you seen anything you like?"

"Ah, yes! Something which is not *casse-pied* swank, just nice and simple. A cruise from Venice around the Mediterranean, including Turkey. Fifteen days—and one doesn't have to dress for dinner. How does that sound, Tome? Every three weeks during May and June, the boat leaves."

"I'm not much in the mood at the moment. Ask Noëlle if she'd go with you. It would do you good."

Tom went upstairs to his room. He opened the bottom drawer of his big chest of drawers. In it was Héloïse's green jacket from Salzburg. At the back on the bottom of the drawer lay a Luger that Tom had acquired just three months ago—from Reeves, oddly enough, though not directly from him but from a man whom Tom had had to meet in Paris to get something the man was delivering, something that Tom had had to hold for a month before posting it. As a favor, really as a kind of payment, Tom had requested a Luger, and it had been given to him—a 7.65 mm. with two little boxes of ammunition. Tom verified that the gun was loaded; then he went to his closet and looked at his French-made hunting rifle. It was loaded also, with the safety on. It was the Luger he would need in case of trouble, Tom supposed, tonight or tomorrow or tomorrow night. Tom looked out the two windows of his room, which gave in two directions. He was looking for cruising cars with dimmed lights, but he didn't see any. It was already dark.

A car approached from the left with a determined air: this was the dear, harmless Cleggs, and they turned in smartly through the gates of Belle Ombre. Tom went down to welcome them.

The Cleggs—Howard, about fifty, an Englishman, and his English wife, Rosemary—stayed for two drinks, and the Graises joined them. Clegg, a retired lawyer, retired because of a heart condition, was nevertheless more animated than anyone else. His neatly cut gray hair, seasoned tweed jacket, and gray flannels lent the air of country stability that Tom needed. Clegg, standing with his back to the curtained front window, Scotch in hand, telling a funny story—what could happen tonight to shatter this rural conviviality? Tom had left his room light on, and he had also turned on the bedside lamp in Héloïse's room. The two visiting cars were parked carelessly on the gravel. Tom wanted his house to present the picture of a party in progress, a party bigger than it was.

Tom knew that this wouldn't really stop the Mafia boys if they chose to toss a bomb, and that he was perhaps putting his friends in danger. But he had the feeling the Mafia would prefer a quiet assassination for him: get him alone and then attack, maybe without a gun—just a sudden beating that would be fatal. The Mafia could do it on the streets of Ville-perce and be away before the townspeople knew what had happened.

Rosemary Clegg, slim and beautiful in a middle-aged way, was promising Héloïse some kind of plant that she and Howard had just brought back from England.

"Are you intending to set any fires this summer?" Antoine Grais asked.

"Not really my dish," Tom said, smiling. "Come out and take a look at the greenhouse-to-be."

Tom and Antoine walked out the French windows and down the steps onto the lawn, Tom with a flashlight. The foundation had been laid with cement and the pieces for the steel frame were stacked alongside—doing the lawn no good, since the workmen hadn't been around for a week. Tom had been warned by one of the villagers about this crew: they had so much work this summer that they hopped from one job to the next, trying to please everybody, or at least keep a lot of people on the hook.

"It's coming along," said Antoine.

Tom had consulted Antoine as to the best type of green-house and had paid him for his services; Antoine had been able to get the materials from him at a professional discount, more cheaply than the mason would have got them. Tom found himself glancing toward the lane through the woods behind Antoine where there were no lights at all, certainly no car lights.

By eleven o'clock, when the four of them were drinking coffee and Bénédictine after dinner, Tom had made up his mind to get both Héloïse and Mme. Annette out of the house by tomorrow. Héloïse would be the easier. He'd persuade her to stay with Noëlle for a few days—Noëlle and her husband had a very large flat in Neuilly—or to stay with her parents. Mme. Annette had a sister in Lyon, and fortunately the sister had a telephone, so something might be arranged quickly. And the explanation? Tom shrank from the idea of putting on an act of being crotchety, such as saying, "I must be alone for a few. days," and if he admitted that there was danger, Héloïse and Mme. Annette would be alarmed. They'd want to alert the police.

Tom approached Héloïse that evening as they were getting ready for bed. "My dear," he said in English, "I have a feeling something awful is going to happen, and I don't want you here. It's a matter of your safety. I would also like Mme. Annette to leave tomorrow for a few days—so I hope, darling, you can help me persuade her to visit her sister."

Héloïse, propped up on pale blue pillows, frowned a little and set down the yogurt she was eating. "*What* is happening that is awful? Tome, you must tell me."

"No." Tom shook his head. Then he laughed. "And maybe I'm only anxious. Maybe it's for nothing. But there's no harm in playing it safe, is there?"

"I don't want a lot of words, Tome. What has happened? Something with Reeves? It is that, isn't it?"

"In a way." It was a lot better than saying it was the Mafia.

"Where is he?"

"Oh, he's in Amsterdam, I think."

"Doesn't he live in Germany?"

"Yes, but he's doing some work in Amsterdam."

"But who else is involved? Why are you worried? What have you done, Tome?"

"Why, nothing, darling!" It was Tom's usual answer under the circumstances. He wasn't even ashamed of it.

"Then you're trying to protect Reeves?"

"He's done me a few favors. But I want to protect you now—and us, and Belle Ombre. Not Reeves. So you must let me try, darling."

"Belle Ombre?"

Tom smiled and said calmly, "I don't want any disturbance

at Belle Ombre. I don't want anything broken, not a pane
of glass. You must trust me. I'm trying to avoid anything
violent—or dangerous."

Héloïse blinked her eyes and said, in a slightly piqued
tone, "All right, Tome."

He knew that Héloïse would ask no more questions—not
unless there was an accusation by the police, or a Mafia
corpse to account for to her. A few minutes later, they were
both smiling, and Tom slept in her bed that night. How
much worse it must be for Jonathan Trevanny, Tom thought
—not that Simone appeared difficult, prying, or neurotic in
the least, but Jonathan was not in the habit of doing anything out of the ordinary, not even telling white lies. As
Jonathan had said, it must be shattering if his wife had
begun to mistrust him. And because of the money it was
natural that Simone would think of crime, of something
shameful that Jonathan couldn't admit.

In the morning, Héloïse and Tom spoke to Mme. Annette together. Héloïse had had her tea upstairs, and Tom
was drinking a second coffee in the living room.

"M. Tome says he wants to be alone and think and paint
for a few days," said Héloïse.

They had decided this was best, after all. "And a little va-
cation wouldn't do you any harm, Mme. Annette. A little
one before the big one in August," Tom added, though Mme.
Annette, sturdy and lively as always, looked in the best of
form.

"If you wish, Madame, M'sieur, of course. That is the
big thing, is it not?" She was smiling, her blue eyes not
exactly twinkling now, but she was agreeable.

Mme. Annette at once agreed to ring her sister Marie-
Odile in Lyon.

The mail came at 9:30 a.m. In it was a square white envelope with a Swiss stamp, the address printed—Reeves's
printing, Tom suspected—and no return address. Tom
wanted to open it in the living room, but Héloïse was there
talking with Mme. Annette about driving her to Paris for the

train to Lyon, so Tom went up to his room. The letter
read:

May 11th

Dear Tom,

I am in Ascona. Had to leave Amsterdam because of a near thing in my hotel, but have managed
to put my belongings in storage in Amsterdam.
God, I wish they would lay off! I am here in this
pretty town, known as Ralph Platt, staying at an inn
up the hill called Die Drei Bären—cozy? At least it's
very out of the way and family pension style. Wish-
ing the very best to you and Héloïse,

As ever,

R.

Tom crushed the letter in his hand, then shredded it
into his wastebasket. It was exactly as bad as Tom had
thought: the Mafia had caught up with him at Amsterdam
and had doubtless got Tom's phone number by checking all
the numbers Reeves had called. Tom wondered what the
near thing at the hotel had been? He swore to himself, not
for the first time, that he'd never have anything more to do
with Reeves Minot. In this case, all he'd provided was an
idea for Reeves. That should have been harmless, and it
was harmless. His mistake, Tom realized, had been to try
to help Jonathan Trevanny. And, of course, Reeves didn't
know that; otherwise he wouldn't have been stupid enough
to ring him at Belle Ombre.

Tom wanted Jonathan Trevanny to come to Belle Ombre
by this evening, even this afternoon, though he knew Jonathan worked on Saturday. If anything happened, the situation
could be more easily handled by two people—at the front
and the back of the house, for instance—because one person
couldn't be everywhere. Who else had he to call on but Jonathan? Jonathan wasn't a promising fighter, and yet in a crisis
he might come through, just as he had on the train. He'd

done all right there, and even yanked him back to safety when he'd surely been going to fall out the train door. He wanted Jonathan to stay the night. He'd have to fetch him, because there was no bus, and Tom didn't want him to take a taxi in view of what might happen, didn't want any taxi driver to recall that he'd driven a man from Fontainebleau to Villeperce, a rather unusual distance.

"You will telephone me tonight, Tome?" Héloïse asked. She was packing a big suitcase in her room. She was going first to her family.

"Yes, my love. About seven-thirty?" He knew Héloïse's parents dined promptly at eight. "I'll ring and say, 'All is well,' probably."

"Is it only tonight you are worried about?"

It wasn't, but Tom didn't want to say so. "I think so."

Around eleven, when Héloïse and Mme. Annette were ready to leave, Tom managed to enter the garage first, even before he helped them with their luggage, though Mme. Annette had the old French school idea that she should carry the luggage because she was a servant. Tom looked under the hood of the Alfa. The motor presented the familiar picture of metal and wires. He started the motor. No explosion. He had gone out and padlocked the garaged doors last evening before dinner, but he believed anything possible when it came to the Mafia. They'd pick a padlock and snap it shut again.

"We will be in touch, Mme. Annette," Tom said, kissing her cheek. "Enjoy yourself!"

"Bye-bye, Tome! Ring me tonight! And take care!" Héloïse shouted.

Tom grinned as he waved goodbye. He could tell that Héloïse wasn't very worried. That was all to the good.

Then he went into the house to telephone Jonathan.

. . .

The morning had been a rough one for Jonathan.

Simone had said, in a pleasant enough tone because she was helping Georges tug himself into a turtleneck sweater, "I don't see how this ambience can go on forever, Jon. Do you?"

Simone and Georges had to leave for Georges's school in a couple of minutes. It was almost eight-fifteen.

"No, I don't. And about that Swiss account—" Jonathan determined to plunge on now. He spoke quickly, hoping Georges wouldn't grasp all of it. "They've made a bet, if you must know. I'm holding the take for both of them. So that—"

"Who?" Simone looked as puzzled and angry as ever.

"The doctors," Jonathan said. "They're trying a new treatment—one is—and somebody's betting against him. Another doctor. I thought you'd think it rather macabre, so I wasn't going to tell you about it. But that means there's really only about two hundred thousand belonging to us. They're paying me that—the Hamburg people—for trying out their pills."

Jonathan could see that she tried, and couldn't believe him. "It's absurd!" she said. "All that money, Jon! For a *bet?*"

Georges looked up at her.

Jonathan glanced at his son and wet his lips.

"Do you know what I think, and I don't care if Georges hears me!" she said. "I think you are holding—concealing dishonest money for that dishonest type Tom Ripley. And of course he's paying you a little, letting you have some of it for doing him the favor!"

Jonathan realized he was trembling, and set his bowl of café au lait down on the kitchen table. Both he and Simone were standing. "Couldn't Ripley conceal his money himself in Switzerland?" he said. His instinct was to go to her and grasp her by the shoulders, tell her that she had to believe him. But he knew quite well that she'd push him back. So he simply stood up straighter and said, "I can't help it if you don't believe me. That's the way it is." Jonathan had had a transfusion last Monday afternoon, the day he had fainted. Simone had gone to the hospital with him, and then he'd gone by himself afterward to Dr. Périer, whom he'd had to ring earlier to make the appointment for the transfusion. Dr. Périer had wanted to see him as a matter of routine. But Jonathan had told Simone that Dr. Périer had given him more of the medications sent by the Hamburg doctor. The Hamburg doctor, Wentzel, hadn't sent pills; the pills he recommended were available in France, and Jonathan had a supply at home now. Jonathan had decided that the Hamburg doctor should be betting "for" and the Munich doctor should be betting "against," but he hadn't got that far with Simone as yet.

"I *don't* believe you," Simone said, her voice gentle and also sinister. "Come along, Georges, we've got to go."

Jonathan blinked, and watched Simone and Georges go up the hall toward the front door. Georges picked up his satchel of books and, perhaps startled by the heated conversation, forgot to say goodbye to Jonathan. Jonathan was silent, too.

Since it was Saturday, Jonathan's shop was busy. The phone rang several times. Around eleven, the voice at the other end was Tom Ripley's.

"I'd like to see you today. It's rather important," Tom said. "Are you able to talk now?"

"Not really." There was a man at the counter in front of Jonathan, waiting to pay for his picture which lay, wrapped, between them.

"I'm sorry to bother you on a Saturday. But I'm wondering how soon you could get to my house—and stay the evening?"

Jonathan was jolted for a second. Close the shop. Tell Simone. Tell her what? "Of course I can. Yes."

"How soon? I'll pick you up. Say at twelve noon? Or is that too soon?"

"No. I'll make it."

"Pick you up at your shop. Or on the street there. One other thing—bring the gun." Tom hung up.

Jonathan attended to the people in his shop, and while there was still someone there, he stuck the FERMÉ sign in his door. He wondered what had happened to Tom Ripley since yesterday. Simone was home that morning, but she was more often out than in on Saturday because she did marketing and chores like going to the dry cleaner. Jonathan decided to write her a note and push it through the letter slot in the front door. He had the note written by twenty to twelve, and went off with it up the Rue de la Paroisse, the quickest way, where there was a fifty-fifty chance of encountering Simone, though he didn't. He stuck the note through the slot marked "Lettres" and walked quickly back the way he had come. He had written:

My dear,

Won't be home for lunch or dinner and have closed the shop. Chance of a big job some distance away, and am being taken there by car.

J.

It was inexplicit, not at all like him. And yet how could things get any worse than they'd been that morning?

Jonathan went into his shop again, grabbed his old mack, and stuck the Italian gun into its pocket. When he went out on the pavement, Tom's green Renault was approaching. Tom opened the door, barely stopping, and Jonathan got in.

"Morning!" Tom said. "How are things?"

"At home?" Jonathan was, despite himself, glancing about

for Simone, who might be anywhere on the streets here. "Not very good, I'm afraid."

Tom could imagine. "But you're feeling all right?"

"Yes, thanks."

Tom made the right turn by the Prisunic into the Rue Grande. "I had another telephone call," Tom said. "Rather, my housekeeper did. Same as before, a wrong number, and she didn't tell him whose house it was, but it's made me nervous. By the way, I've sent my housekeeper and my wife away. I have a hunch something might happen. So I called on you to hold the fort with me. I have no one else to ask. I'm afraid to ask the police to keep watch. If they were to find a couple of the Mafia around my house, there'd be unpleasant inquiries as to why they were there, of course."

Jonathan knew that.

"We're not there yet," Tom went on, passing the monument and entering the road that led toward Villeperce, "so there's time for you to change your mind. I'll gladly drive you back, and you needn't apologize if you don't want to join me. There may be danger and there may not. But it's easier for two people to be on the lookout there than for one."

"Yes." Jonathan felt curiously paralyzed.

"It's just that I don't want to leave the house." Tom was driving rather fast. "I don't want it to go up in smoke or be blown up like Reeves's place. Reeves, by the way, is in Ascona. They tracked him to Amsterdam and he had to run."

"Oh?" Jonathan experienced a few seconds of panic, of nausea. He felt that everything was collapsing. "You've—have you seen anything odd around your house?"

"Not really." Tom's voice was cool. His cigarette stuck up at a jaunty angle.

Jonathan was thinking that he *could* pull out. Now. Just say to Tom he didn't feel up to it, that he might faint if it came to the crunch. He could go home and be safe. Jonathan took a deep breath and lowered the window a bit more.

He'd be a bastard if he did that, a coward and a shit. He could at least try. He owed it to Tom Ripley. And why should he be so concerned about his own safety? Why now suddenly? Jonathan smiled a little, feeling better. "I told Simone about the bet on my life. It didn't go down too well."

"What did she say?"

"The same thing. She doesn't believe me. What's worse, she saw me with you yesterday—somewhere. Now she thinks I'm holding money for you—in my name. Dishonest money, you know."

"Yes." Tom saw the situation. But it didn't seem important compared to what might happen to Belle Ombre, to himself, and maybe to Jonathan, too. "I'm no hero, you know," Tom said out of the blue. "If the Mafia got me and tried to beat some facts out of me, I doubt if I'd be as brave as Fritz."

Jonathan was silent. He sensed that Tom was feeling as queasy as he had a few seconds ago.

It was a particularly fine day, the air liquid with summer, the sunlight brilliant. It was a shame to have to work on such a day—to have to be indoors, as Simone would be this afternoon. She didn't have to work any more, of course. Jonathan had wanted to say that to her for the past couple of weeks.

They were entering Villeperce now, a quiet village of the kind that would probably have only one butcher and one bakery.

"That's Belle Ombre," Tom said, nodding toward a domed tower that showed above some poplars.

They had driven perhaps half a kilometer from the village. The houses on the road were far apart and large. Belle Ombre looked like a small château, its lines classic and sturdy, but softened by four rounded corner towers that came all the way down to the grass. There were iron gates, and Tom had to get out and open them with a huge key he had taken from the glove compartment. Then they rolled onto the gravel in front of the garage.

"What a beautiful place!" Jonathan said.

Tom nodded and smiled. "A wedding present from my wife's parents, mainly. And lately, every time I arrive, I'm delighted to see that it's still standing. Please come in!"

Tom had produced a key for the front door, too.

"Not used to locking up," Tom said. "Usually my house-keeper's here."

Jonathan walked into a wide foyer paved with white marble, then into a square living room—two rugs, a big fire-place, a comfortable-looking yellow satin sofa. And a harpsi-chord stood beside French windows. The furniture was all good, Jonathan saw, and it was well cared for.

"Take off your coat," Tom said. For the moment, he felt relieved. Belle Ombre was quiet, and he hadn't seen any-thing out of the ordinary in the village. He went to the hall table and took his Luger from the drawer. Jonathan watched him, and Tom smiled. "Yes, I'm going to carry this thing all day—hence these old trousers. Big pockets. I can see why some people prefer shoulder holsters." Tom put the gun into a pocket of his trousers. "Do the same with yours, if you don't mind."

Jonathan did.

Tom was thinking of his rifle upstairs. He was sorry to get down to business so quickly, but thought it might be for the best. "Come up. I want to show you something."

They climbed the stairway, and Tom took Jonathan into his room. Jonathan at once noticed the *commode de bateau* and went over for a closer look.

"A recent present from my wife. Look"—Tom was hold-ing his rifle—"there's this. For long range. Fairly accurate, but not like an army rifle, of course. I want you to look out this front window."

Jonathan did. There was a nineteenth-century three-story house across the road, set well back and more than half obscured by trees. Trees bordered the road on either side in a haphazard way. Jonathan was imagining a car pausing on the road outside the house gates, and that was what Tom was talking about: the rifle would be more accurate than a pistol.

"Of course, it depends on what they do," Tom said. "If they intend to throw an incendiary bomb, for instance, then the rifle will be the thing to use. And there are back windows, too. And side windows. Come this way."

Tom led Jonathan into Héloïse's room, which had a window looking out on the back lawn. There were denser trees beyond the lawn, and poplars bordering the grass on the right.

"There's a lane going through those woods. You can just see it on the left. And in my atelier—" Tom went into the hall and opened a door on the left. This room had windows on the back lawn and in the direction where the village of Villeperce lay, but only cypresses and poplars and the tiles of a small house were visible. "We might keep a lookout on both sides of the house, not that we have to stay glued to the windows, but— The other important point is that I want the enemy to think I'm alone here. If you—"

The telephone was ringing. Tom thought for a moment that he wouldn't answer it, then that he might learn something if he did. He took it in his room.

"*Oui?*"

"M. Ripley?" said a Frenchwoman's voice. "*Ici* Mme. Trevanny. Is my husband there by any chance?"

She sounded very tense.

"Your husband? *Mais non,* Madame!" Tom said with astonishment in his voice.

"*Merci,* M'sieur. *Excusez-moi.*" She hung up.

Tom sighed. Jonathan was indeed having troubles.

Jonathan was standing in the doorway. "My wife."

"Yes," Tom said. "I'm sorry. I said you weren't here. You can send a telegram, if you like. Or telephone. Maybe she's in your shop."

"No, no, I doubt that." But she could be, because she had a key. It was only quarter past one.

How else could Simone have gotten his number, Tom thought, if not from Jonathan's notation in his shop?

"Or if you like, I'll drive you back now to Fontainebleau. It's really up to you, Jonathan."

"No," Jonathan said. "Thanks." Renunciation, Jonathan thought. Simone had known Tom was lying.

"I apologize for lying just now. You can always blame me. I doubt if I can sink any lower in your wife's mind, anyway." Tom at that moment didn't give a damn, didn't have the time or the inclination to sympathize with Simone. Jonathan wasn't saying anything. "Let's go down and see what the kitchen has to offer."

Tom drew the curtains in his room almost closed, but open enough so that they could see out without stirring the curtains. He did the same in Héloïse's room and downstairs in the living room. Mme. Annette's quarters he decided to leave alone. She had windows on the lane side and the back lawn.

There was plenty of Mme. Annette's delicious ragout from last night. The window over the kitchen sink had no curtains, and Tom made Jonathan sit out of view at the kitchen table, with a Scotch-and-water.

"What a shame we can't potter in the garden this afternoon," Tom said, washing lettuce at the sink. He had a compulsion to glance out the window at every passing car. Only two cars had passed in the last ten minutes.

Jonathan had noticed that both garage doors were wide open. Tom's car was parked on the gravel in front of the house. It was so quiet that any footstep would be heard on the gravel, Jonathan thought.

"And I can't turn on any music because I might drown out some other noise. What a bore," Tom said.

Though neither ate much, they spent a long time at the table in the dining area off the living room. Tom made coffee. Since there was nothing substantial for dinner that evening Tom telephoned the Villeperce butcher and asked for a good steak for two.

"Oh, Mme. Annette is taking a short holiday," Tom said, in response to the butcher's question. The Ripleys were such good customers that Tom had no hesitation in asking the butcher to pick up some lettuce and a nice vegetable of some kind at the grocery next door.

The very audible crunching of tires on gravel half an hour later announced the arrival of the butcher's van. Tom had jumped to his feet. He paid the genial butcher's boy, who was wearing a blood-spattered apron, and tipped him. Jonathan was now looking at several books on furniture and seemed quite content, so Tom went upstairs to pass some time tidying his atelier, a room which Mme. Annette never touched.

A telephone call just before five came like a scream in the silence, a muffled scream to Tom, because he had dared to go out in the garden and was messing about with the pruning sheers. Tom ran into the house, though he knew Jonathan wouldn't touch the telephone. Jonathan was still lounging on the sofa, surrounded by books.

The call was from Héloïse. She was very happy because she had rung Noëlle and learned that a friend of Noëlle's, Jules Grifaud, an interior decorator, had bought a chalet near Grenoble, and was inviting Noëlle and her to drive there with him and keep him company for a week or so while he arranged his things in the house.

"The country around is so beautiful," Héloïse said. "And we can help him. . . ."

It sounded deadly to Tom, but if Héloïse was enthusiastic, that was what mattered. He had known she wouldn't go on that Adriatic cruise, like an ordinary tourist.

"Are you all right, darling? . . . What are you doing?"

"Oh—a little gardening. . . . Yes, everything is *very* tranquil."

Around 7:30 p.m., when Tom was standing at | **19** | the front window of his living room, he saw the dark blue Citroën—the same one he'd seen last evening, he thought—cruise past the house, this time at a faster speed, but still not as fast as a car usually went to get somewhere. Was it the same? In the dusk, colors were deceiving—the difference between blue and green. But the car was a convertible with a dirty white upper trim, like the other one. Tom looked at the gates of Belle Ombre, which he had left ajar but which the butcher's boy had closed. Tom decided to leave them closed but not locked. They creaked a little.

"What's up?" Jonathan asked. He was drinking coffee. He hadn't wanted tea. Tom's unease was making him uneasy, since as far as he had been able to find out, Tom had no real reason to be so anxious.

"I think I saw the same car I saw last evening. A dark blue Citroën. The other one had a Paris plate. I know most of the cars around here, and only two or three people have cars with Paris plates."

"Did you see the license just now?" It looked dark to Jonathan. He had a lamp on beside him.

"No. —I'm going to get the rifle." Tom went upstairs as if borne on wings, and returned at once with the rifle. He had left no lights on upstairs. He said to Jonathan, "I definitely don't want to use a gun if I can avoid it, because of the noise. It's not the hunting season, and a shot might bring the neighbors—or *someone* might investigate. Jonathan—"

Jonathan was on his feet. "Yes?"

"You might have to wield this rifle like a club." Tom illustrated that the weightiest part of it, the butt, could be used to best effect. "See how it works, in case you have to shoot with it. Safety's on now." Tom showed him.

But they're not here, Jonathan was thinking. At the same

time, he was feeling odd and unreal, as he had felt in Hamburg and in Munich, when he had known that his targets were real and that they would materialize.

Tom was calculating how much time it would take the Citroën to cruise or drive around the circular road that led back to the village. They could, of course, turn at some convenient place on the road and come straight back. "If anyone comes to the door," Tom said, "I have the feeling I'm going to be plugged when I open it. That would be the simplest for them, you see. Then the fellow with the gun jumps into the waiting car and off they go."

Tom was a bit overwrought, Jonathan thought, but he listened carefully.

"Another possibility is a bomb through that window," Tom said, gesturing toward the front window. "Same as Reeves had. So if you're—um—agreeable—" He stopped. "Sorry, but I'm not used to discussing my plans. I usually play it by ear. But if you're willing, would you hide yourself in the shrubbery to the right of the door here—it's thicker on the right—and clout *anyone* who walks up and rings the doorbell? They may not ring the bell, but I'll be watching with the Luger for signs of bomb-throwing. Clout him fast if he's at the door, because he'll be fast. He'll have a gun in his pocket, and all he wants is a clear view of me." Tom went to the fireplace, where he had meant to light a fire and had forgotten, and took one of the third of a log pieces from the wood basket. This he put on the floor to the right of the front door. It was not as heavy as the amethyst vase on the wooden chest, but much easier to handle.

"How about," Jonathan said, "if *I* open the door? If they know what you look like, as you say, they'll see I'm not you and—"

"No." Tom was surprised by Jonathan's courageous offer. "First, they might not wait to see—just fire. And if they did look at you, and you said I don't live here, or I'm not in, they'd only push in and see or—" Tom gave it up with a laugh, imagining the Mafia blasting Jonathan in the stomach and pushing him into the house at the same time. "I think you should take up the post by the door now, if you're willing. I don't know how long you'll have to stay there, but I can always bring you refreshments."

"Sure." Jonathan took the rifle from Tom and went out. The road in front of the house was quiet. Jonathan stood in the shadow of the house and practiced a swing with the rifle, high up to catch a man standing on the steps in the head.

"Good," Tom said. "Would you care for a Scotch, by any chance? You can leave the glass in the bushes. Doesn't matter if it breaks."

Jonathan smiled. "No, thanks." He crept into the shrubbery—laurel and cypress-like bushes four feet high. It was very dark there, and Jonathan felt absolutely concealed. Tom had closed the door.

Jonathan sat on the ground, his knees under his chin, the rifle near his right hand. He wondered if this could last an hour? Longer? Was it a game Tom was playing? Jonathan couldn't believe it was entirely a game. Tom wasn't out of his head. He believed something might happen tonight, and that small possibility made it wise to take precautions. Then, as a car approached, Jonathan felt a start of real fear, an impulse to run straight into the house. The car went by at a fast clip. Jonathan didn't even have a glimpse of it through the bushes and the house gates. He leaned his shoulder against a slender trunk of something and began to feel sleepy. Five minutes later, he lay at full length on his back, but still quite awake, beginning to feel the chill of the earth penetrating his shoulder blades. If the telephone rang again, it might well be Simone. He wondered if, in some frenzy of temper, she would come to Tom's house in a taxi? Or would she ring her brother Gérard in Nemours and ask him to bring her in his car? A bit more likely. Jonathan stopped thinking about that possibility, because it was so awful. Ludicrous. Unthinkable. How would he explain lying outside the house in the shrubbery, even if he concealed the rifle?

Jonathan heard the house door opening. He had been dozing.

"Take this blanket," Tom whispered. The road was empty, and Tom stepped out with a steamer rug and handed it to Jonathan. "Put it under you. That ground must be awful." Tom's own whispering made him realize that the Mafia boys might sneak up on foot. He hadn't thought of that before. He went back into the house without another word to Jonathan.

Tom went up the stairs and, in the dark, surveyed the situation from the windows, front and back. All looked calm. A streetlight glowed brightly—but without extending its light very far—on the road about a hundred yards to the left in the direction of the village. None of its light fell in front of Belle Ombre, as Tom well knew. It was very quiet, but that was normal. Even the footsteps of a man walking on the road might be heard through the closed windows, Tom thought. He wished he could put on some music. He was about to turn from the window when he heard the faint *crunch-crunch-crunch* of someone walking on the dirt road, and then he saw a weak flashlight beam, moving from the right toward Belle Ombre. Tom felt sure this wasn't a person who would turn in at Belle Ombre, and the figure didn't, but went on and was lost to view before it reached the streetlight. Male or female, Tom couldn't tell.

Jonathan might be hungry. That couldn't be helped. Tom was hungry, too. But of course that could be helped. He went down the stairs, still in the dark, his fingertips on the banister, and into the kitchen—the living room and kitchen were lighted—and made some caviar canapés. The caviar was left over from last night, in its jar in the fridge, so the job was quick. Tom was bringing a plate for Jonathan when he heard the purr of a car. The car went past Belle Ombre from left to right, and stopped. Then there was a feeble click, the sound a car door made when it hadn't quite closed. Tom set the plate down on the wooden chest by the door and pulled out his gun.

Steps crunched firmly, at a polite-sounding pace, on the

road, then the gravel. This wasn't a bomb-thrower, Tom thought.

The doorbell rang.

Tom waited a few seconds, then said in French, "Who is it?"

"I would like to ask a direction, please," the man's voice said, with a perfect French accent.

Jonathan had been crouching with the rifle since the approach of footsteps, and now he leaped out of the bushes just as he heard Tom slide the bolt of the door. The man was two steps up from Jonathan, but Jonathan was still almost as tall, and he swung the rifle butt with all his power at the man's head, which had turned just slightly toward him because the man must have heard something. Jonathan's blow caught him behind the left ear, just under the hat brim. The man swayed, bumped the left side of the doorway, and dropped.

Tom opened the door and dragged him by the feet into the house, Jonathan helping, lifting the man's shoulders. Then Jonathan recovered the rifle and came in the door, which Tom closed softly. Tom picked up the piece of firewood and walloped the man's blondish head with it. The man's hat had fallen off and lay upside down on the marble floor. Tom extended his hand for the rifle, and Jonathan handed it to him. Tom came down on the man's temple with the steel butt.

Jonathan couldn't believe his eyes. Blood flowed onto the white marble. This was the husky bodyguard with crinkly blond hair who had been so upset on the train.

"Got that bastard!" Tom whispered with satisfaction. "This is the bodyguard. Look at the gun!"

A gun had fallen half out of the man's jacket pocket.

"Farther into the living room," Tom said, and they hauled and pushed the man across the floor. "Mind the rug with that blood!" Tom kicked the rug out of the way. "Next guy's due in a minute, no doubt. Bound to be two, maybe three."

Tom took a handkerchief—lavender, monogrammed—

from the man's breast pocket and tidied a splotch of blood on the floor near the door. He kicked the man's hat and sent it flying over the body. It fell near the hall door to the kitchen. Then Tom bolted the front door, holding his left hand over the bolt so it wouldn't make a noise. "Next one might not be so easy," he whispered.

There were footsteps on gravel. The bell rang—twice, nervously.

Tom laughed without making a sound and pulled out his Luger. He motioned for Jonathan to take his gun, too. Tom was suddenly convulsed, and doubled over to repress his mirth, then straightened and grinned at Jonathan, and wiped the tears from his eyes.

Jonathan didn't smile.

The bell rang again, a long steady peal.

Jonathan saw Tom's face change in a split second. Tom frowned, grimaced, as if he didn't know what he should do.

"Don't use the gun unless you have to," Tom whispered. His left hand was extended toward the door.

Tom was going to open the door and fire, Jonathan supposed, or cover the man.

Then steps crunched again. The man outside was walking toward the window behind Jonathan, a window now covered by the curtains. Jonathan edged away from the window.

"Angie? *Angie!*" a man's voice whispered.

"Ask him, at the door, what he wants," Tom whispered. "Talk in English—as if you were the butler. Let him in. I'll have him covered. Can you do it?"

Jonathan didn't care to think whether he could or not. There was a knocking, then another ring of the bell. "Who is it, please?" Jonathan called to the door.

"Je—je voudrais demander mon chemin, s'il vous plaît." The accent was not so good.

Tom smirked.

"Whom did you wish to speak to, sir?" Jonathan asked.

"Le chemin! S'il vous plaît!" the voice yelled. Desperation had set in.

Tom and Jonathan exchanged a glance, and Tom gestured for Jonathan to open the door. Tom was immediately to the left of the door to anyone standing outside, but out of sight if the door was opened.

Jonathan slid the bolt, turned the knob of the automatic lock, and opened the door partway, fully expecting a bullet in his abdomen, but he stood tall and stiff, with his right hand in his jacket pocket on the gun.

The somewhat shorter Italian, wearing a hat like the other man, also had his hand in his pocket and was plainly surprised to see a tall man in ordinary clothes in front of him.

"Sir?" Jonathan noticed that the man's left jacket sleeve was empty.

As the man came into the house, Tom poked him in the side with his Luger.

"Give me your gun!" Tom said in Italian.

Jonathan's gun was also pointed at him now. The man heaved his jacket pocket up as if to fire, and Tom pushed him in the face with his left hand. The man didn't fire. His left sleeve was limp, Tom noticed. This was the bodyguard who'd had his arm amputated.

"Reeply!" the Italian said, in a tone of mingled terror, surprise, and maybe triumph.

"Never mind that—give us the gun!" Tom said in English, poking the man again in the ribs and knocking the door shut with his foot.

The Italian got the idea, at least. He dropped the gun on the floor when Tom indicated that that was what he wanted. Then the Italian saw his friend on the floor a few yards away, and started, wide-eyed.

"Bolt the door," Tom said to Jonathan. Then Tom said in Italian, "Any more of you?"

The Italian shook his head vigorously, which meant nothing, Tom thought. Tom saw that his arm was in a sling under his jacket. So much for the newspaper reports.

"Cover him while I do this," Tom said, beginning to frisk

the Italian. "Off with your jacket!" Tom took the man's hat off and threw it in Angie's direction.

The Italian let his jacket slide off and drop. His shoulder holster was empty. There were no weapons in his pockets.

"Angie—" said the Italian.

"Angie *è morto*," Tom said. "So will you be if you don't do what we say. You want to die? What's your name? What's your *name?*"

"Lippo. Filippo."

"Lippo. Keep your hands up and don't move. Your hand. Go stand over there." He motioned for Lippo to stand by the dead man. Lippo lifted his good right arm. "Cover him, Jon, I want to have a look at their car."

With his Luger ready, Tom went out and turned right on the road, approaching the car cautiously. He could hear the motor. The car was at the side of the road with parking lights on. Tom stopped and closed his eyes for a few seconds, then opened them wide, trying to see if there was any movement at the sides of the car or behind the back window. He advanced slowly and steadily, expecting a shot from the car. Silence. Could they have sent only two men? Tom, in his nervousness, had forgotten to bring a flashlight. With his gun pointed at someone who might be crouched in the front seat, he opened the left side door. The interior light came on. The car was empty. He closed the door enough to shut the light off, stooped, and listened. He didn't hear anything. He trotted back and opened the gates of Belle Ombre, then returned to the car and backed it onto the gravel. A car passed just then on the road, coming from the direction of the village. Tom turned off the ignition and the lights in the Citroën. He went to the door, knocked, and announced himself to Jonathan.

"It seems this is all of them," Tom said.

Jonathan was standing where Tom had seen him last, pointing his gun at Lippo, who now had his good arm down and hanging a little out from his side.

Tom smiled at Jonathan, then at Lippo. "All alone now,

Lippo? Because if you're lying, it's *finito* for you, get me?"

Mafia pride seemed to be returning to Lippo, and he merely narrowed his eyes at Tom.

"*Rispondi,* you!"

"*Si!*" said Lippo, angry and scared.

"Getting tired, Jonathan? Sit down." Tom pulled up a yellow upholstered chair for him. "You can sit down, too, if you want to," Tom said to Lippo. "Sit next to your pal." Tom spoke in Italian. His slang was returning.

But Lippo remained standing. He was a bit over thirty, Tom supposed, about five feet ten, with round but strong shoulders and a paunch already starting—hopelessly dumb, not *capo* material. He had straight black hair, a pale olive face that was now faintly green.

"Remember me from the train? A little bit?" Tom asked, smiling. He glanced at the blond hulk on the floor. "If you behave well, Lippo, you won't end up like Angie. All right?" Tom put his hands on his hips and smiled at Jonathan. "Suppose we have a gin-and-tonic for fortification? You're all right, Jonathan?" Jonathan's color had returned, Tom saw.

Jonathan nodded with a tense smile. "Yep."

Tom went into the kitchen. While he was pulling out the ice tray, the telephone rang. "Never mind the phone, Jonathan!"

"Right!" Jonathan had a feeling it was Simone again. It was now quarter to ten.

Tom was wondering how to force Lippo to get his pals off his trail. The telephone rang eight times and stopped. Tom unconsciously counted the rings. He went into the living room with a tray of two glasses, ice, and an open tonic bottle. The gin was on the bar cart near the dining table.

Tom handed Jonathan his drink and said, "Cheers!" He turned to Lippo. "Where's your headquarters, Lippo? Milano?"

Lippo chose to maintain an insolent silence. What a bore. Lippo would have to be beaten up a little. Tom glanced with distaste at the splotch of drying blood under Angie's head, set his glass down on the wooden chest by the door, and went back to the kitchen. He wet a sturdy floor cloth—called a *torchon* by Mme. Annette—and mopped up the blood from Mme. Annette's shiny parquet floor. Tom pushed Angie's head aside with his foot and stuck the cloth under it. No more blood was coming. With sudden inspiration, Tom searched Angie's pockets thoroughly—trousers, jacket. He found cigarettes, a lighter, small change. A wallet in the breast pocket, which he left. There was a wadded handkerchief in a hip pocket, and when Tom pulled it out, a garrote came with it. "Look!" Tom said to Jonathan. "Just what I wanted! Ah, these Mafia rosaries!" Tom held it up and laughed with pleasure. "For you, Lippo, if you're not a good boy," Tom said in Italian. "After all, we don't want to make any noise with guns, do we?"

Jonathan looked at the floor for a few seconds as Tom strolled toward Lippo. Tom was whirling the garrote around one finger.

"You are of the distinguished Genotti family, *non è vero,* Lippo?"

Lippo hesitated, but very briefly, as if it only flitted across his mind to deny it. *"Sì,"* he said firmly, with a trace of *orgoglio.*

Tom was amused. The families had strength in numbers, in togetherness. Alone, like this one, they turned yellow, or green. Tom was sorry about Lippo's arm, but he wasn't torturing him yet, and Tom knew the tortures the Mafia put its victims to if they didn't come across with money or services—yanked toenails and teeth, cigarette burns. "How many men have you killed, Lippo?"

"Nessuno!" cried Lippo.

"No one," Tom said to Jonathan. "Ha-ha." Tom went to rinse his hands in the little bathroom opposite the front door. Then he finished his drink, picked up the piece of log beside the door, and approached Lippo with it. "Lippo, you're going to telephone your boss tonight. Maybe your new

capo, eh? Where is he tonight? Milano? Monaco di Bavaria?"
Tom gave Lippo a swat over the head with the wood, just
to show he meant business, but the blow was fairly hard,
because Tom was nervous.

"Stop it!" yelled Lippo, staggering and near collapse, one
hand pitifully on top of his head. "Me a guy with one arm?"
he shrieked, talking like himself now, the gutter Italian of
Naples, Tom thought—though it could have been of Milan,
Tom wasn't an expert.

"*Sissi!* And two against one!" Tom replied. "We don't
play fair, eh? Is that your complaint?" Tom called him something unspeakable, and turned on his heel to get a cigarette.
"Why don't you pray to the Virgin Mary?" Tom said over
his shoulder. "Another thing," he said to Lippo in English,
"no more shouting or you'll get this over your head in no
time flat!" He came down with the piece of firewood in the
air—*whish!*—to show what he meant. "This is what killed
Angie."

Lippo blinked, his mouth slightly open. He was breathing shallowly and audibly.

Jonathan had finished his drink. He was holding the gun
pointed at Lippo, holding it in two hands because the gun
had become heavy. He was not at all sure he could hit Lippo
if he had to fire it, and anyway Tom was frequently between
him and Lippo. Now Tom was shaking the Italian by his
belt. Jonathan couldn't understand all of what Tom was
saying, some of it being in clipped Italian, the rest in French
and English. Tom was mostly muttering, but his voice finally
rose in anger, and he shoved the Italian back and turned
around. The Italian had said hardly anything.

Tom went to the radio, pressed a couple of buttons, and
a cello concerto came on. Tom made the volume medium.
Then he made sure the front curtains were completely closed.
"Isn't this dreary," Tom said apologetically to Jonathan.
"Sordid. He won't tell me where his boss is, so I've got to
hit him a bit. Naturally he's as afraid of his boss as he is of

me." Tom gave Jonathan a quick smile, and went and changed the music. He found some pop. Then he picked up the wood with determination.

Lippo brushed the first blow aside, but Tom bashed him in the temple with a backhand stroke. Lippo yelped and cried, *"No! Lasciame!"*

"Your boss's number!" Tom yelled.

Crack! That was a swat at Lippo's middle, which caught the hand Lippo had put there to protect himself. Glass particles fell on the floor. Lippo wore his watch on his right wrist. The watch had shattered, and Lippo held his hand in pain against his abdomen while he looked at the glass on the floor. He gasped for breath.

Tom waited. The log was poised.

"Milano!" Lippo said.

"All right, you're going to—"

Jonathan missed the rest.

Tom was pointing to the telephone. Then he went to the table near the front windows where the telephone was and got a pencil and paper. He was asking the Italian the number in Milan.

Lippo gave a number and Tom wrote it down.

Then Tom made a longer speech, after which he turned to Jonathan and said, "I've told this guy he's going to be garroted if he doesn't ring his boss and tell him what I want him to say." Tom adjusted the garrote for action, and as he turned to face Lippo, the sound of a car came from the road, the sound of a car stopping at the gates.

Jonathan stood up, thinking it was either Italian reinforcements or Simone in Gérard's car. He didn't know which would be worse, both seeming a death of sorts at that moment.

Tom didn't want to part the curtains to look out. The motor purred on. Lippo's face showed no change, no sign of relief that Tom could see.

Then the car moved on, toward the right. Tom looked between the curtains. The car was going on, very much on, and all was well unless the car had let out a few men to hide in the bushes and fire through the windows. Tom listened for several seconds. It might have been the Graises, Tom thought. It might have been the Graises who had telephoned a few minutes ago. Maybe they'd seen the strange car on the gravel inside the gates and decided to go on, thinking the Ripleys had visitors.

"Now, Lippo," Tom said calmly, "you're going to telephone your boss, and I'm going to listen with this little gadget." Tom picked up the round earpiece that was clipped to the back of his telephone, which the French employed as a second ear to augment the sound. "And if everything doesn't seem *perfect* to me," Tom continued in French now, which he could see the Italian understood, "I won't hesitate to pull this tight suddenly, you see?" Tom illustrated with the noose around his wrist. Then he walked toward Lippo and flipped the garrote over his head.

Lippo jerked back a little in surprise, then Tom led him forward, like a dog on a leash, toward the telephone. He pushed Lippo down in the chair by the phone so Tom was in a position to apply strength on the garrote.

"Now I'll get the number for you—collect, I'm afraid. You will say you are in France, and you and Angie think you are being followed. You will say you have seen Tom Ripley, and Angie says he is not the man you were looking for. Right? Understand? Any funny words, code words and —this—" Tom tightened the garrote, but not so tight that it disappeared in Lippo's neck.

"*Sissi!*" said Lippo, staring in terror from Tom to the telephone.

Tom dialed the operator, and asked for the long-distance operator for Milan, Italy. When the operator asked for his number, as French operators always did, Tom said it was a collect call.

"From whom?" asked the operator.

"Lippo. Just Lippo," Tom replied. Then he gave the number. The operator said she would ring Tom back. He said to Lippo, "If this turns out to be a corner grocery or one of your girl friends, I'll choke you just the same! *Capish?*"

Lippo squirmed, looking as if he were desperate to try to escape, but as if he didn't know how as yet.

The telephone rang.

Tom motioned for Lippo to pick the telephone up, then took the earpiece and listened. The operator was saying that the call would be accepted.

"*Pronto?*" a male voice said at the other end.

Lippo held the telephone with his right hand to his left ear. "*Pronto*. Lippo here. Luigi!"

"*Si,*" said the other voice.

"Listen, I—" Lippo's shirt was sticking to his back with sweat. "We saw—"

Tom jerked the garrote a little to make Lippo get on with it.

"You are in France, no? With Angie?" the other voice said with some impatience. "*Allora*—what's the matter?"

"Nothing. I—we saw this fellow. Angie says he is not the man. . . . No . . ."

"And you think you are being followed," Tom whispered, because the connection wasn't good and he had no fear that the man in Milan could hear him.

"And we think—maybe we're being followed."

"Followed by *who?*" asked Milan, hottening up.

"I dunno. So what the ———— should we do?" Lippo asked, in fluent argot with a word Tom didn't understand. Lippo sounded genuinely scared now.

Tom's ribs tensed with laughter, and he glanced at Jonathan, who was still dutifully covering Lippo with his gun. Tom couldn't understand quite all of what Lippo was saying, but Lippo didn't seem to be pulling any tricks.

"Return?" said Lippo.

"*Si!*" said Luigi. "Abandon the car! Take a taxi to the nearest airport! Where are you now?"

"Tell him you've got to hang up," Tom whispered, gesturing.

"Got to sign off. *Rivederch*, Luigi," said Lippo, and hung up. He looked up at Tom with eyes like a miserable dog's.

Lippo was finished and he knew it, Tom thought. For once, Tom was proud of his reputation. He had no intention of sparing Lippo's life. Lippo's family wouldn't have spared anyone's life under the circumstances.

"Stand up, Lippo," Tom said, smiling. "Let's see what else you've got in your pockets."

When Tom started to search him, Lippo's good arm twitched back as if to strike him, but Tom didn't bother ducking. Just nerves, Tom thought. Tom felt coins in one pocket, and a crumpled bit of paper, which on inspection turned out to be a decrepit strip of Italian bus ticket, then in the hip pocket a garrote, this one a *sportif* red-and-white striped cord that reminded Tom of a barber's pole, fine as catgut.

"Look at this! Still another!" Tom said to Jonathan, holding up the garrote as if it were a pretty pebble he had found on a beach.

Jonathan barely glanced at the dangling string. The first garrote was still around Lippo's neck. Jonathan didn't look at the dead man, who was hardly two yards from him, one shoe turned inward in an unnatural way on the parquet floor, but he kept seeing the prone figure in the margin of his vision.

"My goodness," Tom said, looking at his watch. He hadn't realized it was late, after 10 p.m. It had to be done now: he and Jonathan had to drive some hours' distance away and get back before sunup, if possible. They would have to dispose of the corpses far away from Villeperce. South, of course, in the direction of Italy. Southeast, perhaps. It didn't really matter, but Tom preferred southeast. Tom took a deep breath, preparatory to action, but Jonathan's presence inhibited him. However, Jonathan had seen murder before, and there was no time to lose. Tom picked up the wood from the floor.

Lippo dodged, flung himself on the floor, or tripped

and fell, as Tom came down twice on his head with the wood. But he didn't put his full strength into it—the thought of not getting more blood on Mme. Annette's floor was in the back of his mind.

"He's only unconscious," Tom said to Jonathan. "He's got to be finished, and if you don't want to see it—go in the kitchen, perhaps."

Jonathan had stood up. He definitely didn't want to see it.

"Can you drive?" Tom asked. "My car, I mean. The Renault."

"Yes," Jonathan said. He had a license from the early days in France with Roy, his friend from England, but the license was at home.

"We've got to drive tonight. —Go in the kitchen." Tom motioned Jonathan away. Then Tom bent to the job of pulling the garrote tight. Not a pleasant task—the trite phrase crossed his mind—but what about people who weren't mercifully unconscious? Tom held tight to the cord, which had disappeared in the flesh, and fortified himself with the thought of Vito Marcangelo succumbing on the Mozart Express by the same means: he had brought that job off, and this was his second.

He heard a car on the road, at first tentative, then rolling up and stopping with a pull of the hand brake.

Tom kept his grip on the garrote exactly the same. How many seconds had passed? Forty-five? Not more than a minute, unfortunately.

"What's *that?*" Jonathan whispered, coming in from the kitchen.

The motor of the car was still running.

Tom shook his head.

They both heard light footsteps trotting on the gravel, then a knock at the door. Jonathan felt suddenly weak, as if his knees would give way.

"I think it's Simone," Jonathan said.

Tom desperately hoped that Lippo was dead. His face looked only dark pink. Damn him!

The knock came again. "M. Ripley? *Jon!*"

"Ask her who's with her," Tom said. "If she's with some-body, we can't open the door. Tell her we're busy."

"Who are you with, Simone?" Jonathan asked through the closed door.

"No one! I've told the taxi to wait. What is happening, Jon?"

Jonathan saw that Tom had heard what she said.

"Tell her to get rid of the taxi," Tom said.

"Pay off the taxi, Simone," Jonathan called.

"He is paid!"

"Tell him to leave."

Simone went away toward the road to do this. They heard the taxi drive off. Simone came back up the steps, and this time she didn't knock, only waited.

Tom straightened up from Lippo, leaving the garrote in place. He was wondering if Jonathan could go out and ex-plain to her that she couldn't come into the house. That they had other people? That they would send for another taxi for her? Tom was thinking of the taxi drivers' im-pressions. Best to have dismissed this one, rather than *not* show signs of letting Simone into a house that plainly had lights and at least one person in it.

"Jon!" she called. "Will you open the door? I would like to speak with you."

Tom said softly, "Can you wait outside with her while I ring for another taxi? Tell her we're talking business with a couple of people."

Jonathan nodded, hesitated an instant, then slid the bolt. He opened the door not widely, intending to slip out him-self, but Simone thrust the door against him suddenly. She was in the foyer.

"Jon! I am sorry to—" Breathless, she glanced around as if looking for Tom Ripley, master of the house, then she saw him, and at the same time saw the two men on the floor. She gave a short cry. Her handbag slipped from her fingers and dropped with a soft thud on the marble. *"Mon Dieu! What is happening here?"*

Jonathan gripped one of her hands tightly. "Don't look at them. These—"

Simone stood rigid.

Tom walked toward her. "Good evening, Madame. Don't be frightened. These men were invading the house. They are unconscious. We had a bit of trouble. Jonathan, take Simone into the kitchen."

Simone didn't walk. She was swaying and leaned against Jonathan for a moment, then lifted her head and looked at Tom with hysterical eyes. "They look dead! Murderers! *C'est une maison de fous!* Jonathan! I cannot believe that it is *you—here!"*

Tom was going to the bar cart. "Can Simone take some brandy, do you think?" he called to Jonathan.

"Yes. We'll go in the kitchen, Simone." He was prepared to walk between her and the corpses, but she wouldn't move.

Tom, finding the brandy more difficult than the whiskey to open, poured whiskey into one of the glasses on the cart. He took it to Simone, neat. "Madame, I realize this is dreadful. These men are of the Mafia—Italians. They came to the house to attack us—me, anyway." Tom was much relieved to see that she was sipping the whiskey, barely grimacing, as if it were medicine that was good for her. "Jonathan helped me, for which I'm very grateful. Without him—" Tom stopped. Anger was rising again in Simone.

"Without him? What is he doing here?"

Tom stood straighter. He went into the kitchen himself, thinking it the only way to draw her from the living room. She and Jonathan followed him. "That I can't explain tonight, Madame. Not now. We've got to leave now— with these men. Would you—" Tom was thinking, had they time, had he time to take her back to Fontainebleau in the Renault, then return to remove the corpses with Jonathan's assistance? No. Tom absolutely couldn't waste that much time—a good forty minutes. "Madame, shall I ring for a taxi to take you back to Fontainebleau?"

"I will not leave my husband. I want to know what my husband is doing here—with such filth as you!"

Her fury was directed entirely against him. Tom wished it would all come out, now and forever, in a great burst. He could never deal with angry women—not that he had had to deal with many. To Tom it was a circular chaos, a ring of little fires, and if he successfully extinguished one, the woman's mind leaped to the next. Tom said to Jonathan, "If Simone could only take a taxi back to Fontainebleau—"

"I know, I know. Simone, it really is best if you go back to our house."

"Will you come with me?" she asked.

"I—I can't," Jonathan said, desperate.

"Then you don't want to. You are on his side."

"If you'll let me talk with you later, darling—"

Jonathan went on in that vein. Tom began to think Jonathan wasn't willing to help, or had changed his mind; he was getting nowhere with Simone.

Tom interrupted, "Jonathan." Tom beckoned to him. "You must excuse us a moment, Madame." Tom spoke with Jonathan in the living room, in a whisper. "We've got six hours' work ahead—or I have. I've got to take these two away and dispose of them—and I'd prefer to be back by dawn or before. Are you really willing to help?"

Jonathan felt lost, in the sense that he might be lost in the middle of a battle. But the situation with Simone seemed already hopeless. He could never explain. Going back to Fontainebleau with her would gain him nothing. He had lost Simone, and what else was there to lose? These thoughts flashed in Jonathan's mind like a single image. "I am willing, yes."

"Good. Thanks." Tom gave a tense smile. "Surely Simone doesn't want to stay here. She could, of course, stay in my wife's room. Maybe I can find a sedative. But for Christ's sake, she can't come *with* us."

"No." Simone was his responsibility. Jonathan felt power-
less either to persuade or command. "I have *never* been
able to tell her—"

"There's some danger," Tom interrupted, then stopped.
There was no time to lose in talking. He glanced at Lippo,
whose face was now bluish, or so Tom thought. At any rate,
his clumsy body had that abandoned look of the dead—not
dreamlike or sleeplike but simply an empty look, as if consciousness had departed forever. Simone was coming in from
the kitchen, where Tom had been heading, and he saw that
her glass was empty. He went to the bar cart and brought
the bottle. He poured more into the glass in her hand,
though she indicated that she didn't want any more. "You
don't have to drink it, Madame," Tom said. "Since we must
leave, I must tell you there is some danger if you stay in this
house. I simply don't know if more of these won't turn up."

"Then I will go with you. I will go with my husband!"

"That you *cannot,* Madame." Tom was firm.

"What are you going to do?"

"I'm not sure, but we have to get rid of these—this car-
rion!" Tom gestured. "*Charogne!*" he repeated.

"Simone, you have got to take a taxi back to Fontainebleau," Jonathan said.

"*Non!*"

Jonathan grabbed her wrist, and with his other hand took
the glass so it wouldn't spill. "You must do as I say. It's your
life—it's my life. We cannot stay and argue!"

Tom leaped up the stairs. He found, after nearly a minute's
search, Héloïse's little bottle of quarter-grain phenobarbi-
tals, which she took so seldom that they were at the back
of everything in her medicine cabinet. He went downstairs
with two of them in his hand, and dropped them casually
into Simone's glass—which he had taken from Jonathan—
as he topped the drink up with a splash of soda.

Simone drank it. She was sitting on the yellow sofa now.
She seemed calmer, though it was too soon for the pills to
have taken effect. Jonathan was on the telephone. Tom pre-

sumed he was phoning for a taxi: the slender Seine-et-Marne directory was open on the telephone table. Tom felt a little dazed—the way Simone looked. But Simone also seemed stunned with shock.

"Just Belle Ombre, Villeperce," said Tom when Jonathan glanced at him.

While Jonathan and Simone waited for the taxi, both standing in terrible silence near the front door, Tom went out to the garden via the French windows, and got a jerrican of spare gasoline from the toolhouse. To Tom's regret, it felt only three-quarters full. He had his flashlight with him. When he came around to the front of the house, he heard a car approaching slowly—the taxi, he hoped. Tom, instead of putting the jerrican in the Renault, set it in the laurels, out of sight. He knocked on the front door and was admitted by Jonathan.

20

"I think the taxi's here," Tom said.

Tom said good night to Simone, and let Jonathan escort her to the taxi, which was waiting beyond the gates. The taxi drove off, and Jonathan came back.

Tom was refastening the French windows. "Good Christ," Tom said, not knowing what else to say, and being immensely relieved to find himself alone with Jonathan again. "I hope Simone isn't too livid. But I can hardly blame her."

Jonathan shrugged in a dazed way. He tried to speak and couldn't.

Tom realized his state and said, like a captain giving orders to a shaken crew, "Jonathan, she'll come around." And she wouldn't ring the police, either, because if she did, her husband would be implicated. Tom's fortitude, his sense of purpose, was returning. He patted Jonathan's arm as he walked past him. "Back in a minute."

Tom got the jerrican from the bushes and put it in the

back of his Renault. Then he opened the Italians' Citroën. When the interior light came on, he saw that the fuel gauge registered slightly over half full. That might do: he wanted to drive for more than two hours. The Renault, he knew, had only a little more than half a tankful, and the bodies were going to be in it. He and Jonathan hadn't had any dinner. That wasn't wise.

Tom went back into the house and said, "We ought to eat something before this trip."

Jonathan followed him into the kitchen, glad to escape for a time from the corpses in the living room. He washed his hands and face at the kitchen sink. Tom smiled at him. Food—that was the answer, for the moment. He got the steak from the fridge and stuck it under the glowing bars. Then he found a platter, a couple of steak knives, and two forks. They sat down, finally, and ate from the same platter, dipping morsels of steak into a saucer of salt and another of horseradish. It was excellent steak. Tom had even found a half-full bottle of claret on the kitchen counter. There'd been many a time when he'd dined worse.

"That will do you good," Tom said, and tossed his knife and fork onto the platter.

The clock in the living room gave a ping, and Tom knew it was eleven-thirty.

"Coffee?" asked Tom. "There's Nescafé."

"No, thanks." Neither Jonathan nor Tom had spoken while they had bolted the steak. Now Jonathan said, "How are we going to do it?"

"Burn them somewhere. In their car," Tom said. "It isn't necessary to burn them, but it's rather Mafia-like."

Jonathan watched Tom rinse a thermos at the sink, careless now of the fact that he stood before an open window. Tom ran the hot water, tipped some of the jar of Nescafé into the thermos, and filled it with steaming water.

"Like sugar?" Tom asked. "I think we'll need it."

Then Jonathan helped Tom carry out the blond man,

who was stiffening. Tom was saying something, making a joke. Then he said he had changed his mind: both bodies were going into the Citroën.

". . . even though the Renault," Tom said between gasps, "is bigger."

It was dark in front of the house, the distant streetlamp not shedding a glow as far as the Citroën. They tumbled the second body onto the first on the back seat of the car, and Tom smiled because Lippo's face seemed to be buried in Angie's neck, but he refrained from comment. He found a couple of newspapers on the floor of the car and spread them over the dead men, tucking them in as best he could. Tom made sure that Jonathan knew how the Renault worked, showed him the turn signals, the headlights, and the bright lights.

"Okay, start it. I'll close the house." Tom went into the house, left one light on in the living room, and came out and closed the front door and double-locked it.

Tom had explained to Jonathan that their first objective was Sens, then Troyes. From Troyes they would go farther eastward. Tom had a map in his car. They would rendezvous first at Sens, at the railway station. Tom put the thermos in Jonathan's car.

"You're feeling all right?" Tom asked. "Don't hesitate to stop and drink some coffee if you feel like it." Tom waved him a cheerful goodbye. "Go ahead first. I want to close the gates. I'll pass you."

So Jonathan drove out first, Tom closed his gates and padlocked them, then soon passed Jonathan on the way to Sens, which was only thirty minutes away. Jonathan seemed to be doing all right in the Renault. Tom spoke to him briefly at Sens. At Troyes, they were again to go to the railway station. Tom didn't know the town, and it was dangerous for one car to try to follow another on the road, but the way to La Gare was pretty well marked in every town.

It was about 1 a.m. when Tom got to Troyes. He hadn't

seen Jonathan behind him for more than half an hour. He went into the station café for a coffee, then a second coffee, and kept a lookout through the glass door for the Renault to pull into the parking area in front of the station. Finally Tom paid and went out, and as he walked toward the Citroën, his Renault came down the slope into the parking area. Tom gave a wave, and Jonathan saw him.

"You're all right?" Tom asked. Jonathan looked all right to Tom. "If you want some coffee here, or to use the toilet, better go in alone."

Jonathan didn't want either. Tom persuaded him to drink some coffee out of the thermos. No one was giving them a glance. A train had just come in, and ten or fifteen people were heading for their parked cars or the cars of people who had come to meet them.

"From here we take the National 19," Tom said. "We'll aim for Bar—Bar-sur-Aube—and meet again at the railway station. All right?"

Tom started off. The highway became clearer, with very little traffic except two or three elephantine trucks, their rectangular rears outlined in white or red lights, moving forms that might have been blind, Tom felt, blind at least to the two corpses in the back of the Citroën under newspapers—such a tiny cargo compared to theirs. Tom was not going fast now, not more than ninety kilometers—around fifty-five miles—per hour. At the Bar railway station, he and Jonathan leaned out of their windows to speak to each other.

"Gas is getting low," Tom said. "I want to go beyond Chaumont, so I'm going to pull in at the next station, okay? And you do the same."

"Right," said Jonathan.

It was now a quarter past two. "Keep on the old N 19. See you at the railway station in Chaumont."

Tom pulled in at a Total station as he was leaving Bar. He was paying the man when Jonathan drove in behind him. Tom lit a cigarette and walked about, stretching his legs. He didn't glance at Jonathan. Then he pulled his car a little aside and went to the toilet. It was only forty-two kilometers to Chaumont.

Tom arrived there at five minutes to three. Not even a taxi stood at the railway station, only a few parked and empty cars. There were no more trains tonight. The station bar-café was closed.

When Jonathan arrived, Tom approached the Renault on foot and said, "Follow me. I'm going to look for a quiet spot."

Jonathan was tired, but his fatigue had switched into another gear: he could have gone on driving for hours, he felt. The Renault handled tightly and quickly, with a minimum of effort on his part. Jonathan was unfamiliar with the country here, but that didn't matter. Now it was easy; he merely kept the red taillights of the Citroën in view. Tom was going more slowly, and twice paused tentatively at side roads, then went on. The night was black, the stars not visible, at least not with the glow of the dashboard before him. A couple of cars passed, going in the opposite direction, and one truck overtook Jonathan. Then Jonathan saw Tom's right indicator pulse, and the Citroën disappeared to the right. Jonathan followed, and barely saw the black gorge that was the road, or lane, when he came to it. It was a dirt road that led at once into forest. It was narrow, not wide enough for two cars to pass, the kind of road often found in the French countryside, used by farmers or men gathering wood. Bushes scraped delicately at the front fenders, and there were potholes.

Tom's car stopped. They had gone perhaps two hundred yards from the main road in a great curve. Tom had cut off his lights, but the interior of the car lit up when he opened the door. He left the door open and walked toward Jonathan, waving his arms cheerfully. Jonathan was at that instant cutting his own motor and lights. The image of Tom's figure, in the baggy trousers and green suède jacket, stayed in Jonathan's eyes for a moment as if Tom had been composed of light. Jonathan blinked.

Then Tom was beside Jonathan's window. "It'll be over in a couple of minutes. Back your car about fifteen feet. You know how to reverse?"

Jonathan started the Renault. The car had backing lights. When he stopped, Tom opened the rear door and pulled out the jerrican. He had his flashlight.

Tom poured gasoline onto the newspapers over the two corpses, then on their clothing. He splashed some on the roof, and on the upholstery—unfortunately plastic, not cloth—of the front seat. Tom looked up, straight up where the branches of the trees almost closed together above the road—young leaves, not yet in their summer fullness. A few would get singed, but it was for a worthy cause. Tom shook the last drops in the jerrican onto the rubbish on the floor of the car—the remains of a sandwich, an old road map.

Jonathan was walking slowly toward him.

"Here we go," Tom said softly, and struck a match. He had left the front door of the car open. He flung the match into the back, where the newspapers flared up yellow at once.

Tom stepped back and grabbed Jonathan's hand as his foot slipped in a depression at the side of the road. "In the car!" Tom whispered, and trotted toward the Renault. He got into the driver's seat, smiling. The Citroën was taking nicely. The roof had started to burn in one thin yellow flame, like a candle.

Jonathan got in on the other side.

Tom started his motor. He was breathing a little hard, but it soon became laughter. "I think that's all *right*. Don't you? I think that's just *great!*"

The Renault's lights burst forward, diminishing the growing holocaust in front of them for an instant. Tom backed, fairly fast, his body twisted so he could see through the rear window.

Jonathan stared at the burning car, which completely disappeared as they backed along the curve in the road.

Then Tom straightened out. They were on the main road.

"Can you see it from here?" Tom asked, shooting the car forward.

Jonathan saw a light like that of a glowworm through the trees, then it vanished. Or had he imagined it? "Not a thing now. No." For an instant, Jonathan felt frightened by this—as if they had failed somehow, as if the fire had died out. But he knew it hadn't. The woods had simply swallowed the fire up, hidden it utterly. And yet someone would find it. When? How much of it?

Tom laughed. "It's burning. They'll burn! We're in the clear!"

Jonathan saw Tom glance at the speedometer, which was climbing to a hundred and thirty. He eased back to a hundred.

Tom was whistling a Neapolitan tune. He felt well, not tired at all, not even in need of a cigarette. Life afforded few pleasures tantamount to disposing of Mafiosi. And yet—

"And yet—" Tom said cheerfully.

"And yet?"

"Disposing of two does so little. Like stepping on two cockroaches when the whole house is full of them. However, I believe in making the effort, and above all it's nice to let the Mafia know now and then that people can diminish them. Unfortunately, in this case they're going to think another family got Lippo and Angie. At least I hope they'll think that."

Jonathan was feeling sleepy now. He fought against it, forcing himself to sit up, pressing his nails into his palms. My God, he thought, it would be hours before they got home—back to Tom's or to his own house. Tom seemed fresh as a daisy, singing in Italian a tune he'd been whistling before.

> ". . . papa ne meno
> Como faremo fare l'amor . . ."

Tom chatted on, now about his wife, who was going to stay with some friends in a chalet in Switzerland.

Then Jonathan awakened a little as Tom said, "Put your head back, Jonathan. No need to stay awake. You're feeling all right, I hope?"

Jonathan didn't know how he was feeling. He felt a bit weak, but he often felt weak. He was afraid to think about what had just happened, about what was happening, flesh and bone being burned, smoldering on hours from now. Sadness came over Jonathan suddenly, like an eclipse. He wished he could erase the last few hours, cut them out of his memory. Yet he had been there, he had acted, he had helped. Jonathan put his head back and fell half asleep. Tom was talking cheerfully, casually, as if he were having a conversation with someone who now and then replied to him. Jonathan had, in fact, never seen Tom in such good spirits. Jonathan was wondering what he was going to say to Simone. Merely to be aware of that problem exhausted him.

"Masses sung in English, you know," Tom was saying, "I find simply embarrassing. Somehow one gives the English-speaking people credit for believing what they're saying, so a Mass in English— You feel either the choir has lost its mind or they're a pack of liars. Don't you agree? Sir John Stainer . . ."

Jonathan woke up when the car stopped. Tom had pulled onto the edge of the road. Smiling, he was sipping coffee from the thermos cup. He offered some to Jonathan. Jonathan drank a little. Then they drove on.

Dawn came over a village that Jonathan had never seen before. The light had awakened him.

"We're only twenty minutes from home!" Tom said brightly.

Jonathan murmured something and shut his eyes again. Now Tom was talking about the harpsichord, his harpsichord.

"The thing about Bach is that he's instantly civilizing. Just a phrase . . ."

Jonathan opened his eyes thinking he had heard harpsichord music. Yes. It wasn't a dream. He hadn't really been asleep. The music came from downstairs. It faltered, recommenced. A sarabande, perhaps. Jonathan lifted his arm wearily and looked at his wristwatch: twenty-two minutes to nine. What was Simone doing now? What was she *thinking?*

| 21 |

Exhaustion sucked at Jonathan's will. He sank deeper into the pillow, retreating. He'd taken a warm shower, put on pajamas at Tom's insistence. Tom had given him a new toothbrush and said, "Get a couple of hours' sleep, anyway. It's terribly early." That had been around seven. He had to get up. He had to do something about Simone, had to speak to her. But Jonathan lay limp, listening to the single notes of the harpsichord.

Tom was fingering the bass of something, and it sounded correct, the deepest notes a harpsichord could pluck. As Tom had said, "instantly civilizing." Jonathan forced himself up, out of the pale blue sheets and the dark blue woolen blanket. He staggered, and with an effort stood straight as he walked toward the door. He went down the stairs barefoot.

Tom was reading the notes from a music book propped in front of him. Now the treble entered, and sunlight came through the slightly parted curtains at the French windows onto Tom's shoulder, picking out the gold pattern in his black dressing gown.

"Tom?"

Tom turned at once and got up. "Yes?"

Jonathan felt worse, seeing Tom's alarmed face. The next thing Jonathan knew, he was on the yellow sofa, and Tom was wiping his face with a wet cloth, a dish towel.

"Tea? Or a brandy? . . . Have you got any pills you take?"

Jonathan felt awful; he knew the feeling, and the only thing that helped was a transfusion. It hadn't been so long since he'd had one. The trouble was that now he felt worse than he usually did. Was it only from losing a night's sleep?

"What?" Tom said.

"I'm afraid I'd better get to the hospital."

"We'll go," said Tom. He went away and came back with a stemmed glass. "This is brandy and water, if you feel like it. Stay there. I'll just be a minute."

Jonathan closed his eyes. He had the wet towel over his forehead, down one cheek, and felt chilly and too tired to move. It seemed only a minute until Tom was back, dressed. Tom had brought Jonathan's clothing.

"Matter of fact, if you put on your shoes and my topcoat, you won't have to dress," Tom said.

Jonathan followed his advice. They were in the Renault again, heading for Fontainebleau, and Jonathan's clothes were folded neatly between them. Tom was asking him if he knew exactly where they should go when they got to the hospital, if he could get a transfusion right away.

"I've got to speak with Simone," Jonathan said.

"We'll do that—or you will. Don't worry about that now."

"Could you bring her?" Jonathan asked.

"Yes," said Tom firmly. He hadn't been worried about Jonathan until that instant. Simone would hate the sight of him, but she would come to see her husband, either with Tom or on her own. "You still have no phone at your house?"

"No."

Tom spoke to a receptionist in the hospital. She greeted Jonathan as if she knew him. Tom held Jonathan's arm. When he had seen Jonathan into the charge of the proper doctor, Tom said, "I'll have Simone come, Jonathan. Don't worry." To the receptionist, who was in nurse's uniform, he said, "Do you think a transfusion will do it?"

She nodded pleasantly, and Tom left it at that, not knowing whether she knew what she was talking about or not. He wished he'd asked the doctor. Tom got into his car and drove to the Rue Saint-Merry. He was able to park a few yards from the house, and he got out and walked toward the stone steps with the black handrails. He'd had no sleep, was in slight need of a shave, but at least he had a message that might be of interest to Mme. Trevanny. He rang the bell.

There was no answer. Tom rang again, and looked along the pavement for Simone. It was Sunday. A market day in Fontainebleau, and she might well be out buying something at 9:50 a.m., or might be at church with Georges.

Tom went down the steps slowly, and as he reached the pavement, he saw Simone walking toward him, Georges beside her. Simone had a shopping basket over her forearm.

"*Bonjour,* Madame," Tom said politely, in the face of her bristling hostility. He continued, "I only wanted to bring you news of your husband. *Bonjour,* Georges."

"I want nothing from you," Simone said, "except to know where my husband is."

Georges stared at Tom alertly and neutrally. He had eyes and brows like his father. "He is all right, I think, Madame, but he is—" Tom hated saying it on the street. "He is in the hospital for the moment. A transfusion, I think."

Simone looked both exasperated and furious—as if Tom were to blame for it.

"May I please speak with you inside your house, Madame? It is so much easier."

After an instant's hesitation, Simone agreed to this—out of curiosity, Tom felt. She unlocked the door with a key that she produced from her coat pocket. It wasn't a new coat, Tom noticed. "What has happened to him?" she asked when they were in the little hall.

Tom took a breath and spoke calmly. "We had to drive nearly all night. I think he is merely tired. But—of course,

I thought you would want to know. I've just brought him to the hospital. He's able to walk. I do think he's not in danger."

"Papa! I want to see Papa!" Georges said rather petulantly, as if he had asked for Papa last evening, too.

Simone had set her basket down. "*What* have you done to my husband? He is not the same man I knew—since he met *you*, M'sieur! If you see him again, I—I will—"

It seemed only the presence of her son that kept her from saying that she would kill him, Tom thought.

She said, with bitter control, "*Why* is he in your power?"

"He is not in my power and never was. And I think the job is finished," Tom said. "It's quite impossible to explain now."

"What job?" Simone asked. And before Tom could open his mouth, she continued, "M'sieur, you are a crook, and you corrupt other people! What sort of blackmail have you subjected him to? And why?"

Blackmail—the French word *"chantage"*—was so off the beam, that Tom stammered as he began to reply. "Madame, no one is taking money from Jonathan. Or anything else. Quite the contrary. And he has done nothing to give people power over him." Tom spoke with genuine conviction, and he certainly needed to, because Simone looked the picture of wifely virtue, probity, her fine eyes flashing and her brows concentrated against him, powerful as the Winged Victory of Samothrace. "We have spent the night cleaning things up." Tom felt shabby saying that. His more eloquent French had suddenly deserted him. His words were now no match for the virtuous helpmeet who stood before him.

"Cleaning what up?" She stooped to pick up her basket. "M'sieur, I will be grateful if you leave this house. I thank you for informing me where my husband is."

Tom nodded. "I would also be happy to take you and Georges to the hospital, if you like. My car is just outside."

"Merci, non." She was standing midway in the hall, looking back, waiting for him to leave. "Come, Georges."

Tom let himself out. He got into his car, thought of going to the hospital to ask how Jonathan was, because it would be at least ten minutes before Simone could get there either by taxi or on foot, but decided to telephone from his house. He drove home. And once home, he decided not to telephone. By now Simone might be there. Hadn't Jonathan said the transfusion took several hours? Tom hoped it wasn't a crisis, that it wasn't the beginning of the end.

He turned on France Music for company, opened his curtains wider to the sunlight, and tidied the kitchen. He poured a glass of milk, went upstairs and got into pajamas again, and went to bed. He could shave when he woke up.

Tom hoped that Jonathan could straighten things out with Simone. But it was a problem: how could the Mafia possibly be tied up with two German doctors?

This unsolved riddle began to make Tom sleepy. And Reeves. What was happening to Reeves in Ascona? Madcap Reeves. Tom still had a lurking affection for him. Reeves was now and then maladroit, but his crazy heart was in the right place.

Simone sat beside the flat bed, more wheels than bed, where Jonathan lay taking blood in through a tube in his arm. As usual, he avoided looking at the jar of blood. Simone was grim. She had spoken with the nurse out of Jonathan's hearing. Jonathan thought his condition wasn't serious, or Simone would have been more concerned about him, kinder. Jonathan was propped on a pillow, and there was a white blanket pulled up to his waist for warmth.

"And you're wearing that man's pajamas," Simone said.

"Darling, I had to wear something—to sleep in. It must've been six in the morning when we got back—" Jonathan broke off, feeling hopeless and tired. Simone had told him that Tom had called at the house to tell her where he was. Simone's reaction had been anger. Jonathan had never seen her so grim. She detested Tom as if he were Landru, or Svengali. "Where's Georges?" Jonathan asked.

"I telephoned Gérard. He and Yvonne are coming to the house at ten-thirty. Georges will let them in."

They would wait for Simone, Jonathan thought, then they would all go to Nemours for Sunday lunch. "They want me to stay here till at least three," Jonathan said. "The tests, you know." He knew she knew. They would probably take another marrow sample, which required only ten or fifteen minutes, but there were always other tests, urine, the spleen-feeling. Jonathan still didn't feel well, and he didn't know what to expect. Simone's hardness upset him further.

"I cannot understand. I cannot," she said. "Jon, why do you *see* this monster?"

Tom was not really such a monster. But how to explain? Jonathan tried again. "Do you realize that last night—those men were killers? They had guns, they had garrotes. *Tu comprends, garrottes.* They came to Tom's house."

"And why were you there?"

Gone was the excuse of paintings that Tom wanted framed. You didn't help Tom kill people, help him get rid of corpses, because you were going to frame a few pictures. And what was the favor Tom Ripley had done him to make him cooperate so? Jonathan closed his eyes, gathering strength, trying to think.

"Madame—" That was the nurse's voice.

Jonathan heard the nurse telling Simone that she should not tire her husband. "I promise you that I will explain, Simone."

Simone had stood up. "I think you cannot explain. I think you are afraid to. This man has trapped you—and why? For money. He pays you. But why? You want me to think that you are a criminal, too? Like that monster?"

The nurse had gone away and couldn't hear. Jonathan looked at Simone through half-closed eyes, desperate, wordless, defeated for the moment. Couldn't he make her see that it was not so black and white as she thought? But Jonathan felt a chill of fear, a premonition of failure, like death.

And Simone was leaving, as if on a final word—*her* word,

her attitude. At the doorway she blew him a kiss, but perfunctorily, like a person in church genuflecting slightly, without thinking, as he passed some object. She was gone. The day ahead stretched like a bad dream to come. The hospital might decide to keep him overnight. Jonathan closed his eyes and moved his head from side to side.

They were almost finished with the tests by 1 p.m.

"You have been under a strain, haven't you, M'sieur?" asked a young doctor. "Any unusual exertions?" Unexpectedly, he laughed. "Moving to another house? Or too much gardening?"

Jonathan smiled politely. He was feeling a little better. Suddenly Jonathan laughed, too, but not at what the doctor had said. Suppose it had been the beginning of the end, this morning's collapse? Jonathan was pleased with himself because he had pulled through without losing his nerve. Maybe he could do that one day with the real thing. They let him walk down a corridor for the final test, the spleen palpation.

"M. Trevanny? There is a telephone call for you," a nurse said. "Since you are so near—" She motioned toward a desk and a telephone, which was off the hook.

Jonathan felt sure it was Tom. "Hello?"

"Jonathan, hello. Tom. How is everything? . . . Can't be too bad if you're on your feet now. . . . That's fine."

Tom sounded really pleased. "Simone was here. Thank you," Jonathan said. "But she's—" Even though they were talking in English, Jonathan couldn't get the words out.

"You had a tough time, I can understand." Platitudes. Tom at his end heard the anxiety in Jonathan's voice. "I did my best this morning, but do you want me to—to try to talk with her again?"

Jonathan moistened his lips. "I don't know. It's not, of course, that she—" He'd been going to say "threatened anything," such as taking Georges and leaving him. "I don't know if you *can* do anything. She's so—"

Tom understood. "Suppose I try? I will. Courage, Jonathan! You're going home today?"

"I'm not sure. I think so. By the way, Simone is with her family in Nemours for lunch this afternoon."

Tom said he wouldn't try to see her till about five. If Jonathan was home then, that would be fine.

It was a bit awkward for Tom, Simone's not having a telephone. On the other hand, if there'd been a telephone, she would probably have given him a firm "No" if he asked if he might come to see her. Tom bought flowers, yellow forced dahlias, from a vendor near the château in Fontainebleau, since he had nothing presentable yet from his own garden. Tom rang the Trevanny doorbell at five-twenty.

There were steps, then Simone's voice, *"Qui est-ce?"*

"Tom Ripley."

A delay.

Then Simone opened the door with a stony face.

"Good afternoon—*bonjour encore,*" Tom said. "Could I speak with you for a few minutes, Madame? Has Jonathan returned?"

"He will be home at seven. He is having another transfusion," Simone replied.

"Oh?" Tom boldly took a step into the house, not knowing if Simone would flare up or not. "I brought these for your house, Madame." He presented the flowers with a smile. "And Georges. *Bonjour,* Georges." Tom extended his hand, and the child took it, smiling up at him. Tom had thought of bringing candy for Georges, but he hadn't wanted to overdo it.

"What is it you want?" Simone asked. She had given Tom a cool *"Merci"* for the flowers.

"I definitely must explain. I must explain last night. That is why I am here, Madame."

"You mean—you can explain?"

Tom returned her cynical smile with a frank and open one. "As much as anyone can explain the Mafia. Of course! Yes! Come to think of it, I could have bought them off—I suppose. What else do they want except money? However, in this case

I'm not so sure, because they have a special grudge against me."

Simone was interested. But this fact didn't diminish her antipathy to Tom. She had taken a step back from him.

"Can't we go into your living room—perhaps?"

Simone led the way. Georges followed them, gazing fixedly at Tom. Simone motioned Tom to the sofa. Tom sat down on the Chesterfield, gently slapped its black leather, and started to pay Simone a compliment on it and didn't.

"Yes, a special grudge," Tom resumed. "I—you see, I happened—just happened to be on the same train as your husband when he was returning from a visit to Munich recently. You remember."

"Yes."

"Muniche!" said Georges, his face lighting up as if in anticipation of a story.

Tom smiled back at him. "Muniche. . . . *Alors,* on this train—for reasons of my own—I will not hesitate to tell you, Madame, that sometimes I take the law into my own hands just as much as the Mafia do. The difference is, I don't blackmail honest people; I don't expect protection money from people who wouldn't need protection if not for my threats." It was so abstract that Tom was sure Georges was not following, despite his intense gaze at Tom.

"What're you getting at?" Simone asked.

"At the fact that I killed one of those beasts on the train, and nearly killed the other—pushed him out—and Jonathan was there and saw me. You see—" Tom was only briefly daunted by the shock in Simone's face, by her fearful glance at Georges, who was following the story avidly, and perhaps thought that "beasts" were indeed animals, or maybe that Tom was making it up as he went along. "You see, I had time to explain the situation to Jonathan. We were on the platform—on the moving train. Jonathan kept a lookout for me—that's all he did. But I'm grateful. He helped. And I hope you see, Madame, that it was for a good cause.

Look at the way the French police are fighting the Mafia down in Marseilles, the drug merchants. Look at the way *everyone* is fighting the Mafia! Trying to. But then you must expect dangerous retaliations from them, you know that. So that's what happened last night. I—" Did he dare say he had asked for Jonathan's help? Yes. "It was entirely my fault that Jonathan was at my house, because I asked him if he would be willing to help me again."

Simone looked puzzled, and highly suspicious. "For money, of course."

Tom had expected this, and remained calm. "No. No, Madame." It was a matter of honor, Tom started to say, but that didn't completely make sense, even to him. Friendship, but Simone wouldn't like that. "It was kindness on Jonathan's part. Kindness and courage. You shouldn't reproach him."

Simone shook her head slowly, disbelieving. "My husband is not a police agent, M'sieur. Why don't you tell me the truth?"

"But I am," Tom said simply, opening his hands.

Simone sat tensely in the armchair, her fingers working together now. "Very recently," she said, "my husband has received quite a bit of money. Are you saying that that has nothing to do with you?"

Tom leaned back on the sofa and crossed his feet at the ankles. He was wearing his oldest, nearly worn-out desert boots. "Ah, yes. He told me a little about that," Tom said with a smile. "The German doctors are making a bet together, and they've entrusted the take to Jonathan. Isn't that right? I thought he'd told you."

Simone merely listened, waiting for more.

"In addition, Jonathan told me they'd given him a bonus —or prize money. After all, they are using him to experiment on."

"He also told me there was no—no real danger in the drugs, so why should he be paid?" She shook her head and laughed briefly. "No, M'sieur."

Tom was silent. His face showed disappointment, and he

meant it to. "There are stranger things, Madame. I'm simply telling you what Jonathan told me. I have no reason to think it isn't true."

That was the end of it. Simone stirred restlessly in her chair, then stood up. She had a lovely face, clear handsome eyes and brows, an intelligent mouth that could be soft or stern. Just now it was stern. She gave him a polite smile. "And what do you know about the death of M. Gauthier? Anything? I understand you often bought things at his shop."

Tom had stood up, and he faced this, at least, with a clear conscience. "I know that he was run over, Madame, by a hit-and-run driver."

"That is all you know?" Simone's voice was a little higher pitched, and it trembled.

"I know that it was an accident." Tom wished that he didn't have to speak in French. He felt he was being blunt. "That accident makes no sense. If you think I—that I had anything to do with it, Madame—then perhaps you will tell me for what purpose. Really, Madame—" Tom glanced at Georges, who was now reaching for a toy on the floor. Gauthier's death was like something in a Greek tragedy. But no, Greek tragedies had reasons for everything.

Her mouth twitched a little, bitterly. "I trust you won't have need of Jonathan again?"

"I won't call on him if I do," Tom said pleasantly. "How is—"

"I would think," she interrupted, "the people to call on are the police. Don't you agree? Or perhaps you are already in the secret police? Of America, perhaps?"

Her sarcasm had very deep roots, Tom realized. He was never going to succeed with Simone. Tom smiled a little, though he felt slightly wounded. He'd endured worse words in his life, but in this case it was a pity because he had so wanted to convince Simone. "No, that I am not. I get into scrapes now and then, as I think you know."

"Yes. I know."

"Scrapes, what is scrapes?" Georges piped up, his blond

head turning from Tom to his mother. He was on his feet, very near them.

Tom had used the word *"pétrins"*—which he'd had to grope for.

"Sh-h, Georges," said his mother.

"But in this case, you must admit to take on the Mafia is not a bad thing." Whose side are you on, Tom wanted to ask, but that would be rubbing it in.

"M. Ripley, you are an extremely sinister personage. That is all I know. I would be most grateful if you left both me and my husband alone."

Tom's flowers lay on the hall table, waterless.

"How is Jonathan now?" Tom asked in the hall. "I hope he's better." Tom was even afraid to say he hoped Jonathan would be home tonight, lest Simone think he intended to use him again.

"I think he is all right—better. Goodbye, M. Ripley."

"Goodbye and thank you," Tom said. *"Au revoir, Georges."* Tom patted the boy's head, and Georges smiled.

Tom went out to his car. Gauthier! A familiar face, a neighborhood face, now gone. It piqued Tom that Simone thought he had had something to do with it, had arranged it, even though Jonathan had told him days ago that Simone thought this. My God, the taint! Well, yes, he had the taint, all right. Worse, he had killed people. True. Dickie Greenleaf. *That* was the taint, the real crime. Hotheadedness of youth. Nonsense! It had been greed, jealousy, resentment of Dickie. And of course Dickie's death—rather, his murder—had caused Tom to kill the American slob called Freddie Miles. Long past, all that. But he had done it, yes. The law half suspected it. But they couldn't prove it. The story had crept through the public—the public mind—like ink creeping through a blotter. Tom was ashamed. A youthful, dreadful mistake. A fatal mistake, you might think; it was just that he had had amazing luck afterward. He'd survived it, physically speaking. And surely his . . . murder since then—

Murchison, for instance—had most certainly been done to protect others as much as himself.

Simone was shocked—what woman wouldn't have been?—at seeing two corpses on the floor when she walked into Belle Ombre last night. But hadn't he been protecting her husband as well as himself? If the Mafia had caught him and tortured him, wouldn't he have come out with the name and address of Jonathan Trevanny?

This made Tom think of Reeves Minot. He thought he ought to ring him. Tom found himself staring with a frown at the handle of his car door. His door was not even locked, and the keys, in his usual style, were hanging in the dashboard.

The evidence of the marrow test, which a doctor took in midafternoon Sunday, was not good, | 22 | and they wanted to keep Jonathan overnight and give him the Vincainestine treatment, a complete change of blood, which Jonathan had had before.

Simone came to see him just after 7 p.m. Jonathan had been told that she had telephoned earlier. But whoever had spoken to her had not told her that he had to stay overnight, and Simone was surprised.

"So—tomorrow," she said, and seemed not to find any more words.

Jonathan lay with his head raised a little by pillows. Tom's pajamas had been changed for a loose garment, and he had a tube in both arms. He felt a terrible distance between Simone and himself. Or was he imagining it? "Tomorrow morning, I suppose. Don't trouble to come here, my dear, I'll get a taxi. . . . How was the afternoon? How's your family?"

Simone ignored the question. "Your friend M. Ripley paid a visit to me this afternoon."

"Oh, yes?"

"He is so—absolutely full of lies, it is hard to know even what smallest part to believe. Maybe none of it." Simone glanced behind her, but there was no one. Jonathan's was one of many beds in the ward, not all of them occupied, although the ones on either side of Jonathan were, and one man had a visitor.

They couldn't talk easily.

"Georges will be disappointed that you don't come back to-night," Simone said.

Then she left.

Jonathan went home the next morning, Monday, around ten. Simone was there, ironing some of Georges's clothing.

"Are you feeling all right? . . . Did they give you breakfast? . . . Would you like some coffee? Or tea?"

Jonathan felt much better—one always did just after a Vincainestine, until his disease got to work and ruined the blood again, he thought. He wanted only a bath. He had one, then put on different clothes: old beige corduroy trousers and two sweaters because the morning was cool, or perhaps he was feeling the chill more than usual. Simone was ironing in a short-sleeved woolen dress. The morning newspaper, the *Figaro,* lay folded on the kitchen table with its front page outermost, as usual, but it was obvious from the looseness of the paper that Simone had looked at it.

Jonathan picked up the paper, and since Simone did not look up from her ironing, he walked into the living room. He found a two-column item in a bottom corner of the second page.

TWO CORPSES INCINERATED IN CAR

The dateline was 14 May, Chaumont. A farmer named René Gault, 55, had found the smoking Citroën early Sunday morning, and had at once alerted the police. The still unburned papers in the billfolds of the dead men identified them as Angelo Lipari, 33, contractor, and Filippo Turoli, 31, salesman, both of Milan. Lipari had died of skull fractures, Turoli of unknown causes, though he was believed to have been unconscious or dead when the car was set alight. There were no clues at the moment, and police were making investigations.

The garrote had been completely burned, Jonathan supposed, and evidently Lippo was so badly burned that the signs of garroting had been destroyed.

Simone came into the doorway with folded clothing in her hands. "So? I saw it, too. The two Italians."

"Yes."

"And you helped M. Ripley to do that. That is what you called 'cleaning up.' "

Jonathan said nothing. He gave a sigh and sat down on the luxuriously squeaking Chesterfield sofa, although he sat rather straight lest Simone think he was retreating on grounds of weakness. "Something had to be done with them."

"And you simply had to help," she said. "Jon—now that Georges is not here—I think we should talk about this." She put the clothes on top of the waist-high bookcase by the door, and sat down on the edge of the armchair. "You are not telling me the truth, and neither is M. Ripley. I am wondering what else you are going to be obliged to do for him." On the last words, her voice rose with hysteria.

"Nothing." Jonathan did feel sure of that. And if Tom asked him to do anything else, he could simply refuse. At that moment, it seemed quite simple to Jonathan. He had to hold on to Simone at any cost. She was worth more than Tom Ripley, more than anything Tom could offer him.

"It is beyond my understanding. You knew what you were doing—Saturday night. You helped to kill those men, didn't you?" Her voice dropped, and it trembled.

"It was a matter of protecting—what had gone before."

"Ah, yes, M. Ripley explained. By accident you were on the same train as he was, coming from Munich, is that right? And you—assisted him in—in *killing* two people?"

"Mafia," Jonathan said. What *had* Tom told her?

"You, an ordinary passenger, assist a murderer? You expect me to believe that, Jon?"

Jonathan was silent, trying to think, miserable. The answer was no. *You don't seem to realize they were Mafia,* Jonathan wanted to repeat. *They were attacking Tom Ripley.* Another lie, at least in regard to the train. Jonathan pressed his lips together and sat back on the generous sofa. "I don't expect you to believe it. I have only two things to say: this is the end of it, and the men we killed were criminals and murderers themselves. You must admit that."

"Are you a secret-police agent in your spare time? *Why* are you being paid for this, Jon? You—a killer!" She stood up with her hands clenched. "You are a stranger to me. I have never known you before now."

"Oh, Simone," Jonathan said, standing up, too.

"I cannot like you and I cannot love you."

Jonathan blinked. She had said that in English.

She continued in French: "You are leaving out something, I know. And I don't even want to know what it is. Do you understand? It is some horrible connection with M. Ripley, that odious personage—and I wonder what," she added with the bitter sarcasm again. "Plainly it is something too disgusting for you to tell me. I shouldn't wonder. You've no doubt covered up some other crime for him, and for this you're being paid, for this you're in his power. Very well, I don't want—"

"I am not in his power! You'll see!"

"I've seen enough!" She went out, taking the clothes with her, and climbed the stairs.

When it came time for lunch, Simone said she wasn't hungry. Jonathan made himself a boiled egg. Then he went to his shop, and kept the FERMÉ sign in the door, because he was not officially open on Mondays. Nothing had changed since Saturday noon. He could see that Simone hadn't been in. Jonathan suddenly thought of the Italian gun, usually in a drawer, now at Tom Ripley's. Jonathan cut one frame, cut the glass for it, but lost heart when it came to driving the nails in. What was he to do about Simone? What if he told her the whole story, just as it had been? Jonathan knew, however, that he was up against a Catholic attitude about taking human life. Not to mention that Simone would consider the original proposition to him "fantastic!—disgusting!" Curious that the Mafia was a hundred percent Catholic, and they didn't mind about human life. But he, Simone's husband, was different. He shouldn't take human life. And if he told her it was a "mistake" on his part, that he regretted it—hopeless. First of all, he didn't particularly believe it had been a mistake, so why tell another lie?

Jonathan went back to his work table with more determination, got the glue and nails in the picture frame, and sealed it neatly with brown paper on the back. He clipped the owner's name to the picture wire. Then he looked over the orders to be filled and tackled one more picture, which, like the other, needed no mat. He went on working until 6 p.m. Then he bought bread and wine, and some ham slices from a *charcuterie,* enough for dinner for the three of them in case Simone hadn't done any shopping.

Simone said, "I am in terror that the police will knock on the door at any moment, wanting to see you."

Jonathan, setting the table, said nothing for a few seconds. "They will not. Why should they?"

"There is no such thing as no clues. They will find M. Ripley, and he will tell them about you."

Jonathan was sure she hadn't eaten all day. He found some leftover potatoes—mashed potatoes—in the fridge, and went about preparing the dinner himself. Georges came down from his room.

"What did they do to you in the hospital, Papa?"

"I have completely new blood," Jonathan replied with a smile, flexing his arms. "Think of that. All new blood—oh, at least eight liters of it."

"How much is that?" Georges spread his arms also.

"Eight times this bottle," said Jonathan. "That's what took all night."

Though Jonathan made an effort, he couldn't lift the gloom of Simone's silence. She poked at her food and said nothing.

Georges didn't understand. Jonathan's efforts, failing, embarrassed him, and over coffee he, too, was silent, not even able to chat with Georges.

Jonathan wondered if she had spoken with her brother Gérard. He steered Georges into the living room to watch the television, the new set which had arrived a few days ago. The programs—there were only two channels—weren't interesting for kids at this hour, but Jonathan hoped he would stay with one of them for a while.

"Did you talk to Gérard, by any chance?" Jonathan asked, not able to repress the question.

"Of course not. Do you think I could possibly tell him —this?" She was smoking a cigarette, a rare thing for her. She glanced at the doorway to the hall, to be sure Georges was not coming back. "Jon—I think we should make some arrangement to separate."

On the television, a French politician was speaking about *syndicats,* trade unions.

Jonathan sat down again in his chair. "Darling, I do know —it's a shock to you. Will you let a few days pass? I know, somehow, I can make you understand. Really." Jonathan spoke with utmost conviction, and yet he realized he was not convinced himself, not at all. It was an instinctive clinging to life, Jonathan thought, his clinging to Simone.

"Yes, of course you think that. But I know myself. I am not an emotional young girl, you know." Her eyes looked straight at him, hardly angry now, only determined, and distant. "I am not interested in all your money now, not any of it. I can make my own way—with Georges."

"Oh, Georges—my God, Simone, I'll support Georges!" Jonathan could hardly believe they were saying these words. He got up, drew Simone up from her chair a little roughly, and some coffee spilled out of her cup into the saucer. Jonathan embraced her, would have kissed her, but she squirmed away.

"*Non!*" She put her cigarette out and started clearing the

table. "I am sorry to say also that I don't want to sleep in the same bed with you."

"Oh, yes, I assumed that." And you'll go to church to-morrow and say a prayer for my soul, Jonathan thought. "Simone, you must let a little time go by. Don't say things now that you don't mean."

"I will not change. Ask M. Ripley. I think he knows."

Georges came back. Television was forgotten, and he looked at them both with puzzlement.

Jonathan touched Georges's head with his fingertips as he went into the hall. Jonathan had thought to go up to the bedroom—but it wasn't their bedroom any more, and any-way what would he do up there? The television droned on. Jonathan turned in a circle in the hall, then took his raincoat and a muffler and went out. He walked to the Rue de France, turned left, and at the end of the street went into the bar-café on the corner. He wanted to telephone Tom Ripley. He remembered Tom's number.

"Hello?" Tom said.

"Jonathan."

"How are you? . . . I telephoned the hospital, I heard you stayed the night. You're out now?"

"Oh, yes, this morning. I—" Jonathan gasped.

"What's the matter?"

"Could I see you for a few minutes? If you think it's safe. I'm—I suppose I could get a taxi. Surely."

"Where are you?"

"The corner bar—the new one near the Aigle Noir."

"I could pick you up. No?" Tom suspected Jonathan had had a bad scene with Simone.

"I'll walk toward the monument. I want to walk a little. I'll see you there."

Jonathan felt better at once. It was spurious, no doubt, it was postponing the situation with Simone, but for the moment that didn't matter. He felt like a tortured man mo-mentarily relieved of the torture, and he was grateful for a few moments of relief. Jonathan lit a cigarette and walked slowly, because it would take Tom nearly fifteen minutes. He went into the Café du Sport, just beyond L'Aigle Noir, and ordered a beer. He tried not to think at all. Then one thought rose to the surface on its own: Simone *would* come round. As soon as he thought about it consciously, he feared that she wouldn't. He was alone now. Jonathan knew he was alone, that even Georges was more than half cut off from him, because Simone was going to keep Georges, but Jonathan was aware that he hadn't yet realized it fully. That would take days. Feelings were slower than thoughts. Sometimes.

Tom's Renault came out of the darkness of the woods in a thin stream of cars into the light around the Obelisque, the monument. It was a little past eight. Jonathan was on the corner, on the left side of the road, and Tom's right. Tom would have to make the complete circle to regain his road homeward—if they went to Tom's. Jonathan preferred Tom's house to a bar. Tom stopped and unlatched the door.

"Evening!" Tom said.

"Evening," Jonathan replied, pulling the door shut, and at once Tom moved off. "Can we go to your place? I don't feel like a crowded bar."

"Sure."

"I've had a bad evening. And day, I'm afraid."

"So I thought. Simone?"

"It seems she's finished. Who can blame her?" Jonathan felt awkward, started to take a cigarette, and found even that purposeless, so he didn't.

"I tried my best," Tom said. He was concentrating on driving as fast as possible without bringing a motorcycle cop, some of whom lurked in the woods at the edge of the road here.

"Oh, it's the money—it's the corpses, good Christ! As for the money, I said I was holding the stake for the Germans, you know." It was suddenly ludicrous to Jonathan, the money, the bet also. The money was so concrete in a way, so tangible, so useful, and yet not nearly so tangible or meaningful as the two dead men that Simone had seen. Tom was driving quite fast. Jonathan felt unconcerned whether they hit a tree or bounced off the road. "To put it simply," Jonathan went on, "it's the dead men. The fact that I helped—or did it. I don't think she's going to change." What is a man profited—Jonathan could have laughed. He hadn't gained the whole world, nor had he lost his soul. Anyway, Jonathan didn't believe in a soul. Self-respect was more like it. He hadn't lost his self-respect, only Simone. Simone was morale, however, and wasn't morale self-respect?

Tom didn't think Simone was going to change toward Jonathan, either, but he said nothing. Maybe he could talk at home, and yet what else could he say? Words of comfort, words of hope for a reconciliation when he didn't really believe there'd be one? And yet who knew about women? Sometimes they appeared to have stronger moral attitudes than men, and at other times—especially in political skulduggery and the political swine they sometimes married—it seemed to Tom that women were more flexible, more capable of double-think than men. Unfortunately, Simone presented a picture of inflexible rectitude. Hadn't Jonathan said she was a churchgoer, too? Tom's thoughts switched to Reeves Minot. Reeves was nervous, for no very strong reason that Tom could see. Suddenly Tom was at the turnoff at Villeperce, guiding the car slowly through the familiar quiet streets.

And there was Belle Ombre behind the tall trees, a light glowing above the doorway—all intact.

Tom had made coffee, and Jonathan said he would join him in a cup. Tom heated the coffee a bit, then brought it with the brandy bottle to the coffee table.

"Speaking of problems," Tom said, "Reeves wants to come to France. I phoned him today from Sens. He's in Ascona staying at a hotel called The Three Bears."

"I remember," Jonathan said.

"He imagines he's being spied on—by people in the street. I tried to tell him our enemies don't waste time with that sort of thing. He should know. I tried to discourage him from coming even to Paris. Certainly not here to my place. I wouldn't call Belle Ombre the safest spot in the world, would you? Naturally, I couldn't mention Saturday night, which might've reassured him. I mean, we at least got rid of the two people who saw us on the train. I'm not sure how long the peace and quiet will last." Tom hitched forward, elbows on his knees, and glanced at the silent windows. "Reeves doesn't know anything about Saturday night—or didn't say anything, anyway. Might not even connect it if he reads the papers. I suppose you saw the papers today?"

"Yes," Jonathan said.

"No clues. Nothing on the radio tonight, either, but the TV boys gave it a spot. No clues." Tom smiled, and reached for one of his small cigars. He extended the box to Jonathan, but Jonathan shook his head. "What's equally good news, not a question from the townsfolk here. I bought bread and went to the butcher's today—on foot, taking my time—just to see. And around seven-thirty Howard Clegg arrived, one of my neighbors, bringing me a big plastic sack of horse manure from one of his farmer friends where he buys a rabbit now and then." Tom puffed on his cigar and relaxed with a laugh. "It was Howard who stopped his car outside Saturday night, re-member? He thought we had guests, Héloïse and I, and that it mightn't be the time to deliver horse manure." Tom rambled on, trying to fill in the time, while Jonathan, he hoped, lost a little of his tension. "I told him Héloïse was away for a few days, and I said I'd been entertaining some friends from Paris, hence the Paris car outside. I think that went down very well."

The clock on the mantel struck nine, with pure little pings.

"However, back to Reeves," Tom said. "I thought of writ-ing him, saying I had some grounds for thinking the situation had improved, but two things stopped me. Reeves might leave Ascona at any hour, and second, things haven't improved for him if the wogs still want to get him. He's using the name Ralph Platt now, but they know his real name and what he looks like. There's nothing for Reeves but Brazil if the Mafia still wants to get him. And even Brazil—" Tom smiled, but not happily.

"But isn't he rather used to it?" Jonathan asked.

"Like this? No. . . . Very few people, I suppose, get used to the Mafia and live to talk about it. They may live, but not very comfortably."

But Reeves had brought it on himself, Jonathan was thinking. And Reeves had drawn him into it. No, he'd walked into it of his own free will, let himself be persuaded—for money. And it was Tom Ripley who had—at least tried to help him collect that money, even if it had been Tom's idea from the start, this deadly game. Jonathan's mind spun back to those minutes on the train between Munich and Strasbourg.

"I *am* sorry about Simone," Tom said. Jonathan's long, cramped figure, hunched over his coffee cup, seemed to illustrate failure, like a statue. "What does she want to do?"

"Oh—" Jonathan shrugged. "She talks about a separation. Taking Georges, of course. She has a brother, Gérard, in Nemours. I don't know what she'll say to him—or to her family there. She's absolutely shocked, you see. And ashamed."

"I do understand." So is Héloïse ashamed, Tom thought, but Héloïse was more capable of doublethink. Héloïse knew he dabbled in murder, crime—yet was it crime? At least recently, with the Derwatt thing, and now the accursed Mafia? Tom brushed the moral question aside for the moment, and at the same time found himself flicking a bit of ash off his knee. What was Jonathan going to do? Without Simone, he'd have no morale at all. Tom wondered if he should try talking to Simone again. But his memory of yesterday's interview discouraged him. Tom didn't fancy another try with her.

"I am finished," Jonathan said.

Tom started to speak, and Jonathan interrupted: "You know I'm finished with Simone—or she is with me. Then there's the old business of how long will I live, anyway? Why drag it on? So, Tom"—Jonathan stood up—"if I can be of service, even suicidal, I'm at your disposal."

Tom smiled. "Brandy?"

"Yes, a little. Thanks."

Tom poured it. "I've spent the last few minutes trying to explain why I think—I *think* we're over the hump. That is, with the wogs. Of course we're not out of the woods if they catch Reeves—and torture him. He might talk about both of us."

Jonathan had thought of that. It simply didn't matter much to him, but of course it mattered to Tom. Tom wanted to stay alive. "Can I be of any service? As a decoy, perhaps? A sacrifice?" Jonathan laughed.

"I don't want any decoys," Tom said.

"Didn't you say once the Mafia might want a certain amount of blood, as revenge?"

Tom had certainly thought it, but he wasn't sure if he had said it. "If we do nothing—they may get Reeves and finish him," Tom said. "This is called letting nature take its course. I didn't put this idea—assassinating Mafiosi—into Reeves's head, and neither did you."

Tom's cool attitude took the wind out of Jonathan's sails a little. He sat down. "And what about Fritz? Any news? I remember Fritz well." Jonathan smiled as if recollecting halcyon days, Fritz arriving at Reeves's flat in Hamburg, cap in hand, with a friendly smile and the efficient little pistol.

Tom had to think for a moment who Fritz was—the factotum, the taxi driver and messenger in Hamburg. "No. Let's hope Fritz has returned to his folks in the country, as Reeves said. I hope he's staying there. Maybe they're finished with Fritz." Tom stood up. "Jonathan, you've got to go home tonight and face the music."

"I know." Tom had, however, made him feel better. Tom was realistic, even about Simone. "Funny, the problem isn't the Mafia any more. It's Simone—for me."

Tom knew. "I'll go with you, if you like. Try to talk with her again."

Jonathan shrugged. He was on his feet now, restless. He glanced at the painting by Derwatt over the fireplace that

Tom had said was called "Man in Chair." He was reminded of Reeves's flat, with another Derwatt over the fireplace, maybe destroyed now. "I think I'll be sleeping on the sofa tonight—whatever happens," Jonathan said.

Tom thought of turning on the news. It wasn't the right time to get anything, though, not even Italy. "What do you think?" he said. "Simone can always forbid me the door. Unless you think it'll make it worse for you if I'm with you."

"Things couldn't be worse. —All right. I'd like you to come, yes. But what'll we say?"

Tom pushed his hands into the pockets of his old gray flannels. In his right pocket was the small Italian gun which Jonathan had carried on the train. Tom had slept with it under his pillow since Saturday night. Yes, what to say? Tom usually relied on inspiration of the moment, but hadn't he already shot his bolt with Simone? What other brilliant facet of the problem could he come up with to dazzle her eyes, her brain, and make her see things their way? "The only thing to do," Tom said thoughtfully, "is try to convince her of the safety of everything—now. I admit that's hard to do. That's hurdling the corpses, all right. But much of her trouble is anxiety, you know."

"Well—are things safe?" Jonathan asked. "We can't be sure, can we? . . . It's Reeves, I suppose."

They were in Fontainebleau at 10 p.m. Jonathan led the way up the front steps, knocked, then put his key into the lock. But the door was bolted inside.

| 23 |

"Who is it?" Simone called.

"Jon."

She slid the bolt. "Oh, Jon—I was worried!"

That sounded hopeful, Tom thought.

In the next second, Simone saw Tom, and her expression changed.

"Yes—Tom's with me. Can't we come in?"

She looked on the brink of saying no. Then she stepped back a little, stiffly. Jonathan and Tom went in.

"Good evening, Madame," Tom said.

In the living room the television was on, some sewing—what looked like a repair on a coat lining—lay on the black leather sofa, and Georges was playing with a toy truck on the floor. The picture of domestic calm, Tom thought. He said hello to Georges.

"Do sit down, Tom," said Jonathan.

But Tom didn't, because Simone showed no sign of sitting.

"And what is the reason for this visit?" she asked Tom.

"Madame, I—" Tom stopped, then stammered on, "I've come to take all the blame on myself, and to try to persuade you to—to be a little kinder to your husband."

"You are telling me that my husband—" She was suddenly aware of Georges, and with an air of nervous exasperation took him by the hand. "Georges, you must go upstairs. Do you hear me? Please, darling."

Georges went to the doorway, looked back, then entered the hall and mounted the stairs reluctantly.

"*Dépêche-toi!*" Simone shouted at him, then closed the living-room door. "You are telling me," she resumed, "that my husband knew nothing about these—events, until he just walked in on them. That this sordid money comes from a bet between doctors!"

Tom took a breath. "The blame is mine. Perhaps—Jon made a mistake in helping me. But can't that be forgiven? He is your husband—"

"He has become a criminal. Perhaps this is your charming influence, but it is a fact. Is it not?"

Jonathan sat down in the armchair.

Tom decided to take one end of the sofa—until Simone ordered him out of the house. Bravely, Tom started again. "Jon came to see me tonight to discuss this, Madame. He is most upset. Marriage—is a sacred thing, you know that well. His life, his courage would be quite destroyed if he lost your affections. You surely realize that. And you should think also of your son, who needs his father."

Simone was a little affected by Tom's words, but she replied, "Yes, a father. A real father to respect. I agree!"

Tom heard footsteps on the stone steps, and looked quickly at Jonathan.

"Expecting someone?" Jonathan asked Simone. She had probably telephoned Gérard, he thought.

She shook her head. "No."

Tom and Jonathan jumped up.

"Bolt the door again," Tom whispered in English to Jonathan. "Ask who it is."

A neighbor, Jonathan thought as he went to the door. He slid the bolt quietly shut. *"Qui est-ce, s'il vous plaît?"*

"M. Trevanny?" said a man's voice.

Jonathan didn't recognize the voice and looked over his shoulder at Tom in the hall.

There'd be more than one, Tom thought.

"Now what?" asked Simone.

Tom put his finger to his lips. Then, not caring what Simone's reaction might be, Tom went down the hall toward the kitchen, which had a light on. Simone followed him. Tom looked around for something heavy. He still had one garrote in his hip pocket, though of course it wouldn't be necessary if the caller was a neighbor.

"What are you doing?" Simone asked.

Tom was opening a narrow yellow door in a corner of the kitchen. It was a broom closet, and here he saw what he might need, a hammer, and besides that a chisel, plus several innocuous mops and brooms. "I might be more useful here," Tom said, picking up the hammer. He was expecting a shot through the door, the sound of the front door being assaulted by shoulders from outside, perhaps. Then he heard the faint click of the bolt being slid—open. Was Jonathan mad?

Simone at once started off boldly into the hall, and Tom heard her gasp. There was a scuffling sound in the hall; then the door slammed shut.

"Mme. Trevanny?" said a man's voice.

Simone's cry was shut off before it became a real cry. The sounds came up the hall now toward the kitchen.

Simone appeared, sliding on the heels of her shoes, man-handled by a thick fellow in a dark suit, who had his hand over her mouth. Tom, to the left of the man as he entered the kitchen, stepped out and hit him with the hammer just below his hat brim in the back of the neck. The man, by no means unconscious, released Simone and straightened up a little, so that Tom had an opportunity to bash him on the nose, and this Tom followed—the man's hat having fallen off—with a blow on the forehead, straightforward and true, as if he had been an ox in a slaughterhouse. The man's legs sank under him.

Simone got to her feet, and Tom drew her toward the broom-closet corner, which was concealed from the hall. As far as Tom knew, there was only one other man in the house, and the silence made Tom think of the garrote. With his hammer, Tom went up the hall toward the front door. Quiet as he tried to be, he was still heard by the Italian in the living room, who had Jonathan on the floor. It was indeed the garrote again. Tom sprang at him with the hammer raised. The Italian—fat, in a gray suit, gray hat—had released the garrote and was pulling his gun from a shoulder holster when Tom hit him in the cheekbone. More accurate than a tennis racket, the hammer! The man, who had not quite stood up, lurched forward, and Tom removed his hat quickly with his left hand and with his right came down again with the hammer.

Crack! Little Leviathan's dark eyes closed, his pink lips relaxed, and he thudded to the floor.

Tom knelt beside Jonathan. The nylon cord was already well into Jonathan's flesh. He turned Jonathan's head this way and that, trying to get at the cord to loosen it. Jonathan's teeth were bared, and he was trying with his own fingers, but feebly.

Simone was suddenly beside them, holding something that looked like a letter-opener. She pried with the point of it into the side of Jonathan's neck. The string loosened.

Tom lost his balance, sat down on the floor, and sprang up again. He yanked the curtains of the front window shut: there had been a gap of six inches between them. About a minute and a half had passed, he thought, since the Italians had come in. He picked up the hammer from the floor, went to the front door, and bolted it again. There was no noise from outside, except for the normal-sounding steps of someone walking past on the pavement and the hum of a passing car.

"Jon," said Simone.

Jonathan coughed and rubbed his neck. He was trying to sit up.

The porcine man in gray lay motionless, with his head propped by accident against a leg of the armchair. Tom tightened his grip on the hammer and started to give the man one more blow, then hesitated because there was already some blood on the carpet. But Tom thought the man was still alive.

"Pig," Tom murmured, pulled the man up a little by his shirtfront and flamboyant tie, and smashed the hammer head into his left temple.

Georges stood wide-eyed in the doorway.

Simone had brought Jonathan a glass of water. She was kneeling beside him. "Go *away,* Georges!" she said. "Papa is all right! Go in the—go upstairs, Georges!"

But Georges didn't. He stood there, fascinated by a scene that was perhaps unsurpassed on television. By the same token, he wasn't taking it too seriously. His eyes were wide, absorbing it all, but he was not terrified.

Jonathan got to the sofa, helped by Tom and Simone. He was sitting up, and Simone had a wet towel for his face. "I'm really all right," Jonathan mumbled.

Tom was still listening for footsteps, front or back. Of all times, Tom thought, when he'd meant to create a peaceable impression on Simone! "Madame, is the garden passageway locked?"

"Yes," said Simone.

And Tom remembered ornamental spikes along the top of the iron door. He said in English to Jonathan, "There's probably at least one more of them in a car outside." Tom supposed Simone understood this, but he couldn't tell from her face. She was looking at Jonathan, who seemed to be out of danger, and then she went to Georges, who was still in the doorway.

"Georges! Will you—!" She shooed him away again, carried him halfway up the stairs, and spanked his bottom once. "Go into your room and close the door!"

Simone was being splendid, Tom thought. Just as at Belle Ombre, it would be a matter of seconds until another man came to the door, he supposed. He tried to imagine what the man in the car would be thinking: from the absence of noise, or screams, of gunshots, the waiting man or men probably supposed that everything had gone as planned. They must be expecting their two pals to come out the door at any moment, mission accomplished, the Trevannys garroted or beaten to death. Reeves must have talked, Tom thought, must have told them Jonathan's name and address. Tom had a wild idea of Jonathan and himself putting on the Italians' hats, making a dash to the Italians' car (if any), and taking them by surprise with—the one small gun. But he couldn't ask Jonathan to do that.

"Jonathan, I'd better go out before it's too late," Tom said.

"Too late—how?" Jonathan had wiped his face with the wet towel, and some blond hair stood on end above his forehead.

"Before they come to the door. They'll be suspicious if their pals don't come out." If the Italians saw the situation here, they'd blast the three of them with guns and make a getaway in their car, Tom was thinking. He went to the window and stooped, looking out just above the sill level. He listened for a car motor idling somewhere, looked for a car stationed with parking lights on. Parking was permitted on the opposite side of the street today. Tom saw it—maybe —to the left, some twelve yards away diagonally. The car's parking lights were on, but Tom couldn't be sure the motor was, because of the other noises on the street.

Jonathan was up, walking toward Tom.

"I think I see them," Tom said.

"What should we do?"

Tom was thinking of what he would do alone: stay in the house and try to shoot anyone who broke in the door. "There's Simone and Georges to consider. We don't want a fight in here. I think we should rush them—outside. Otherwise they'll rush us here, and it'll be guns if they break in. —I can do it, Jon."

Jonathan felt a sudden rage, a desire to guard his house and home. "All right—we'll go together!"

"What are you going to do, Jon?" Simone asked.

"We think there might be more of them—coming," Jonathan said in French.

Tom went to the kitchen. He got the hat from the floor near the dead man, stuck it on his head, and found that it fell over his ears. Then he suddenly realized that this Italian —and the other one, too—had a gun in his shoulder holster. Tom took the man's gun from the holster. He went back into the living room. "These guns!" he said, reaching for the gun of the man on the floor. It was under his jacket. Tom took the man's hat, found that it fitted him better, and handed Jonathan a gun and the hat from the kitchen. "Try this. If we can look like them till we cross the street, it's a slight advantage. But don't come with me, Jon. It's just as good if one person goes out. I just want them to move off!"

"Then I'll go," Jonathan said. He knew what he had to do: scare them off, and perhaps shoot one first, if he could, before he was shot himself.

Tom handed a gun to Simone, the small Italian gun. "It

might be useful, Madame." But she looked shy of taking the gun, and he laid it on the sofa. The safety was off.

Jonathan pushed the safety off the gun in his hand. "Could you see how many are in the car?"

"Couldn't see a thing inside." On his last words, Tom heard someone walking up the front steps, cautiously, with an effort to be silent. Tom jerked his head at Jonathan. "Bolt the door after us, Madame," he whispered to Simone.

Tom and Jonathan, both wearing hats now, walked up the hall, and Tom slid the bolt and opened the door in the face of the man standing there. At the same time, Tom bumped him and caught him by the arm, turning him back down the stairs again. Jonathan had grabbed his other arm. At a glance, in the darkness, Tom and Jonathan could be taken for his friends but Tom knew the illusion wouldn't last more than a second or two.

"To the left!" Tom said to Jonathan. The man they held was struggling, though not yelling yet, and his efforts nearly lifted Tom off his feet.

Jonathan had seen the car with its parking lights on, and now he saw the lights come full on, and heard the motor revving. The car backed a little.

"Dump him!" Tom said, and he and Jonathan, like a pair who had rehearsed it, hurled the Italian forward, and his head hit the side of the slowly moving car. Tom was aware of the clatter of the Italian's drawn gun on the street. The car had stopped, and the door in front of Tom was opening: the Mafia wanted their pal back, apparently. Tom pulled his gun from his trousers pocket, aimed at the driver, and fired. The driver, with the aid of a man in back, was trying to get the dazed Italian into the front seat. Tom was afraid to fire again, because a couple of people were running toward them from the Rue de France. And a window opened in one of the houses. Tom saw, or thought he saw, the other back door of the car being opened, someone being pushed out onto the pavement.

One shot came from the back of the car, then a second,

just as Jonathan stumbled or walked right in front of Tom. The car was moving off.

Tom saw Jonathan slump forward, and before he could catch him, Jonathan fell in the place where the car had been. Damn it, Tom thought, if he'd hit the driver, it must have been only in the arm. The car was gone.

A young man, then a man and a woman came trotting up.

"What's happening?"

"He's shot?"

"Police!" The last was the cry of a young woman.

"Jon!" Tom had thought Jonathan had merely tripped, but Jonathan wasn't getting up, and was barely stirring. With the assistance of one of the young men, Tom got him to the curb, but he was quite limp.

Jonathan had been shot in the chest, he thought, but he was mainly aware of numbness. There had been a jolt. He was going to faint soon, though maybe it was more serious than fainting. People dashed around him, shouting.

Only now did Tom recognize the figure on the sidewalk —Reeves! Reeves was crumpled, apparently trying to recover his breath.

"Ambulance!" a Frenchwoman's voice was saying. "We must call an ambulance!"

"I have a car!" a man cried.

Tom glanced at the windows in Jonathan's house and saw the black silhouette of Simone's head as she peeked through the curtains. He shouldn't leave her there, Tom thought. He had to get Jonathan to the hospital, and his car would be quicker than any ambulance. "Reeves! Hold the fort, I'll be back in one minute. . . . *Oui,* Madame," Tom said to a woman (now there were five or six people around them), "I'll take him to the hospital in my car!" Tom ran across the street and banged on the house door. "Simone, it's Tom!"

When Simone opened the door, Tom said, "Jonathan has been hurt. We must go to the hospital at once. Just take a coat and come. And Georges, too!"

Georges was in the hall. Simone didn't waste time with a

coat, but she did grope in a coat pocket, in the hall, for her keys, then hurried toward Tom. "Hurt? Was he shot?"

"I'm afraid so. My car is to the left. The green one." His car was several feet beyond where the Italians' car had been. Simone wanted to go to Jonathan, but Tom assured her that the most useful thing she could do was open his car doors, which were unlocked. There were more people, but no policeman yet, and one officious little man asked Tom who in hell he thought he was taking charge of everything?

"Stuff yourself!" Tom said in English. He was struggling with Reeves to lift Jonathan in the gentlest way possible. It would have been wiser to have brought the car closer, but having got Jonathan off the ground, they continued, and a couple of people assisted, so that after a few steps it was not difficult. They braced Jonathan in a corner of the back seat.

Tom got into his car, dry in the mouth. "This is Mme. Trevanny," Tom said to Reeves. "Reeves Minot."

"How do you do?" said Reeves with his American accent.

Simone got into the back, where Jonathan was. Reeves took Georges in beside him, and Tom pulled out, heading for the Fontainebleau hospital.

"Papa has fainted?" Georges asked.

"*Oui*, Georges." Simone had begun to weep.

Jonathan heard their voices, but couldn't speak. He couldn't move, not even a finger. He had a gray vision of a sea running out—somewhere on an English coast—sinking, collapsing. He was already far away from Simone, whose breast he leaned against—or so he thought. But Tom was alive. Tom was driving the car, Jonathan thought, like God himself. Somewhere there had been a bullet, which somehow no longer mattered. This was death now, which he had tried to face before and yet had not faced, tried to prepare for and yet hadn't been able to. There was no preparation possible; it was merely a surrender, after all. And what he had done, misdone, accomplished, striven for—all seemed absurdity.

Tom passed an ambulance just coming up, wailing. He

drove carefully. It was a drive of only four or five minutes. The silence among all of them in the car became eerie to Tom. It was as if he, Reeves, Simone, Georges, and Jonathan —if he was conscious of anything—had been frozen in one second that went on and on.

"This man is *dead!*" said an intern in an astonished voice.

"But—" Tom didn't believe it. He couldn't get another word out.

Only Simone gave a cry.

They were standing on the walk at the entrance to the hospital. Jonathan had been put on a stretcher, and two helpers held the stretcher poised, as if they didn't know what to do next.

"Simone, do you want—" But Tom didn't even know what he had been going to say. And Simone was now running toward Jonathan, who was being borne inside, and Georges followed her. Tom ran after Simone, thinking to get her keys from her, to remove the two corpses from her house, do *something* with them; then he stopped so abruptly that his shoes slid on the cement. The police would be at the Trevanny house before he was. The police were probably already breaking in, because the people in the street would have told them that the disturbance started from the gray house, that after the shots one person (Tom) had run back to the house, and he and another man had taken the man who was shot, a woman, and a small boy away in a car.

Simone was now disappearing around a corner, following Jonathan's stretcher. It was as if Tom saw her already in a funeral procession. Tom turned and walked back to Reeves.

"We take off," Tom said tiredly, "while we can."

He and Reeves got into the car. Tom drove off, toward the monument and home.

"Jonathan's *dead*—do you think?" Reeves asked.

"Yes. Well—you heard the intern."

Reeves slumped and rubbed his eyes.

It wasn't sinking in, Tom thought, not to either of them. Tom was apprehensive lest a car from the hospital be trailing him, even a police car. One didn't deposit a dead man and drive off with no questions asked. What was Simone going to say? They'd excuse her for not saying anything this evening, perhaps, but tomorrow? "And you, my friend," Tom said, his throat hoarse. "No bones broken, no teeth knocked out?" He'd talked, Tom remembered, and maybe at once.

"Only cigarette burns," Reeves said in a humble voice, as if burns were nothing compared to a bullet. Reeves had an inch-long beard, reddish.

"I suppose you know what's at the Trevannys' house— two dead men."

"Oh. Good. Yes, of course I know. They're missing. They never came back."

"I'd have gone by the house to do something, try to, but the police must be there now." A siren behind Tom made him grip the wheel in sudden panic, but it turned out to be a white ambulance with a blue light on its roof, which passed Tom at the monument and whisked away in a quick turn toward Paris. Tom wished it had been Jonathan being taken to a Paris hospital where they were better able to deal with him. Tom thought that Jonathan had deliberately stepped between him and the gun in the car. Was he wrong? No one overtook them, or sirened them to a stop, in the drive to Villeperce. Reeves had fallen asleep against the door, but he woke up when the car stopped.

"This is home sweet home," Tom said.

They got out in the garage, and Tom locked it, then opened his house door with a key. All was serene. It was rather unbelievable.

"Do you want to flop on the sofa while I make some tea?" Tom asked. "Tea is what we need."

They had tea and whiskey, more tea than whiskey. Reeves, with his usual apologetic manner, asked Tom if he had any anti-burn ointment, and Tom produced something from the downstairs bathroom medicine cabinet. Reeves retired there to dress his wounds, which he said were all on his stomach.

Tom lit a cigar, not so much because he craved it as because it gave him a sense of stability—perhaps illusory, but it was the illusion, the attitude toward problems, that counted. One simply had to have a confident attitude.

When Reeves came into the living room, he took note of the harpsichord.

"Yes," Tom said. "A new acquisition. I'm going to see about taking lessons in Fontainebleau—or somewhere. Maybe Héloïse will take lessons, too. We can't go on twiddling on the thing like a pair of monkeys." Tom felt curiously angry, not against Reeves, not against anything specific. "Tell me what happened in Ascona."

Reeves sipped his tea and whiskey again, silent for a few seconds like a man who had to drag himself back inch by inch from another world. "I'm thinking about Jonathan. Dead. . . . I didn't want that, you know."

Tom recrossed his legs. He was thinking about Jonathan, too. "About Ascona. What did happen there?"

"Oh. Well, I told you I thought they'd spotted me. Then a couple of nights ago—yes—one of these fellows approached me on the street. Young fellow, summer sports clothes, looked like an Italian tourist. He said in English, 'Get your suitcase packed and check out. We'll be waiting.' Natch, I—I knew what the alternative was—I mean if I'd decided to pack my suitcase and run. This was around seven Sunday evening. Yesterday?"

"Yesterday was Sunday, yes."

Reeves stared at the coffee table, but he sat upright, one hand delicately against his midriff, where perhaps the burns were. "By the way, I never took my suitcase. It's still in the lobby of the hotel in Ascona. They just beckoned me out the door and said 'Leave it.' "

"You can telephone the hotel," Tom said, "from Fontaine-bleau, for instance."

"Yes. So—they kept asking me questions. They wanted to know the mastermind of it all. I told them there wasn't any. Couldn't have been *me*, a mastermind!" Reeves laughed weakly. "I wasn't going to say *you,* Tom. Anyway it wasn't you who wanted to keep the Mafia out of Hamburg. So then —the cigarette burns started. They asked me who'd been on the train. I'm afraid I didn't do as well as Fritz. Good old Fritz—"

"He's not dead, is he?" asked Tom.

"No. Not that I know of. Anyway, to make this disgraceful story short, I told them Jonathan's name—where he lived. I said it—because they were holding me down in the car in some woods somewhere, giving me the cigarette burns. I remember thinking that if I screamed like mad for help, no one would hear me. Then they started holding my nose, pretending they were going to suffocate me." Reeves squirmed on the sofa.

Tom could sympathize. "They didn't mention my name?"

"No."

Tom wondered if he could dare believe that his action with Jonathan had come off. Perhaps the Genotti family really thought that Tom Ripley had been a wrong trail. "These were the Genotti family, I presume."

"Logically, yes."

"You don't know?"

"They don't mention the family, Tom, for goodness' sake!"

That was true. "No mention of Angie—or Lippo? Or a *capo* called Luigi?"

Reeves thought. "Luigi—maybe I heard the name. I'm afraid I was scared stiff, Tom—"

Tom sighed. "Angie and Lippo are the two Jonathan and I did in Saturday night," he said in a soft voice, as if someone might overhear him. "Two of the Genotti family. They came to the house here, and we— They were incinerated in their own car, miles from here. Jonathan was here and he was marvelous. You should see the papers!" Tom added, smiling. "We made Lippo phone his boss Luigi and tell him that I wasn't the man he wanted. That's why I'm asking you about the Genottis. I'm very interested to know whether it was a success or not."

Reeves was still trying to remember. "They didn't mention your name, I know. Killed two of them here. In the house! That's something, Tom!" Reeves sank back on the sofa with a gentle smile, looking as if it were the first time he'd relaxed in days. Perhaps it was.

"However, they know my name," Tom said. "I'm not sure whether the two in the car recognized me tonight. That's—in the stars." He was surprised at the phrase coming from his lips. He meant it was fifty-fifty, something like that. "I mean," Tom continued on a firmer note, "I don't know whether their appetites are satisfied by getting Jonathan tonight or not."

Tom stood up, turning away from Reeves. Jonathan dead. And Jonathan hadn't even needed to go out to the car with Tom. Hadn't Jonathan deliberately stepped in front of him, between him and the pistol pointing from the car? But Tom wasn't quite sure he'd seen a pistol pointing. It had all happened so quickly. Jonathan had never reconciled Simone, never had a word of forgiveness from her—nothing but those few minutes of attention she had given him after he'd been nearly garroted.

"Reeves, shouldn't you think about turning in? Unless you'd like to eat something first. Are you hungry?"

"I think I'm too bushed to eat, thanks. I'd really like to turn in. Thanks, Tom. I wasn't sure you could put me up."

Tom laughed. "Neither was I." Tom showed Reeves up to the guest room, apologized for the fact that Jonathan had slept for a few hours in the bed, and offered to change the sheets, but Reeves assured him that it didn't matter.

"That bed looks like bliss," Reeves said, weaving with exhaustion as he started to undress.

Tom was thinking, if the Mafia boys tried another attack tonight, he had the bigger Italian gun, plus his rifle, and the Luger, too, with a tired Reeves instead of Jonathan. But he didn't think the Mafia would come tonight. They would probably prefer to get a great distance from Fontainebleau. Tom hoped he had at least wounded the driver, and badly.

The next morning, Tom let Reeves sleep on. Tom sat in his living room drinking coffee, with the radio tuned to a popular French station which gave the news every hour. Unfortunately it was just after nine. He wondered what Simone was saying to the police, and what she had said last night. She wouldn't, Tom thought, mention him, because that would expose Jonathan's part in the Mafia killings. Was he right? Couldn't she say that Tom Ripley had coerced her husband—but how? By what kind of pressure? No, it was more likely that Simone would say, more or less, "I can't imagine why the Mafia (or the Italians) came to our house." "But who was the other man with your husband? The witnesses say there was another man—with an American accent." Tom hoped none of the bystanders would remark on his accent, but probably they would. "I don't know," Simone might say. "Someone my husband knew. I have forgotten his name. . . ."

Things were a bit uncertain at the moment.

Reeves came down before ten. Tom made more coffee, and scrambled some eggs for him.

"I must take off, for your sake," Reeves said. "Can you drive me to—I was thinking of Orly. Also I want to telephone about my suitcase, but not from your house. Could you take me to Fontainebleau?"

"I can take you to Fontainebleau and Orly. Where are you headed?"

"Zurich, I think. Then I could swoop back to Ascona and get my suitcase. Although if I telephone the hotel, they might send the suitcase to Zurich care of American Express. I'll just say I forgot it!" Reeves laughed a boyish, carefree laugh—or, rather, forced one out of himself.

Then there was the money situation. Tom had about thirteen hundred francs in cash in the house. He said he could easily let Reeves have some for the plane ticket and to change into Swiss francs once he got to Zurich. Reeves had travelers' checks in his suitcase.

"And your passport?" Tom asked.

"Here." Reeves patted his breast pocket. "Both of them. Ralph Platt with the beard, and me without. Had the picture taken by a friend in Hamburg, me wearing a phony beard. Can you imagine, the Italians didn't take the passports off me? That's luck, eh?"

It certainly was. Reeves was unkillable, Tom thought, like a slender lizard flitting over stone. Reeves had been kidnaped, cigarette-burned, intimidated God knew how, dumped, and here he was eating scrambled eggs, both eyes intact, not even his nose broken.

"I'm going back to my own passport. So I'll shave off my beard this morning, take a bath, too, if I may. I came down in a hurry because I thought I'd slept pretty late."

Tom telephoned while Reeves was bathing and found out about planes to Zurich. There were three that day, the first taking off at 1:20 p.m., and the girl at Orly said there should be a single seat available.

Tom was at Orly with Reeves a few minutes past noon. He parked his car. Reeves telephoned The Three Bears in Ascona about his suitcase, and the hotel agreed to send it to Zurich. Reeves was not much concerned, not as concerned as Tom would have been if he'd left behind an unlocked suitcase with an interesting address book in it. Reeves would probably recover his suitcase, with all its contents undisturbed, tomorrow in Zurich. Tom had insisted on Reeves's taking one of his small suitcases with an extra shirt, a sweater, pajamas, socks, and underwear, and Tom's own toothbrush and toothpaste, which he thought essential for a suitcase to look normal. Somehow Tom hadn't wanted to give Reeves the toothbrush that Jonathan had used only once. He also gave Reeves a raincoat.

| 24 |

Reeves looked paler without the beard. "Tom, don't wait to see me off; I'll manage. Thanks infinitely. You saved my life."

That wasn't quite true, unless the Italians had been going to plug Reeves on the pavement, which Tom doubted. "If I *don't* hear from you," Tom said, with a smile, "I'll assume you're all right."

"Okay, Tom!" A wave of the hand, and he vanished through the glass doors.

Tom got his car and drove homeward, feeling wretched and increasingly sad. He didn't care to try to shake it off by seeing people this evening, not the Graises again, or the Cleggs either. Not even a film in Paris. He'd ring Héloïse around seven, and see if she'd departed on the Swiss jaunt. If she had, her parents would know her telephone number in the Swiss chalet, or some way of reaching her. Héloïse always thought of things like that, leaving a telephone number or an address where she could be found.

Then, of course, he might have a visit from the police, which would put an end to his efforts to shake off his depression. What could he say to the police—that he had been home all last evening? Tom laughed, and the laugh was a relief. He ought to find out first, of course, what Simone had already said, if he could.

But the police didn't come, and Tom made no effort to speak with Simone. He suffered his usual apprehension that the police were spending time in amassing evidence and testimony before they dumped it on him. He bought some things for his dinner, practiced finger exercises on the harpsichord, and wrote a friendly note to Mme. Annette in care of her sister in Lyon:

My dear Mme. Annette,

Belle Ombre misses you painfully. But I hope you are relaxing and enjoying these beautiful days of early summer. Everything is all right here. I will tele-

phone one of these evenings and see how you are.
All the best wishes.

Affectionately,

Tom Ripley

The Paris radio reported a "shoot-up" in a Fontainebleau
street, three men killed, no names given. The Tuesday papers (Tom bought *France-Soir* in Villeperce) had a five-inch-
long item: Jonathan Trevanny of Fontainebleau shot dead,
and two Italians killed in Trevanny's house. Tom's eyes
glided over their names as though he didn't want to remember them, though he knew they would linger a long time in
his memory: Alfiori and Ponti. The Italians had invaded
the house for no reason that Mme. Simone Trevanny knew,
she had told the police. They had rung the doorbell, then
burst in. A friend, whom Mme. Trevanny did not name,
had aided her husband, and later driven them both, with
their small son, to the hospital in Fontainebleau, where her
husband had been found dead on arrival.

"Aided." Tom thought with amusement of the two Mafiosi
with their skulls bashed in in the Trevanny house. Pretty
handy with a hammer, that friend of the Trevannys, and
Trevanny too, maybe, considering they had been up against
five men with guns. Tom began to relax, even to laugh—
and if there was a little hysteria in the laugh, who could
blame him? He knew that more details were going to come
out in the newspapers, and if not the newspapers then via
the police themselves—direct to Simone, direct to him, perhaps. But Mms. Trevanny was going to try to protect her husband's honor and her nest egg in Switzerland, Tom believed,
otherwise she would have told them a bit more already. She
could have mentioned Tom Ripley, and her suspicions of
him. The newspapers could have said that Mme. Trevanny
promised to make a more detailed statement later. But evidently she hadn't.

Jonathan Trevanny's funeral was to be held Wednesday

afternoon, May 17th, at 3 p.m. in the Church of Saint-Louis. Tom wanted to go, but he felt it would have been exactly the wrong thing to do from Simone's point of view, and, after all, funerals were for the living, not the dead. Tom spent that time in silence, working in his garden. (He must prod those blasted workmen about the greenhouse.) He became more and more convinced that Jonathan had shielded him on purpose from that bullet by stepping in front of him.

Surely the police were going to question Simone in the days to come, demand to know the name of the friend who had aided her husband. Hadn't the Italians—probably identified by now as the Mafia—been in pursuit of the friend, perhaps, not Jonathan Trevanny? The police would give Simone a few days to recover from her grief, and then they would question her again. Tom could imagine Simone's will strengthened even more in the direction in which she had started: the friend didn't want his name given, he was not a close friend, he had acted in self-defense, as had her husband, and she wanted to forget the whole nightmare.

About a month later, in June, when Héloïse was long back from Switzerland, and Tom's speculations on the Trevanny affair had come true—there had been no further statements from Mme. Trevanny in the newspapers—he saw Simone approaching on the sidewalk in the Rue de France in Fontainebleau. He was carrying a heavy urn-like thing for the garden, which he had just bought. Tom was surprised to see Simone, because he had heard that she had already removed herself and her son to Toulouse, where she had bought a house. He had heard this news via the young aggressive owner of the new and expensive delicatessen shop into which Gauthier's art-supply shop had been converted. So—with his arms nearly giving out from the load which he had almost entrusted to the clerk at the florist, the unpleasant memory of céleri rémoulade and herrings-in-cream in his mind instead of the as yet odorless tubes of paint, virgin brushes, and canvases that he was used to seeing in Gauthier's premises, plus the belief that Simone was already hundreds of miles away

—Tom had the feeling he was seeing a ghost, having a vision. He was in shirt sleeves, beginning to crumple, and if it hadn't been for Simone, he might have set the urn down to rest for a moment. His car was at the next corner. Simone saw him and at once began to glare. She paused briefly beside him, and as Tom came almost to a stop, thinking at least to say "*Bonjour,* Madame," she spat at him. She missed his face, missed him entirely, and plunged on toward the Rue Saint-Merry.

That, perhaps, corresponded to the Mafia revenge. Tom hoped that would be all that there was to it—either from the Mafia or Mme. Simone. In fact, the spit was a kind of guarantee—unpleasant, to be sure, whether it hit or not. But if Simone hadn't decided to hang on to the money in Switzerland, she wouldn't have bothered spitting and he would be in prison. Simone was just a trifle ashamed of herself, Tom thought. In that, she had joined much of the rest of the world. Tom felt, in fact, that her conscience would be more at peace than that of her husband, if he were still alive.

A NOTE ON THE TYPE

This book was set on the Linotype in a type face called Baskerville. The face is a facsimile reproduction of types cast from molds made for John Baskerville (1706–75) from his designs. The punches for the revived Linotype Baskerville were cut under the supervision of the English printer George W. Jones. John Baskerville's original face was one of the forerunners of the type style known as "modern face" to printers—a "modern" of the period A.D. 1800.

This book was composed by
The Colonial Press Inc., Clinton, Massachusetts,
and printed and bound by
The Haddon Craftsmen, Scranton, Pennsylvania.